MI

Trey stood at her approach, and Alana was struck anew by how dashing he looked in his evening clothes. She wondered fleetingly if he, too, had experienced the same magnetic pull she had felt a moment ago.

"Your performance tonight was extraordinary."

"Thank you. That's very kind of you, Mr. Matthews."

"Mr. Matthews?" He quirked a dark brow. "Isn't that a bit formal for a man who came to the rescue of a fair damsel in distress, not once but twice?"

"Then Trey it shall be. Or—" she laughed—"perhaps Sir Trey would be more fitting. My own personal knight in shining armor."

So she thought of him as a knight, did she? The comparison didn't displease him, he realized with a start. He'd gladly slay dragons for her.

Midnight Rain

Elizabeth Turner

AVON BOOKS NEW YORK

AVON BOOKS
A division of
The Hearst Corporation
1350 Avenue of the Americas
New York, New York 10019

Inside cover author photo by Gorback Photography
Published by arrangement with the author
Library of Congress Catalog Card Number: 93-90969
ISBN: 0-380-77371-6

First Avon Books Printing: June 1994

Printed in the U.S.A.

RA 10 9 8 7 6 5 4 3 2 1

To my impatient Bob
for his patience.

This one's for you.

Special thanks to Joan Avery,
who put me back on track every time I derailed.

Chapter 1

Late October
San Diego, 1886

Hot and unforgiving.

Conceived in the scorched Utah desert, the winds swooped down from high inland plateaus, twisting and winding through narrow mountain canyons as they barreled toward the sea. A storm without rain—the dreaded Santa Ana sirocco.

From her suite above the Gilded Lily, Alana Van Dorne Fairchild stared aimlessly across the rooftops of buildings that had cropped up almost overnight. In the distant mountains, forest fires, fanned by raging winds, cast a copper glow in the moonless sky. As she watched, a tree, appearing no larger than a matchstick, exploded amid a shower of sparks and shot skyward.

A chill slid down her spine. Alana shivered in spite of the unrelenting heat. God, how she hated the Santa Anas. Ever since her arrival in California, the winds were harbingers of ill luck. Would this year be different?

It was nearly time for her performance. With a sigh that was part regret, part resignation, Alana pulled the pins from her hair. A shake of her head sent the waist-length mass of blond curls tumbling down her back and swirling around her shoulders. Already she could feel tendrils clinging damply to the nape of her neck. Wearing it loose was Colin's idea, part of the image he had created for her. The customers will love it, he had insisted, and, she acknowledged ruefully, he had been right.

Suddenly, gunshots rang out. Whirling around, Alana picked up the skirt of her raspberry satin gown and raced down the back staircase. Pushing aside the swinging door that opened into the bar, she anxiously searched through the thick blue cloud of cigar smoke for her friend and employer.

She let out a sigh of relief when she spotted Colin O'Shea's dapper figure, apparently unscathed, standing near the bar. Colin's hot temper had sparked half a dozen altercations with more than one close call, she thought grimly as she pushed her way through the boisterous crowd to be at his side.

A muscle ticked in Colin's jaw. "Haven't had it a week, and it's broken already," he said by way of a greeting.

Alana's gaze followed his. Colin's pride and joy, a twelve-foot mirror adorned with a bevy of lounging satyrs and dancing nymphs that had hung above the bar, was now reduced to a few jagged shards of silvered glass clinging to the wall in blatant defiance of gravity. She placed a restraining hand on his arm. "Please don't do anything rash. It can be replaced."

Colin riveted his glare on Stubs, the heavyset, balding man behind the bar. As if feeling the force of his employer's glowering look, Stubs glanced up, shifted his chewed-off cigar from one corner of his mouth to the other, then nodded in the direction of two men seated at a nearby table. Shaking off her touch, Colin plowed through the throng with Alana close behind him.

The noisy babble of voices grew hushed. Alana swept an encompassing glance over the saloon. She was dismayed by the avid expressions the men wore. Bright-eyed and eager for trouble, they were so rabidly thirsty for bloodshed it sickened her.

Colin planted himself directly in front of the table Stubs had indicated, feet braced, hands on hips. "All right, which of you gentlemen fancies himself Buffalo Bill?"

In the unnatural stillness, Alana could hear a rhythmic tapping, the cadence as soft as a heartbeat, as ominous as a drum roll. The sound pulled her gaze downward. A snub-nosed, pearl-handled pistol rested on a stack of ten-dollar bills so casually it might have been a paperweight on a scholar's desk. Mere inches from the small but deadly revolver, strong, lean fingers drummed against the scarred pine table.

And Colin wasn't armed.

The thought flashed through Alana's brain. It would be just like him to provoke a gunfight when he didn't even carry a weapon. Instinctively, she clutched his sleeve in warning.

"I thought Californians admired sharpshooters," an indolent voice drawled.

Colin snorted in disgust. "My name's not P. T. Barnum. I run a saloon, not a circus."

Alana raised her gaze, ready to challenge the stranger. China-blue eyes clashed with cool green ones as the two took each other's measure. Pistol or no pistol, this man was trouble. Beneath a shock of hair so dark it was almost black, his devilishly handsome face was all harsh planes and intriguing angles, the kind women were drawn to—contrary to common sense and their mothers' dire warnings. Cynicism, ruthlessness, and self-confidence were all evident in varying degrees. Though by his dress he would be classified a gentleman, Alana doubted he was a gentle man.

The stranger's appraisal of her was equally frank. His gaze wandered slowly over the golden tresses spilling in wild abandon over her bare shoulders, memorized her features, lingered on the tantalizing expanse of creamy white flesh that welled above the low-cut bodice, then slid down her slender curves. Assessing. Measuring. Judging.

Alana had seen that hot, speculative gleam a hundred times. Easy prey, it seemed to say, his for the price of a jeweled trinket or a pouch of gold. Damn him anyway, she thought rebelliously. Damn them all.

Raising her chin a fraction, she snapped, "Proving one's marksmanship doesn't mean destroying another's property."

"That right?" he asked with a coldly amused smile.

"Had that mirror shipped all the way from St. Louis. Cost me plenty." Colin placed both palms on the table and leaned forward until he was almost nose to nose with the dark-haired man. "Now pay up."

Neither man looked about to back down.

Driven by impulse, Alana snatched the pistol from the table. While the crowd gaped in surprise, she clicked open the cylinder, emptied the bullets from the chamber, and cupped them in her hand. She stared at them blankly for a second before her expression turned resolute. "If you don't mind, gentlemen, I'll keep these until your tempers cool." One by one, she dropped the bullets down the front of her gown.

"Way to go, girlie." A whiskey-roughened shout broke the strained silence.

"I've got somethin' you can keep warm, honey," another yelled.

Amid raucous laughter and more lewd comments, the customers of the Gilded Lily returned to their drinks and games of chance.

Alana felt the cold metal nestle in the hollow between her breasts as she bent to pick the money off the table. "Here." She handed the currency to a bemused Colin. "Consider this partial payment."

The green-eyed stranger took a slow swallow of bourbon, his eyes still fixed on Alana. "Send me the bill—care of the California Southern," he said.

The second man at the table spoke for the first time, his words slurred. "Didn't like the way one of the girlies on your goddamn mirror kept watchin' me. Reminded me of my wife, so I took aim." He mimicked firing a gun.

Colin pocketed the cash. "So you're the culprit."

"Not bad for an amateur." He chuckled.

Alana inspected the dark-haired man's companion more closely. At first glance, his thinning sandy hair, round face, and pudgy build made him seem as harmless as a tabby cat. However, on closer inspection, his glassy eyes and slurred speech told her he was inebriated. A year in a saloon had shown her that drink made men unpredictable. "Next time, mister, practice your target shooting somewhere else," she warned.

"No two-bit whore is gonna give me orders." His face a blotchy red, he struggled to his feet.

Alana flinched inwardly at the insult, but experience had taught her to school her features not to betray her hurt.

"That's no way to speak to a woman, Pierce. Sit down." The dark-haired man's voice cracked with authority. When the man he called Pierce obediently plopped back down, he continued in a more conversational tone, "You've already caused enough commotion tonight. Next thing you know, Dorothea will get wind of this and all hell will break loose."

Chastened by the mention of what was evidently his wife's name, Pierce sloshed more whiskey into his nearly empty glass.

"California Southern, eh?" Colin asked, his amiability restored.

Knowing the volatile situation had been defused, Alana allowed herself to relax. It was common knowledge that railroad men favored the Gilded Lily. Their drinking and gambling added a substantial sum to the saloon's coffers. Colin wouldn't risk losing his bread and butter over a silly mirror, no matter how fond he was of it.

"My associate will see that you're fully reimbursed." The handsome stranger extended his hand to Colin. "I'm Trey Matthews. This is my colleague, Carter Pierce."

Colin returned the handshake. "Pleased to make your acquaintance. I'm Colin O'Shea, proprietor."

"Nice place." Pierce rocked back in his chair, his bleary eyes fixed on the empty space above the bar. "Just didn't like that goddamn mirror."

Trey Matthews signaled a passing barmaid and ordered a bottle of their best bourbon and two extra glasses. "Allow us to make amends by buying you and your lovely . . . lady friend . . . a drink."

The deliberate hesitation over his choice of words brought an angry sparkle to Alana's eyes. "Perhaps another time." Her haughty tone did credit to her blue-blooded mother.

Carter Pierce hooted with laughter and turned to Trey. "That, my friend, is the first time I ever heard a woman put you in your place. Usually they swarm over you like bees over honey."

Colin slipped an arm around Alana's waist, his fingers digging into her rib cage as he said to her, "Surely you didn't intend to offend one of our guests, did you, mavournin."

Colin's Gaelic charm left her unmoved. "Certainly no more than Mr. Matthews intended to offend me." She pried free from his hold. She'd suffer another of his lectures on the importance of pleasing the customers, rather than endure Trey Matthew's arrogance a minute longer. "Excuse me, gentlemen, I just heard Jimmie play my cue."

Turning, Alana walked toward a small, raised platform that spanned the back wall, oblivious of the appreciative stares that followed the graceful sway of her bustled gown. The tinny sound of an upright piano at the base of the makeshift stage could barely be heard above the din.

Colin pulled out a chair and joined the railroad men. " 'Music to soothe a savage beast,' " he cheerfully misquoted. "You're in for a rare treat. Alana's the finest songstress west of the Mississippi."

Alana?

Trey sat up straighter. Alana was an uncommon name. In fact, he had heard it only once before—a year ago in Baltimore. A vision of his mother's contorted face, her mouth twisted to one side, her eyes filled with stark terror, danced in front of him. *If it weren't for Alana Van Dorne, Robert wouldn't be in his grave.* Those had been the last words his mother had uttered just before her collapse. Trey's hands tightened around the tumbler of whiskey. Could there be a connection between a saloon singer in San Diego and a society bitch from Baltimore? Highly unlikely, but . . . He resolved to ask O'Shea the singer's surname later on. After all, there was no hurry. For now, he was content simply to admire the woman's uncommon beauty.

"If the lady's half as good as you claim, O'Shea,"

Carter Pierce was saying, "she should head for New York. With her looks, she'd have people standing in line to see her on stage."

Colin pulled a cigar from his vest pocket. "Just wait. Her voice can charm the birds right out of the trees."

Trey leaned forward, all his attention concentrated on the shapely blond ascending a short flight of steps to a small stage. Even if she couldn't sing a note, her speaking voice was a pleasure to listen to, each word slow and distinct. Hearing her brought to mind the contented purr of a feline or the smoky smooth taste of expensive whiskey. At her nod, a black man at the piano began a popular ballad.

Then she began to sing. Her voice, sultry yet sweet, curled around each note, each phrase, until they tugged at raw emotion. The song spoke of unrequited love, and Trey doubted that there was a solitary man in the audience left untouched. Unwillingly, he succumbed to the magic of her music, mellowing, gentling under the spell she wove.

When the ballad ended, the piano player struck up a livelier tune. In a heartbeat, the singer's pensive mood switched to one of gaiety. By turns coy, then seductive, she flirted outrageously from behind a plumed fan. She was a temptress. With the face of an angel, the body of Venus, and the voice of a nightingale, she embodied every man's dream—Trey's included. And that glorious mane of golden curls . . . It lent her that disheveled, just-out-of-a-man's-bed kind of look. Trey felt his manhood harden. He wondered what it would take to lay claim to that delectable combination of femininity. Did she want to be wooed with compliments and candlelight? Or was she the mercenary type who liked expensive baubles and cold cash? Whatever the price, he was willing to pay it.

The performance concluded amid a thunderous chorus of cheers, whistles, and foot stomping. As Alana rose from a deep curtsy, her eyes met Trey's across the footlights. With slow, mocking deliberation, he raised his glass in a silent salute.

There was absolutely no doubt in Alana's mind that Trey Matthews wanted her. She recognized raw desire, had seen it stamped on dozens of different faces. By now, she should be immune to men's baser instincts. Yet anger and resentment bubbled anew. And along with the resentment and anger came another sensation. For some irrational reason, she wanted him to know she wasn't typical of the women who inhabited the Stingaree District. That she was of a finer caliber.

Irritated by her thoughts, she broke the eye contact and exited the stage to lingering applause. Mr. Matthews would discover soon enough that it took more than a handsome face and a pocketful of money to win her favors. She was no longer the silly, foolish girl she had once been. Quite simply, she wasn't for sale.

Jimmie, the piano player, took a swig of beer, then flashed her a wide grin. "That ought to bring 'em back fer more, miss."

Alana returned the black man's friendly smile before making her way to the bar. "The usual, Stubs," she said, addressing the barkeep.

Stubs reached for a pitcher he kept below the bar. "Customers are restless. Spoilin' fer a fight."

"It's the winds." She gratefully accepted the soothing blend of iced tea laced with honey and took a long swallow, savoring the cold sweetness trickling down her throat. "The Santa Anas affect people that way."

Finishing her drink, she knew it was time to circulate among the customers. She spotted Colin still drinking with the two railroad men. Ignoring his motions for her to join them, she began to wend her way among the tables.

A ruddy-faced man with bushy sideburns beckoned to her. "Let me buy you a drink—anything you want. How about champagne?"

"Champagne sounds wonderful. Maybe later." Alana smiled and moved on.

A fashionably dressed gentleman, his nut-brown hair parted high on one side and slicked down with Macassar oil, caught her arm. "How about joining me for a late supper in my room at the St. James?"

Alana recognized him as Ronald Cooper, one of the town's wealthiest businessmen—and one of the Gilded Lily's biggest spenders. She was also aware that the man's friends, their card game temporarily forgotten, watched their exchange with undisguised interest. Her practiced smile remained intact. "I've already had my dinner," she replied, firmly disengaging her arm from his grasp.

A portly gentleman with the cherubic face of an aging choirboy winked at her. "If a girl doesn't watch her waistline, the gentlemen won't either."

"If I know Ron, he's interested in more than just her waistline," another of Cooper's companions added with a smirk.

"Meet me later," Ronald persisted. He took a key from his pocket and pressed it into her palm. "Room 224."

Alana stared at the key for a long moment, her mouth curved bitterly. In her entire life, she had shared only one man's bed, that of her husband, but she doubted anyone here would believe that. Holding the offensive object between thumb and forefinger, she took aim. The key landed in his drink with a satisfying *plink.* "Mother taught me never to borrow. I believe the rule applies to other women's husbands as well."

The group exchanged uneasy glances.

A vein throbbed in Ronald Cooper's temple. "Keep my wife out of this," he snarled. "Your kind isn't fit to empty her chamber pot."

Alana was saved a reply by an argument that erupted at a nearby table.

"You cheated!"

"Did not!"

"You sonofabitch, I saw you."

"Liar!"

Ronald Cooper forgotten, Alana looked around frantically for Colin, but he had left the railroad men and was nowhere in sight. Chairs scraped against the planked floor, the sound grating on her nerves like chalk screeching against a blackboard. Her attention swung back to the arguing pair.

Pistols drawn, the two gamblers stood facing each other. Alana's heart slammed painfully against her ribs. The air was thick, heavy, difficult to inhale. Dear Lord, she prayed, wasn't anyone going to stop them?

A pall hung over the saloon as the unruly crowd turned watchful.

Knowing only that she couldn't stand idle while one man gunned down another, Alana took a tentative step forward, hoping, foolishly perhaps, that she could persuade the pair to settle their differences peacefully. Before she could take a second step, a gunshot desecrated the hushed silence.

Both men were still standing, guns drawn, frozen in a macabre tableau. The sulfuric stench of gunpowder pervaded the air. Numb with horror, Alana watched one man slowly sink to the floor. His body jerked spasmodically, then lay motionless. Blood pumped from a gaping hole in the victim's chest to form an ever-widening stain on his white brocade vest, like an obscene boutonniere. The man was young, she realized dazedly, with jet-black curls . . . just like Phillip's.

Her memory pinwheeled backward. To a year ago . . . to a dusty street in Dodge City . . . to Phillip. Present merged with past. She was no longer in a San Diego saloon but in a lawless Kansas town. There, filled with despair, she had cradled her bridegroom's head in her lap while his life's blood stained his white brocade vest.

"Phillip . . ." The name escaped, a mere whisper of sound. With a roaring in her ears, a gray mist obscuring her vision, Alana slid into a seductive oblivion.

Chapter 2

Trey caught Alana's limp form inches from the floor. From the corner of his eye, he had seen her step forward. What had the fool woman been thinking of? he wondered furiously, looking at her ashen face. Was she crazy? No one in his right mind placed himself between a gambler's pistol and a man caught cheating at cards.

Colin shoved his way through the gawkers. "Someone fetch the police!" His scowl softened as it rested on Alana. "Thought my heart would stop when I saw what she was trying to do. Take her to my office." He pointed to a door at the far end of the barroom. "I'll join you as soon as I straighten out this mess."

Trey nodded, his mouth set in a grim line. The crowd of curious onlookers parted to let him through, then closed tighter than a miser's pursestrings. The door Colin had indicated stood ajar. Trey stepped inside, nudging it shut behind him. A quick glance revealed a surprisingly tidy room with a desk piled high with ledgers, an oak file cabinet, and a leather sofa. An oil lamp, its wick trimmed low, sat on a small corner table along with a tray holding a bottle of whiskey and several glasses. Trey crossed the room and carefully deposited the songstress's still form on the sofa.

Stepping back, he anxiously studied the woman.

Her respirations were so shallow she appeared to be scarcely breathing; her skin had the pale translucence of fine porcelain. Worse yet, she showed no signs of regaining consciousness. Sweat trickled down his neck. "Blasted heat," he muttered, running his finger around the rim of his starched collar.

Trey mentally reviewed his options. He could try forcing some whiskey down her throat. That would either bring her around or choke her. At that moment, he would have gladly emptied the money from his pockets for smelling salts. He thought fleetingly of collecting Pierce and leaving the Gilded Lily. He wasn't a nursemaid. Let the woman's boyfriend tend to her. What the devil was keeping O'Shea anyway? He cast a glance at the door, hoping the glib Irishman would appear. Then, with a sigh of resignation, he dropped to one knee, picked up the woman's hand, and began chafing her wrist.

She was a beauty, no doubt about it. In repose, her face, free of sophistication, held an innocent allure. But he had watched her tonight and knew she was far from innocent. He had seen her boldly swill a glass of liquor, brazenly fend off amorous advances, and bravely, albeit foolishly, attempt to divert a gunfight.

His gaze fell on the lush curve of her breasts and lingered there. A dun-colored bullet, one of six she had earlier emptied from his gun, nestled between two rounded globes. Not pausing to weigh the consequences, Trey, using his thumb and index finger, extracted the metal slug. A mistake, he realized as desire jolted through him like lightning, racing down his nerve endings, heating his blood. Her flesh was warm velvet . . . and addictive. He had to fight the urge to retrieve the other shells as well. Until tonight, until this very moment, he had never imagined himself the sort to take advantage of an unconscious woman. But from the instant their eyes had met, she had brought out his darker side. Uncivilized. Primal. She was the type of woman who could entice a man to lose his head, his morals, his very soul.

And perhaps even his life?

Images flooded back. As long as he lived, he'd never forget the horror of finding Robert's dead body slumped across his desk, a pistol clutched in one hand. And the blood . . . it had been everywhere. Trey's jaw clenched as he tamped down the despair that threatened to overwhelm him whenever he remembered that moment. The first anniversary of Robert's death had recently passed, but the pain was still fresh, the wound still raw. And he still grieved. Fast on the heels of despair came rage.

Trey's hands balled into fists of impotent fury. His eyes took on the cold, emerald brilliance his adversaries feared. Not for the first time, he wondered whatever had become of the elusive "Alana" who had driven his half-brother to take his own life. If he ever found her, God help her. He would make her life a living hell.

On a sigh of protest, Alana opened her eyes. Her first instinct was to shrink back into the cushions. The expression on the face of the man watching her was frightening. It was filled with the cunning watchfulness of a panther about to spring on an unwary victim.

"So," he said, rising to his feet, "you've decided to wake up."

"You," she breathed.

His mouth curved in a parody of a smile. "What, no 'thank you' for coming to your rescue?"

Alana closed her eyes. The scene in the saloon a vivid memory, she could still hear the blast of the pistol, smell the gunpowder, see a body sink to the floor. Bile rose in her throat, and she swallowed it back. When she reopened her eyes, their clear blue depths held a haunted look.

Trey crossed the room and splashed bourbon into a glass. Returning, he thrust it at her. "Here," he ordered. "Drink!"

"No, thank you, I—"

"I said drink, dammit. Or I'll pour it down your throat myself."

Although he didn't raise his voice, one quick glance told Alana he wouldn't hesitate to carry out his threat. Mutely, she levered herself on one elbow and accepted the glass. With an unsteady hand, she brought the glass to her lips and sipped. The bourbon burned like lye, bringing a sheen of moisture to her eyes.

"Another."

Too shaken to resist, Alana obeyed. She relaxed slightly as she felt the bourbon's searing heat begin to thaw the bone-deep chill that seemed to encase her.

"Who's Phillip?" Trey fired the question at her.

She tensed. Her hand trembled so violently that bourbon sloshed over the rim to puddle on her raspberry satin gown.

"Who's Phillip?"

She cupped her hands tightly around the glass. "He was my husband," she answered, her voice a husky whisper.

"*Was* your husband?" Trey persisted, his curiosity unappeased.

"He's dead." A faraway expression on her face, Alana absently rolled the tumbler between her palms. "Phillip was killed in a gunfight in Dodge City. The young man who was shot tonight bore a close resemblance to him." A dull ache began to build behind her eyes. She didn't want to think about Phillip, didn't want to remember crimson staining white brocade, didn't want to be reminded how quickly dreams turned to ash.

Trey muttered a curse. He might occasionally be called insensitive, but he wasn't heartless. He recognized suffering when he saw it. He, too, had experienced the excruciating pain of losing a loved one. Perhaps he was being overly harsh because she bore the same first name as the woman responsible for Robert's suicide.

It wasn't fair to condemn the girl for what was likely just a coincidence. In truth, he had never learned the name of the man the infamous Alana Van Dorne had run off with. In the rush of grief and chaos following the discovery of Robert's body and arrangements for his funeral, he had never quizzed his mother about the man's identity. She had only referred to him as *that horrid young Englishman.* And the night of the funeral, she had suffered a massive stroke that robbed her of the ability to speak. The name of Robert's so-called friend would forever remain a mystery.

Trey blamed himself for the oversight. He ought to have made it his duty to know all of Robert's friends. But he hadn't. If only he hadn't been so damned involved with business. Work and traveling had consumed so much of his life, he had even taken rooms closer to the office, spending less and less time with his mother and Robert. Trey sighed heavily. Regrets—so many, so late.

Taking a handkerchief from his pocket, he stooped down and blotted the whiskey from her skirt. The action brought his head level with hers. A half-formed apology on his lips, he ceased dabbing at the stain and glanced up.

At close range, Alana could see tiny flecks of gold in

his green eyes. For the first time, she noticed the slight cleft in his chin and wanted to touch that shallow indentation with her fingertips. The effect he was having on her was far more potent than the bourbon she had swallowed. It was as though all the oxygen had been suddenly sucked out of the room, leaving her giddy and light-headed. Blood thrummed through her veins at a dizzy pace. Quite irrationally, she wanted him to kiss her.

Trey, too, felt the pull. Her mouth was tempting, as soft and succulent as sun-ripened fruit. Instead of the cloying fragrance he half-expected, hers was the subtle scent of white flowers on a summer's eve. He was achingly aware of her breasts straining the bodice of her gown and remembered the petal softness of her skin. With an effort, Trey pushed aside wayward fancies and straightened.

Though not a word had been exchanged, Alana sensed his withdrawal. Confused and inexplicably hurt by his defection, she watched him turn and walk to the corner table, where he poured himself a generous drink.

He observed her through narrowed eyes from across the room. "Didn't it occur to you that you might have been killed?"

"Someone had to try to stop them," she replied. His brusque tone had put her on the defensive. She swung her feet to the floor and assumed a sitting position.

"So you appointed yourself?" he asked, unreasonably angered that she had risked her life. "Does that make you brave, I wonder, or just slow-witted?"

The lassitude that had held her in its thrall suddenly dissipated. "Neither," she snapped, getting to her feet. "I've had quite enough of your rudeness for one evening. Get out!"

Colin appeared in the doorway. "You heard the

lady, Matthews. She's tired of your company." He held out his arms, and Alana rushed into them. "Ah, darlin'," he crooned in a thick Irish brogue, "ye took ten years off me life tonight."

Trey's gaze flicked from the saloon owner to the beautiful woman in his embrace. There was no mistaking O'Shea's proprietary air. It confirmed what he had suspected earlier. The pair were lovers. Yet minutes ago, Trey could have sworn she would have been his for the taking. So much for the woman's loyalty, he thought in disgust.

Colin gave Trey a cocky grin and pulled Alana closer. "Thanks for tending my girl. Your next drink is on the house."

Reaching into his jacket pocket, Trey brought out the single bullet. He weighed it thoughtfully in the palm of his hand, then casually tossed it in the air and caught it.

The action wasn't wasted on Alana. She let out a startled gasp, her hand flying to the bodice of her gown.

"Another time." With a satisfied nod, Trey turned and left.

It wasn't until later that he realized he still hadn't found the solution to the riddle. Were the saloon singer in San Diego and the Baltimore belle one and the same? He'd find the answer.

Soon.

Alana stood on the corner of Fifth and E Streets and read the gaily painted sign above the shop, MRS. A. TIDWELL. MILLINERY. FANCY GOODS. DRY GOODS. Her grip tightened on her handbag. She had just left the First National Bank across the street. Her account there was small but growing steadily. Someday, if she was frugal and the Gilded Lily continued to thrive, she would own a similar shop. This was something she could do, run a business—a respectable business. She had more in common with her Dutch father than blond hair and blue eyes; she had inherited his business acumen as well. She'd leave saloon life and make a fresh start where no one knew her, perhaps in San Francisco.

With a spring in her step, she pushed open the door. It was clearly a woman's store down to the last hat pin. Dainty blue and white floral paper covered the walls. A rainbow of pastel ribbons hung from the ceiling and festooned cabinets and shelves. A long glass case to her left displayed spools of ribbon, sprays of flowers, and feathery plumes. Another held bone crochet hooks, silk embroidery floss, delicate bird-shaped scissors, brass buckles, silver thimbles, and papers of pins. An assortment of elaborately trimmed bonnets rested atop hat stands on shelves behind the cabinet, impressive examples of Mrs. Tidwell's handiwork.

The clerks were all busy with customers, so Alana contented herself with browsing. She was considering the purchase of an aigrette hair ornament when a little girl with sandy curls and a doll tucked under one arm sidled up to her.

"You're pretty," the child blurted.

"Why, thank you." Alana smiled down at her young admirer, whom she guessed to be six or seven. "You're pretty, too. What's your name?"

"Sarah."

"It's a pleasure to meet you, Sarah. My friends call me Alana."

Sarah held up her doll for Alana's approval. "My daddy gave her to me. I call her Madelaine, but I like the name Alana better."

Alana dutifully examined the exquisite French bisque creation. Her throat tightened painfully. "My father gave me a doll just like yours when I was about your age."

"What happened to her?"

The simple question was difficult to answer. The imported doll had been a special gift, a rare token of affection from her undemonstrative father, one she had cherished. She had debated taking it with her the night she had eloped with Phillip, but at the last minute had left it behind, mute evidence of her discarded girlhood.

Before Alana could frame a reply, a tall, fashionably dressed woman came up and grabbed the little girl's arm. "Wait for me by the door, young lady!"

"But Mother . . ."

"Sarah Louise Cooper, I don't want to hear another word out of you."

The child's lower lip quivered at her mother's sharp rebuke, and her eyes filled with tears. Lowering her head, she did as she was told.

Sarah Louise *Cooper?* Alana quickly made the connection between her insistent suitor of the night before and the charming little girl. What she couldn't understand was why a man would rather spend each evening in a smoky saloon instead of at home with his family. Judging from her irate expression, Ronald Cooper's wife wasn't at all happy with the situation.

"I know who you are, you Jezebel." Miriam Cooper made no effort to lower her voice. "How dare you come in here and mingle with good, God-fearing townspeople?"

"Mrs. Cooper, I realize you're upset—"

"I may be upset, but I'm not stupid!" she blazed. "Every night, you hussies with your low-cut gowns and painted faces lure respectable men away from their loved ones. Your kind ought to be run out of town."

Alana met the attack head on. "My kind? How dare you make presumptions about me?"

"You're a tramp, that's all I need to know."

"And you, Mrs. Cooper, are an evil-minded shrew." Alana moved away, only to feel the woman's bony fingers dig into her arm and jerk her around.

"Stay away from my husband," Miriam hissed, her reddened face inches from Alana's. Then she turned and marched out, dragging the hapless child in her wake.

As Alana waited for her own temper to cool, she became aware of the profound silence. Slowly, she looked about her. Censure was stamped on the faces of clerks and customers alike. The little scene had been enacted before a hostile audience who had cast her in the role of villainess. Well, Alana decided grimly, it was time to bring down the curtain and make a quick exit. With a forced smile, she inclined her head. "When you think of entertainment, kindly remember the Gilded Lily. Good day, ladies."

Head held proudly, Alana left the shop. Though humiliated, she had the ultimate satisfaction of knowing she hadn't let it show. *A lady never publicly displays emotion.* Her mother's admonition rang in her ears. And, after all, her mother had been a Howard of Baltimore. Good manners be damned, Alana thought irritably. She had almost surrendered to the impulse to tell those sanctimonious biddies a tidbit or two that would wipe the smug looks off their faces.

As Alana strolled the blocks separating the business section of town from the Stingaree District, the scenery changed, subtly at first, then more blatantly. Offices and shops were soon outnumbered by fish stalls, vegetable stands, and Chinese laundries. Interspersed with these were the opium dens, gambling halls, and Chinese cribs, the lowest of the city's brothels. There girls, painted and crimped, waited for clientele behind lace-curtained windows. Alana was painfully aware of the vast differences that existed between the churchgoing population and those who preferred pleasure of another sort.

It was a different world from the one she had grown up in. The pampered life of a Baltimore debutante had little in common with the one she now led. How shocked her mother would be if she knew the truth about her elder daughter. God, would she ever stop being homesick for her family? Alana wondered miserably. All her letters had been returned unopened. Her presence went unacknowledged; she had ceased to exist. As far as her family was concerned, she might as well be dead.

Colin, she reflected upon nearing the Gilded Lily, had considered himself fortunate in purchasing the present lot. Time had proven it a wise choice. Located near Third and I Streets, it was at the heart of San Diego's Barbary Coast, where dozens of saloons and bawdy houses competed for trade.

Alana rounded a corner and stopped. Midway down the block, she spotted Trey Matthews climbing down from a lacquered buggy pulled by a strapping bay. Still smarting from her confrontation at the milliner's, Alana didn't want to hazard a sparring session with a man she found both attractive and infuriating. Instead, she ducked into the narrow passageway between two adjacent buildings. This, she knew, led to an alley that ran behind the Gilded Lily. From there, it would be a simple matter to slip through the rear entrance unnoticed and up the back staircase to her quarters.

As she moved deeper into the alley, she discovered two men arguing. The first was tall and lean, his derby set at a rakish angle. The second was Chinese, clothed in traditional garb, his long braid trailing to his waist.

"Ling Ho, you dirty little chink, I'm not paying you another cent."

"You forget deal, English." Ling Ho tightened his grip on a battered leather satchel.

"You're a greedy bastard!"

"No money, no poppy!"

The man in the derby narrowed his eyes and smiled, a smile so cold that Alana felt ice crystals form in the pit of her stomach. Then, while she watched in horror, he pulled a knife.

The Chinese man stepped back and, pulling his own blade, made a quick lunge forward. With the speed of an adder, the man called English latched on to Ling Ho's wrist with bone-crushing brutality. At the same time, he thrust his knife deep into the Chinese man's throat.

With a gurgling sound that Alana was certain would visit her dreams, Ling Ho crumpled to the dirt, satchel still clutched in one hand. Blood spewed from a gaping wound in his neck. Alana gasped, unable to suppress the involuntary cry.

The murderer looked up—straight into her frightened face.

Alana stood transfixed, unable to move, scarcely able to breathe. The man called English appeared just as stunned to see her. He was the first to recover. With a calm more terrifying than wrath, he stepped around the dead body and started toward her. Sunlight glinted off the lethal steel blade in his right hand.

He meant to kill her. There wasn't a doubt in Alana's mind. "No," she whispered, taking a tentative step backward. Her handbag dropped unnoticed to the ground. "No," she repeated.

Panic engulfed her in its mindless thrall, then receded, leaving in its wake a wild desperation to flee. She whirled, hitching up her skirts in both hands, and raced down the narrow passage from which she had emerged just minutes ago. Maybe fifty feet in length, the distance seemed more like fifty miles. The activity on the street beyond beckoned her. If only she reached it in time . . .

Alana opened her mouth to scream for help, but no sound came out. Close behind, she heard her pursuer's footsteps. Or was it merely the frantic pounding of her heart? It was hard to distinguish between the two when fear blurred reality. She felt mired in her own worst nightmare, but somehow knew this wasn't a dream.

She was halfway to safety when her view of the street was suddenly cut off by a delivery wagon pulled by a team of stout draft horses. The wagon rolled to a stop at the end of the alleyway, so close its broad side scraped whitewash from the buildings flanking the alley's entrance.

So close it might have been a boulder sealing a tomb—her tomb.

Chapter 3

"Nowhere to run, my pretty? Too bad."

Alana's feet dragged to a halt. Slowly, she turned around. Ling Ho's murderer stood less than eight feet away. Though his eyes remained shielded by his derby, his features were chiseled and cruel, his nose crooked from countless brawls, his mouth a colorless slash. It was not a face she was likely to forget.

Her gaze locked on the blade he held in a bloody fist, she slowly retreated step by step until her back pressed against rough sawn siding of the building. She offered up a desperate prayer that the delivery wagon would move on. Her mouth was so dry she could barely utter a plea, much less a scream. "Please," she begged, "don't hurt me. I won't tell, I swear . . ."

"Time to pay the piper." English smiled that same mirthless twitch of the lips he had displayed seconds before driving his knife into the Chinese man's throat.

Alana recoiled at the thought. She could almost feel the steel plunge into her flesh, slicing muscle and sinew until it mortally plundered vital organs. She knew with certainty that no miracle would be forthcoming. Unless she acted—and acted quickly—her blood would mingle with Ling Ho's on the evil weapon. Spurred by the most primitive instinct of all, she dashed to the front of the building, hoping against hope that there would be space enough between it and the wagon to squeeze through. But there wasn't, she discovered with a whimper of disappointment. Her gaze darted about the narrow passage. Then she saw it—a golden sliver of sunlight shining beneath the low wagon bed.

Without a second to spare, Alana dove beneath the wagon. Gravel shredded her soft kid gloves and abraded her palms. A seam in her favorite blue walking dress ripped; her pert bonnet with its saucy plume was knocked askew. Bent on her escape, Alana was impervious to all of this. Digging her elbows and knees into the dirt, she clawed her way toward safety.

"Oh, no, you don't," her tormentor snarled. His hand manacled her slender ankle, and he began to drag her backward.

Alana kicked. English merely cursed and tightened his hold. Sprawled on her stomach beneath the wagon, she could see a jumble of disembodied feet and legs. But, oddly, they all seemed an exaggerated distance away, as though she were viewing them through the wrong end of opera glasses. "Help," she cried. "Help, please." Her voice lacked the strength to startle a sparrow. No one seemed to hear it. In spite of her efforts, she felt herself lose ground. She sucked in a great lungful of air, then let it out. This time her voice didn't fail her. Her scream was powerful enough to shatter crystal.

She didn't have time to savor her victory. The ominous creak of wood and the rumble of wheels heralded a new threat. Out of the corner of her eye, Alana saw the wagon bolt forward. Any second now, she would be crushed under its heavy weight.

"Control the horses!" a man shouted. "There's someone under the wagon!"

A pair of strong hands locked around her wrists, and Alana held on with tenacity. Her attacker was equally tenacious in refusing to relinquish his grip. Alana felt torn asunder, a human pawn in a life-or-death game of tug-of-war.

As the heavy conveyance ground to a halt scant inches from her prone form, Alana's walking boot slipped from her foot, and she was unceremoniously hauled into the brilliant sunlight.

Alana blinked, hardly able to believe her good fortune.

"What the hell . . . ?" a familiar male voice asked in disbelief.

She blinked again, and Trey Matthews's features came into focus. At that given moment, his was the dearest face in all the world. Without him, she would have perished. Alana fought the urge to cling, to lean against him and borrow his strength.

"Hey, lady! Whatja tryin' ta do? Git yerself killed?" The driver, color rapidly returning to his face, clambered down from the delivery wagon.

At the mention of the word *kill*, Alana wasn't able to suppress the tremor that rippled through her. Trey's hands, warm and comforting, reached out to steady her, and she lacked the willpower to shake them off.

A crowd began to form around them. "That was some close call," someone observed.

"Thought for sure she was a goner," another added.

Trey held her at arm's length. A stirring of sympathy began before he could squelch it. The songbird was a sorry sight to behold. Her bonnet dangled by its satin ribbons; her dress was torn and soiled. Her hair had come free of its moorings and straggled down her back in an unkempt tangle of pale gold.

But it was her dazed expression that tugged at his heart. The pupils of her eyes, which nearly eclipsed the irises, attested to her shock. Not a hint of color marred the alabaster purity of her complexion. Resolutely, he set aside the unwanted feelings of concern.

"What happened?" he demanded.

"A man . . . in the alley," she stammered. "He tried to kill me."

"Why would someone want to kill you?"

Alana licked her dry lips. "I saw him stab someone . . . a Chinaman by the name of Ling Ho." She was achingly aware that Trey still held her loosely. As soon as she regained her composure, she rationalized, she would let him know she was not a hothouse flower in need of protecting . . . in just a moment, or maybe two.

The group of men shuffled their feet and talked among themselves. Trey took command, his orders crisply slicing through their inactivity.

He pointed at a trio of longshoremen. "You there, go take a look in the alley." His next orders were directed at the deliveryman. "Move your blasted wagon out of the way. And be quick about it."

Hustling to obey, the driver climbed back on his perch and slapped the reins. The wagon lumbered slowly off. The burly longshoremen, always ready for action, quickly disappeared between the two buildings.

Rigid with tension, Alana watched them go. To her immense relief, Trey remained behind, as though sensing her reluctance to be left alone.

His questioning gaze bored into her, but she deliberately refused to meet it. The incident had left her emotionally bruised and battered, and feeling very vulnerable. While she sorely need solace, pride kept her from burrowing into his embrace. But even though she maintained a tight rein on her impulses, she was more aware of Trey Matthews than she wanted to be. She inhaled a deep, calming breath and inhaled his unique essence of soap, sandalwood, and sheer male. His light touch conveyed coiled strength.

A taut silence quivered between them.

She was grateful when the seamen returned. One of them carried her leather boot. Neither had her missing handbag.

"The chink's dead all right."

"His throat's slit ear to ear."

"Jest layin' in a pool of blood with his eyes wide open."

Alana's knees felt like water, and she feared they might buckle. Trey wrapped his arm more securely around her shoulders, lending his support. "Call the police," he directed. "I'm taking the lady home. If they want to ask questions, they can find her at the Gilded Lily."

One shoe on, one shoe off, Alana hobbled beside him, aware of what an incongruous sight they presented to any curious onlookers.

At midmorning the saloon was nearly deserted. A group of diehard poker players occupied a back corner, their bloodshot eyes and bearded stubble mute testimony of an all-night card game. The only other patron was a slender, swarthy man at the bar wearing a serape and a wide brimmed sombrero.

"When the police come to see . . ." It dawned on Trey that he didn't know Alana's surname. "They can find her," he resumed, "in Mr. O'Shea's office."

Once inside Colin's office, he urged Alana down on the sofa, then sat next to her. Awkwardly, he untied the ribbons of her bonnet and set it aside. "Care to tell me what happened?"

Alana clasped her hands together to still their nervous movement. She winced from the light pressure and, glancing downward, was surprised to find her kid gloves shredded beyond repair.

"If it upsets you . . ."

She shook her head and summoned a smile. "If it wasn't for you, that man would have killed me. I'm indebted to you for saving my life."

Trey cleared his throat, uncomfortable to be cast as this woman's savior. He was spared a reply by the noisy arrival of Colin O'Shea, who was still tucking his shirttail into his pants. Directly behind him came a blue-uniformed policeman.

"Jaysus, Alana!" Colin exclaimed, "you look like hell! What the devil's goin' on?"

"I'll ask the questions, if you don't mind, O'Shea." The law officer assumed a cocky stance in front of Alana, then took out a small pad of paper and a stubby pencil. "Now, miss, what the devil's goin' on?"

Alana sensed Trey's interest. Somehow his presence lent her courage. Her voice gained confidence as she related the events from the moment she entered the alley until her timely rescue. She was careful to omit that Trey Matthews was the reason she had ducked down the alley in the first place.

"Would you recognize this man called English if you saw him again?" the policeman asked when she concluded her story.

Alana met his look without wavering. "Yes. I'll never forget his face."

"What does your department plan to do about this?" Trey asked.

"Do?" The lawman stuffed his pad and pencil inside his jacket pocket.

Trey rose to his feet. A muscle ticked in his jaw.

"Yes, do, goddammit! The lady just witnessed a murder and nearly got herself killed in the bargain."

"Listen, mister, I don't know where you come from, but around here no one makes a fuss about a dead Chinaman. Fact is, no one would give a damn if a boatload of 'em got their throats slit."

"This is a hell of a way to wake up," Colin grumbled, running his fingers through his already disheveled locks. "You'll have to make allowances for Mr. Matthews. He's from back East, Officer—?" Bleary-eyed, he squinted at the policeman's badge.

"*Sergeant* Walters." The policeman gave his badge a quick buff with his coat sleeve.

"Surely there must be something you can do." Alana stood, distress etched on her pale features.

"Perhaps your superior is the one we should talk to, Sergeant. I doubt he would condone such a poor attitude," Trey said.

"Police Chief Coyne?" Walters snorted. "He's got more important fish to fry."

"Don't know about the rest of you, but I could use a drink." Colin went over to the corner table and poured a whiskey. "Any takers?" he asked, holding out the glass.

Sergeant Walters didn't hesitate to accept the offer of a free drink. "I am a might thirsty, now that you mention it." He drained the glass in one long swallow.

"So you're going to pretend nothing happened?" Trey asked in disbelief.

"I'm gonna file a report." The policeman leveled a finger at Trey's chest. "Best teach yer girlfriend to stay out of alleys. She might not be so lucky next time."

Alana recalled English's face and shivered.

* * *

Alana grabbed the inkwell just in time to prevent it from toppling, then glared at the intruder. "How many times do I have to tell you? Don't sneak up on me!"

"Quit being so damn jumpy." Colin pushed away from the door frame and sauntered into his office. "I can't help it you were so busy scribbling you didn't hear the door open."

"I'm trying to balance accounts." Alana swept her arm in an encompassing gesture over the paper-strewn desk. "It would make my job much easier if you told me whenever you wrote a bank draft."

"Don't get in a dither. We both know the Gilded Lily takes in far more than we pay out." Colin sank down on the sofa, crossed his legs, and lounged back. "You're looking peaked these days. Still fretting over that dead Chinaman?"

Alana tossed down the pen she was using. "You'd worry, too, if you had been a murder witness."

Colin stifled a yawn. "In all likelihood, the culprit probably decided to lay low and hightailed it out of town."

"I sincerely hope so." Alana smoothed her hand over the reassuring bulge in the pocket of her skirt. Since her ordeal in the alley a week ago, she never went anywhere without her trusty derringer.

"What you need, pet, is to have some fun. A picnic is just what Dr. O'Shea ordered to pull you out of the doldrums."

"A picnic?"

"How about some Sunday I rent a buggy and the two of us ride out to Point Loma?"

"I'm not sure, Colin . . ."

"Nonsense." He brushed aside her reservations with a flick of his wrist. "I'm told the view from the lighthouse is spectacular. Maybe, if we're lucky, we can even spot a school of whales on their trip south."

"Whales?"

"It's settled." Colin got to his feet and strolled toward the door. Halfway there, he stopped and turned. "By the way, I booked a large private party for tonight. They requested that you provide the entertainment."

"You could have had the decency to ask me first. I don't know if I'm ready."

Colin's affable expression hardened. "It's time, Alana. Your self-imposed absence is starting to hurt business."

"I just need a little longer."

"How long, Alana?" Colin walked over to the desk, flattened his palms on the surface, and leaned forward until he was eye level with her. "How long do you plan to hole up in a stuffy office afraid of your own shadow? Another week? A month? Two?"

Alana didn't have a ready reply.

Colin's lip curled in disdain. "I never thought you were a coward."

"I'm not!" she fired back.

"Then be downstairs at nine sharp! No excuses."

Six hours later, as she waited in the wings for Jimmie to play her cue, Alana decided Colin was right. She was being a coward. However, the threat English posed was quite real. Of that she had no doubt. She had watched him kill a man without batting an eye and knew he would have killed her just as easily. But she was tired of cringing like a whipped puppy. She had allowed a madman to intimidate her long enough. It was time to come out of hiding and start living again. While she would continue to be vigilant, she refused to spend another evening behind locked doors.

The houselights dimmed. A nervous fluttering started in the pit of her stomach just as it always did prior to a performance. She drew in a deep, calming breath, then stepped into the spotlight.

Peering coquettishly over the edge of an oversized fan made from peacock feathers, she crooned in a sultry voice, "Who wants to buy me a diamond ring?"

The enthusiastic response from the roomful of men made her glad she had saved this new number she and Jimmie had worked on for a special occasion. The turquoise silk gown with its low-cut beaded bodice was sophisticated, yet a bit risqué. The lines flattered her figure, and the rich hue accentuated her coloring. Knowing she looked her best bolstered her lagging spirits and gave her confidence. A purely feminine, feline smile curved her mouth. Colin wanted a performance, did he? Well, she'd give him one he wouldn't quickly forget. With a toss of her tawny ringlets, she lowered her fan and proceeded to captivate the entire male audience.

Smoke spiraling lazily from the cheroot clamped between his teeth, Trey Matthews studied the lovely blond singer. Overriding any vague suspicions he might harbor, Trey admitted to a strong, physical attraction for the woman. She had become a craving he needed to appease, an itch he needed to scratch. She made him restless, irritable. He burned at the thought of caressing her lush curves and feeling her supple form yield beneath his.

He leaned toward the elderly man seated on his right. "I told you she was good," he said in a low voice.

The man nodded in agreement. "Yes, very," he murmured absently.

Trey leaned back and returned his attention to the stage. The woman intrigued him far more than he cared to admit. The interest he felt went more than skin-deep. No coy or simpering miss was she, but rather a woman both direct and forthright. Even after witnessing a gruesome murder, she hadn't succumbed to hysterics like most would have done under the circumstances. Though he had felt the tremors rippling through her supple body, she had shown surprising strength. The softness of a midsummer night and the resilience of tempered steel: an unbeatable combination.

Trey's companion thoughtfully sipped his bourbon. "She certainly bears a striking resemblance to a girl I once knew."

Trey merely grunted. He drew on his cheroot, then blew out a thin stream of smoke, giving no other indication he had heard the man's comment. Were Alana and O'Shea lovers, he wondered. Could he have been mistaken about their relationship? He fervently hoped so. Then and there, he made up his mind to give the Irishman a run for his money.

Heady from her successful performance, Alana exited the stage to find Colin waiting just beyond the footlights. "Bravo!" He kissed her soundly. "You were sensational."

Smiling, Alana pulled away and tucked her hand into the crook of his arm. "To be honest, it felt wonderful to be singing again."

Colin patted her hand. "Aren't you glad you listened to Uncle Colin? Sorry if I was a bit harsh with you this afternoon, but it was for your own good."

And for the good of the Gilded Lily, she added silently, not fooled by Colin's solicitous manner. "You failed to tell me earlier who it was that booked the Gilded Lily for the entire evening."

"Come and see for yourself." He steered a path around the crowded tables. "I think you'll discover tonight's party will show a sizable entry in the profit column of your precious ledger."

Alana, her blue eyes alight with pleasure, graciously accepted bouquets of extravagant compliments as she and Colin wove their way through the packed saloon. Her eyes were still sparkling when they encountered Trey Matthews seated at a nearby table. Even though his back was turned, she instantly recognized him by the way his dark hair curled slightly above his starched collar and by the breadth of his shoulders. He negligently held a thin cigar, and, not for the first time, she found herself admiring his hands with their long, tapering fingers. Artist's hands; the phrase popped to mind.

Sensing her presence, Trey glanced over his shoulder. His eyes captured, then held hers. Time hung suspended. Seconds ticked by. Alana forgot to breathe; her heart slowed. The noise of the saloon faded.

Trey was staring at her with an unnerving intensity that seemed to plumb the depths of her soul. And Alana responded to his interest as a flower does to sunshine.

"Hey!" Colin nudged her side. "You're not getting sick, are you?"

The spell broken, Alana scrambled to collect her wits. "I-I'm fine." But she didn't feel fine. She felt vaguely disoriented—as though awakening from a deep sleep, or a dream.

His hand riding the small of her wrist, Colin propelled her forward. "Mr. Matthews is responsible for all this. He's hosting a gathering of railroad officials from all over the country."

Trey stood at their approach, and Alana was struck anew by how dashing he looked in his evening clothes. She wondered fleetingly if he, too, had experienced the same magnetic pull she had felt a moment ago.

"Your performance tonight was extraordinary." A warm smile curved his mouth. "Carter was right when he said you could have a career on the New York stage."

"Thank you." Alana treasured this man's simple praise more than the flowery accolades she had received from a dozen faceless admirers. "That's very kind of you, Mr. Matthews, but I have no desire for a career in the theater."

"Mr. Matthews?" He quirked a dark brow. "Isn't that a bit formal for a man who came to the rescue of a fair damsel in distress, not once but twice?"

"Then Trey it shall be. Or"—she laughed—"perhaps Sir Trey would be more fitting. My own personal knight in shining armor."

So she thought of him as a knight, did she? A rueful smile tugged at the corners of his mouth. The comparison didn't displease him, he realized with a start. He'd gladly slay dragons for her. "I'm happy to see you suffer no ill effects after your harrowing experience."

Alana felt the reassuring weight of the derringer concealed deep within the folds of her gown. She had carried off the evening with a bravado she didn't feel. Trey, or anyone else for that matter, would never suspect the fear that had nearly incapacitated her. She had spent the past week looking over her shoulder, jumping at her own shadow, and listening for stealthy footfalls in the hall outside her rooms. "I've quite recovered from my ordeal, thanks to a little prodding from Colin."

Trey's expression hardened at the mention of Colin O'Shea. "There's someone here I'd like you to meet." He placed his hand on the shoulder of the distinguished gray-haired gentleman seated next to him. "Leland Hastings is an associate of mine from the Baltimore and Ohio Railroad."

Alana's smile froze, and the sparkle in her eyes dimmed as she stared into the face of an old family friend.

Behind wire-rimmed spectacles, Leland Hastings's eyes widened in shocked recognition. Before he could voice his surprise, Alana clutched his hand in hers. An almost imperceptible shake of her head warned him to keep her secret. "A pleasure to meet you, Mr. Hastings. I hope you enjoyed tonight's show."

"Yes. Yes, indeed," he muttered, responding to the pleading in her big blue eyes.

Alana let out a sigh of relief. She had already done enough to disgrace the family name. She didn't need it bandied about the Stingaree that her father was an influential banker or that her mother's family one of the most respected in Baltimore. If nothing else, she could at least spare them that humiliation.

Chapter 4

Trey hurriedly rinsed off the grime of travel, then scraped a day's growth of whiskers from his lean cheeks and added a splash of cologne. The week had seemed impossibly long. He had pushed hard to return to San Diego, when it would have been much simpler and far less arduous to spend another night on the road. But he was eager to see Alana again. Even though the hour was late, he knew the Gilded Lily would still be open to entice a few diehard gamblers to part with precious dollars.

He pulled a freshly laundered shirt out of a drawer and shrugged into it. While searching through a carved teak box for his onyx shirt studs and cuff links, he accidentally brushed the silver-framed picture he kept on his dresser. He picked it up and gazed at the three images. His mother stern and unsmiling, a much younger version of himself, and his half-brother Robert stared back at him. In the past week he had been away, he had inspected, and rejected, three parcels of land. None seemed quite as he and Robert had long ago envisioned for their ranch. "Sorry, brother," he murmured. "Maybe next time we'll get lucky."

The sight of Robert's engaging grin sent memories swirling through Trey's mind like wisps of smoke, choking out the present, clouding the past . . .

"You stupid, lazy boy!" Estelle Prescott berated her younger son.

Robert's face blanched. He studied the carpet, the toe of his shoe tracing the intricate swirls of navy, burgundy, and camel. "I'm sorry, Mother."

"How do you ever expect to carry on your poor deceased father's business when you can't bring home a decent grade in any subject except poetry?"

"I tried, Mother. I really did."

Estelle slapped the schoolmaster's report on the mahogany desk, the sound as sharp as flesh striking flesh. "Well, you obviously didn't try hard enough. I can't hold my head up when I hear friends brag about their sons' accomplishments."

"I'm sorry," Robert repeated miserably. "I promise to work harder."

"You certainly will. I hired a private tutor to see that you do just that."

"A tutor?"

"You heard me," Estelle snapped. "He arrives on Monday."

"Monday?" Robert's voice filled with dismay. "I thought we were going to spend the summer in Newport."

"I'll be summering in Newport—alone. Trey is home from college. It will be his job to keep an eye on you. Now get out of my sight before I lose my temper."

Trey, who had been listening just outside the library door, followed Robert upstairs. He pushed open the door to his half-brother's room and found Robert facedown on the bed. He sank down on the edge of the mattress and placed a hand on his shoulder. "Hey, don't take it so hard. Newport isn't the only place to spend the summer. We'll find plenty of things to do right here in Baltimore. Besides, it'll give us a chance to spend some time together. With me away at Harvard, we don't get to see much of each other anymore."

Robert turned a tear-streaked face toward his brother. "Mother always makes me feel as though I can never do anything right. Nothing I do ever pleases her. I just wish I could get away—far away." He sniffed loudly. "California, maybe."

Trey tried to cheer him up. "California again, eh?"

"I heard land's real cheap there. I'd like to get me a place where I'd be my own boss, with no one telling me what to do or that I'm not doing it right. Maybe a ranch." Robert scrubbed tears away with his shirtsleeve.

Trey frowned thoughtfully. "I read somewhere that many of the Spanish land grants are being subdivided and sold in parcels—"

Robert cut him off, animation back in his voice. "That's what I'd like—a ranch. A ranch with just you and me running it. A place with a high bluff. We could ride there before daybreak and watch the sun rise over the mountaintops. A place I could go when we weren't busy. Then I'd sit under a big shade tree and write poetry."

As Trey's thoughts returned to the present, he carefully replaced the photograph on the dresser. A sad smile flickered across his face as he gazed at Robert's image. Sunrise and poetry. The two seemed precious little to expect from life. "Never you mind, little brother. I'll find us a ranch." It was a promise he'd made years ago.

A promise he intended to keep.

The days had dragged by. Another week had passed—a week that felt more like a month. Specters, both good and evil, haunted its passage. To Alana's surprise—and dismay—she discovered that greater than her dread of finding the man called English among her audience was her dream of seeing Trey Matthews. His continuing absence formed a void in her heart.

Reluctant to relinquish the fragile hope that even though the hour was late Trey might still appear, Alana peered through her reflected image in the saloon window to the street beyond. Though it was past midnight, occasionally men, either singly or in pairs, would drift down I Street in search of a last shot of whiskey or a final game of chance. But Trey was never among them. Disappointed, Alana turned away.

The crowd inside the Gilded Lily had started to thin. Near the foot of the stage, Jimmie lazily plunked out the notes of "My Old Kentucky Home." His half-empty beer glass formed a wet ring on the piano top. Polishing rag in hand, Stubs manned his post behind the bar. Alana cast a lingering glance at the doorway, then heaved a sigh before catching herself.

Stop it, she scolded silently. Stop mooning over the man. In no time at all, Trey Matthews had effortlessly reduced her to a schoolgirl in the throes of her first crush. How humiliating, how demeaning. She was accustomed to men seeking her out, not her yearning for them. Ever since she could remember, boys, and later men, had flocked to her. Not the other way around. Somehow, Trey Matthews had managed to reverse the norm. Squaring her shoulders, Alana made her way to the bar.

Catching sight of her, Stubs ceased his conversation with a scrawny cowpoke. The man tugged the dusty brim of his Stetson on lower and sidled off. Stubs shifted his chewed-off cigar from one side of his mouth to the other. "What can I getcha?"

"Another iced tea with honey," she answered absently, looking around for Colin.

Stubs splashed tea into a glass and added a small chunk of ice.

Alana watched as Carter Pierce staggered into the Gilded Lily. He leaned against the bar and loudly ordered a whiskey. She hesitated a moment before approaching the already inebriated railroad man. "Drinking alone tonight, Mr. Pierce? Where's your friend?"

Pierce drew his brows together in concentration. "What friend? I've gotta lot of friends."

Alana tried to inject a nonchalance into her voice as she casually surveyed the crowd. "Mr. Matthews—the gentleman who hosted the party for the railroad officials. I haven't seen him around lately."

"Neither have I. Don't know what he's up to these days."

Alana took a small sip of tea. "I hope he wasn't disappointed with the Gilded Lily."

"He doesn't confide in me." Carter drained his glass. "A new saloon opened down the block. Maybe he found it more to his liking."

"Could be." Competition for business was fierce among the Stingaree's saloons and gambling houses. Perhaps Trey had found another place to while away the evenings, another singer to flatter with smoldering looks.

The notion depressed her.

"I'd better get home before Dorothea raises hell," Pierce mumbled. Pushing away from the bar, he turned abruptly. His equilibrium adversely affected by a night of heavy drinking, he stumbled and would have fallen if Alana hadn't caught him. He swayed against her like a dancer in a drunken embrace. His head lolled against her shoulder. Alana stiffened beneath his weight.

Carter Pierce gave her a slack-mouthed grin. "How about you and me havin' us a little party somewhere private?"

Careful to hide her distaste, Alana put her arm around his waist and steered him toward the door. "If you're not home soon, Dorothea will round up the temperance ladies and come after you."

"Her and those damn women are always lookin' for ways to ruin my fun," Carter grumbled. He shook loose from Alana and wove an unsteady path down the boardwalk and away from the Gilded Lily.

Shaking her head, Alana went back inside.

Candy, a well-endowed red-haired barmaid with an abundance of freckles, approached the bar. After giving Stubs the drink order, Candy turned to Alana. "How 'bout joinin' my boyfriend and me fer a few laughs and a beer or two after closin'? Jake's got this friend who's dyin' to meet you."

Alana shook her head. "I don't think so."

"Why not?" Candy demanded, hands on hips. "You always got some lame excuse. You too highfalutin to have a drink with Jake and me?"

"You know I don't socialize much." Alana took another small sip of tea.

"I told Jake you were an uppity one." Candy transferred the beer mugs from the bar to her tray with enough force to send foam sloshing over the rims and down the sides. "Well, I got news for you, honey. You're no better'n me."

Alana's cheeks grew warm. Although Stubs wiped a glass with a concentration that would have done credit to a diamond cutter, she could tell from his smirk that he was eavesdropping. "I'm sorry if I gave that impression," she replied stiffly.

Candy's voice rose. "I'm sick of your fancy airs."

As Alana carefully set her glass on the bar, she swept a surreptitious glance around to see if anyone was listening. Two cowhands seated at a nearby table were watching the exchange with undisguised interest. A third, nursing a whiskey at the bar, angled his rangy body for better viewing. Alana knew they'd love nothing better than a name-calling, hair-pulling catfight to liven up an otherwise dull evening. "This is hardly the time or place to discuss this," she said quietly.

Candy's cinnamon-brown eyes glittered with malice. "You work in the Stingaree same as me. No-account white trash, that's how the rest of the world sees us. Better get used to it, honey!" Hefting the heavily laden tray, she marched off with a twitch of her bustle.

"Don't mind her," a soft voice counseled. "She's been in a foul mood ever since Madame Rose's Arsenic Complexion Wafers that she ordered all the way from Chicago didn't take away her freckles like they was supposed to."

Alana turned to find Lottie, a petite brunette whose large hazel eyes turned her from plain into almost pretty. Alana had objected that Lottie hardly seemed the type to work in a saloon, but Colin had reminded her of the dire straits she had been in when they'd first met. That had silenced her further objections.

"Candy's jealous, is all," Lottie stated matter-of-factly.

"Jealous?"

Lottie nodded vigorously, her small face serious. "You're much prettier than she is. You could easily have your pick of any man in San Diego—maybe even the whole state of California."

"Why, thank you, Lottie." Another time Alana might have found the girl's extravagant flattery amusing, but not tonight. Tonight she was in sore need of a friend. She studied the girl more closely. Kohl heavily rimmed eyes that hinted of sadness.

Rouge inexpertly applied highlighted the girl's pale cheeks and small mouth. The low-cut vermilion gown trimmed with cheap black lace did little to enhance her appearance. Yet there was something about her, a friendliness, an innate kindness, a willingness to please, that was appealing.

Alana returned Lottie's tentative smile.

Encouraged, Lottie continued, "Candy would like to keep all the men to herself. She ain't used to sharin' the spotlight." Lottie set a bottle of whiskey and two glasses on a tray and half-turned to go. "Looks like she's found a new admirer. Leastways, she won't be botherin' you for a while."

Curious, Alana followed the direction of Lottie's nod. *Trey.* He had slipped in unnoticed while she and Lottie were talking. Alana's stomach swooped, then plummeted. Her heart beat triple time before settling into a natural rhythm.

Candy, on the other hand, must have spotted him immediately. While Alana watched from across the room, Candy sashayed over, pulled out a chair, and without waiting for an invitation, plopped down. Resting both arms on the table, the redhead leaned toward Trey until her breasts pushed above the bodice of her gown like twin loaves of white bread. While Candy's actions didn't surprise Alana, Trey's response did. From where Alana stood, Trey appeared to invite, not repel, Candy's blatant flirtation.

Alana seethed. Watching Trey smile at Candy with none of his usual reserve made her angry. Then jealousy—until now a sensation totally foreign to her—sank its lethal fangs into her.

"I—uh—better get these to my customers." Sensing but not understanding the undercurrents, Lottie edged prudently away.

Determination firmed the delicate set of Alana's jaw and added a dangerous glint to her eyes. Her gaze swept over the Gilded Lily, alighting on Colin. A cigar clamped between his teeth and a whiskey glass within easy reach, Colin was in the middle of a poker game. Normally, Alana would leave him to gamble uninterrupted, but not tonight. Not when he sat a mere table away from Trey Matthews.

Alana smoothed her hair. Reassured that the lush purple flower fastened above one ear with a tortoiseshell comb was intact, she advanced toward Colin with deliberate, unhurried steps.

Though pretending not to, she observed Trey out of the corner of her eye. If he noticed her approach, he gave no indication. Indeed, he was too involved with Candy to notice much of anything. Alana's irritation escalated. Fine, she thought, her chin high. She'd ignore him, too. Then she thought better of it.

"Why, Mr. Matthews," she drawled as she drew up alongside his table. "What a surprise."

Trey pulled his attention away from Candy and glanced up. "A pleasant one, I trust."

The lack of warmth in his greeting chilled her. To compensate, Alana tried to infuse some in hers. "Of course. We like to see our customers on a regular basis. Their satisfaction is important to us."

Did that include Carter Pierce? Trey wondered in disgust. Through the window outside the saloon, he had been treated to an unobstructed view of the two embracing. He had watched Alana slip her arm around the man with the familiarity of an old friend and walk him to the door. Trey had watched his associate lurch down the boardwalk. Then his conscience had kicked in. He couldn't permit Pierce to try to find his way home in his present condition. As he had helped him board a horsecar, Pierce had boasted the singer had suggested a private party, but he had refused. "Wouldn't want to chance Dorothea gettin' wind of it." Carter had chuckled before slouching down in the seat and closing his eyes. Hearing this had made Trey feel like a fool. The lady clearly had an unending abundance of admirers.

Trey smiled at Alana coolly. "Your attitude toward your customers is commendable."

A compliment, or sarcasm? Alana couldn't be sure. Her feeling of awkwardness increased. Resorting to a bald-faced lie, she forged ahead. "Colin was afraid you had found another saloon more to your liking."

"O'Shea wouldn't give an tinker's damn if I never stepped foot inside this establishment again."

"That's not true."

"Are you sure it wasn't you, not O'Shea, who did the wondering?"

Candy hooted with approval.

Trey might have called her bluff, but Alana wasn't ready to fold. She met his look squarely. "Colin's a businessman, Mr. Matthews. To put it bluntly, you're good for business."

"Mr. Matthews? Come, Alana, I thought we were past such formality. You agreed to call me Trey, remember?"

Bait then retreat. Thrust then parry. Alana was certain he was playing a game with her. But why? She studied him warily.

He lounged back in his seat, his benign gaze trained on her face, his head cocked. "Have you missed me?"

Candy's curiosity knew no boundaries. Her head swung back and forth as she tried to make sense out of what was going on.

Matthews's arrogance was galling. With a toss of her head, Alana sent her hair flying over her shoulder. "Don't be absurd."

"Have you?" he persisted.

Yes! she screamed silently, but she'd bite off her tongue before she'd admit it out loud. "When pigs fly," she snapped, whirling away with a swish of skirts.

Even as she turned, she couldn't escape the feeling that their strange exchange had been less of a conversation and more of a gauntlet thrown. Instinct warned her the stakes were high, the price more than she could afford.

"Stick around, pet." Colin welcomed her with a smile. "You can be my lucky charm."

Dear, straightforward, uncomplicated Colin. Alana resisted the urge to smooth back the shock of auburn hair that dipped across his brow as she took her place directly behind him.

"Match your hundred, and raise you fifty." Colin added three rumpled fifty-dollar bills to the pile on the table.

"Too rich for my blood." The whiskered gentleman on Colin's right threw down his hand.

"Deal me out." Hank Mulroy, a land speculator, pulled out his pocket watch and checked the time. "I've lost enough money for one night."

The remaining man, John Clark, was nonplussed. He calmly transferred a stack of gold pieces to the pile in the center of the table. "You're on."

Alana watched the play, her hand resting familiarly on Colin's shoulder. A second card was dealt faceup, then another, until each player had five cards.

Colin reached out and tipped up the edge of the card in the hole.

Alana pressed closer for a better view.

A triumphant grin spread across Colin's face. "A seven," he crowed, picking it up and fanning his cards on the table. "Three of a kind beats two pair."

John Clark flung his hand down in disgust. "I guess the lady was your lucky charm, O'Shea."

Colin wrapped his arm around Alana's waist and drew her alongside him. "I knew that the first time I laid eyes on her." He winked at her. "C'mon, Clark. Let's go another round. Winner takes all."

"No thanks." Clark shoved back his chair and got to his feet. "Unlike some, I know when to quit."

Colin merely laughed. "Only an amateur quits when he's on a winning streak. Any takers?" he called out, looking around.

"I never back down from a challenge."

Heads swiveled toward the voice. Though Trey's words had been directed at Colin, Alana sensed they were meant for her: another coded message she could try to decipher later.

Trey Matthews unwound Candy's arm from his, rose from the chair, and sauntered over. Candy followed close at his heels.

"The railroad man has guts." Colin tipped back in his seat and grinned cockily at Trey through a haze of cigar smoke. "Now let's see if he knows how to lose."

Alana sucked in her breath. Colin's brash manner offended more often than it charmed. She studied Trey as he pulled out the chair opposite Colin. His expression gave no clue to his thoughts. If he was annoyed with Colin, it didn't show. At their first meeting, she had sensed a certain ruthlessness in him. Nothing since had altered that impression.

Colin leaned forward, eager for the game to begin. "All right, Matthews, I'll take on a city slicker."

Quicker than a brushfire, word of the high-stakes poker game spread throughout the Gilded Lily. Within minutes, patrons left their tables and places at the bar to cluster around the table. A few waged side bets on the outcome.

Colin straightened his cuffs with a flourish, then reached for the cards.

"Not so fast, O'Shea." Trey laid a restraining hand over Colin's.

"Getting cold feet?"

"Two stipulations."

"Go on. I'm listening."

"Fresh deck."

Colin nodded.

"And the lady deals." Trey inclined his head to indicate Alana.

Her small gasp of surprise was lost in the buzz of speculation. Both men were watching her closely. Though Trey's expression was bland, his eyes were bright and alert. Colin, on the other hand, looked clearly suspicious.

Colin's eyes darted from Alana to Trey, then back again, weighing the advantages and disadvantages. Finally, his mouth sullen, he shrugged. "All right. We're wasting time."

Trey watched Alana leave Colin's side and take her place at the table, where she gracefully arranged her skirts. With her fancy airs, one could imagine her at some high-class finishing school for young ladies, pouring tea and simpering with the best of them.

Alana held out her hand for a new deck of cards. "I'm ready, gentlemen, if you are. Shall we make it five-card stud?"

Colin grunted his assent. With a slight nod of his head, Trey indicated that he, too, was agreeable.

Alana shuffled the deck and, with practiced ease,

dealt each player a card in the hole, followed by a second faceup.

"All right, Matthews," Colin directed, "time to see the color of your money."

Trey withdrew his wallet and produced ten crisp one-hundred-dollar bills, which he added to the pot. "This ought to match what's on the table."

A ripple of anticipation went up from the onlookers as they inched closer for a better view.

Candy draped her arms around Trey's neck. "Show 'em how it's done, sugar," she cooed in his ear.

Alana dealt each man a third card faceup, then a fourth. Tension caused men to shuffle their feet and trade uneasy looks. In mute disbelief, Alana stared at the cards splayed on the table.

Colin puffed his cigar and grinned at Alana. "Two pairs. You did right by me, pet."

Alana hazarded a glance at Trey. His expression remained shuttered, unreadable. She had dealt him the ten, jack, king, and ace of diamonds. A worthless hand. The odds of his drawing one card out of fifty-two was almost nil.

Colin triumphantly turned over his remaining card. His grin turned gloating. "Another jack. That makes a full house."

Most of the onlookers headed toward the bar. Candy untwined her arms from around Trey's neck and stepped aside.

"Aren't you forgetting something, gentlemen?" Trey asked calmly, stopping them in their tracks. "The last card hasn't been played." He slowly uncovered the last card.

The queen of diamond's enigmatic smile mocked the disbelievers.

Trey's mouth curved upward. "Even city slickers like me know that a straight flush beats a full house."

The color washed out of Colin's face, then rushed back, staining his skin a dull red. "You're one lucky bastard, Matthews. How about one more hand?" He rummaged through his pockets for extra cash.

But Trey was already on his feet, gathering up his winnings. "No thanks, O'Shea. I might be an amateur, but I know when to quit."

Colin swallowed noisily, his gaze glued to the pile of money disappearing into Trey's pockets. "C'mon," he wheedled. "What's one more round?"

"Sorry."

Colin jumped to his feet. "You sonofabitch! You'll regret this one day." Turning, he stomped off.

Trey's glance slid to Alana, but she avoided his look.

"Hey, sugar, I'd be happy to help you spend all that money." Candy latched on to Trey's arm and rubbed up against him like a bitch in heat. "Let's go someplace—private."

"Lead the way." Smiling at the redhead, Trey tucked her arm in his, and together they strolled toward the door. A redhead for a blond, he thought. An even trade. One woman was as good as another, he tried to tell himself. He paused on the threshold and looked back in time to see Alana vanish through the batwing doors at the rear of the saloon. Whom was he trying to fool? One was gold, the other dross.

Candy followed the direction of his glance. "Forget her, sugar. Let Candy take care of you. I know ways of pleasing a gentleman."

Trey extricated himself from her grasp.

The fact that Trey was no longer smiling escaped Candy's notice. "Just say the word. I'll ditch my boyfriend and meet you at your hotel."

Trey took one of the bills out of his pocket, placed it in the palm of her hand, and wrapped her fingers around it. "Don't break your date on my account."

"Aw c'mon, honey," she wheedled. "We can have ourselves a real good time."

Trey's cool green gaze swept over her, cataloging then dismissing her flagrant charms. "I don't think so."

"Humph," she sniffed. "Not good enough, am I? You and Miss Hoity-Toity deserve each other. You're two of a kind." She marched off in a huff, the money clutched tightly in one fist.

Leaving the Gilded Lily, Trey opted to walk the short distance to his hotel. The pearl-handled pistol tucked into the waistband of his pants gave him a sense of security. After nightfall, the Stingaree District teemed with pickpockets and ruffians. Even in broad daylight, it could be a dangerous place. Especially for a woman. Particularly for Alana.

Unbidden, he recalled her close brush with death. He remembered the feel of her body against his after he had pulled her from beneath the wagon. She had been quaking like an aspen in a gale. It had seemed perfectly natural, not at all studied. In her panic, she had clung to him. And, God help him, he had wanted nothing more than to hold her, protect her. He could even remember the elusive scent of her perfume.

Damn! He wanted her. Wanted her more than he ever wanted a woman in his entire life.

One glance at Trey's scowling countenance sent a prostitute veering in the opposite direction. He lengthened his stride. He had gone to the Gilded Lily that evening not to indulge in a stupid, insignificant game of cards, but to see Alana. Where she was concerned, he was quickly becoming an addict.

Chapter 5

Colin slapped the reins and the rented buggy rolled down Third Street at a brisk pace. "Jaysus, Alana," he grumbled. "I'm glad Lottie turned down your invitation to join us. I like the girl well enough, but three's a crowd."

Alana adjusted the angle of her parasol to shield her face from the sun. "Lottie doesn't have many friends. I thought she'd enjoy going to Point Loma with us."

"Did you stop to think that not everyone likes getting up this early on a Sunday morning?"

"Nonsense, it's not that early. Besides, Lottie told me she grew up in the country."

He slanted her a skeptical look. "Since when have the two of you become such good friends?"

"I'm not sure you can describe us as good friends. We're still getting acquainted."

"She's hardly the sort I'd have thought you'd choose for a friend. You two are as different as night and day."

Alana's expression turned introspective. "In some ways, Lottie reminds me of myself," she said quietly. "Of the way I was when I first arrived in California—lonely, scared, thousands of miles from home, and feeling more than a little lost."

"I still remember spotting you on that train out of

Dodge." Colin smiled at the memory. "There I was with a satchel full of money, enough to finance the saloon of my dreams, and there you were—flat broke. Yet you had the one thing all the wealth in the world couldn't buy—class."

Alana swallowed the lump in her throat. "I don't know what I would have done without you."

Colin reached over and patted her hand. "You would have survived, pet, trust me."

"I'm not so sure, Colin. If you hadn't befriended me, offered me a job . . ." She shuddered, knowing Lottie's quiet desperation might easily have been her own if not for Colin O'Shea. Resolutely, she shrugged off the unpleasant thought. "Regardless of Lottie's background, we both have one important thing in common. She needs a friend, and so do I."

"How can you say that when you've got me?" Colin asked indignantly.

Alana smiled and squeezed his hand. "You're the best friend a person could ever have. I can never repay you."

"You don't owe me a thing." Colin focused his attention on an imaginary spot somewhere between the horse's ears. "Alana"—he cleared his throat—"I know I promised not to bring this up again, but . . ."

Alana studied his profile, dread churning her stomach. "Colin, please," she entreated, "we've been over this before."

"Are you angry that I see other women?" His voice was as tight as his hands on the reins. The horse tossed its head skittishly, protesting its rough handling.

"No, of course not." Alana clenched her hands together and prayed the beast would settle down. Ever since she was a child, horses had made her nervous.

Muttering a curse, Colin lightened his grip, and

once again the horse resumed its steady pace. "You're the only woman who matters to me. Just one word of encouragement, and I promise I'll be faithful."

"Colin, don't . . ."

"You'd make me the happiest man in all of California if you'd be my wife."

"Colin, I'm sorry, but I can't marry you." Distress deepened the hue of her eyes from blue to indigo. Regret thickened her voice to a throaty whisper. "You're my dearest friend in the whole world, but I don't love you the same way you love me."

"That could change." Colin set his jaw stubbornly.

Alana gazed sightlessly at passing buildings. "I'm not sure if I'll ever marry again. Perhaps when I have enough money set aside, I'll move away from San Diego and open a shop."

"Hogwash!" Colin scoffed. "A beautiful woman isn't meant to waste her life selling bonnets. She needs a husband to look after her."

A husband, home, children.

Respectability.

Alana exhaled a ragged sigh. Why did things she had once presumed were her birthright now seem so far out of reach? Where had her life taken a wrong turn? When she eloped with Phillip? She had loved Phillip Fairchild with all the passion of a girlish heart. He had been charming and handsome, and so full of life. Marrying him had seemed one grand adventure—a short-lived adventure that had ended in tragedy. They had had so many plans, so many dreams. With the promise of a job beckoning him, the future had seemed bright.

Unfortunately, her parents hadn't shared her optimistic view. They had discouraged Phillip's courtship and, when that failed, her father had outright forbidden Alana to see him. Arne Van Dorne claimed Phillip was only interested in her family's wealth and social position. That was grossly unfair, Alana had tearfully charged. Phillip loved her. And she loved him. Using the last of his small inheritance to finance the trip West, she and Phillip had eloped. All their plans and dreams along with their bright future were now laid to rest with Phillip in a Boot Hill cemetery.

Soon Colin headed the buggy north, away from the city. Alana's spirits lifted at the sheer beauty of the day. Clouds floated across the sky like frothy dollops of meringue in an azure bowl. The sun beamed down, imparting a benevolent warmth. A gentle zephyr swept across San Diego Bay, carrying the salty tang of ocean and teasing the fringe on Alana's parasol.

"What a city," Colin exhorted. "What a great place to be! I tell you, Alana, coming here when we did was a stroke of genius. San Diego is booming. Just yesterday, I heard a man claim the railroads bring in two to three thousand folks a month."

In Alana's mind, the idea of railroads led directly to Trey Matthews. Her thoughts drifted to the enigmatic stranger who had aroused her interest as no other man had. By turns, he confused, then irritated, but always fascinated her. Though he was outwardly cool and aloof, she had seen fire in his green eyes often enough to know he wanted her. She tried to deny her attraction to him, but an answering heat deep within her told her she wanted him, too.

"There's a building frenzy going on," Colin continued, extolling the merits of San Diego. "Offices, stores, hotels, and banks are going up all over the place. Everyone's talking about the Coronado Beach Company and the grand hotel they play to build out on the peninsula. It'll be the largest hotel in the world, one too gorgeous to be true. I'm thinking of investing in it myself."

"You, investing?" Alana snapped back to attention. "Do you think that's wise?"

"You can't always be cautious, Alana, or life passes you by. Sometimes a person has to take chances."

But some people were lucky, and others weren't, she thought.

"Well, here we are," Colin announced cheerily, slowing the buggy.

Alana looked around her with interest. Point Loma poked into the Pacific like an arthritic finger. Ahead of her, along a spine of land, rose the lighthouse, a squat sandstone building with a rolled tin roof. It was crowned with a brick tower that sported an iron and brass housing for the lighting apparatus that served as both a harbor light and a coastal beacon.

Colin followed her gaze. "Heard that light came all the way from France. In clear weather, sailors can see it twenty-five miles out to sea." He steered the buggy to a grassy clearing where a dozen or so carriages loaded with wicker picnic hampers were parked. He climbed down, and after securing the rented buggy to a low growing shrub, lifted Alana to the ground.

"This must be a popular spot for Sunday excursions," Colin observed with satisfaction.

Smoothing the wrinkles from her gown, Alana glanced around her. People were gathered in small knots, talking and laughing together. Suddenly, she felt out of place and unwelcome. "Perhaps coming here wasn't such a good idea."

"Stop being so sensitive. It's a beautiful day, let's not spoil it." Tipping the brim of his derby at a rakish angle, he proferred his arm with a flourish. "Shall we?"

She resolutely set aside her lingering misgivings.

Colin was right, she assured herself. The day was much too beautiful to waste it worrying about what others might think. With a smile, she accepted Colin's arm. He looked particularly dapper in a plaid jacket, brown pants, and derby. She, too, had taken pains with her appearance, selecting her favorite day dress of rose-colored watered silk with its matching bonnet and parasol. As they began to stroll the perimeter of the peninsula, she knew that outwardly they presented a striking pair.

Women chatted in small clusters; men smoked cigars and talked among themselves; children darted everywhere. While Colin was greeted by various business acquaintances, Alana's presence went ignored. Men she recognized as regular patrons of the Gilded Lily acted as if she were invisible. Afraid, Alana presumed, to risk their wives' ire. The women, as though fearing contamination by the town whore, collectively drew their skirts aside as she passed. Alana's smile grew strained as she listened to Colin's grandiose plan to capitalize on San Diego's land boom.

"Alana!" a male voice hailed her. "Wait."

Hearing her name called, she stopped abruptly. She watched as Leland Hastings separated himself from a group that included Trey Matthews. Leland forgotten, she felt her attention cling to Trey like a magnet. His dark head was bent attentively while he listened to the animated conversation of a lovely brunet. A couple, whom she guessed to be the girl's parents, beamed their approval, no doubt thinking what a fine match Trey would make for their darling daughter. Jealousy roared through Alana, the impact fierce and unexpected. Drawing in a ragged breath, she fought the urge to shove her way between Trey and the girl, and demand he look at her instead.

While she watched from a distance, Trey threw

back his head and laughed. Humor wrought a dramatic change on his darkly brooding features. All traces of arrogance and cynicism vanished; charm and good humor radiated. The overall effect left Alana dazed and slightly light-headed. She realized that this was the first time she had ever seen Trey laugh. A yearning welled deep within her. She wanted to be the woman at his side, the one he smiled at—the one who made him laugh. Shaken by the realization, she dragged her gaze away.

"What a stroke of luck," Leland said, his black walnut walking stick swinging in time to his steps. "I didn't expect to see you here today. Do you mind, O'Shea, if I speak to the lady in private? Family business," he added.

"No problem," Colin relinquished Alana's arm. "I want to see if anyone's interested in making a wager on next week's game between the Young Americans and the Golden Eagles."

"Baseball," Alana explained when Leland looked baffled. "It's the favorite sport here in San Diego."

Before turning away, Alana cast a final sidelong glance in Trey's direction. He had ceased his conversation with the pretty dark-haired girl and was watching her. Flustered by the intensity of his stare, Alana glanced hastily away.

Leland took her arm and steered her in the opposite direction. "I was planning on stopping by—what's the name of the establishment you sing at? The Golden Swan?"

"The Gilded Lily," she corrected automatically, still shaken by the expression on Trey's face.

"Ah, yes, that's it."

They strolled to a vantage point that overlooked the ocean. Far out in the bay, a ship steamed toward the harbor. A sidewheeler and coal burner with a full set of sails, the boat was a familiar sight. "The *Orizaba*," Alana told her companion. "In the early years before the railroads, it brought most of the people to San Diego."

"I'm quite taken with the climate here in your city," Leland remarked amiably. "I've heard Point Loma is an excellent spot from which to observe the migration of the gray whale each winter."

"Colin promised to bring me back again. He said that if you scan the water beyond the kelp beds, you can often see them shoot great spouts of water."

Leland turned his back on the view. Resting both hands on the gold head of his walking stick, he regarded her soberly. "I must confess, my dear, when I left Baltimore for California I never expected to find Alana Van Dorne singing in a cheap saloon. I still remember you as a comely young miss performing at her mother's musicales."

A hot flush crept into her cheeks. "I'm no longer Alana Van Dorne. I'm Alana Fairchild."

"So the scoundrel married you, did he?"

"Phillip could hardly be termed a scoundrel. He was a fine young man from a good family."

"Was?" Leland's voice rose indignantly. "What happened to the chap? Don't tell me he ran off and deserted you?"

"Phillip died from a bullet wound in Dodge City a week after we were married."

"Then why didn't you simply return home? Surely under those tragic circumstances, your family would have forgiven your impetuous marriage."

"It was more complicated than that." She sighed. "Phillip had lost all of our money gambling. All I had left was my ticket to San Diego. After what happened, I couldn't stay in Dodge. As soon as I buried Phillip, I took the first train out of town."

"You poor child!" Leland clucked his tongue sympathetically. "I had no idea. Is there anything I can do? If money's a problem, just speak up."

Embarrassment swept over her. "How very kind of you to offer, Mr. Hastings, but I'm no longer in need of financial assistance."

It was Leland's turn to be embarrassed. "*Hrummph.*" He cleared his throat. "Of course not. Foolish of me to speak out of turn. A beautiful woman such as yourself wouldn't go long without a protector. O'Shea must see that you're well provided for."

Pride and anger collided in a heated rush. How dare he assume Colin was her lover? A hot denial sprang to Alana's lips, but she bit it back. She didn't owe Leland—or anyone—an explanation. Let him assume what he wished, she thought defiantly. "You mentioned you wanted to see me?"

"Ah, yes." Leland rocked back on his heels. "I plan to return to Baltimore later this week. I thought perhaps you might like me to deliver a message to your family. If so, I'm at your disposal."

What could she possibly say to her family after a year's absence? Would they be eager to receive word from her? To welcome her back? Maybe by now enough time had elapsed and her father was willing to forgive her. Alana's mind spun with possibilities—and with hope.

"In a recent correspondence with your father, he mentioned your younger sister—Laura—was recently engaged to the son of a wealthy shipbuilder."

"Laura, my baby sister, engaged?"

Leland nodded. "I believe your father said they're planning a Christmas wedding. By the way, my dear, I took the liberty of telling him of the astonishing coincidence of my finding you on stage at the Gilded Lily."

Speechless, Alana stared at him. Her fledgling hope of being reunited with her family had been thoughtlessly destroyed. Given time, Alana had trusted her father would forgive her elopement with Phillip Fairchild. She had prayed that someday he would even pardon her greater offense—singing in a saloon. But now that his respected colleagues also knew of her shame, the disgrace would be too great for Arne Van Dorne to overlook.

Leland, unaware of the devastation he had caused, tugged on the watch fob swagged across his vest and consulted a good pocket watch. "Must be off. If you should want to send a message home, I'm staying at the Brewster Hotel."

A bone-chilling numbness fell over her. Home? Thanks in part to Leland Hastings, she no longer had a home. No longer had a family.

Chapter 6

Alana felt encased in an icy shell, a shell so brittle that she could shatter and break. She needed time alone, away from everyone, even Colin—time to absorb the ramifications of Leland's unknowing perfidy. Tears waited below a calm facade, a tempestuous sea contained by a thick crust of winter ice.

Head high, she wandered in search of solitude, a place far from prying eyes, where she could vent the hopelessness that threatened to overwhelm her. As she searched, she passed a group of women that included Miriam Cooper.

"The brazen hussy," she heard Miriam say. "Doesn't have the sense to know where she doesn't belong."

"I thought her sort slept all day and caroused all night," sniped another woman.

"Do you suppose she gets that hair color out of a bottle?" a third questioned.

"I wonder if she uses a breast enhancer."

A stunned silence was followed by a burst of tittering. "Martha, really! Where do you get such notions?"

Alana ignored the catty remarks and kept walking.

It was then that she noticed Trey stood nearby. Her cheeks flamed with humiliation as she realized he must have overheard the women discussing her.

Even without turning her head, she felt his eyes follow her progress.

His companion must have noticed his attention stray. "Who *is* that woman?" the girl demanded petulantly.

"No one you'd know." He dismissed the question with a casualness that cut deep. "Just a saloon singer from the Stingaree."

No one important. Just a saloon singer.

Those two curt sentences seemed to sum up Alana's life. A lump lodged in her throat. Is that all she would ever be? A saloon singer? The prospect added to her growing depression.

Eyes straight ahead, she continued her walk. Along the eastern border of the peninsula, she discovered a narrow footpath zigzagging down the steep bluff to the beach below. After a second's hesitation, she decided to investigate.

The sharp descent required all her concentration. Using her closed parasol as a walking stick, she carefully navigated down a trail lined with buckwheat, sage, and yucca. A rabbit darted out of the brush, startling her. Then, before her heart rate returned to normal, it vanished back from where it had come. Recovering from her fright, Alana continued on her way.

At the foot of the bluff, she paused to catch her breath. She snapped open her parasol to shield her eyes from the sun's glare and stared out to sea. Here, at last, she found the solitude she craved. The Pacific stretched in front of her, an endless bolt of sapphire satin. Whitecaps decorated its shimmering surface like frilly strips of lace. Overhead, gulls glided effortlessly on wind currents, their mournful cries an echo of her own unhappy thoughts. The air was redolent with brine, the salty tang reminding her of home. Home . . .

Lost forever.

All because of Leland Hastings's innocuous letter. Her father, Arne Van Dorne, was stubborn and proud. His standing in the community meant everything to him. As a young man, he had emigrated from Amsterdam, penniless but possessing a university education and a shrewd mind for finance. His talent quickly won him a series of promotions at the bank and eventually the coveted title of director. Marriage to the only daughter of a wealthy, established family had cemented his social position. Two accomplished daughters and a socially prominent wife served as visible symbols of his success. He had taken great pride in them. Until a year ago . . .

Tears blurring her vision, she turned and ambled along the shoreline. The narrow ribbon of rocky beach ended in a jumble of rocks a short distance away. Tidepools, wells of saltwater, pockmarked this section of coastline. Farther out, waves crashed over jagged boulders that protruded from the ocean floor, then continued their relentless surge toward shore, where they broke with frothy vengeance.

Alana watched for a while and was about to turn back when she noticed a scrap of blue fluttering among the rocks guarding the tidepools. Distracted from her gloomy contemplation, she stared at it curiously. The blue scrap disappeared from sight, then almost instantly reappeared in its entirety. Alana blinked in surprise. Little Sarah Louise Cooper, garbed in a bright blue dress, her sandy curls tied with a satin hair ribbon, stepped out from behind a rock.

"Sarah?"

Sarah Cooper looked up guiltily, then her face broke into a grin. "Alana, I'm exploring. Come see what I've found."

The little girl's enthusiasm was so infectious it almost made her smile. Alana schooled her features along stern lines. "Does your mother know you're down here?"

"Uh—no." Sarah's sandy curls bounced in denial. "She'd only scold. Come see what I found."

Carefully circumventing several large rocks, Alana stepped closer for a better look. "What is it?"

"A sea anemone."

Alana leaned closer as Sarah squatted down on a rock and stuck her finger into the water. A flower with stubby petals, vaguely resembling a dahlia from her mother's garden, closed around the girl's index finger tighter than a newborn's fist.

"Have you ever seen anything like it?"

"It's quite fascinating, Sarah," Alana replied, sounding properly impressed, "but your parents are going to be worried about you."

Sarah jumped up and hopscotched across the rocks comprising the tidepool. "In a minute. Just as soon as I show you the starfish I found. It's right over here." She leaped toward a boulder.

And missed.

Alana's breath caught in her throat as Sarah's head disappeared below the water's surface. Before she could react, Sarah emerged, coughing and sputtering, waist-deep in water. Her once perky hair ribbon trailed down her face like seaweed.

Perilously close to tears, Sarah shook the ribbon out of her eyes. Her lower lip trembled. "My new dress is all wet. Mother is really going to be mad at me now."

Alana smiled at the child, trying to mask her concern. "It's all right, honey. I'll explain what happened."

Sarah's eyes lit with hope. "Would you?"

"Of course." Alana forced the thought of another

confrontation with Miriam Cooper from her mind. Rucking up her skirts, she carefully started across the sea-slicked rocks toward the frightened child. Twice the slippery leather soles of her shoes threatened to slide out from under her. She dropped her skirts and, arms flailing, twice righted herself just in time to keep from falling. When she was closer to the child, she extended the handle of her parasol. "Just grab on to this and climb out."

Sarah grasped the parasol and tugged. Nothing happened. She tried again—and failed. Her face puckered. "I can't. My foot's stuck between two rocks."

A breaker burst over the boulder directly behind her, liberally dousing Sarah with cold water. "Alana," she wailed. "Help me, please."

Even before the sound of Sarah's plea faded, Alana tossed her parasol aside and pulled off her shoes. Sharp edges of rock cut into her stockinged feet. Her mind worked frantically for a way to rescue Sarah short of entering the water herself. Where were Sarah's parents when she needed them? Alana wondered angrily. A quick glance over her shoulder confirmed her fear that the stretch of beach as well as the bluff above were deserted. Miriam was probably too busy gossiping to realize her child was missing.

"Alana!"

The terror in Sarah's scream made Alana's blood curdle.

"Cr-crabs . . . Hundreds of crabs . . ."

As she watched in horror, the rock to which Sarah clung for support became a living, crawling mass. Crabs skittered from crevices, pincers waving, and skated across the uneven surface in their peculiar sideways motion. Still another variety with shiny black shells covered the granite like an unsightly disease. Alana's hand flew to her mouth to stifle a cry. She thought she was going to be ill.

Alana hoped—no, prayed—that the girl's screams could be heard above the pounding surf. But there was no time to waste. Sarah's rescue depended on her. Swallowing back her revulsion, she took a deep breath and stepped off the rock on which she was standing into thigh-deep water.

"H-hurry, Alana. I'm so sc-scared."

"I'm coming, sweetie. It's all right." Rose silk billowed around her waist as she waded toward the little girl. At first the frigid water was painfully cold against her legs. Then, mercifully, a numbing sensation spread through her lower limbs.

"Alana, quick, I can feel one crawling down by back. Hurry, please hurry!" Sarah's voice rose with hysteria as she twisted around, straining to see over her shoulder.

Indeed, there was a dark, ungainly scavenger marching awkwardly down Sarah's blue dress. Alana knocked it off with the back of her hand. Then, giving Sarah a reassuring smile, she smoothed a lock of wet hair from her frightened face. "It's gone."

"What if you can't get my foot unstuck?"

Worry zipped through her at the sight of Sarah's blue-tinged lips. She injected confidence in her voice, a confidence that was shaky at best inside. "Don't worry. I'll get you out of here in a jiffy."

Alana closed her mind to the hideous sight of crabs scrabbling over the rock. Bending her knees slightly, she eased her arms into the water and grasped Sarah's leg. "When I count to three," she instructed, "pull as hard as you can. One . . . two . . . three!"

Sarah pulled and pulled, but her foot remained

trapped. Alana bit her lip to keep back her disappointment.

Tears rolled down Sarah's paper-white cheeks. "I t-told you it was st-st-stuck." Her voice caught on a sob.

Alana gritted her teeth. She knew what she had to do. The knowledge filled her with revulsion. She called forth every ounce of courage she possessed. At that particular moment, the task facing her seemed more daunting than stepping between two men holding pistols, more daunting than facing a cold-blooded killer named English. Before she could reconsider, she sucked in a great lungful of air, bent double at the waist, and stuck her head beneath the water.

An even greater number of crabs inhabited the underwater world. The second Alana opened her eyes, she saw them stuck everywhere she looked. Blocking out the loathsome creatures, she concentrated instead on Sarah. Angling her head slightly, she distinguished the girl's foot wedged solidly between two rocks. Placing her hands around Sarah's ankle, she exerted all her strength to pull back and up.

Her lungs burned from a lack of oxygen. She thought she felt the foot give a fraction and tried harder. This time she was successful. Sarah's foot popped free.

Alana quickly straightened, shaking water from her eyes and breathing deeply.

Sarah watched her, a tremulous smile on her lips. "Your hat is all wet," she offered shyly.

Alana touched the sodden mass atop her head that had once been a stylish bonnet. Then reaching out, she tweaked Sarah's straggling satin hair ribbon. A giggle of pure relief erupted. "Aren't we a sight!"

Sarah giggled, too, a weak sound but a giggle nevertheless, and Alana felt a small measure of tension melt away.

"Let's get out of here before your parents send out a search party." Alana wrapped her hands around the child's waist and boosted her out of the water onto the nearest level surface. Next she hauled herself out. Taking Sarah's small, cold hand in hers, she carefully moved with the child from rock to rock and finally onto the pebbly band of beach.

Sarah stood shivering on the sand. "I'm freezing."

Alarm raced through Alana anew. She feared for Sarah's well-being. It was well-known that lung fever claimed many young lives every year. Kneeling down, she bunched Sarah's dress in her hands and squeezed out seawater. Briskly, she chafed the small body, trying to restore a modicum of warmth.

"Sarah! Sarah, are you all right?"

Great was Alana's relief when she looked up to find Ronald Cooper running down the beach toward them. Trey followed close on his heels.

"Sarah, baby, are you hurt?" Cooper knelt down and opened his arms.

Sarah flung herself into them. "I'm sorry, Daddy."

"There, there, baby. There's nothing to be sorry about." He hugged his daughter tight, all the while glaring at Alana. "Miss Fairchild should have more sense than to bring you down here. These tidepools can be dangerous. You might have drowned."

"But, Daddy—"

Cooper took off his jacket, threw it over Sarah's shoulders, then scooped her up. "Hush, baby. I'm taking you back to your mother. You gave her quite a scare."

Over his daughter's head, he glowered at Alana. "I could press charges. Let this be a warning. Stay away from my daughter, or I'll have you arrested." Alternately scolding and comforting, he started toward the bluff with Sarah clutched tightly in his arms.

Stunned by his accusation, Alana stared after him, all the while aware that she wasn't alone. For the second time that day, Trey Matthews had witnessed her abject humiliation. She squared her shoulders, conscious of how she must look, wet and dripping in her salt-stained gown and ruined bonnet. She pushed her straggling hair back from her face. She wished she could vanish rather than face the censure that she would surely see in Trey Matthew's clear green gaze.

Would this horrendous afternoon ever end? she wondered bleakly. She couldn't bring herself to meet his look. Stalling for time, she grabbed a sodden handful of silk and wrung it out. Her favorite day dress was ruined. This little episode had given the term *watered silk* an entirely new meaning. A nervous giggle threatened to escape, then she sobered. She wished Trey would speak, break the terse silence that stretched interminably between them. Did he agree with Cooper? Did he, too, believe she would endanger an innocent child?

Cooper had succeeded in frightening her with his charges. Could he really have her arrested? The notion was ludicrous. Preposterous. But who would take the word of a woman whom the town branded a whore over one of its leading citizens?

The answer was appallingly simple. No one. Bitterness flooded through her.

Eyes blazing, she raised her gaze to meet Trey's. "Don't just stand there, go ahead, say it," she challenged, needing a scapegoat for her wounded self-image. "You agree with Cooper, don't you?"

"Cooper's a fool," Trey retorted softly. He plucked a strand of seaweed from her bonnet.

Alana stared at him in disbelief. She had been

prepared to heatedly defend herself; his ready capitulation left her speechless.

He closed the distance between them. "That notwithstanding, he's acting like a typical parent who's been half out of his mind with worry. Give him time. He'll come to his senses."

The last thing Alana had expected from Trey Matthews was sympathy. "It's not only Ronald Cooper." She made a broad, sweeping gesture. "It's all of them."

Trey reached out and briskly rubbed her arms, much as she had done minutes ago to Sarah. "Who do you mean, *all* of them?"

"The whole town." She knew she sounded like a madwoman, but she was beyond caring. "I'm tired of being treated like a leper."

"I don't see you that way at all. I think you're the most amazing woman I've ever met."

Surprise stunned her into silence. "Do you really?" she finally asked, her voice suddenly husky. He stood close. Close enough for her to see tiny amber flecks in his green eyes. His nearness left her feeling strangely unsettled and off balance.

"Really," he assured her. The wistfulness in her tone struck a chord deep inside him. For a beautiful woman, she seemed oddly vulnerable. His hands ceased their movement. When they resumed a heartbeat later, the pressure had gentled, the rhythm had changed. The palms of his hands languidly stroked her from shoulder to elbow and back again. "You have more courage than most men I've known."

Alana struggled to combat the sensual haze fogging her mind. His touch burned away her chill, sent rivers of fire coursing through her veins. She shivered from the riot of emotions cascading through her.

Wordlessly, Trey tugged off his jacket and draped

it around her shoulders. He gripped the lapels firmly, holding her captive as he thoughtfully perused her face, feature by feature. It was true, he realized bemusedly, she was the most amazing woman he'd ever met. A captivating blend of grace and spirit. A woman to stand side by side with him during the golden days of summer. One to grow old with in the twilight of winter. His head lowered to hers, and his breath whispered across her lips. "You're a rare woman, Alana Fairchild. In fact, I find you quite irresistible."

"Trey," she sighed, then all coherent thought fled as his mouth claimed hers. Hot and insistent, his lips moved over hers with powerful mastery. Needs, long suppressed, swept through her, uprooting resistance, scattering reservation. When his tongue slipped between her parted lips, she felt her knees buckle. If he hadn't still been holding on to the lapels of his jacket, she would surely have slid to the ground.

Reluctantly, Trey ended the kiss. He made no move to step back but rather held her secure in the circle of his arms. "Is it so important to you what others think?"

"The townspeople just make me so angry. I'm every bit as good as they are." Her voice was muffled against his chest. "My family is one of the most respected in Baltimore."

Baltimore? Trey stiffened.

Alana sensed the sudden tension in his body. Her mind grabbed the most obvious reason for this change in him. "You don't believe me, do you? But it's the truth, I swear."

"Tell me about your family," he prompted in a carefully controlled voice.

Alana drew a shaky breath and fought to recapture her self-righteous indignation. "I attended the finest schools, shopped at the most exclusive stores, vacationed at Newport every summer. Everywhere I went, I was treated with deference and courtesy. Then I carelessly tossed respectability aside, never realizing its true value. Never realizing"—her voice hardened with bitterness—"until it was too late—until my reputation was in ruins."

Trey wondered: Could the woman he held so tenderly in his arms be the same woman who had driven Robert to end his life? Had her late husband and Robert's friend been one and the same? Impossible . . . or was it? "Your reputation," he said slowly. "It means a lot to you?"

"Yes," she whispered. "It means everything."

"Alana!" Colin's voice carried on the breeze.

Trey released her abruptly and stepped back. Feeling as though she'd been cast adrift, Alana struggled to collect her wits. Nervously, she moistened her lips, which tasted of salt—and Trey. She darted a glance at him, but his expression was impassive. If he was affected by what had just transpired between them, he gave no indication.

Colin sprinted toward them, coattails flapping. He drew up short in front of Alana, and eyed her wet clothing in disgust. "Jaysus, Alana, you look like a drowned rat. You certainly picked a fine time for a swim."

She laughed, but even to her own ears it rang false. "You're absolutely right, Colin. Next time you take me to a beach, I'll bring my bathing costume."

Colin whipped Trey's jacket from around her shoulders. "Take your jacket, Matthews," he growled, shoving it at him. "I'm here now. I'll take care of the lady." He replaced the jacket with his own.

Alana didn't protest as Colin placed a proprietary arm around her and led her away. Neither did she look back. She didn't have to. She could sense Trey's gaze following them. A drowned rat, Colin had called her. Indeed, the description must be apt, she thought as she plodded up the beach, her sodden skirts dragging in the sand.

Trey watched them disappear up the winding trail along the bluff. Then, hands behind his back, he paced the narrow expanse of beach. He wasn't ready to rejoin the group congregated at the lighthouse above. He needed time to think. Word by word, phrase by phrase, he recalled his conversation with Alana. He had never been one to believe in coincidence.

Until now.

As much as he wanted to, he couldn't ignore Alana's startling disclosures. Her family was the cream of Baltimore society. She and Robert would surely have traveled in the same social circles. Trey didn't want to believe it. God help him, he didn't want to believe it. But as hard as he struggled to deny it, the glaring truth leaped out at him: *Alana Fairchild and Alana Van Dorne were one and the same.* Her precious Phillip had been Robert's young English friend. At last, he had learned the bastard's name.

Remembered pain and fresh anger twisted his gut into a cold, tight knot. Fate had landed Alana Fairchild back in his life just as though it were Christmas morning and she were gift wrapped and tied with a silver ribbon.

Chapter 7

Gift wrapped and tied with a silver ribbon. Alana plucked the bow a final time, then nodded, pleased with the results. The package looked as pretty as the gift inside. She had spent the entire day searching for just the right present to mark her sister's betrothal and had finally decided on a lovely Valenciennes lace shawl. Now all that remained to do was to deliver it to Leland Hastings.

Alana alighted from the horsecar and walked the short distance to the Brewster Hotel situated on the southeast corner of Fourth and C. A rococco palace that catered to commercial travelers, it was the first building in San Diego to boast an elevator. Alana stepped inside and looked around the lobby with interest. She had the impression of mahogany paneling, plush Oriental carpets, and a miniature jungle of greenery. The stale smell of tobacco hung in the air. Men stood in groups of twos and threes talking and smoking. Still others moved through the lobby with a sense of purpose in their stride. It was clearly a man's domain. With a start, she realized that as the only female present, she was the object of whispered speculation among the hotel's patrons.

Spying the front desk, Alana renewed her grip on the package and resolutely crossed the lobby, ignoring the interested stares that followed her. At her approach, the desk clerk, a man in his forties who sported an ample girth and thinning hair slicked over a bald spot, looked up from his ledger.

"Good afternoon, madam." He favored her with an unctuous smile. "I'm Tucker Bixby. How may I be of service?"

"Could you tell me if Mr. Leland Hastings is in?"

"Hmm . . . Hastings?" He drummed his pudgy fingers on the polished desktop and pretended to ponder the matter.

"He's an elderly, rather distinguished-looking gentleman," she supplied helpfully.

"Ah, yes, Mr. Hastings!" He beamed. "A fine gentleman indeed. From back East, I believe."

"Yes, that's the one." Alana schooled the impatience from her tone. "Is he in?"

"No, I'm afraid not," Bixby said with a sympathetic wag of his head. "He left on business not thirty minutes ago."

"Oh, I see." Disappointed, Alana stood for a moment trying to decide whether to leave the package with a brief note or to return later.

Tucker Bixby rested an arm on the desk and leaned forward. "Can't get rid of the feeling that I've seen you somewhere before. I pride myself on the fact that I never forget a face. Especially a beautiful one such as yours."

Alana ignored the remark. "Did Mr. Hastings happen to mention when he'd return?"

"Can't say that he did." Bixby frowned as though giving the matter considerable thought, then his frown melted into a lecherous smile. "But he obviously wasn't expecting such a charming guest."

Alana had had enough of this odious desk clerk. She started to turn away when he suddenly snapped his fingers.

"It's the hair!" he exclaimed.

She turned back. "I beg your pardon?"

"That's why I didn't recognize you sooner. You're wearing your hair differently. Usually all those pretty blond curls are hanging nearly to your waist. Drives the men wild. Course you're dressed different, too." He gave a deep-throated chuckle that ended in a hacking cough. "You're that saloon singer from the Stingaree, aren't you?"

"You're familiar with the Gilded Lily?"

"Sure. Make it my business to see what goes on in this town. People expect me to know these things. No accounting for some tastes, if you catch my drift."

"Would you kindly tell Mr. Hastings that I came by."

"I take it the gentleman wasn't expecting you?"

"No," Alana admitted tightly. "I wanted to surprise him."

"You still can." Tucker Bixby dropped his voice conspiratorially and motioned her closer. "If you're real nice to me, I could give you a passkey to Mr. Hastings's room. Then you could make yourself all comfy until he returns."

Angry color flagged her cheeks. "I merely came to deliver a package. Please tell Mr. Hastings that Alana Van Dorne Fairchild called while he was out."

"And a nicely wrapped package if I do say so myself," he said with a broad wink.

Alana knew the lewd comment had nothing to do with her sister's gift. Intent on fleeing, she turned and collided with Trey Matthews.

As he reached out to steady her, the package fell to the floor. He stopped to retrieve the gift, then flicked his glance over the neatly written name tag. "Laura Van Dorne," he read quietly.

Until he had actually heard Alana say it aloud, until he had seen her handwriting on the gift tag, Trey had nurtured the hope that he was wrong about her. But the truth was staring him in the face. The Stingaree saloon singer who attracted him like no other woman ever had was the same unfeeling bitch who had killed his brother. How could that be? Could a polished red apple be rotten at the core? Could such beauty mask an evil, cunning soul?

He schooled his features into a polite smile. "Someone's birthday?"

"No, it's an engagement gift for my sister." Alana snatched the gift from him. How much of the conversation with the repugnant Tucker Bixby had Trey overheard? she wondered. Blood rushed to her face anew, this time in acute embarrassment.

Trey studied her flushed cheeks a moment longer before switching his attention to the desk clerk. "Correct me if I'm mistaken, Bixby, but I'm under the impression that the Brewster advertises its hospitality."

Tucker Bixby squirmed uncomfortably. "Yes, sir."

"So if the manager learned that Mrs. Fairchild was prevented from delivering a package to one of your guests, he'd be happy to rectify it. Isn't that right, Bixby?"

"Quite, sir."

Trey took the gift from Alana and placed it on the polished desk surface squarely beneath the clerk's nose. "Then delivering this package to Mr. Hastings shouldn't be a problem, should it?"

"No, sir."

"Good." Trey smiled coldly. "See that Mr. Hastings gets it the minute he returns."

Tucker Bixby grasped his lapels with both hands and tugged to close his jacket, which could not cover his considerable paunch. "I'll see to it personally, Mr. Matthews."

Alana barely suppressed a smile as she observed the exchange. She admired the authoritative way Trey had handled the problem. Tucker Bixby hadn't stood a chance. She doubted there were many men brave enough to challenge a simple request from Trey Matthews. Certainly none foolish enough to defy an order.

Trey took her elbow and escorted her across the lobby. "I've been thinking of you a great deal since Sunday," he said, lowering his voice. "As a matter of fact, I planned to stop by the Gilded Lily this evening to speak with you."

She tilted her head to see his face better and was struck anew by his good looks. He was by far the most attractive man she had ever met. Dark, intelligent, brooding; a compelling combination. Alana was suddenly inordinately grateful that for once during one of their chance encounters she wasn't either torn and tattered or sodden wet. She felt confident knowing she presented a picture of studied elegance in her mauve suit with its ruffled skirt and embroidered basque trimmed with matching ribbons.

"You've piqued my curiosity. I hope you won't keep me in suspense," she said.

"Curious, eh?" He pushed open the door leading to the street and waited for her to precede him. "Tell me, Alana, do you also admit to being impatient? Perhaps even impulsive?"

"I'm not sure I'd describe myself in those terms," she hedged.

"I must confess, you intrigue me, but then you probably have had that effect on men since you were in the cradle."

She frowned thoughtfully. Was a subtle thread of sarcasm woven through the flattery? "Is that a compliment? With you, I can never be quite sure."

"Was there ever a man alive who was impervious to your considerable charms, Mrs. Fairchild?" he countered with a small smile. "Rest assured I'm no different from legions of others."

Before she could think of a suitable reply, he grasped her elbow and steered her down the street. She tried to disengage her arm from his grip, but he held her securely. "Where are you taking me?"

"There's a cozy little tearoom just down the block. I thought we might get better acquainted over tea and biscuits. Afterward, I'll escort you home." He slanted her a look. "As you well know, the Stingaree can be a dangerous place for a lady even in broad daylight."

Tea and biscuits? The incongruity of the invitation almost made her laugh. Trey Matthews struck her more as a steak and bourbon type. What could the two of them possibly have to discuss over tea and biscuits? But it would have been churlish to refuse. Besides, Trey's assumption was correct. She had always been curious.

The tearoom he selected was charming. It had been decorated to resemble a miniature garden. Wisteria-patterned wallpaper covered the walls. Ivy climbed a latticework arbor in the center of the room. Colorful blooms filled small pots on each table. It was the sort of place her mother would have frequented, Alana reflected as a pink-cheeked girl in a starched white apron led them to a corner table.

Trey held out the wicker chair for Alana, then after seating himself opposite her, gave the waitress their order. As soon as the girl left, he flashed Alana a sympathetic smile. "From the bit of conversation I overheard, I gather Bixby was giving you a hard time."

Alana carefully unfolded the linen napkin and

spread it across her lap. Trey's remark answered her earlier question. He had heard the desk clerk's sly innuendos. "The man has a filthy mind. He assumed I was there to visit Mr. Hastings for . . . other reasons."

"I'll speak to the manager about him."

Her gaze flew to his face. "Why would you do that for me?"

"Why not?"

Alana was spared an immediate response by the arrival of the waitress. The girl poured tea from a china pot painted with forget-me-nots and placed a plate of iced cakes in front of them. Nervously the girl looked at Trey for approval, then blushed profusely when he complimented her efficiency. She bustled off.

"Bixby had no call to insult you." Trey raised a brow. "Are you always so suspicious when someone tries to help you?"

She took a sip of tea and tried to sound casual. "No one has come to my defense in a very long time."

"I find that hard to believe. Your friend O'Shea seems quite devoted."

"Oh, he is." Alana jumped to Colin's defense. "Only . . ."

"Only . . .?" Trey observed her closely as she bit daintily into a pastry. Her finishing-school manners were impeccable, but she must have been absent the day they taught how to snag a rich husband. If not, she wouldn't have passed up the opportunity to marry the heir to the Prescott fortune. Poor Robert. According to their mother, the lad had been so besotted he would have given her the moon on a silver platter. Instead, Robert had given her something infinitely more precious—his life. As Trey remembered, his rage burned hotter.

"Colin tells me not to mind what others think," Alana said. "That it's natural for people to assume that any woman who sings in a saloon is a woman of low virtue. He said I'm being overly sensitive."

The woman was as unfeeling as a brick wall, Trey reflected bitterly. If she was as sensitive as she professed, Robert might still be alive. "Nonsense, I disagree wholeheartedly," he said. "A woman such as yourself, raised by an upstanding family, must be very conscious of her social position. Correct me if I'm wrong," he said, leaning back in his chair and studying her, "but you probably attended the very best school for young ladies, had a houseful of servants, and had parents who orchestrated every aspect of your life down to the correct fork to use. Since childhood, you were groomed to marry a rich young man from a family just like your own. Am I right?"

At his apt description, her lips curved into a smile more bitter than sweet. "And I've been a terrible disappointment to them."

He wondered how disappointed her parents would be to learn their precious daughter was a murderer. "Because you married someone they disapproved of?"

She broke off a small piece of cake. "My elopement with Phillip Fairchild was a blow to their pride, but they might have recovered. My father claimed Phillip was a wastrel who was only after my money, but he was wrong. Phillip and I cared about each other deeply. My reputation was damaged beyond repair when I began singing at the Gilded Lily."

"Why did you? Surely you must have known the harm it would cause."

Alana fidgeted with the handle of her teacup. "In certain situations, a person doesn't stop to analyze long-term consequences. They simply do what they must to survive."

He looked at her, unsmiling, weighing her words. "Yes," he answered at length, "I understand perfectly."

He sounded sincere, looked sincere, she thought. It would be easy—oh, so very easy—to believe that he did understand. Clearing her throat, she stood and picked up her handbag. "I really must be getting back. I need to go over tonight's material with my piano player."

Trey rose, paid the waitress, and followed Alana. Outside, he offered his arm. "My buggy is in front of the hotel. I insist on giving you a ride home."

He stopped before a stylish plum-colored buggy with gold striping tied to a hitching rail. He helped her inside, then climbed into the driver's side. The sturdy bay responded to the slap of the reins, and the buggy merged into traffic.

"Earlier you mentioned that you planned to drop by the Gilded Lily this evening to speak with me. You still haven't mentioned why."

"I spoke with Ronald Cooper about the incident with his little daughter at Point Loma on Sunday."

"I see," she murmured. Her stomach knotted with tension. Although she tried not to dwell on it, Cooper's threat to press charges distressed her. He was in a position to cause trouble. Because he was a highly respected citizen, his word would hold greater sway than hers. She didn't need more notoriety. The notion of defending herself against the unfair charges was repugnant. "And what was the outcome of your discussion?"

"I was able to convince Cooper his charges were completely unfounded."

Her eyes widened in disbelief. "Why?" she asked

when she found her voice. "Why would you go to so much trouble on my account?"

Trey concentrated on steering the buggy around a dray loaded with lumber. "Because I felt you were innocent. If anything, your efforts to save the child should be commended."

"How did you ever convince him when just a few days ago he was so certain that I had lured Sarah onto the rocks?"

He shrugged dismissively. "I merely let the facts speak for themselves."

Alana shook her head in confusion. "But you weren't there. How could you possibly know what happened?"

"I made a simple deduction from the way your shoes and parasol were scattered on the beach. You had obviously discarded the items in a hurry. It's not the way a lady who was going to leisurely explore the tidepools would leave her belongings."

"Were you able to convince the Coopers of this?"

"Once Sarah calmed down, she told them the whole story. They had little choice but to accept my theory. I expect an apology will be forthcoming."

Alana stared blindly at the passing shops and buildings. She was touched beyond words by Trey's effort on her behalf. She was merely a singer in a tawdry saloon; he was a respectable businessman. What did he have to gain by pleading her case? Nothing. Absolutely nothing. Yet in Trey Matthews, she had discovered an unlikely champion.

He reined to a halt in front of the Gilded Lily.

"Ever since our first meeting, I constantly find myself in your debt," Alana said. "Thank you again for your intercession on my behalf."

"No thanks are necessary. I was glad to be of help."

Silence stretched between them. Still, both seemed reluctant to part. Alana wanted to ask when she would see him again, but didn't want him to think her bold. Then another thought occurred to her. Perhaps he planned to leave San Diego with Leland Hastings. The idea staggered her. She didn't want him to leave. "Are you . . . ?" There was a husky catch in her voice, so she cleared her throat and tried again. "Are you planning to return to Baltimore with Leland?"

"No." He smiled inwardly, seeing through her ruse. "California is all that I hoped it would be. I plan to buy property here and settle permanently."

"Well." She smiled brightly. "From what Colin says, San Diego is ripe with opportunity."

"I've always been one to take advantage of every opportunity." With that, he climbed down from the buggy, circled it, and helped her alight.

His hands around her waist were strong, capable—and warm. So was the rest of his body. She could feel its heat burn through her layers of clothing like the summer sun on bare skin. "Thank you for seeing me safely home." Her voice dropped to a sultry whisper.

Unexpectedly, Trey reached out and traced the outline of her lips with his index finger. "I wouldn't want anything to happen to such a pretty lady."

The action seemed more intimate than a kiss. Desire pooled heavy and wet between her thighs. Her lips parted; her eyelids felt weighted. With difficulty, she restrained the urge to take a playful nip of his fingerpad, then soothe it with her tongue. She had never experienced anything quite like this, certainly never with Phillip. In spite of what others assumed about her, she had never considered herself a particularly sensual woman. The realization of how deeply

Trey Matthews could stir her with a simple touch frightened her.

"I don't want to keep Jimmie waiting." She picked up her skirts and fled into the saloon without even saying goodbye.

Trey watched her retreat. That was precisely what it was—a retreat. He should be pleased with himself. He had seen the hue of her eyes deepen, her breathing quicken. She was as responsive to his touch as tinder to a match. Yet that very fact angered him. She was a sensuous female who welcomed not only his touch, but undoubtedly the touch of countless others before him. Damn it all! It shouldn't bother him.

But it did.

He was in the audience that night. Afterward, she found a gift waiting in her room. Nestled in a prettily wrapped box were four iced cakes from the tearoom they had visited that afternoon.

The following evening, Alana had just finished singing "Lorena" when she saw him again. That night a hatbox arrived bearing the name A. TIDWELL. MILLINER. Raising the lid, she exhaled a sigh of delight as she lifted out the frilly pink bonnet she had admired in the woman's shop. The note read: *To replace the one that was ruined the day you suddenly decided to go for a swim*. Even without a signature, she knew Trey had sent it.

This went on for an entire week. More gifts followed: chocolates, roses, a painted fan, an antique filigree locket. Never once during this period did Trey approach her. He was always present during her performance, then left afterward without a word. So great was her awareness of his presence, Alana could sense him even before she saw him.

Trey was different from other men she had met. He

didn't press his attentions, but made her acutely aware of his interest with a look, a smile, a thoughtful gesture.

His restraint, while admirable, was driving her insane. He was playing a game of cat and mouse, and her nerves were on edge as she waited for him to make the next move. Colin was oblivious to her mounting tension. Only Lottie knew of what was becoming a nightly ritual.

"He's here," Lottie said in an excited whisper just before Alana was scheduled to go on stage.

Alana didn't have to ask whom she meant. Though she remained outwardly calm, her stomach did a queer flip in anticipation. Through the screen of her lashes, she saw Trey seated alone at a corner table, his eyes somber, mouth unsmiling, expression impassive. Frowning slightly, she nodded to Jimmie, who took a swig of beer before jangling the opening bars on the battered piano. She drew in a calming breath, released it slowly, then stepped onto the stage.

His gaze unwavering, Trey raised his glass in a mocking salute. From his vantage point, he had watched Alana smile and flirt. He had heard her laughter ring out. It wasn't fair that she blithely went on her merry way without having to suffer the consequences of her actions. It wasn't fair to Robert—or to his mother. He was the only one left to avenge his family. If all went according to plan, he'd teach her a lesson she wouldn't quickly forget. He'd use her, then discard her—just as she had callously discarded Robert's tender declarations of devotion.

Trey sipped his bourbon without tasting it. Thoughtfully, he studied the lovely blond singer he had deliberately set out to seduce. Bedding her would be no hardship, he admitted as his eyes charted her shapely curves. All week, he had carefully baited the trap with a series of small gifts designed to appeal to a woman. Yet he had dallied over each selection: a bonnet the exact shade of pink as the one ruined, a locket of exquisite workmanship, hand-dipped chocolates from San Diego's best confectionery. He set his glass down with a bang. Damn! he swore in disgust. His actions mirrored serious courtship more than a simple seduction.

He hoped it would soon be over. If tonight's offering was well-received, his trap would spring shut on its unsuspecting, but not blameless, victim. Finishing his drink, Trey shoved to his feet.

Alana wasn't singing for the audience; she was singing for Trey. She sang her first song with such zest, patrons were tapping their toes in time to the music. For her finale, she sang "I'll Take You Home Again, Kathleen," wringing forth so much emotion from the haunting ballad that more than one hardened gambler furtively dabbed at his eyes. The applause was thunderous.

Before her final bow was over, she sensed Trey had disappeared. She was filled with disappointment.

Lottie hurried up to her the minute she descended the stage. "Well, what do you suppose he sent this time?"

Alana laughed indulgently at her friend's enthusiasm. Lottie's anticipation was nearly as great as her own. Under Alana's tutelage, Lottie's appearance had drastically improved. She had abandoned the heavy makeup and garish colors for more flattering shades. The only thing Alana hadn't been able to alter was the sadness that filled the girl's expressive hazel eyes whenever she thought no one was watching.

"Let's go look."

"You mean now?" Lottie frowned worriedly as she scanned the packed saloon. "Gee, I don't know, it's awfully busy. Mr. O'Shea might get mad."

"We'll only be gone for a minute. No one will miss us." Alana clasped Lottie's hand and tugged gently. "And if they do, I can handle Mr. O'Shea."

After snaking their way through the crowd, they dashed up the back staircase as fast as their long skirts would allow.

"Look, Alana," Lottie squealed, pointing down the hall. "Another present."

A package the size of a shoebox, covered in silver paper, sat in front of her suite of rooms. She quickly scooped it up and went inside, where she perched on a small settee, the gift on her lap. Lottie sat on the edge of a Queen Anne chair and leaned forward. Alana's fingers trembled with excitement as she loosened the bow, unwrapped the box, and pried off the lid. A sigh of pleasure rushed out at the exquisitely wrought gift inside.

"What is it? Let me see." Lottie craned her head for a better view.

Alana gingerly withdrew a black lacquered music box embellished with intricate red and gold figures of fire-breathing dragons. She lifted the lid experimentally and, to her delight, an enchanting melody poured into the room.

"This fell out of the box." Lottie bent and picked up a small envelope.

Alana handed the music box over for Lottie's inspection. Savoring the anticipation sweeping through her, she held the envelope for a moment. It seemed heavier, bulkier than just a casual note. Slowly she slid her finger along the seal. Two tickets fluttered to her lap. She picked one up and examined it. It was to a performance of *The Mikado*, Gilbert and Sullivan's newest operetta, to be performed by a touring company direct from London.

Along with the tickets was a note: *Please join me for what promises to be an unforgettable evening. T.M.*

How could she resist?

Chapter 8

The white dress was too virginal. The blue one too plain. The gray too drab. Alana carelessly tossed the gowns aside.

"Sweet Jaysus, Alana! Have you been robbed?"

Alana spun around to face Colin. "No, I haven't been robbed," she replied irritably. "How many times must I tell you not to sneak up on me?"

Colin assumed an offended air. "I did knock. Swear on my mother's grave." He held his hand to his heart, his expression as innocent as a choirboy's.

Shaking her head in exasperation, Alana turned back to her wardrobe. "Which do you think, Colin?" she asked, holding up a gown of teal-green for his inspection. "This, or the pink?"

Colin scooped a mound of silk and satin from a chair, deposited it on the bed, then sat down. Crossing his legs, he lounged back and pondered the matter. "I'm partial to the green, but that's the Irish in me."

Alana hugged the gown to her and studied her reflection in the mirror. "Mmm . . . I don't know. Maybe the lavender . . ."

"Whichever you choose, you'll knock 'em dead. What's the occasion?"

"I've been invited to attend *The Mikado*. It received

encore after encore when it opened in London last year. I didn't think you'd mind if I took a night off."

His stony silence put her on the defensive. "Since I've worked for you, I've never taken a vacation, and I'm almost never sick. You always say I work too hard. Surely one night isn't too much to ask."

"If you wanted to go so much, why didn't you say something? I could've gotten tickets."

She hated the hurt that crept into his voice. It made her feel guilty when she had nothing to feel guilty about. *Except the fact that he loved her. And she didn't love him.*

"Who's the lucky gent?" Colin took a cigar from an inner pocket and was about to light it when he remembered Alana forbade smoking in her suite and put it back.

Alana avoided his eyes as she answered. "Trey Matthews."

"Matthews, is it? I might have known. He's a smooth operator, all right. How much do you know about him?"

Alana spread the teal gown across the bed. How much did she know about Trey? She shrugged. "Very little," she answered truthfully.

Colin crossed, then uncrossed his legs. "Precisely! I hate to remind you, but you haven't always shown the best judgment where men are concerned. Your precious Phillip wasn't the catch of the season. He made you a bride and a widow within a week—and a penniless one to boot."

"That isn't fair. We were both very young. I'm older now—"

"But not necessarily wiser. Did you bother to find out whether or not Matthew's married?"

"He doesn't wear a wedding band."

Colin snorted in disgust. "Neither does Ronald Cooper and we both know he's married."

"You're just angry because Trey beat you at your own game."

"That has nothing to do with it!" Colin snapped, leaping to his feet. "There's something about him. I can't put my finger on why, but I don't trust the man. Mark my words, Alana. He's trouble."

Colin stormed out, leaving Alana to stare after him. He's jealous, she told herself. He sees Trey as a threat to his male pride. Well, she wasn't going to allow Colin's petty jealousy to ruin what promised to be a wonderful evening.

Lottie arrived early to help Alana arrange her hair. A romantic at heart, the girl bubbled with excitement. She began to pull a hairbrush through Alana's long blond tresses. "Mr. Matthews is the handsomest man I've ever seen. He reminds me of a prince in a fairy tale."

Fairy tale? Alana tipped her head to one side and contemplated her reflection in the mirror above the dressing table. The naive Baltimore debutante had vanished, replaced by a woman whose eyes were shaded with a wisdom far beyond her years. Yet, once upon a time, like Lottie, she, too, had believed in fairy tales. But no longer. Fairy tales were for children. She had abandoned them along with her childhood dreams on a dusty Dodge City street the day her bridegroom's blood had seeped into the Kansas soil. "Do you believe in fairy tales, Lottie?"

Lottie stilled, the brush in her hand forgotten. Her eyes met Alana's in the mirror. All traces of excitement vanished, replaced by a haunting sadness. "No," she whispered. "Not anymore."

Alana wished she could take back the question. "I'm sorry, Lottie, I didn't mean to pry."

"It's all right." Lottie pointed to a picture in a silver frame on Alana's dressing table. "Is that your family?"

"Yes. It was taken shortly after Father was named director at the bank." She picked up the photograph and studied it wistfully before setting it carefully back down. "I just heard that my baby sister will be getting married soon. I still think of her as a little girl waiting for her first ball."

"You miss them. I can hear it in your voice. I miss my family, too." Lottie reapplied herself to the task of arranging Alana's hair. "My pa is a preacher back in Ohio. I've got me a sister, Mary, and two little nieces, too. Sure wish I could see them all again."

Lottie's circumstances were so much like Alana's it was frightening. "Is it a matter of money? Colin said there's a rate war brewing between the railroads. Tickets are going to get even cheaper. I've some money saved—"

"I can't go home." Lottie's voice cracked. She swallowed hard, then focused her attention on smoothing a curl into place. "I'd only embarrass my pa, him being a preacher and all. Folks still remember how I ran off with Johnnie Morrissey. Pa and Mary both begged me not to see Johnnie. They tried to tell me he was a no-account, but I wouldn't listen."

"What happened to Johnnie?" Alana asked quietly.

"He promised he'd marry me, but he lied. He ran off with another girl soon after we got to California. Took our money with him."

"I'm sorry, Lottie."

Lottie shrugged her shoulders. "It don't matter no more."

"Someday you'll meet a man who appreciates you. One who won't run off."

"The only men I seem to meet these days are the kind who wonder how much I charge for a quick tumble between the sheets. I'm not that kind."

"I know what you mean," Alana commiserated. She fastened a dangling jet earring in each lobe. "They all seem to think I have a price tag. I thought Trey Matthews was like that, too, when I first met him, but I was mistaken. He's a gentleman who treats me with courtesy and respect."

Belatedly, she remembered the bullet he had kept. Her face pinkened at the thought of his retrieving it from her bodice when she was unconscious. But perhaps she was doing him a disservice. Perhaps it had simply fallen out of her gown the evening she had fainted and he had carried her into Colin's office. Perhaps he had simply picked it up off the floor . . .

"A man as handsome and rich as Mr. Matthews can have his pick of any woman in town," Lottie chatted on.

"That's why I was so flattered he invited me to go with him this evening," Alana replied. "The townspeople will be out in full force for tonight's performance. Unlike the others, he's not ashamed to be seen in public with me." Absently, she reached for a cut-glass perfume bottle and removed the stopper.

Was it too good to be true? Why would an esteemed businessman be eager to flaunt a saloon singer as his companion? Surely he must realize the gossip it would create. Didn't he care? Or did he like courting attention? Stop it, she chastised herself. She had grown cynical. Why was she so determined to look for hidden motives? Why couldn't she just accept the fact that Trey wanted her companionship for an evening?

Perfume forgotten, she replaced the glass stopper with more force than was necessary. "Trey never once believed I was responsible for leading little Sarah Cooper down to the tidepools. He even defended me to her parents. That meant a great deal to me." She spoke vehemently, trying to convince not Lottie but herself of Trey's merits.

"He's a fine gentleman all right." Lottie shoved in the last hairpin and stepped back to view her handiwork. A cluster of pale gold curls hugged the back of Alana's head, the overall effect simple yet elegant. Lottie reached into a box and, withdrawing a waxy white gardenia from a bed of tissue, pinned it among the curls. The sweet floral scent wafted through the room. "Perfect," she declared with satisfaction. "Mr. Matthews's flower sure does smell pretty."

Alana eyed her reflection critically, then smiled her approval. "Give me a minute to slip into my dress, then if you'll be so good as to fasten it for me . . ." She rose and stepped behind a painted screen. Minutes later she emerged in a stunning black evening gown fashioned of velvet and lace. A lace ruffle edged the neckline, which was cut high at the back and low in the front. More lace trimmed the sleeves and hem. Around her neck, tied with a black velvet ribbon, she wore the antique locket that Trey had given her.

She presented her back to Lottie, who adroitly fastened the tiny row of covered buttons, then turned for her friend's final approval. "Well, Lottie, do you think Mr. Matthews will rue his invitation?"

Lottie's awed gaze gave Alana the assurance she needed. "Oh, no," she breathed. "You're beautiful. All my life I wished I could look like you. Instead I'm as plain as bread pudding."

"I don't want to hear you talk like that." Alana

filled a jet evening bag with items from her dressing table. "You *are* very pretty, Lottie. Believe me, beauty isn't always a blessing. Sometimes it can be a curse."

Lottie let out a short bark of laughter. "Surely, you gotta be jokin'."

"On the contrary, I'm deadly serious." Picking up a pair of long black gloves, Alana worked them over her fingers. "Ever since I can remember, I've had to contend with its drawbacks. Other women see you as competition. They're either intimidated by your appearance or they're afraid you might steal their beaus. Back in Baltimore, even though I had many suitors, I could never be certain if they were really interested in me or in my family's money and social position. Here," she said, warming to her subject, "men seek you out because they're attracted to your looks. They don't care who you are inside. They just want to be seen in your company. It makes them feel important. To them you're no more than a trophy to be put on display, a boast of their prowess."

Lottie listened with a dubious look on her face.

A small enameled clock on the dressing table chimed the hour. Alana snatched up her handbag and a fringed shawl. "It's time. I don't want to keep Trey waiting."

"Have a wonderful evening," Lottie said wistfully as she watched Alana leave.

Alana pushed through the doors at the rear of the saloon. She immediately spotted Trey standing at the bar talking with Colin. As she moved toward them, both men looked up and watched her approach. Her gaze darted anxiously from one to the other. Heat and ice. Two extremes. Trey coldly contained, all emotion hidden, as dangerous as an iceberg set to rip through the hull of an unsuspecting ship. Colin ready to explode in a blaze of anger and resentment. Abruptly, he turned his back, and the fleeting impression vanished like a puff of smoke.

Trey stepped forward as she drew near. Alana was dimly aware of the hush that had fallen over the Gilded Lily. The saloon patrons gawked unabashedly. She felt as though she were center stage and she, Trey, and Colin were the principal actors. She smiled on cue and accepted the hand that Trey held out to her. He raised her hand to his lips and brushed a kiss across the back of it. The pleasurable tingle that traveled up her arm caught her unaware. Her breath hitched in her throat.

Startled by her response, she raised her eyes to his and caught him gauging her reaction with smug satisfaction. Disturbed, disappointed, and angered by his expression, she tried to pull free from his grasp, but he held fast.

"I didn't think it possible, but you manage to look more beautiful every time I see you."

"Do you suppose the fact that I'm neither covered with dust and grime, nor sopping wet and trailing seaweed might be responsible for the improvement?" she asked archly.

A grudging smile quirked his lips. "Personally, I'm partial to seaweed."

"I'll try to remember." She returned the smile, pleased to discover he had a latent sense of humor. The exchange helped dispel some of the tension between them.

He tucked her hand in the crook of his arm. "I'm honored you elected to join me this evening. It should be a memorable night."

She drew upon ingrained social skills. "I've no doubt it will be."

Colin listened to their exchange, his mouth sullen.

Tossing back his whiskey, he studied her through narrowed eyes. "I see you ignored my advice and didn't wear the green."

Alana's hand tightened on Trey's arm. Appalled by Colin's deliberately provocative remark, she gave Trey a sidelong glance. He was watching her, too, a dark brow lifted askance. The unspoken question hung between them. A silent challenge.

Colin rocked back on his heels with a self-satisfied grin. He apparently relished the notion of being a nettle under his rival's skin. "As I've often told Alana, even if she wore a feed bag, she'd put other women to shame."

"I doubt such a resourceful and lovely woman would ever need a feed bag to clothe herself," Trey replied coldly. "I'm sure she must have legions of admirers who would be happy to come to her aid."

Alana had had enough of their subtle competition. The two men had been adversaries since their first meeting. "Hardly a legion," she answered lightly in an attempt to diffuse hostilities, then smiled up at Trey. "Shall we go? I wouldn't want to miss the opening curtain."

As Trey started to lead her away, she gave Colin a final glance. His expression was so crestfallen that her heart ached in sympathy. Impulsively, she rested a gloved hand on his arm. "Thank you for not making a fuss about my taking the night off."

"Sure, you deserve one," Colin mumbled. He gave her a quick peck on the cheek. "Be careful, love," he cautioned, his tone uncharacteristically serious.

Alana glanced at him sharply, wondering what he meant by his warning, then shook her head in exasperation. There, she was doing it again. Looking for hidden motives. She exited the saloon on Trey's arm, knowing Colin was still scowling after them.

* * *

The Mikado had been hailed as the social event of the season. As their buggy neared Horton's Hall where the performance was to be held, the street became congested with carriages. People clogged the area surrounding the theater. The air crackled with gaiety and excitement as friends hailed one another. The men were resplendent in evening garb with silk top hats. Many jauntily swung elaborate walking sticks. The ladies were decked out in their frilliest gowns of silk, satin, and lace, all lavishly trimmed with beads and bows, feathers and flowers.

A quiver of trepidation shot through Alana. These were the same ladies who had whispered among themselves behind gloved hands at Point Loma. The same good women who had driven her from Mrs. Tidwell's shop with their tightly pursed lips and censorious comments. The same ones who filleted her reputation as easily as a plate of fish.

An avalanche of second thoughts struck Alana, nearly sweeping away her self-confidence. As desperately as she had wanted to view Gilbert and Sullivan's latest success, now her desire wavered. Perhaps it would have been prudent to refuse the offer. This evening could prove an embarrassment to both her and Trey. In the shifting and surging crowd, she caught a glimpse of the lovely brunet Trey had been talking with at Point Loma. Lottie's remark came back to taunt her. *A man as handsome and rich as Mr. Matthews can have his pick of any woman in town.* Trey's theater invitation would have been welcomed by a dozen women more suitable than she. She caught her lower lip between her teeth. She had hoped for a special evening, not one marred by malicious gossip. "Trey," she began tentatively, "perhaps my being here with you is a mistake."

"A mistake? In what way?"

She gestured toward the crowd. "I don't fit in with these people. At least not anymore."

"Nonsense. You have no reason to feel uncomfortable."

"But I don't want you to regret asking me. My reputation is already ruined beyond redemption, but have you given any consideration to your own? When people see us together, they'll gossip and draw all sorts of conclusions. In no time, they'll start to question your morals. Next they'll refuse to admit you to their homes. They'll forbid their precious daughters to spend time alone with you."

He regarded her with a wry expression. "You're concerned about *my* reputation?"

The skepticism in his tone made her defensive. "You don't know what it's like to lose something dear to you."

"You're making presumptions," he said sharply, his eyes narrowed and looking straight ahead. "When you know me better, you'll realize how very wrong you are. The loss I've suffered is irreplaceable. Something I valued above all else was heartlessly stolen from me. Not a day passes that I don't grieve. Not a day passes that I don't vow to avenge that loss . . . to make the person responsible suffer." His grip on the reins tightened, causing the horse to prance nervously.

Alana clutched the side of the buggy in alarm. Passion smoldered inside the man like a volcano ready to erupt and destroy without warning. She hoped she wouldn't be witness to such unleashed fury. "I'm sorry if I sounded presumptuous. I didn't know."

With an effort, he brought his temper under control. He slackened his grip on the reins and maneuvered the carriage into an empty space at the rail.

"Put all thoughts of ruining my reputation aside. Trust me, my reputation is of sufficient strength to shelter both of us. No one dares impugn my good name. But if it makes you so uncomfortable, we won't attend the theater."

"No," she replied quietly. "If you're prepared to weather the flurry of unkind speculation, then I am, too."

Trey swung down from the carriage, handed the reins to an eager young lad, and helped Alana alight. He took her firmly by the elbow and steered her through the milling throng. As Alana had predicted, heads turned and eyebrows rose at their passage. Trey seemed unperturbed by the stir they were creating. Bending his head, he whispered, "If people gawk, it's only because you are by far the loveliest woman here tonight. They cannot take their eyes off of you." His warm breath feathered her ear, sending delicious sensations spiraling through her. Alana smiled up at him, and he smiled in return.

Arm in arm, they entered the lobby. Trey stopped occasionally to chat with acquaintances. He introduced Alana simply as Mrs. Fairchild, as though she were a highly respected yet unknown member of the community. Friends followed his cue. In spite of her earlier misgivings, she began to relax. Groomed since childhood in the social intricacies, she moved through the situation with practiced ease. She managed to be gracious and cordial, even when her overtures were not readily reciprocated. But it was Trey who paved the way for her, she acknowledged. He was her champion. Knowing he stood ready to come to her defense, she found that her earlier apprehension faded.

She had almost convinced herself that her fears were groundless when she spied Ronald and Miriam

Cooper chatting with friends. There was no way to avoid them; the couple stood directly in their path. A quick intake of breath alerted Trey to her sudden distress. He placed his hand over hers and gave it a quick, reassuring squeeze.

"Cooper," Trey said, extending his hand to Ronald Cooper. "Nice to see you again."

"Matthews." Cooper pumped Trey's hand, but his attention rapidly strayed to Alana. The gleam in his brown eyes was hot and bold, silently questioning her preference for Trey over him. "You should be complimented on your good taste."

"Good taste, dear?" Miriam's tone was acidic. "Whatever are you referring to?"

"Why the play, my dear, the play. I was merely referring to Mr. Matthews's good taste for fine theater," Ronald answered smoothly, giving his wife a patronizing smile. "It's quite the rage."

Watching the couple, Alana couldn't help but wonder if Miriam Cooper knew that her husband reserved a room at the St. James which he used exclusively for his extramarital romps. A closer look at Miriam's pinched features gave her the answer. With a woman's sixth sense, Alana realized that Miriam knew but was powerless to prevent it. She was a bitterly unhappy wife.

Ronald Cooper injected a false jocularity in his voice. "According to the *San Diego Union,* tonight's performance should be a rare treat."

"Yes," Miriam concurred woodenly. "I understand it was a magnificent success at the Savoy in London. We're fortunate the touring company is stopping here before moving on to San Francisco."

"I once saw *H.M.S. Pinafore* in New York," Alana said. "It was wonderfully witty and amusing. My family and I enjoyed it immensely."

Miriam's brow lifted in obvious disbelief. She opened her mouth to comment, but was silenced by her husband's discreet nudge in her rib cage.

"Mrs. Fairchild, or Alana, if I may be so forward . . ." Ronald cleared his throat and continued. "Matthews here set us straight about what really happened at the tidepool last Sunday, and Sarah confirmed it. My wife and I are both very grateful you were there to help her."

"I planned to drop you a note, Mrs. Fairchild, and personally thank you for rescuing our Sarah."

Though Miriam Cooper's apology sounded rehearsed, Alana knew the effort the single sentence had cost her. "I'm glad I was able to help. I rather doubt Sarah will wander off like that in the future."

The blat from a tuba and the warble of a flute could be heard above the hum of conversation. "Time to take our seats," Trey announced. "Enjoy the performance." He steered Alana away from the Coopers.

They joined the others who trooped up the stairs. An usher took their tickets, then led them down the aisle and indicated two seats center stage five rows back.

As soon as they were settled, Alana turned toward Trey. "Even if the play is horrid, you've already made my evening very special."

He studied her solemnly for a heartstopping moment. Then his beautifully molded mouth curved into one of his rare smiles. He picked up her gloved hand and threaded his fingers through hers. "My pleasure."

Chapter 9

The houselights dimmed; programs rustled. The audience shifted a final time before settling into an expectant silence. The conductor, a distinguished silver-haired gentleman with a Roman nose, stepped from the wings to a spontaneous outpouring of applause. He bowed to the audience, then faced his musicians and raised his baton. The result was magic. Pure magic.

The music embraced Alana like a lover's arms, transporting her, delighting her. She squeezed Trey's hand, and he returned the slight pressure. Their shoulders brushed in the darkened theater, increasing the aura of intimacy that enveloped them.

The feel of Trey's hand holding hers heightened Alana's already sharpened perceptions. Violins sang and she felt her blood hum. The kettle drum boomed in rhythm with her heart. Soprano blended with baritone and tenor, and she felt at one with the man beside her.

The lyrics of "I've Got a Little List" made them both laugh. Simultaneously, they turned to each other. Alana's smile was arrested at the sight of Trey's. She had thought his sternly handsome face appealing before, but now it was even more engaging. Laugh lines creased the corners of his incredible green eyes. How could she ever have thought those eyes cool, she wondered bemusedly, when they looked as inviting as a glen on a midsummer day? Even his laugh, deep and resonant, was pleasing to her ear.

Alana reluctantly returned her attention to the stage where three actresses garbed in colorful satin kimonos and elaborate black wigs shuffled into a make-believe garden. In high-pitched voices, they began to sing "Three Little Maids From School." The audience clapped wildly. Although Alana joined in the applause, she was struck by the ironic parallel with her own education at an exclusive finishing school—and her blissful naivete. When an enraged Katisha exited the stage, the curtain came down on the first act, signaling the intermission.

"Shall we find some refreshments before the final act?" Trey suggested.

Together they joined the throng filing up the aisle and spilling into the lobby. Everyone seemed to be talking at once. Trey snatched two glasses of lemonade off the tray of a passing waiter and handed one to Alana.

"I don't have to ask if you're enjoying yourself. One look at your face tells me you are. You're absolutely radiant. Have you ever been tempted to try your luck on the stage? You really are quite talented."

"It's very kind of you to say so."

"I didn't mean it as idle flattery. Your range is remarkable, and you have good stage presence. Few women could quiet a noisy saloon with just a few notes the way I've seen you do at the Gilded Lily."

Alana sipped her drink. She hoped she wouldn't embarrass herself by blushing like a schoolgirl. Somehow, Trey Matthews didn't strike her as the type of man who passed out lavish praise, but rather one who doled it out sparingly. Sensing this, she treasured the compliment all the more.

"Matthews!" a male voice boomed. "I thought I glimpsed you earlier." A portly gentleman with a wreath of white hair circling a shiny pink dome elbowed his way through the crowd. A pleasant-faced woman as plump as a partridge followed close behind him.

"Felix." Trey pumped the man's hand. "Nice to see you and Mrs. Osterman again."

"Haven't set eyes on you since the board of directors meeting last week. Thought maybe you headed East with your friend Hastings."

"No. I find the climate here much more to my liking. I'm thinking of purchasing some land in this area."

Eliza Osterman beamed her approval. "The climate here is truly exceptional, and now that the railroad has finally arrived, San Diego is being developed beyond Alonzo Horton's greatest expectations."

Alana recognized the name of the man whom many long-time residents referred to as the father of San Diego.

Mrs. Osterman regarded Alana with friendly curiosity. "I don't believe we've met, dear."

Trey promptly performed the introductions.

"Are you new in town, Mrs. Fairchild?" Felix Osterman inquired.

"Actually I've been here only a short time."

Eliza Osterman fluttered her fan. "Strange our paths have never crossed."

"I doubt that we travel in the same social circles, Mrs. Osterman." Alana took another small sip of lemonade.

"A pretty young woman such as yourself needs to get out and make friends. I'm an officer of the Women's Christian Temperance Union. You should attend one of our meetings. I'd be happy to introduce you to some other young ladies."

Alana tensed. The conversation was rapidly getting out of hand, and Trey's help was conspicuously absent. "I'm afraid I wouldn't be a welcome addition to your group, Mrs. Osterman."

"Nonsense, child." Eliza waved away her objections with a flick of a bejeweled wrist. "They're as fine a group of women as you're likely to meet anywhere. Right now we're in a midst of a fund-raising project. With the money we collect, we hope to buy a home for indigent gentlewomen."

Alana's fingers tightened around the frosted glass. Trey seemed to be waiting, testing her reaction. She should have known better than to think she could rely on someone other than herself. She raised her chin proudly, steeling herself against the reaction that was sure to come. "You're very kind, Mrs. Osterman, but I'm afraid you don't understand the reason for my hesitation. You see, I earn my living singing in a saloon in the Stingaree District."

Eliza's mouth opened and closed. Her husband turned beet-red. Another time Alana might have found their expressions humorous. For the moment, however, she felt only the sting of humiliation.

"Mrs. Fairchild is being modest." Trey stepped into the breach at last. "Alana is a gifted vocalist. It was only because of her great love of music that I was able to persuade her to join me this evening. She couldn't resist the chance to see *The Mikado.*"

"I'm an ardent admirer of Gilbert and Sullivan's

works." Alana took a swallow of lemonade. It no longer tasted sweet, but tart.

"If she had chosen to do so," Trey continued, placing his hand protectively at the small of her back, "I'm convinced Alana could have had a career on the stage. She'd make a delightful Yum-Yum."

"You don't say," Felix murmured, and noisily cleared his throat.

Trey took Alana's half-empty glass and, setting it aside, tucked her hand into the crook of his arm. "I believe the second act is about to begin. If you'll kindly excuse us."

"Don't let the encounter with the Ostermans spoil your evening," Trey said as they took their seats. "Eliza's intentions are good. However, she's led a very sheltered life and tends to be rather narrow-minded."

"You needn't make excuse for your friends." Alana gave him a bitter smile. "Their response is typical of many in this city."

With an effort, Alana blocked the Ostermans' shocked faces from her mind and concentrated on the music. Once again, Trey reached for her hand. She found the gesture oddly comforting and disconcerting at the same time.

The second act passed quickly, bringing the popular operetta to its conclusion amid thundering applause and three curtain calls. Alana felt a distinct pang of regret. The evening had been wonderful—and like the operetta, it was over all too quickly.

She and Trey exited the theater, swept along by a chattering, exuberant crowd. While they waited for Trey's carriage, quite a few people stopped to talk with Trey. Judging from their manner, Alana surmised he was a well-respected, well-liked member of the business community. Men addressed him deferentially; women, even the married ones, openly courted his favor. As long as Alana was at his side, she fell under his protection. To her vast relief, everyone was at least civil to her, though not overtly friendly. No one seemed willing to risk Trey's ire with insults, subtly veiled or outright.

When the carriage drew up, Trey flipped the lad a coin, helped her inside, and climbed in after her. "I thought a late dinner might be a fitting end to a delightful evening," he said. "I took the liberty of reserving a table in the Persian Room. Unless, of course, you'd rather go somewhere else."

"No," she replied quickly, eager to prolong the evening. "Dinner sounds lovely."

Ten minutes later, they arrived at the restaurant. Trey climbed down from the buggy, and, reaching up, he encircled Alana's waist and swung her to the ground. Her palms rested lightly on his shoulders; his hands stayed at her waist. They stood poised like two dancers—or two lovers. Instinctively, she raised her face to his, yearning for his kiss, uncaring that they stood on a public street. His head dipped toward hers.

Just then a carriage drew up behind them. The spell was broken. Alana quickly lowered her arms. Trey released her and moved back. "Later . . ." he said softly.

Later? What did he mean by *later?* But she knew. She had to be honest with herself. Deep in her heart, she knew exactly what he meant. She couldn't deny that whenever they were together, an undisputed chemistry simmered just below the surface. The correct combination of ingredients would trigger an explosion.

Trey escorted her into the restaurant, where the maitre d' greeted them with an obsequious smile. "Ah, Mr. Matthews. So good to see you again, sir. The table you requested is ready. If you will kindly follow me."

The Persian Room was packed with many of the people Alana had seen at *The Mikado.* As they had at Horton's Hall, curious stares and whispered comments followed their progress. Alana focused her attention on the maitre d's stiff back. She was left with only a vague impression of dark wood paneling, red-flocked wallpaper, and a profusion of potted palms and leafy ferns. Trey seemed oblivious to the speculation their appearance generated as he nodded and smiled at acquaintances.

The maitre d' led them to a table near a window and held out a chair for Alana. "I hope you will find everything satisfactory." He handed each of them a leather-bound menu and departed.

Before they could study the menu, a waiter arrived with a bottle of champagne nestled in a bucket of ice. Alana raised a brow and looked at Trey. He shrugged. "I ordered it when I made the reservation. You do like champagne, don't you?"

"I don't usually imbibe, but tonight I'll make an exception."

Trey eyed her skeptically. "Would you prefer something stronger? Whiskey, perhaps?"

"Good heavens, no!" Alana laughed. "Champagne will do nicely."

The waiter filled their glasses, then withdrew discreetly. "Allow me to propose a toast." Trey raised his glass. "To an unforgettable evening."

The intensity of his gaze held hers captive. As he brought the glass to his lips, Alana found herself watching his mouth. *Later,* he said. *Later.* The word tantalized, hinting of untold delights yet to be discovered. Her hand not quite steady, she raised her glass and took a sip of the bubbly wine.

The waiter returned shortly, and Alana listened while the two men discussed the merits of tenderloin of beef versus those of roast leg of mutton. As for herself, it didn't make the least difference. Cardboard could be substituted, and she probably wouldn't notice. Being with Trey was more heady than wine.

"Have you dined here before?" Trey asked after the waiter left with their order.

"No, I haven't."

"I must confess that surprises me."

A bemused smile curved her mouth. "Now why should that come as a surprise?"

"You're a lovely woman. I've seen the way men behave at the Gilded Lily. Surely they must ply you with dinner invitations."

"Most of the invitations I receive come from men who are already married. As far as I'm concerned, they can eat their dinner at home where they belong." Alana stared pensively out the darkened window. In the daylight, it probably afforded a view of an enclosed garden. Now only her mirrored reflection stared back, mocking her. "None of them are willing to flaunt their association with a saloon singer for fear their wives might hear of it. As for the rest"—she shrugged—"they only want what can be easily found with any of the sporting women in the Stingaree."

"Are you always so forthright?"

"I know what I want." She met his gaze over the rim of her champagne glass. "And what I don't want."

Trey leaned forward, his voice low, his expression unreadable. "What don't you want?"

"I'm not interested in a shoddy affair."

He nodded, seemingly satisfied. "And what is it you do want?"

Alana twirled the stem of her glass and debated how much to reveal about herself. In spite of her attraction to Trey Matthews, he was still a stranger, and she was not ready to bare her soul. He already knew far too much about her, while she knew virtually nothing about him.

Trey reached across the table and captured her hand. Turning the palm up, he sketched lazy circles with his thumb along the inside of her wrist. Her pulse jerked. "Why the hesitation? Afraid to answer my question?"

The waiter arrived with the first course, and Alana withdrew her hand.

"Saved by the soup," Trey quipped with a knowing smile.

The turtle soup was followed by salmon in caper sauce. While they waited for the main course to be served, Alana asked a question that had festered all evening. "Why aren't you afraid to be seen in public with a woman of my reputation? Parents with marriageable young daughters won't find you a suitable companion."

"You're the only woman I'm interested in. Trust me, Alana, my reputation is strong enough for both of us. No one will dare offend you while you're in my company."

How wonderful it would be, she mused, to rely on someone else's strength, not to have to fight the battle alone. To be assured someone stronger would be there to deflect the blows. "You have a chivalrous nature, Trey Matthews," she said softly. "Your mother must be proud to have a son like you."

Trey's expression hardened. "If you knew me better, you wouldn't call me chivalrous."

His tone sent a ripple of apprehension racing down her spine. This man could be dangerous. She had nearly forgotten her first impression. The waiter brought the main course just then, and she was grateful for the interruption.

Trey attacked his dinner with gusto while Alana merely nibbled on hers. She searched for a topic that would return them to firmer ground. Remembering her mother's advice that men always enjoyed talking about themselves, she tried to draw him out. "I understand you're from out East," she ventured. "Exactly where are you from?"

"Maryland." Trey sliced off a piece of beef. "Though in recent years, I've spent a great deal of time in New York and abroad."

"You're from Maryland? So am I. What a coincidence!"

His lips twisted in a parody of a smile. "Yes, quite a coincidence."

She speared a glazed carrot. "Does your family still live there?"

"No," he replied shortly. He turned a brooding look out the darkened windowpane.

Alana put down her fork, her meal forgotten. "Forget that I asked. It's none of my business."

With a visible effort, he dredged up a smile and an apology. "No, I'm the one who was out of line. I had no call to snap at you. In answer to your question, I have no family." He shoved back his plate. "My half-brother died after an unfortunate incident last year. In her grief, my mother suffered a stroke that left her paralyzed and unable to speak. She passed away recently."

"I'm sorry." Alana touched his hand lightly.

He didn't trust himself to look at her. His hands clenched into fists, then, drawing a deep breath, he slowly forced them to relax. He signaled the waiter. "Two cognacs."

"Make mine tea, please."

Tea? So much for his not too terribly original plan to get the lady tipsy before he seduced her. All during dinner, she had only sipped at her champagne, and now she was ordering tea of all things. He'd have to rely on charm alone if he wanted to get into her bed. Even so, it shouldn't be difficult. The woman was an extremely sensual creature. He would bet his last gold piece on that. He need barely touch her to see her eyes darken to cobalt and to hear her breath catch in her throat. Desire pumped through him, hardening his shaft. God help him! Making love to her would be no burden.

He raised an eyebrow inquiringly. "You, a teetotaler? Perhaps the Women's Christian Temperance Union would be a fitting place for you after all."

Alana laughed. "Couldn't you just picture Colin's expression when I told him what group I just joined?"

A spark of humor briefly lit his eyes. "Correct me if I'm mistaken, but I could swear I've seen the barkeep at the Gilded Lily pour you a drink after each of your performances."

"Cold tea and honey." Alana's smile broadened. "A voice teacher once recommended it for my throat."

"Aha," he exclaimed. "All this time, I thought you harbored a fondness for hard liquor, when it's tea you prefer."

They lingered over tea and cognac. After an awkward start, conversation flowed more freely. Waiters were clearing off tables as they left the nearly deserted Persian Room. Alana draped her shawl over her shoulders against the crisp night air. Overhead, a million tiny pinpricks of light spangled the midnight sky.

A boy, his cap pulled low, dozed beside the carriage at the hitching rail. Trey shook his shoulder to awaken him, then pressed a coin in his hand. "Off with you, lad. It's late." The boy scrambled to his feet and loped off.

Both Trey and Alana fell silent as the carriage headed southward. The arc lamps looming above the buildings lent the sky a pinkish glow. They were approaching the Stingaree when they came upon an overturned wagon blocking the road. Cabbages, potatoes, and heads of lettuce littered the street. A second wagon with JOHN LITTLE'S BREADS, CAKES & PIES lettered on the side was parked diagonally across the boardwalk. The two drivers, ignoring the mess the collision had created, gestured wildly and shouted obscenities, each blaming the other for the accident. Muttering under his breath, Trey turned the carriage about and took a different route.

The detour brought them closer to the harborfront. Alana tensed. Living in the Stingaree District, she knew that crime was rampant south of H Street. Gangs of hoodlums and roving youths bent on trouble roamed the streets at night. Added to this was the fear that someday she would unexpectedly confront the murderer known as English. She clutched her handbag and glanced around uneasily.

Suddenly, Trey sat up straighter, more alert.

"What's wrong?" Alana instinctively lowered her voice to a whisper.

A slight shake of his head warned her to keep silent. Then she heard it, too—a muffled cry for help.

She peered through the darkness. Wordlessly, she caught his sleeve and pointed. In a vacant lot between two buildings, three men were beating a fourth.

Pulling the carriage to a halt, Trey tossed the reins in Alana's lap and vaulted from the seat. "Go!" he ordered. "Get out of here."

She didn't have the faintest inkling of how to manage a horse and buggy. Even if she did, she couldn't drive off and leave Trey behind. Feeling completely helpless, she watched him join in the fray.

He grabbed the first man he reached by the scruff of his neck, then, hauling back his right arm, plowed his fist into the man's jaw. The thug's body fell to the ground, limp and unconscious.

The remaining two ruffians turned on Trey as one. Their victim laid doubled up in the dirt, moaning.

"Well, well, whatta we got here?" the larger of the two chortled.

The smaller one grinned. "Don't look much like a fighter to me. Whatta ya think, Bugsy?"

"I think mebbe, Charley, we should give the fancy man a boxin' lesson."

"Mebbe we should, but the price don't come cheap." The two men separated, flanking Trey. "It'll cost 'im the cash in his pocket."

"And I've got a hankerin' fer a gold watch. The one he's wearin' will do nicely."

What was Trey thinking of? Alana wondered frantically. He was a railroad man, not a prizefighter. Even a prizefighter would think twice when outnumbered three to one. She gnawed her lower lip and fervently wished for her trusty derringer. Unfortunately, her gown possessed no pockets and her handbag was too small to accommodate it. Besides, she'd thought herself safe with Trey.

"C'mon, fancy man, show me yer best punch," Bugsy challenged.

Trey swung, but Bugsy dodged the blow. Trey jerked his arm back, but before he could aim another punch, Charley slipped behind him, catching both his arms and pinning them behind his back.

"Lesson number one, fella," Bugsy said, balling up a fist. "Bring a friend." A punch to Trey's midsection drove the air from his lungs. "Lesson number two—if ya wanta win, fight dirty."

Alana clamped a hand over her mouth to stifle a cry as Bugsy's fist smashed into Trey's face.

Trey reared back, nearly toppling his captor, and kicked Bugsy in the groin. Bugsy went down with both hands cupping his privates. Trey followed up with a vicious jab of his elbow into Charley's rib cage, which earned his release.

"Lesson number, three," Trey growled, shaking blood from his eyes. "Don't underestimate your opponent."

Muttering a string of expletives, Charley spun Trey around, pummeling him with short vicious punches about the head and torso.

Alana watched in horror. The *thud* of flesh striking flesh, punctuated by grunts and groans, marred the stillness. The magical evening had suddenly been transformed into a nightmare. Unable to sit still any longer, she gathered her skirts and scrambled down from the carriage, her plan of action yet unformed.

She hesitated on the outer fringe of the vacant lot. Trey, bloody and disheveled, drew back his arm and landed a blow that knocked Charley off his feet. But the ever tenacious Charley stuck out his foot. Trey fell to the ground, where the two men rolled over and over until they were a wild tangle of arms and legs.

The sound of men talking among themselves drew Alana's attention. Casting a hopeful glance up the street, she saw two helmeted policemen, nightsticks swinging, strutting on down the boardwalk. "Help, police!" she cried loudly.

Firearms drawn, the policeman raced toward her. They assessed the situation at a glance and overpowered the hoodlums within moments.

Alana ran over and knelt at Trey's side. Blood trickled from a gash over his left eye and a split lip. The bruised flesh on one cheekbone hinted of a black eye before dawn. "Are you all right? You could have been killed." She dug through her handbag for a handkerchief.

Trey raised himself to one elbow and gingerly felt his jaw. "You're a fine one to talk."

One of the policemen kept his gun trained on the would-be thieves. The other snapped handcuffs on the trio, then helped the dazed victim to his feet. "Well, if it ain't Bugsy and Charley and their buddy Spence. Ain't you boys ever goin' to learn?"

"Can't scare us, copper," Bugsy snarled.

"Yeah," Charley seconded. "Police courts so jammed up, we'll be back on the streets by daybreak."

A look of frustration passed between the policemen. "Down to the station you go." The policeman with the handlebar mustache indicated the beating victim. "You, too, mister. We'll need you to press charges."

Trey got to his feet and dusted off his trousers. "My name's Matthews. If you need me, you can find me either at the California Southern or the Brewster Hotel."

"Next time, Matthews, think twice before interfering. These dudes are mean customers." The officer prodded his prisoners in the back with a nightstick. "Get a move on, fellas."

As the hapless victim shambled after the two policeman and his assailants, Alana dabbed at the cut on Trey's lip. "You need to see a doctor."

"No, I'm fine. All I want to do is go back to my hotel room and lie down."

"Then I'm going with you." Alana stood her ground. "If you're too stubborn to see a doctor, the least I can do is make sure there is no permanent damage. I insist," she added when it looked as though he might argue.

"Very well." Trey sighed wearily. "I'm in no mood to fight another battle this evening."

Alana wrapped her arms around his waist, and they slowly made their way back to the carriage. He climbed gingerly inside. His cautious movements told Alana that he was in more discomfort than he was willing to admit. As the horse moved forward, Alana slanted him a sideways look. His evening clothes, once so elegant, were coated with grime. His tie was missing. Dark hair fell over his forehead, making him look very human, and very, very appealing.

Thank goodness the police had arrived when they did, or the outcome could have been different. She shivered at the ugly possibility. Trey had plunged into the fight with no thought to his own safety. Brave, foolish, heroic. Her bold knight.

The carriage rolled to a stop in front of the Brewster Hotel and they carefully alighted.

The desk clerk watched with interest as Alana, her

arm around Trey's waist, crossed the deserted lobby. Her head held high, she ignored him, sweeping up the stairs with all the poise she possessed. Her reputation was already past redemption, so his gossip couldn't hurt her, she told herself. Besides, Trey's health was far more important than whatever people might think of her.

Chapter 10

Trey fished a key from his jacket pocket and unlocked the door to his room, then stood aside for Alana to enter. She froze on the threshold. Common sense collided with ingrained values. The lack of propriety hit her. A lady *never* visited a gentleman's quarters. It was simply unheard of. This had been drummed into her since the day she had switched to long skirts. *Nonsense,* a little voice argued. She was no longer a child, but a grown woman. And Trey needed her.

"Worried about your reputation?" Trey asked, a quiet challenge in his voice.

"Reputation?" Alana gave a humorless laugh and stepped inside. "I left that behind long ago."

Meager light filtered into the room, shrouding it in inky shadows. Alana blinked, waiting for her eyes to adjust to the darkness. She could barely make out Trey's tall, black-clad figure as he moved like a specter deeper into the gloom. A portent of change starved the oxygen from the room. Fear and excitement poured through her veins in equal portions. The urge to turn tail and run warred with a stronger desire to remain.

Then a pale, rosy glow filled the room, dispelling fanciful illusions. Trey, no longer a mysterious phantom but flesh and blood, stood in the center of a spacious room. He winced slightly as he lowered his arm from the brass gasolier suspended from the ceiling.

His grimace of pain reminded Alana why she was in his hotel room. She set her handbag and shawl on a chair and tugged off her gloves. "Let me help you remove your coat."

"I can manage."

Alana waited for him to slip out of his evening jacket. His movements were stiff and awkward, lacking their usual masculine grace. His vest followed. Alana's heart wrenched in sympathy at the sight of him looking battered and unutterably weary. Needing something to do, she went to the bed, folded back the counterpane, and plumped the pillows. "Why not lie down and rest? Let me take care of you."

He turned slowly and took her measure. Though his body had taken a beating, his eyes gleamed clear and sharp. For an unguarded moment, Alana would have described his expression as predatory. Then as quickly as a shutter dropping down, his expression was wiped clean and only fatigue remained. Wordlessly, he nodded his assent. He sank onto the edge of the bed and bent to remove his shoes. Sucking in his breath, he pressed one hand to his rib cage.

Without hesitation, Alana knelt in front of him, unlaced his shoes, and slipped them off. The simple act was oddly intimate. A warm, not unpleasant sensation spread through her. "There, just put your feet up. I wish I had some ice for your face. Colin says it's best to keep down the swelling, but I don't suppose at this hour of the night . . ." She trailed off, realizing she was babbling to cover her sudden nervousness. "Cold water will have to do."

Alana went into the bathroom and was pleased to

discover that the Brewster Hotel offered the almost unheard-of luxury of hot and cold running water. Armed with towels, washcloths, and soap, she returned to the bedside and perched on the edge of the mattress. "You really should see a doctor." She frowned at the nasty gash above his left eye. "This could leave a scar unless you have some stitches."

"I don't want some strange doctor poking and prodding. I'm in your hands."

She concentrated on the laceration, not daring to meet his cool green gaze. The water in the basin turned pink before Alana was satisfied the wound had stopped oozing blood. She flicked a quick glance at him, but his eyes were closed now, his breathing slow and even. He might have been sleeping, but she knew he wasn't.

He possessed the kind of face young girls were introduced to in picture books, the kind that chased them into sleep and pursued them in dreams. But was he hero or villain? she wondered. Surely he was no coddled, pampered storybook prince, but rather lord of the manor, a battle-hardened knight of the realm.

Her attention skidded to his mouth. A cut marred one corner and blood had dribbled down his chin. She hesitated, cloth in hand. Then, drawing a steadying breath, she dipped the cloth in cold water and carefully dabbed at that firm, sensual lower lip that could wreak such havoc on her senses. She itched to explore the subtle indentation in his chin with her fingertips. The warmth she was feeling crept up another notch. She shifted uneasily. "Hold this on your mouth. It will keep the swelling down."

"You're the doctor." Without opening his eyes, Trey reached for the cloth.

Alana gasped. "Your poor hand!" She captured it

and cradled it in hers. For some inexplicable reason, she wanted to weep at the sight of his raw, swollen knuckles. She had admired his lean, elegant hands the first time she had seen them. Indeed, she had loved his hands before she'd loved his face.

Loved? Ridiculous! There were a great many qualities she admired about the man, but love? The idea unsettled her. Loving Trey Matthews, she imagined, would be rather like walking on thin shale: one moment the ground solid beneath your feet, the next splintering into tiny pieces. *Love?* she scoffed. Why, she barely knew the man. Resolutely, she set these disturbing thoughts aside.

With the utmost gentleness, she bathed the torn flesh of first one hand, then the other. Though her actions were purposeful, her thoughts continued to be unruly. His hands conveyed strength and assurance, the same traits she admired in his character. He possessed the unique ability to make her feel safe and protected, to make her feel that she wasn't merely existing, but alive and vibrant. Impulsively, she brushed a feather-light kiss across his abraded knuckles, a mere whisper of touch.

Trey sighed, a ragged escape of air. Alana carefully placed his hand on the counterpane. Could it be that her touch had the power to stir him? The notion sent butterflies dancing in her stomach.

She cleared her throat. "I need to check for injuries." Careful to avoid looking at his face, she unbuttoned his shirt. Nervousness made her movements clumsy. As she unfastened the last button, she paused for a heartbeat, then pulled the shirttails out of his pants. His shirt spread wide, Trey's chest was exposed for her perusal. The sight made her blood pound. Wanton, she chided. What was wrong with her tonight? She had seen a man's bare chest before. After all, she had been married, albeit briefly.

But Phillip's body had never elicited such a powerful, elemental desire in her. Where Phillip's torso had been slender and smooth, Trey's was well-muscled, tapering from broad shoulders to a narrow waist. A springy mat of black curls converged into a scrollwork of fine hair that disappeared into the waistband of his pants. A fine tremor palsied her hands as she placed one on either side of his rib cage. With methodical thoroughness, she traced each rib, probing for breaks—and enjoying the feel of him more than was proper.

"There are bruises, but I don't think any ribs are broken," she said in a voice as lush as the rich black velvet she wore.

Trey snaked his left hand around her wrist and jerked hard. Alana fell sprawled across his bare chest. Her eyes widened in surprise. He stared back, his green eyes mesmerizing, intense. His right hand cupping the base of her skull, he gently forced her head down.

"Trey, we shouldn't, you're hurt . . ." Even to her own ears, her protest sounded feeble. "Another time. Later . . ."

"Not later. Now . . ." His mouth crushed hers, forcing her lips apart. Tasting, feasting, devouring.

Her token resistance melted like a snowflake in the sun. She moaned helplessly when his lips trailed a heated path across her cheek and nibbled at an exquisitively sensitive spot on her jaw.

"Trey . . . this isn't . . . we shouldn't . . ." Through a haze of sensation that was rapidly scrambling her reason, Alana struggled to mount an offensive. The attempt was a miserable failure. She couldn't think, couldn't speak. The desire burning in her rendered her incoherent.

Trey's nimble fingers pulled first the gardenia, then the pins from her hair and spread the golden tresses around her shoulders in a riot of curls. "Ah, yes," he murmured, "this is the way I imagined you." His lips continued their sensual assault, down the slender column of her neck to the wildly beating pulse in the hollow of her throat.

Alana moistened her lips with the tip of her tongue. A mistake, she realized as she tasted Trey's kiss. "I don't think . . ."

"Shh, don't think, vixen. Let yourself feel."

Alana was only dimly aware of the dexterous fingers unfastening her gown until cool air wafted across her overheated flesh. Before she could voice an objection—before she could decide whether she wanted to—Trey rolled over, taking her with him. His weight pinned her to the mattress, a willing and eager prisoner. His eyes glowing with the hard brilliance of emeralds, he stared at the full breasts straining the confines of an apricot satin corset trimmed in black lace. "Your body was made for a lover's touch," he murmured. "Luscious . . . ripe . . . beautiful."

Her heart thundered in her ears. A sweet, heavy sensation started in the pit of her stomach and traveled downward to pool between her legs.

Trey dragged off her gown and cast it aside. Her petticoats followed. Alana's eyes drifted shut. She shuddered at the feel of his moist tongue making light forays across her collarbones. His whisker-roughened cheeks rubbed against her breasts, the sensation so highly erotic that her body arched against his, as if instinctively seeking closer contact.

"You want more, don't you, vixen? Let me hear

you say it." Trey's nimble fingers unhooked the fastenings of her corset.

"Yes," she whispered. "Oh, yes . . ." Sensations washed over her, sweeping away any lingering reservations.

At last she lay clad only in a lace-trimmed chemise and drawers. Beneath white lawn so delicate it was almost transparent, her rosy nipples were clearly outlined, pebble-hard and as succulent as sun-ripened berries. Trey brought his mouth down to fasten around a dusky aureole. With a strong, sucking motion, he drew it into his hot, wet mouth and laved it with his tongue. Pleasure, painful in its intensity, speared through her. She drew in a swift breath. He repeated the action on the other breast until her hips began to writhe.

Hooking his hand in the delicate fabric of her chemise, he yanked downward. A loud rent filled the room as the lawn gave way. Alana's eyes flew wide at the unexpected violence of his action. Before she could utter a protest, her drawers suffered the same demise. Trey balled up the remnants of her undergarments and hurled them across the room.

She stared up at him, words, half-formed, clogging her throat. Like some ancient warrior, he loomed over her, his battered face taut with triumph. Victory gleamed in his eyes. A shiver rustled through her. This man was dangerous. Dangerous, yet the attraction she felt for him was undeniable. She shivered again even as she surrendered to his kiss. His mouth plundered hers, and her fears scattered under the onslaught of passion. Looping her arms around his neck, she returned the kiss full measure.

He gently kneaded her breast, then captured its stiff peak, rolling the nub between thumb and forefinger until it throbbed for more. Alana tossed her head from side to side, ready to plead, to beg, for what she couldn't be sure. Nothing she had ever experienced had prepared her for the mindless desire surging through her.

Trey's hand left her breast and traveled lower, brushing her hip, then trailing over her abdomen, where it lingered just long enough to tantalize. She moaned and he swallowed the small burst of sound. Ever so slowly, he moved his hand lower until it rested lightly over the mound of her femininity. Alana's hips moved to a primitive rhythm. Trey swept his head lower still, his long, tapered fingers parting the soft petals guarding the entrance to her inner core.

"You'll never know the many nights I dreamed of you this way," Trey said, his voice husky. Slick moist heat, proof of her resounding passion, awaited him. He stroked the tiny bud with infinite finesse.

Breathing became a chore for Alana. She squeezed her eyes shut and writhed uncontrollably beneath the wizardry of his fingers, his lips. A sensation unlike anything she had ever imagined began building and building within her, climbing toward an invisible crest. Alana cried out as it peaked, spilling her into a wild, headlong, yet exhilarating, plunge toward fulfillment.

Trey tore his pants open and mounted her, driving his manhood deep inside her velvety sheath. With maddening control, he thrust in and out until Alana wanted to scream, to urge him faster, deeper, harder. She dug her nails into his back and wrapped her legs around his waist to pull him closer to her heat.

"Vixen," Trey ground out through clenched teeth. His tempo quickened. Perspiration sheened his skin.

Alana flung her head back, her throat arched and vulnerable. Need began to mount anew, mightier, more powerful than before, lifting her higher and higher toward a shimmering summit. When she feared she would die of this exquisite torment, need crested in a soul-shattering burst of ecstasy. She shuddered violently as wave after wave of passion crashed over her.

Trey's face contorted, his teeth bared. With a primal groan, his body went rigid before convulsing as his seed spilled forth.

Later, feeling as though she were floating on a gauzy cloud of sheer contentment, she sighed. "I never knew it could be like this . . ."

Trey stroked her cheek. "Neither did I, vixen. Neither did I."

Alana fell asleep, a smile curving her lips, her head resting in the hollow of his shoulder.

He stared broodingly at the ceiling. He hadn't wanted to feel anything when he took her. Yet he had. There was an innate sweetness, a gentleness about her that touched him. And a passionate nature that had set him ablaze. Silently, he cursed his weakness.

A persistent tapping on the door nudged Alana toward wakefulness. She burrowed deeper into the covers, wishing the noise would cease.

"Maid service," repeated a voice muffled by the wood.

Alana rolled onto her back. Her body ached in strange places. Maid service? Reality inched back in slow degrees. Trey Matthews and *The Mikado*. Trey and dinner at the Persian Room. Trey, the fight, and afterwards . . .

She flung one arm over her eyes to block out the light. Without turning her head, she sensed that Trey was no longer in bed next to her. She reached out and found only rumpled bed linens. A coldness stole over her, and with it came shame. What had possessed her to give herself to Trey so freely? Did she fancy herself in love with a man she barely knew?

"You want maid service or not?"

"Come back later."

The linen cart rattled down the hall. Alana opened her eyes and stared dry-eyed at the high ceiling. Waking up in a man's hotel room was a new and rather unpleasant experience. What was it about Trey Matthews that had made her abandon caution? Ever since Phillip, she had jealously guarded her heart—and her reputation. Phillip had been the first and only man ever to make love to her, and on those brief, hurried occasions, passion had never burst into full bloom. Last night, in Trey's arms, had been a revelation.

But midnight's fires left morning's ash.

Maybe, just maybe, she was being too pessimistic. She sat up and shoved the hair from her eyes. After all, Trey was a busy man. He couldn't afford to loll the morning away. He probably had business to conduct, meetings to attend. A smile tugged at her mouth at the thought of him quietly shaving and dressing, careful not to disturb her. She should thank him for his consideration, not vilify him.

She threw back the bedclothes and swung her feet to the floor. With a sigh, she began gathering up the scattered articles of clothing. Her once-elegant gown formed a crumpled velvet puddle on the floor. Her petticoats decorated a marble-topped table like an oversized doily. Corset and bustle reclined at a drunken angle in a far corner of the room. Frowning, she gingerly picked up what was left of her undergarments. The memory of Trey ripping them off her sent embarrassment rushing through her. She shook her head to banish the image.

The mirror above the dresser captured the quick movement of her head. Clutching her clothes to her breasts to cover her nakedness, Alana gazed at the reflection. She barely recognized the stranger with the unkempt mane of tawny curls and kiss-swollen mouth who stared back at her. But it was the eyes that gave the most damning evidence. Gone were any lingering vestiges of girlish innocence. Instead, darkening the blue depths with inky shadows, was the carnal knowledge of a woman experienced in the ways of the flesh. The full import of her actions struck her. What had she done? Where was her pride? Her self-respect?

A bone-chilling cold descended over her, numbing the pain that would undoubtedly come later. Their lovemaking had meant everything to her; it had meant nothing to him. Whore, harlot, slut. That's all she had been to him. The knowledge ate like acid on her damaged self-esteem, corroding her pride, eating away what remained of her self-respect. *Whore.* The epithet resounded through her. Trey Matthews's opinion of her couldn't possibly be any lower than her own. Blinking back tears, Alana turned away.

She dressed quickly. Without her customary chemise and drawers, she felt half-naked, as though strangers could look at her and instantly know she wasn't wearing underclothes. Not wanting the maid to find them, she hastily stuffed the tattered remnants into her handbag. Next, she tried to tame her wild tumble of curls into some semblance of order. Most of her hairpins had disappeared. She crawled along the floor, searched under the bed, and ran her hand over the carpet until she came up with a meager handful.

Loath to take or use anything that belonged to him, she refused to touch even the tortoiseshell hairbrush bearing the initials *TM*. Instead, she used her fingers to comb her hair and arranged it as best she could. She jabbed in hairpins haphazardly, uncaring that they scraped her scalp. The discomfort was a welcome distraction from an encroaching sense of hurt and betrayal. After smoothing the hopelessly wrinkled skirt of her velvet evening gown, she squared her shoulders and left the room.

She shunned the elevator in favor of the stairs, hoping she wouldn't encounter a soul. She congratulated herself on making it to the first floor undetected, but there her luck ended. The lobby teemed with people. Every chair and sofa was occupied. A long line formed at the front desk as men waited to settle their accounts and check for messages. This was no time for cowardice. Alana drew a steadying breath, then, keeping her gaze locked on the street entrance, resolutely crossed the crowded lobby.

She knew with certainty what it meant to walk a gauntlet. Lewd comments marked her passage. Out of the corner of her eye, she saw the odious desk clerk give her a broad wink. Her cheeks burned in humiliation, but she forced herself to maintain a sedate pace. She alternately cursed Trey Matthews for putting her in this situation, and her own stupidity for allowing him to do so.

Once outside, she caught a horsecar. Passengers looked at her curiously, but she ignored them. She walked the remaining block to the Gilded Lily, hoping Colin would be nowhere in sight. She wasn't in the mood for his probing.

She considered using the rear entrance to the saloon, but ever since witnessing the Chinese man's murder, she was squeamish about entering the alley.

Cautiously, she shoved the front door open and let out a sigh of relief when she found the saloon deserted. The odors of spilled beer and stale smoke greeted her like old friends. From a back storage room came the jingle of bottles, telling her either Stubs or Colin was overseeing the delivery of the weekly liquor supply. Knowing they could appear at any second, she quickly crossed the empty saloon. The Louis heels of her evening slippers clicked a sharp tattoo on the pine floorboards.

"Just sign my name, Stubs. I'm already late for a meeting." Colin emerged from his office. He stopped short when he caught sight of Alana. His gaze traveled from her disheveled hair down to her crumpled black velvet gown before coming back to rest on her face.

Stubbornly, she refused to meet his look.

"Well, well," he drawled. "Look who just strolled in. Aren't you a little overdressed for so early in the day, darlin'?"

She tried to sweep past him, but he blocked her path.

A cynical smile curled his mouth. "Don't tell me you've been to the bank? Or was it the milliner's?"

Alana mutinously clamped her lips shut. She didn't owe him an explanation. He had no right to cross-examine her.

He caught a long strand of her hair that had escaped the hairpins and tucked it behind her ear. "God knows you've accused me often enough of not being observant, but," he said, cocking his head to one side, "isn't that the same gown you were wearing when you left here last night?"

A hot rush of blood stained her cheeks bright pink. She had no reason to feel guilty, she told herself—no reason at all. After all, she wasn't married to

Colin—he was only a friend. She had never led him to believe otherwise.

Colin caught a fold of her wrinkled skirt between thumb and forefinger and, holding it out, shook his head in mock dismay. "Your fancy new gown's a mess, darlin'. What did you do, sleep in it?"

She jerked the fabric free. "What I do is none of your business."

She sidestepped him, but he grabbed her arm and spun her around. "You spent the night with Matthews, didn't you?"

They stood toe to toe, so close Alana could smell the spicy tang of his cologne, see that his hair was still damp after he had run a comb through it. So close she read the censure—and the betrayal—in his eyes.

Alana opened her mouth to deny his charge, but no words came out. She couldn't—wouldn't—lie to Colin. He deserved better. They were good friends. And he knew her far too well.

"Why, Alana?" His hold on her arm tightened painfully. "What the sam hill makes this man so unique? What did he offer that no one else has? Money, undying devotion, matrimony? Tell me, dammit!" His voice rose angrily.

Devotion? Alana stifled a hysterical laugh. Hardly. One would have to care first, and the only thing Trey cared about was slaking his lust. Matrimony? When cows flew. Money? That would have been the ultimate insult. At least he had spared her that humiliation.

Her throat aching with unshed tears, she jerked free and ran upstairs, too blinded by her own pain to notice Colin's.

* * *

Alana didn't know how she managed to get through yet another evening, but somehow she did. Even her choice of music reflected her melancholy. There had been no word from Trey in more than a week. It was over between them, over before it had begun. She spent every waking moment trying to convince herself she didn't care, and every night tossing sleeplessly because she did.

"Sure you're not comin' down with somethin'?" Lottie asked for the third time as she set her tray on the bar.

"I'm fine." Alana idly traced the rim of her glass of iced tea. "Really," she added without conviction.

"If you want," Lottie offered, "I can give you the name of my doctor. He's got all kinds of remedies."

Alana shook her head and summoned a weak smile. "Thank you, Lottie, but no."

"Suit yourself." Lottie loaded two mugs of beer and a shot of whiskey on her tray. "Let me know if you change your mind."

Alana watched her friend circulate among the tables. She spotted Colin, who as usual was involved in a poker game at a corner table. He glanced up, and when he found her watching, he raised a hand and signaled her over. With a sigh of resignation, Alana went to join him.

"Alana, my pet, you're looking far too gloomy with the Christmas season upon us." He hooked his arm around her waist and grinned up at her through a haze of cigar smoke. "You know all these gentlemen, don't you?"

Alana pasted on a smile reserved for patrons of the Gilded Lily. Its brightness dimmed when it met that of Carter Pierce, Trey's railroad associate. Pierce raised his bourbon in a salute.

"Mr. Pierce," she said, recovering from her surprise. "Have you used any more mirrors for target practice lately?"

An angry flush crept up his neck. He tossed back his drink. "Our little songbird sounded a mite unhappy tonight. Can it be she's pining for a certain dark-haired ladies' man I happen to know?"

"Of course not," Alana snapped. She hadn't liked the man before; she liked him less now.

"Glad to hear it. Because you'd be out of luck."

"What do you mean by that?" Alana hated herself for asking but couldn't help it.

Carter Pierce studied the cards in his hand, then discarded a nine of clubs. "Because," he said, grinning triumphantly, "Trey Matthews has left San Diego."

Chapter 11

"What did I tell you! It's perfect," exclaimed Averil Drewery, land agent from Los Angeles.

It *was* perfect, Trey agreed silently. But a shrewd business sense kept him from betraying his growing excitement. "The house is a shambles, Drewery. We both know this place has been on the market for some time, and the heirs are eager to settle the estate."

"B-but," the agent sputtered, the sweet scent of flowers fading, "it's a prime piece of property. With a little work, a smart man like you could make it into a showplace. A great place to found a dynasty." Averil Drewery gestured expansively.

"I'm not interested in a showplace, Drewery. Give me time to think it over. I'll meet you at the hacienda."

"Sure, take all the time you need." Drewery turned his horse and headed back in the direction they had come.

Trey watched the agent disappear down the hillside, then dismounted, looped the reins around the branch of scrub pine, and climbed the bluff. At the top, he stood, one hand braced against the bark of a live oak, and gazed eastward. Range after range of snow-capped mountain peaks stretched before him as far as the eye could see. A profound sense of peace settled over him. His search had ended; he had found what he had been looking for. He would have bought the place for this view alone.

This land was mean to be his. If not for Alana, it would have been Robert's, too.

A light breeze ruffled his hair and seemed to whisper Robert's words.

The only thing more beautiful than watching the sun rise over the ocean would be to watch the sun rise over range after range of snow-capped mountains.

It was a desire Trey had heard his brother express at least a dozen times over the years, but never more poignantly than the first time—the summer after his stepfather had died. Trey remembered it well. Robert had been nine; he had been fourteen.

"No need to spend the summer in this sweltering heat when we could be in Newport," Estelle Matthews Prescott declared. "It's not fair to you boys. I don't want to disrupt your lives any more than Alfred's untimely death already has."

But once in Newport, Trey had sensed his mother's resentment of the restrictions recent widowhood imposed on her activities. She thrived on being in the center of things; mourning cramped her style. At the slightest provocation, she would lash out at her sons. Robert, being the younger and weaker of the two, was the more frequent target of her rapier-sharp tongue. One incident in particular stood out in Trey's mind. Robert had been goaded into fisticuffs with the only son of a prominent family.

"You young ruffian!" Estelle screamed at Robert. "How dare you embarrass me in front of my friends!" In a fit of anger, she boxed Robert's ears until he cowered whimpering in a corner. Trey couldn't let the attack continue. He

grasped his mother's wrists and brought her hands slowly down to her sides.

"The fight wasn't Robert's doing," Trey tried to explain. "The other boy was bigger, meaner. Don't you care that Robert could have been hurt?"

Estelle didn't listen. All that mattered was that her offspring had sent Billy Ormsby home crying with a bloody nose. As bad luck would have it, Billy was the only son of Baltimore's reigning social doyen.

Trey wakened before dawn the following morning to discover Robert missing. He found his brother huddled under a tree at his favorite spot, a vantage point overlooking the Atlantic. "Mother wishes I was the one who died instead of Father. I know it's wrong, but sometimes I wish I had died, too," Robert said, not looking up.

"Don't talk like that." Trey sank down and put his arm around him. More than the dank predawn air, Robert's admission chilled him to the marrow of his bones.

"I can't help it." Robert shrugged his narrow shoulders. "It's just the way I feel."

"Forget about Mother, think about something else. Think about things that make you happy."

"If I were bigger, I'd run away. Go someplace far, maybe California . . ."

"California?" Trey grasped on to the topic as a way to divert Robert's morbid thoughts.

Robert drew his legs under his chin and darted Trey a hopeful smile. "You could come with me. We could raise cattle . . . or horses. Or maybe both." He brightened at the prospect.

"I'll come with you on one condition." Trey gave Robert an affectionate hug. "Promise me there will be no more talk about wishing you were dead. Whenever you're unhappy, think of the two of us in California on a grand adventure."

"Promise," Robert agreed in a small voice. The two sat

side by side and watched the first rays of dawn tint the horizon. The sun began its slow ascent, turning the water pale pink, bright rose, then fiery red as it climbed into the sky. The boys observed the awesome display in a silence broken only by the occasional cry of a gull.

Robert was the first to break the stillness, his voice dreamy. "I think the only thing more beautiful than watching the sun rise over the ocean would be to watch the sun rise over range after range of snow-capped mountains."

Now, spread out in front of Trey like a sumptuous feast, were the snow-capped peaks of Robert's boyhood dream. Trey's chest felt tight. He swallowed the lump in throat. God, how he still missed his brother. "You'll be here in spirit, little brother," he vowed softly. "Every time I stand here and witness a sunrise, you'll be here with me."

Turning his back on the view, turning his back on painful memories, Trey went to find Averil Drewery . . .

And fulfill Robert's dream.

During the long ride back to San Diego, Trey found himself recalling the land agent's words. *A great place to found a dynasty.* Trey's mouth curled into a hard smile. To found a dynasty, one must have a wife. Alana's image flashed in his mind as sharply—and as unwelcome—as a bolt of lightning.

Alana.

He had foolishly believed he could exorcise her hold over him by seducing her. But he had been mistaken. Very, very mistaken. If anything, her hold on him was more tenacious than ever. He had been the one seduced, not she. He had sought to punish her for her role in Robert's death, to prove her the slut his mother claimed her to be. To prove to himself she was unworthy of Robert's love—and his own lust. Instead, he had let himself become hopelessly, emotionally entangled with her.

He hated her for what she had done to Robert. He hated her for arousing unquenchable desire in himself. And still, he wanted her. Had to have her. The need to possess her was stronger, fiercer, than the urge to buy his and Robert's dream ranch. The realization gnawed at him.

What kind of man was he? The woman was responsible for his brother's death, yet he coveted her flesh. She had killed Robert as surely as if she had pulled the trigger. Trey deliberately fanned the flames of his hatred hotter, brighter. She should be made to suffer for what she had done to his brother. To experience remorse so deep that it touched her very soul. Trey owed that to his brother's memory.

But how could he exact retribution if Alana was in a San Diego saloon and he was a hundred miles away? "Impossible," he muttered under his breath. One night hadn't been enough. He wanted her to pay dearly over a period of days, months, maybe years. He needed more time with her for his sake as well as Robert's. As with any other malady, he needed time to recover from his obsession with her. Time to see her for the coldhearted bitch she really was. Then, and only then, would he be free of his infatuation. "There has to be a way."

Even as he spoke the words, a plan began to form in his head, a plan that would satisfy both his craving to possess her and his need for revenge. Before he reached the city's outskirts, his nebulous ideas had solidified into a course of action.

His first stop in town would be the jeweler's.

* * *

Christmas Eve dinner had always been a family tradition in the Van Dorne home. Aunts, uncles, and cousins would gather in the dining room for a feast befitting royalty. Alana sank down on the bench in front of her dressing table. Closing her eyes, she pretended that she was in Baltimore. In her imagination, she could see the crystal chandelier entwined with ivy. The table was spread with her mother's finest lace tablecloth. Crystal, china, and sterling silverware sparkled in the light. Decanters filled with cordials had been set in one candlelit corner. In another was a gleaming silver tea service. Prettily wrapped presents tied with elaborate bows marked each place setting. Not even the chairs had escaped her mother's festive touch. Hothouse roses and ribbons decorated every chair back. The room was perfumed with the sweet scent of roses and the spice of bayberry candles. A reminiscent smile curved Alana's lips as she drew in a deep breath, hoping to recapture their distinctive fragrance. Then her smile faded. She wondered sadly if anyone would miss her tonight.

She opened her eyes and stared at her mirrored image, not liking what she saw. Her eyes were large and somber, her expression lost and unhappy. Disillusionment tugged at the corners of her mouth. Heaving a long sigh, she rose and began to pace the length of her bedroom. It was far too quiet tonight. Too much time to reflect, to remember, to regret. Colin had given everyone the evening off, then left to spend the holiday with friends. She had approached Lottie about sharing Christmas together, but Lottie had pleaded a headache. A worried frown puckered Alana's brow when she recalled their conversation earlier that day. Lottie had expressed the desire to go to bed and not wake up until Christmas was over.

As she paced, the silk velvet folds of her dressing

gown swirled around her ankles. The woman in the shop had described the color as claret. Alana would have purchased it for that reason alone. How her father had loved claret cup. Each Christmas, Cook would prepare the drink from red Bordeaux wine, oranges, and spices. As a final touch, she included a sprig of borage, which she grew under glass all year round for the express purpose of lending the concoction the delicate hint of fresh cucumber.

In her mind, Alana could readily picture her father. He presented a striking portrait as he raised his cup for a holiday toast, his golden hair threaded with silver, his blue eyes twinkling behind steel-rimmed spectacles. The rest of the year he was a stern and sober banker, but on Christmas Eve, he became a gentler, kinder man—and a more loving parent. Tears pricked her eyelids, and she blinked them back.

Colin didn't stock Bourdeaux, but Stubs kept a bottle of cheap red wine under the bar. It wouldn't be claret cup, but it would do. Even though she was estranged from her family and thousands of miles from home, she'd toast her loved ones. Sniffing back tears, she picked up a lamp and hurried downstairs to the empty barroom.

In the distance, a church bell pealed a clear and poignant summons to worship. Alana paused, lamp in hand. Services at St. Paul's Episcopal Church were another important part of the Van Dorne Christmas. Sitting in the family pew, listening to the Gospel according to Matthew, and then joining the choir in "O Little Town of Bethlehem" never failed to move her. The lump in her throat felt the size of a fist.

Alana crossed the room and set the lamp on one of the empty tables. Rounding the bar, she sorted through the bottles until she found what she was searching for. She pulled out the cork and filled a glass half-full of red wine. From the boardwalk outside the saloon, she heard two drunks hopelessly slur the chorus of "Jingle Bells" as they passed the Gilded Lily. She waited until their song faded, then lifted her glass. "To my family. God bless us every one!"

"Merry Christmas to you, too." Trey stepped out of the shadows and into the stingy light.

The glass slipped through her nerveless fingers and shattered on the floor.

Stunned by his sudden appearance, Alana at first could only stare at him. "How did you get in here?" she asked when she could find her voice.

He held up a key, then casually pocketed it. "I came by earlier and bribed Stubs to give this to me."

"Why?"

"He said you were going to spend Christmas Eve alone, and I wanted to talk to you." He studied her from beyond the circle of light. With golden curls cascading over her shoulders and red velvet molding curves that made him ache with wanting, she looked like an angel atop a Christmas tree. An angel fallen from grace. "Sorry. I didn't mean to frighten you."

"I'm not frightened," she denied too quickly. "Just startled."

"So startled you dropped your drink?"

Alana stared blankly at the spilled wine, the shards of glass.

Trey's gaze followed hers. Ruby-red wine soaked into the floorboards like bloodstains. The soul-rendering horror of finding Robert's dead body washed over him anew. And with it his reason for being here. He vowed not to be as easily swayed by her beauty. Before he was through with Alana Fairchild, he would see her suffer.

His thoughts spun backward—to another time, another place, another life. *"If it weren't for Alana Van*

Dorne, Robert wouldn't be in his grave," Estelle Prescott railed the day of the funeral after everyone had left and she and Trey were alone. "She was all he talked about. How wonderful she was, how beautiful. That blond strumpet had young and old alike dancing to her tune."

Trey watched his mother pull a single long-stemmed rose from one of the many floral arrangements. "Not only did that Van Dorne hussy reject Robert, she had the audacity to run off with his friend, some Englishman he had met on his grand tour. Robert gave his heart to that little slut—and she destroyed him." Seemingly unmindful of her actions, Estelle plucked at the rose petals. One by one, they drifted to the floor, where they lay on the carpet like bright splashes of blood. "God! How I hate her!"

Those were the last words she had uttered before suffering a debilitating stroke. She had survived, the right side of her body paralyzed, her mouth unable to articulate even a simple request. For nearly a year, Trey had watched his mother's eyes light with frustration and, whenever Robert's name was mentioned, flicker with sorrow, then burn with intense hatred. Now revenge was within his grasp.

Alana clenched her hands into fists. "Please leave. You and I have nothing more to say to each other."

"You're wrong, Alana. We have a great deal to talk about."

"I disagree. Besides, considering the last time we were together, I don't think it is my conversation that interests you."

"You have every right to be angry with me."

"You're damn right I do. You used me, then left without even saying goodbye. Well, I allowed that to happen once, but never again. Go and leave me alone."

Trey realized at once that he had underestimated

her fury. "I'm here to make amends," he said placatingly, taking a half-step forward.

She held up a hand to stay his advance. "Save your smooth talk for someone more gullible. I refuse to allow you make a fool of me a second time. I made my own seduction so remarkably easy, it must have been laughable," she said bitterly. She stared at him with eyes the hard, clear brilliance of precious gems. "Did you even stage the fight you were in that evening?" She didn't give him time to answer. "I felt so worried about you afterward that I practically invited myself to your hotel room. No, that isn't true. I *insisted* on returning to your room."

"I won't deny that I wanted you in my bed from the first moment I set eyes on you. But one night wasn't enough. I want more than that."

"The Stingaree is full of women who would be happy with such an arrangement. I'm not one of them."

A heavy silence fell. Still Trey made no move to leave. Alana returned his stare for as long as she could, but found its intensity unnerving. It made her want what she couldn't have. Feel what she shouldn't. Wish for the impossible. She dropped her gaze to the barroom floor, where broken glass littered the pine boards. Broken glass like broken dreams. One moment whole, the next in pieces. Shattered beyond repair. Bending down, she slowly began to pick up the shards.

Trey placed the flower he had brought with him on the bar and stooped to help her. Their eyes met, his hooded, hers wary. "You don't belong in the Stingaree, Alana. You're much too fine for such a place. I want to take you out of the saloon, away from here."

Blood rushed to her cheeks, flagging them with anger. "If you think for one minute I'd consent to be your mistress, you're sadly mistaken." Fury vibrated in each word, each syllable.

"I don't want you as my mistress. I want you for my wife."

"You're wasting your time if you expect—" Alana's eyes widened in shock as the full import of his words struck her. "Your wife . . .?"

Trey helped her to her feet, but she shook free from his touch. Carefully, as though it were expensive crystal, she set the jagged pieces of glass on a scarred table. "Is this some kind of joke?" She shook her head in disbelief.

Trey knew he was going about this all wrong, but he was determined to salvage the situation. "I treated you abominably. How can I make amends except to say I'm sorry?"

"How arrogant to think that you can arrive like an unexpected gift on Christmas Eve and assume I'd leap at the chance to be your wife."

Trey had the grace to look shamefaced. He had been so single-minded in his quest to possess her, he had given little thought to her reaction. His plans hadn't taken into account the true depth of her anger, hurt, and humiliation. Alana shifted nervously under his steady regard and hugged her arms around her midriff. The action drew his attention to the velvety soft swell of her breasts straining the lush fabric. Desire pumped through him, hot and potent. He ached to touch her, to feel her nipples respond to his light caress.

Hoping that distance would dilute the powerful spell Trey cast over her like an ancient sorcerer, Alana moved until a table stood between them. Her effort was a dismal failure. As always, Trey loomed larger than life. His presence elicited a response that made every cell of her body tingle in awareness.

He took a step closer. Glass crunched beneath the soles of his shoes. "Marry me, Alana."

"Why, Trey? Why me?"

"Why does a gentleman usually ask a lady to marry him?" he replied, answering her question with a question.

She held her ground. "I deserve a better answer than that."

"Because . . ." He flung out a hand and floundered for an explanation that would appease her. "Because you're in my blood. Like the poppy seed that can sap a person's will, you've become an addiction to me. The way you smell, the way you taste, the sound of your voice—" He broke off, realizing he spoke the truth. Vengeance for his brother notwithstanding, some primitive urge that he didn't pretend to understand dictated that he possess her.

Confusion settled over Alana like a heavy woolen mantle. She had never thought to see this man again. She didn't think he liked her. She was certain he didn't respect her. Now here he was, asking her to be his wife. She took a half-step backward. "I-I don't know what to say."

Trey advanced until he stood directly in front of her. "Just say yes."

"I'm all wrong for you." She was wrong for him, she knew, but it was . . . oh, so tempting. She laced her fingers together to stop their trembling. "You're an important man. You need a wife who's accepted by society, not shunned by it."

"I'll decide what I need and what I don't need."

His voice cracked like a whip, and Alana felt its sting. Instinctively, she retreated until the hard edge of the bar pressed against her back.

"Forgive me." He tempered the sharpness of his

words with a smile. "Try to understand I'm a novice at this. I've never proposed to a woman before."

Alana kept her eyes on the snowy collar of his shirt. "Your friend Pierce said that you had left San Diego. I thought you were gone for good."

Trey placed the fingers of one hand along her throat, while his thumb gently forced her chin up so she that she had to meet his gaze. "I couldn't get you out of my mind, Alana. I had to come back."

Her heart tripped like a field drum in a marching band. Should she believe him? He looked sincere. Why would he lie to her? Still, she hesitated. She desperately wanted to believe she mattered to him. "This is all so sudden . . ."

"After what we shared, I thought you cared about me. Was I mistaken? If so, tell me, and I'll never bother you again." He started to draw back.

"No!" The denial burst from her lips.

"Then what's troubling you? I'm a wealthy man, Alana. I want to take care of you, to protect you. If you agree to become my wife, you'll be able to resume your rightful place in society." The pitch of his voice deepened, mesmerized. "You'll no longer have to fight your battles alone. I'll be there to defend your honor. If anyone dares insult you, they'll face my wrath."

This man is a virtual stranger, her common sense counseled. *Don't be hasty. Give yourself time. Learn more about him.*

But you do know him, came her heart's rebuttal. *He's everything you admire in a man. He's brave and strong. A bold knight riding to your rescue.* She searched his face, seeking her answer.

"It was wrong of me to come tonight." Trey lightly trailed his fingertips down her throat and along the deep vee of her dressing gown. "Obviously, the depth of your feelings doesn't mirror the depth of mine. Goodbye, vixen." He dropped his hand and stepped away.

Panic seized her. He was leaving, she realized, perhaps for good. Fast on the heels of panic came an overwhelming sense of loss. And faster still came her decision to throw caution to the winds. *Sometimes a person has to take chances,* Colin had once said. Perhaps it was time she did. "Please don't go." She reached out to stop him.

"Does this mean you'll marry me?"

"Yes." She drew a shuddering breath. "Yes, I'll marry you."

Trey retrieved the flower from where he had placed it on the bar. Smiling thinly, he held out a single long-stemmed rose, a bloom identical to the one his mother had ruthlessly shredded on the day of Robert's burial. A macabre symbol, he had decided. A fitting tribute. "This is for you."

Feeling suddenly shy in his presence, she held up the rose and inhaled its sweet fragrance. A glimmer in the center caught her attention. Puzzled, she gently parted the petals. There, nestled in the heart of the flower, sparkling like a drop of early-morning dew, was a magnificent diamond ring.

"Go ahead," he urged. "Try it on."

Alana's fingers shook so hard that Trey took pity on her. Removing the ring from its hiding place, he slipped the large tear-shaped solitaire on the third finger of her left hand. "Perfect," he announced, pleased with his choice.

Her face radiant with love and joy and wonder, Alana gazed up at him. She threw her arms around his neck, and, standing on tiptoe, pressed her cheek to his. "I swear you'll never regret asking me to marry you. I'll never do or say anything to dishonor you or your family."

Hesitating a fraction of a second, Trey returned her embrace. The trap had sprung shut. Silly, unsuspecting woman, he thought. She didn't have a clue to the true irony of her words. She had no inkling of the dishonor his family had already suffered at her hands. But she would . . . soon.

Colin O'Shea was spoiling for a fight. Balling his hands into fists, he jammed them into the pockets of his jacket. Damn Trey Matthews to hell and back. The lying, sneaky, lowdown sonofabitch. He'd as soon pound him in the face as look him in the eye. Trouble, the man was nothing but trouble. He should have known it the first time he laid eyes on him.

Jaw set pugnaciously, Colin paced back in forth in front of the bar. Stubs and the handful of customers in the Gilded Lily gave him wide berth.

For months, Colin had been trying to convince Alana to marry him. Matthews had been in the picture just a short time, and he was about to carry off the prize that should have been his own. What was so hellfire great about the man anyway? What did Matthews have to offer that he didn't? With a short, vicious kick, Colin knocked a chair out of his way. From the corner of his eye, he saw Stubs diligently apply more elbow grease to an already shiny bar. Who was he kidding? Matthews had more of everything. Looks, money, class. You name it, he had it all. And now he had Alana, too.

The knowledge soured Colin's stomach. But that was insignificant compared to the ache in his heart. Where he was concerned, it had been love at first sight. He had waited patiently, giving her time to mourn her precious Phillip before declaring his intentions. While Alana had never given him more than a friendly peck on the cheek, he knew she was fond of him. Deep inside, he nurtured the hope that someday she might return his love. But that wasn't to be. Like a thief in the night, Trey Matthews had sneaked in and stolen Alana's love.

"Speak of the devil," Colin muttered, his mouth twisting as the object of his diatribe strode into the saloon.

"Good evening, O'Shea," Trey greeted him, oblivious to Colin's surly mood. "I suppose you've heard that congratulations are in order. This is a perfect time to collect the drink you still owe me. How about joining me?"

Colin couldn't believe the man's audacity. He stuffed his hands in his pockets, clenching them into fists, and debated the merits of beating this man to a bloody pulp. Only the thought of Alana's horrified reaction prevented him. Then another option occurred to him. He almost smiled. Maybe this was time for brains not brawn. "Stubs," he called out. "Bring us a bottle of the house's finest."

When the two men were seated, Colin poured each of them a generous drink and raised his glass. "To Alana. You're getting yourself a real prize. And I should know." Grinning, he tossed back the bourbon.

Trey remained silent, sipping his drink.

Irritated when Trey didn't rise to the bait, Colin persisted. "Alana and I go back a long ways. We've shared a lot in the past." He refilled his glass. "Yessiree, we shared a lot."

"If you're trying to make me jealous, O'Shea, you can save yourself the trouble. What you're telling me hardly comes as a surprise."

Colin's cocky grin collapsed. "Doesn't it bother

you? What kind of man are you?" he asked, genuinely puzzled by Trey's indifference.

"I'd be a fool if I believed a woman as beautiful as Alana hadn't had her share of lovers. Trust me, O'Shea, I've been called a lot of names but never a fool."

Colin tried another tack. "What if I told you she's only marrying you for your money? She's partial to the title of Mrs. Trey Matthews and all that comes with it."

Trey lounged back in his chair and shrugged. "I'd say that the lady is no fool, either."

"Dammit, Matthews!" Colin slammed his glass down on the table. "You're a coldhearted bastard."

"Just practical."

Colin leaned forward, his drink forgotten. "Do you love her?"

The question hung between them. Trey's silence supplied the answer.

"You sonofabitch!" Colin exploded. "Alana deserves better than the likes of you. What do you hope to gain by this? Trying to shock your family by marrying a saloon singer? Or do you want to flaunt your own importance by ramming her down the throats of your society friends?"

Trey pushed away from the table and stood. "That's enough, O'Shea."

"Enough of what?" Alana asked, coming up behind them.

Colin bit back a heated retort. He took a long swallow of bourbon and waited for his temper to cool.

"Nothing for you to be concerned about, darling." Trey smiled and put his arm around her waist. "Are you all packed? I have a suite reserved for you at the Florence Hotel. Did you tell your friend here"—he flicked a glance at Colin—"that we're to be married New Year's Eve?"

"New Year's Eve?" Colin sputtered, the color draining from his face. "Why, that's only five days away."

Alana smiled with something akin to regret. "I wanted to tell you myself, but never found the right opportunity."

"I'm not giving my fiancée a chance to change her mind."

Colin watched Trey leave with Alana. Her beauty, as always, hit him like a punch in the gut. Today, she was absolutely glowing. Dammit! She looked . . . happy.

He reached for the bottle.

"Congratulations, Mr. Matthews." Josiah Stanton, attorney-at-law, pumped Trey's hand. "You've just bought yourself a prime piece of real estate. Yes, sir, a choice piece of property."

"Thanks, Stanton." Trey rose. "It's exactly what I hoped to find when I came to California. This has been a dream of mine for years."

"What are you planning to do? Raise cattle or grow citrus?"

"Thought I'd try my hand at both. If it's a bad year for one, the other should see me through."

"Sounds sensible to me." Stanton reached into the humidor on his desk, pulled out two cigars, and offered one to Trey, but he declined.

"You will see that a crew is sent out to clean up the place and make the necessary repairs?"

"Rest assured, I'll take care of the matter personally." Stanton walked his client to the door, then slapped Trey heartily on the back. "By the way, Matthews, if I don't see you again, congratulations on your upcoming wedding. You're the envy of every man in San Diego. I understand that your bride's a real beauty."

"That she is, Stanton. I can't believe my own luck."

Trey bounded down two flights of stairs to the street. His step was purposeful as he turned up Broadway. Yes, he was a lucky man. Not everyone had not one, but three, of his fondest wishes granted. The ranch, revenge—and Alana. All tied up in a neat package.

Chapter 12

"New Year's Eve," Lottie enthused. "What a perfect time for a wedding. Off with the old, on with the new. A whole new life. Do you realize how lucky you are? I envy you so." She secured the garland of pearls, moonstones, and mistletoe that encircled the coronet of curls atop Alana's head.

"A whole new life," Alana repeated dreamily. "You don't know how grateful I am for a chance to start fresh. The fact that I sang in a saloon doesn't seem to bother Trey in the slightest. He assured me that in time people will accept me and might even view the years at the Gilded Lily as some sort of exotic adventure."

"That's what I want most—a fresh start." Lottie sighed wistfully. "A chance to go back home and pretend running off with Johnnie Morrissey never happened. I know it's impossible, my pa bein' a preacher and all, but that's what I dream of."

Sympathy squeezed Alana's heart so hard that her chest hurt. She gave her friend an affectionate hug. "Hold on to your dreams, Lottie. Sometimes they come true. Just look at me. I'm living proof."

"You look like a bride." Lottie's expressive hazel eyes were luminous with unshed tears. Resolutely, she sniffed them back. "Your gown is such a pretty color."

"The saleslady called the color magnolia." Alana was pleased by the compliment. "I have to confess I've been terribly extravagant. I emptied my entire bank account. Not that it was so much money," she said with a deprecatory laugh, "but Trey is an important man. I'm sure we'll be going out a lot and will eventually do some entertaining. I didn't want him to be ashamed of me. I needed a wardrobe befitting the wife of a respectable businessman."

"Where will you two live after your wedding?"

"Trey hasn't told me yet. He said he's keeping that for a surprise."

"You don't think you'll be leaving San Diego, do you?"

The question caught Alana by surprise. She had never stopped to consider the possibility. With all the wedding preparations to attend to, she had simply been too busy to give the matter much thought. She had been content to leave the question of where they would live afterward entirely in Trey's capable hands. "I'm sure Trey would have said something if we were."

Lottie nodded. "He probably bought you one of those fancy big houses that are going up near this hotel. Or maybe one on Golden Hill."

"It isn't important as long as we're together." As she said the words, Alana realized that she spoke the truth.

There was a sharp rap on the door. The two women looked first at each other, then at the enameled clock on the dressing table. There was still a full ten minutes until the ceremony was scheduled to begin.

"I'll get it," Lottie volunteered. "If it's Mr. Matthews, you want me to send him away? It's bad luck for the groom to see the bride before the wedding."

Before Alana could answer, Lottie opened the door a crack and peeked through. "It's Mr. O'Shea come to wish you well." She opened the door wide enough to allow him entry.

Alana turned, a mixture of relief, gratitude, and anxiety rushing through her. Colin, unsure of his welcome, stood just inside the door, took off his derby, then smoothed his hair.

"Colin!" Alana hurried over and threw her arms around him. "I was afraid you weren't coming."

He returned the hug, his eyes suspiciously bright, then held her at arm's length. "Matthews is a lucky man. You make a beautiful bride."

Lottie fidgeted with the brooch on her dress. "Um . . . I think I'll go downstairs and find me a spot to watch from where I won't be noticed." She slipped out the door.

Colin swallowed noisily and cleared his throat. "The last time we were together we argued. I didn't want our friendship to end that way."

"Oh, Colin, we'll always be friends. Nothing will ever change that," she said, feeling a great rush of affection for the rogue who had befriended her when she so desperately needed a friend.

Colin shook his head sadly. "He doesn't love you, Alana. I don't know why he's marrying you, but, trust me, it's not out of love."

Alana stiffened and stepped away. "I don't want to hear any more of that talk. If that's all you came to say, you can leave."

"No. I promised myself before I came that the subject was closed, but"—he shrugged—"I had to give it one last try." He reached into the pocket of his jacket and withdrew an envelope. "Here, this is for you."

Alana reached out slowly and accepted it.

"Take it. It's not going to bite. Consider this my wedding present. Just go ahead and open it."

Sliding her fingers under the flap, she opened the envelope and pulled out a legal-looking document. Quickly, she scanned the contents. The sheet of paper gave her ten percent interest in the Gilded Lily. "Colin . . . I don't know what to say."

He shrugged off her gratitude. "To my thinking, pet, this way you're still part of the Gilded Lily—no matter where you are."

Alana wiped the tears rolling down her cheeks. "You're the best friend I've ever had, Colin," she said in an emotion-choked voice.

"Have a good life, mavournin." Giving her a grin that was endearingly lopsided, he left, quietly closing the door behind him.

Then it was time.

Alana was scared to death. She had been married, but she had never had a wedding. She had had a bridegroom, but never a husband. Now she was getting both. Her knees felt like custard, her palms were clammy, she thought she was going to be sick.

The music started. Summoning all her reserves of strength, Alana put on a calm face and stepped into the private dining room where her wedding was to take place. Two dozen strangers turned to stare. Her step faltered. Panic surged through her. Every instinct screamed to bolt and run. In that instant, Colin's dire warnings crashed down on her. What *did* she know about this man she was pledging her life to? Colin had caustically alluded to the fact that where men were concerned her judgment was unsound. He pointed to her brief marriage to Phillip Fairchild as proof of his theory. But Trey wasn't anything like Phillip. He was strong where Phillip had been weak. He would protect her where Phillip hadn't. It was time she relearned to trust her instincts. This time she could trust her heart.

From the opposite side of the room, she felt the full brunt of Trey's gaze and looked up. He stood tall, erect, and unsmiling in front of a mantel flanked with white poinsettias and draped with pine boughs. Even from a distance, the hypnotic green brilliance of his eyes beckoned her. Though he remained statue-still, she felt him reach out and urge her forward. The intensity emanating from him was frightening. His will seemed to overpower, then dominate hers. A strange sense of unreality descended over her. Drawing in a deep breath, she slowly started down the short aisle.

Out of the corner of her eye, she spotted Lottie trying to look inconspicuous behind a potted palm. As she passed by, Lottie waggled her fingers and offered a feeble smile of encouragement. The rest of the people were a faceless blur. Countless white tapers in candelabra cast a benevolent glow over the proceedings. The room was scented with evergreen and beeswax. Judge Willard J. Morgan, a portly gentleman with iron-gray hair, bushy sidewhiskers, and a mustache, stood next to Trey.

"If the two of you will kindly turn and face me, the ceremony will begin." Without further ado, Judge Morgan opened an official-looking black book. "My dear friends," he intoned, "we are are gathered here this evening to witness . . ."

Alana clutched her bouquet of stephanotis and white roses tighter to keep her hands from trembling. Certain phrases leaped out with painful acuity.

Keep thee only unto her for so long as you both shall live . . .

To love and to cherish . . .

Till death do you part . . .

Trey repeated the vows in a firm, steady voice. *He*

sounds so sure of himself, Alana marveled while the enormity of the solemn vows left her weak.

Then it was her turn. She felt mired in uncertainty. Once again, she felt the force of Trey's gaze. She raised her head and found him watching her with that same powerful intensity. At close range, his eyes were unfathomable pools of green so deep one could drown without a trace. A small crease bisected the edge of his left brow, a reminder of his fight with the three thugs. Somehow that small scar made him seem very human—unexpectedly vulnerable.

The judge cleared his throat. "Wilt thou, Alana Faith Van Dorne Fairchild . . ."

Taking a steadying breath, she spoke her vows in a barely audible voice.

"Those whom God hath joined together, let no man put asunder." Judge Morgan beamed at them with avuncular approval. "You may kiss your bride."

In the brief moment before Trey's lips claimed hers, Alana was vaguely aware of a fleeting smile of triumph curving his sensual mouth. Then her qualms were forgotten. Under the persuasive pressure of his kiss, she responded like a flower unfurling beneath the summer sun. Sweet flames licked at her, gentle fires that brought pleasure without pain. Doubt melted. Fear dissolved. Alana pressed her body closer to Trey, nearer to the source of heat.

A flurry of well-wishes interrupted a kiss that was much too brief to suit Alana. Guests gathered around them in an atmosphere of determined gaiety. Acquaintances slapped Trey on the back and pumped his hand. Light kisses brushed Alana's cheeks. Words of congratulations, though somewhat restrained, were generously exchanged. She couldn't fault the impeccable breeding of the wedding guests.

There were some familiar faces after all, she realized. Carter Pierce and his wife, Dorothea, who was every bit as formidable as Trey had intimated, were present, along with Felix and Eliza Osterman, the couple they had met at *The Mikado*. Even Miriam and Ronald Cooper were in attendance. She was disappointed, however, that Colin had elected not to witness the nuptials. Lottie, too, had managed to slip away unnoticed.

With Trey's hand riding possessively at her waist, Alana felt her earlier tension dissipate. Before this gathering of friends and associates, he had vowed to love and to cherish her. She assured herself that her earlier fears had been nothing more than an attack of nerves, something she had heard was not uncommon in brides.

"You look lovely, my dear." Eliza Osterman smiled kindly at her. "That pale pink is very becoming."

"Yes, very," agreed a plump woman with curly brown hair.

"Thank you," Alana murmured, wondering why the woman looked so familiar. Then it occurred to her that this was Martha, the woman who at Point Loma had been questioning her possible use of breast enhancers. Alana trusted the cut of her wedding gown would remove any lingering doubt.

Dorothea Pierce directed her attention at Trey. "Where will you and your bride live?"

Carter rocked back on his heels, looking smug. "Trey's keeping it to himself. Wants it to be a surprise."

"How romantic," Dorothea cooed, smiling coyly at Trey and batting her lashes.

Why, the woman was flirting with Trey! Alana realized in disgust, developing an instant dislike of Dorothea Pierce. No one, she thought uncharitably, had ever questioned Dorothea's need for a breast improver. Indeed, her profile resembled the prow of a ship.

A man Alana had been introduced to earlier as the hotel manager approached the group and spoke to Trey in a low voice. With a smile of apology, Trey excused himself.

Felix Osterman and Carter Pierce began talking business between themselves and were soon joined by Ronald Cooper.

Miriam Cooper bestowed a frosty smile on Alana. "Congratulations. You caught yourself a prize."

"Thank you." Alana's smile was equally cool. She easily read the subtly veiled message beneath the polite words. You've got your own man, Miriam was telling her, leave mine alone. She wished Trey would reappear and rescue her from the spiteful women.

"I was saying, dear," Eliza Osterman's voice cut into her pondering, "now that you're no longer singing in that nasty saloon, maybe you'll reconsider attending one of the meetings of the Women's Christian Temperance Union. We'd love to have you join us."

The other women looked aghast at Eliza Osterman's innocent suggestion. They exchanged uneasy glances and seemed to breathe a collective sigh of relief when Dorothea changed the subject. "Your maiden name was Van Dorne?" She didn't wait for Alana's reply. "Carter mentioned you're from Baltimore. I have relatives there. My second cousin once removed married a man in the import business. I'll have to write and tell her we've met."

"Maybe they know Alana's family. Wouldn't that be a coincidence!" Martha tittered. "What line of work is your father in?"

"He's a banker."

She lifted a brow and subtly nudged Dorothea. "A banker? Hmm . . ."

Alana ignored the cattiness. The mention of her family started her along a new train of thought. How would her family react to the news that she had remarried? More importantly, would they even acknowledge her existence? A dull ache started behind her eyes. Memory of her last communication with her father was still painful. Following Phillip's untimely death, she had written home informing him of her dire financial straits and begging for his help. Instead of the aid she had pleaded for, a trunk had arrived with the last of her belongings. In a curt note, Arne Van Dorne charged that she had disgraced the family name and that he never wanted to hear from her again. Neither her mother nor her sister dared disobey his edict.

His business concluded, Trey rejoined the group. "Sorry for the interruption, ladies," he said smoothly, taking Alana's elbow. "As soon as everyone's seated, dinner will be served."

Trey had spared no expense in the elaborate feast which followed. He sat beside Alana at a long table spread with snowy linen and decorated with holly. Champagne flowed freely. The combination of a wedding and New Year's Eve seemed to put everyone in a celebratory mood. When the clocks chimed and church bells heralded the hour of midnight, Trey rose for a toast. "To friends. My wife," he gave Alana a benign smile, "and I thank you for sharing this special evening with us. There will be dancing in the ballroom for anyone who cares to stay. Unfortunately, Alana and I must bid you farewell. We depart San Diego early tomorrow morning for our ranch."

"Our ranch?" Alana's surprised cry was lost in the buzz that followed Trey's announcement.

"Mi casa es su casa." Trey held his champagne glass aloft. "My house is your house."

Amid another chorus of well-wishes, Trey shepherded a dazed Alana from the dining room.

The door of their suite had barely closed behind them when she turned to face him. "Our ranch?"

Trey made no move to turn on the gaslight. An eerie mix of light and gloom prevailed. Moonbeams bathed the bridal suite in a silvery fairyland glow. Dark, massive furniture along the perimeter of the room cast sinister shadows. "I wanted to surprise you. Disappointed?"

Alana strained to read his expression in the near dark. But the compelling planes and angles of the handsome face staring back at her betrayed no clues. However, she couldn't dismiss the notion that there had been a hint of menace in his voice. She shrugged uneasily. "You never mentioned a ranch. I just assumed we'd be living here in town."

"You expected I'd buy you a mansion? Perhaps something to rival Alonzo Horton's big white house on the hill?"

He made her feel . . . mercenary. "No, of course not," she denied quickly. "I never expected anything of the kind."

"Are you absolutely certain about that? Are you sure that deep down you didn't want to play the role of ex-saloon girl turned society matron? To right any wrongs done to you, either real or imagined? If so, don't be afraid to admit it." He pulled his necktie loose.

Alana moistened her lips with the tip of her tongue. There was a grain of truth to Trey's words, she admitted with brutal honesty, but that wasn't why she had married him. Should she confess she had simply followed her heart? And if she did, would he believe her? It wasn't an issue she was ready to test—at least not yet. "Where, exactly, is this ranch of ours?" she asked, changing the subject.

"About a hundred miles north of here."

"A hundred miles?" she echoed.

"Does the thought of moving so far away upset you?" he asked, his voice silky smooth.

"No, of course not." His secretiveness disturbed her far more than the notion of leaving San Diego. She shifted her weight from one foot to the other, aware that he was watching her like a hawk eyeing a sparrow. "I just need a little time to adjust to the idea."

"You'll have all the time in the world," he drawled. He shrugged out of his dinner jacket and tossed it aside.

A warm flush spread through her, heating her blood, making her skin tingle. Were they going to spend what remained of their wedding night talking? She wished that he would take her in his arms. That he would kiss her. "The important thing is we'll be together."

" 'Whither thou goest, I will go; and where thou lodgest, I will lodge,' " he quoted. "See, I know my Bible. A very noble sentiment."

The strange conversation kept going in circles, but it always came back to the same issue. Trey believed she had married him for his money. She doubted all the words in Webster's dictionary would convince him otherwise. It hurt her to know he had so little faith in her—and in himself. Then a bubble of optimism rose to the surface. Hadn't he just said they had all the time in the world? In the end, time and patience might prove more eloquent than words.

Setting aside her bridal bouquet, she laid her

hands lightly on his chest. "Don't underestimate your worth, Trey Matthews. You have many fine qualities I admire."

Trey stared at her, his eyes narrowed. In her gown the color of a maiden's blush and with a golden halo of curls framing her lovely face, she could have been an apparition, an angel. But she was neither, he reminded himself. Dressed in her bridal finery, she looked more virginal than she had a right to. He steeled himself against her allure. This woman with her limpid gaze, beguiling mouth, and lush curves was far from innocent. She had entertained men for a living, had O'Shea as a lover. His gut twisted at the thought. "Fine qualities?" He laughed, a short humorless bark. "Beware, vixen, lest you bestow virtue where there isn't any."

The stillness, the shadows, the faint scent of roses charged the room with intimacy. Reaching up, she pulled the wreath from her hair, then the hairpins one by one. With a shake of her head, her waist-length tresses tumbled down her back and curled around her bare shoulders. "It's a little late for warnings, don't you think?"

"Much too late," he agreed. All his plotting, all his planning had borne fruit. She was his. Trey traced her delicate jaw and the slender column of her throat with his index finger, then let it trail over the tempting swell of her breasts to the deep cleft between. Like the Santa Anas, desire swept through him, hot and unforgiving.

"Trey . . ."

The catch in her voice unleashed the last of his restraint. He pulled her against his chest, and his mouth crushed hers. For a split second, he felt her stiffen. Then the tension dissolved, and she flowed against him, her body soft and malleable. Her lips parted under his. Quick to take advantage, Trey slid his tongue into her mouth, exploring, savoring, plundering. Her taste was more heady than bourbon and sweeter than honey. He felt as though he could drink and drink and never slake his thirst.

He broke off his kiss reluctantly. Dazed, Alana stared back at him, her passion-glazed eyes the deep shade of indigo, her mouth red, swollen, tempting. He could understand a battle-hardened soldier falling victim to her spell. A boy like Robert must have been putty. God forgive him, but he wanted her. Wanted her with a fierceness that jolted him to his core. "Turn around," he ordered.

Wordlessly, she obeyed.

Feeling like a callow youth ready to test his manhood for the first time, Trey unfastened the row of satin-covered buttons at the back of her gown and shoved the bodice off her shoulders. The gown fell in a shimmering pool at her feet. Her petticoats promptly followed in a froth of white. Bending his head, he lightly nipped the juncture of her neck and shoulder. "Delicious," he breathed.

Her head lolled back, and she leaned weakly against him.

He wrapped one arm around her waist and held her tightly. With his other hand, he cupped the heavy fullness of her breast and gently pressed upward until it overflowed the confining corset and chemise. He caught the pink bud of her nipple and expertly played with it until she moaned with pleasure. Her hips rotated against his manhood. The fire inside him roared hotter.

Turning her around to face him, he hastily stripped off her undergarments and tossed them aside. His features granite-hard, he swept her up in his arms. Alana wrapped her arms around his neck and held fast. He carried her across the room and placed her on the bed.

Legs braced apart, he loomed above her. This should be his moment of glory. Yet his conscience stung. He wished she wasn't gazing back at him with so much trust. Wished he didn't see the hope shining in her eyes. Think of Robert, he told himself fiercely. Think of your mother. Remember the suffering—the anguish—this woman heaped upon your loved ones. His resolve hardened.

His eyes riveted on her, he slowly shed his clothes. "I've waited a long time for this."

"And I've waited all my life." She held up her arms in ageless invitation.

He sank down beside her and gathered her close. All thought of Robert fled under the onslaught of passion. Naked, they came together. Soft, yielding woman and hard-muscled male. Skin against skin. Her flesh branded his. A spark flared. Desire ignited. Passion raged. Together they created a fire that burned out of control.

"Trey . . . Trey . . ." She sighed his name like an invocation as his hands boldly roamed her body, charting gentle curves and mapping subtle valleys. She slid her fingers into his thick dark hair, trying to pull him closer still.

"Beautiful . . ." he murmured. "Your body could drive a man insane." His lips followed the path his hands had traveled. His breath bathed her skin with sultry heat. Moist kisses covered her breasts, then trailed liquid heat down over her abdomen, then lower still.

"Trey . . . no . . ."

"Oh, yes, vixen."

He spread her legs. His mouth hot and wet, he thoroughly explored the apex of her thighs. She uttered incoherent protests while her body sang for more. With slow delicious strokes, his tongue stroked the tiny nub guarding the vault of her femininity. She gave a strangled cry. Her fingers tangled in his hair. Tiny convulsions of pleasure tore through her. Unaware that she did so, she arched against him. "Please," she whispered.

He slid his body over hers. Bracing his elbows, he stared into her passion-glazed eyes. "You're mine now, Alana Matthews, all mine." He lowered himself and plunged into her. He fought for control, then a shudder ran though his muscular frame as he surrendered to an urge as primitive as man.

Unmindful of the world around them, they sped toward an invisible goal. They raced faster and faster, their bodies joined, until they no longer seemed bound to the earth but were part of the heavens. Higher and higher, they rocketed skyward until the universe splintered in a glorious, shimmering explosion of light, heat, and magic.

The room still cloaked in shadows and moonbeams, they lay sated in each other's arms, breastbone to breastbone. Their two hearts pounded in synchronized harmony. The clock struck one. The marriage was consummated; an annulment was out of the question.

Trey faced a moment of bitter truth. The cruel irony staggered him. Against all reason, he was irresistibly drawn to his brother's murderer. Every time he took Alana in his arms, kissed her, loved her, he betrayed Robert's memory. Guilt bubbled up around him. Dark, oily, deadly. Sucking him down. Suffocating him. Choking him with remorse and self-loathing.

He struggled to break free of the quagmire that threatened to engulf him. Guilt, anger, frustration, and confusion swirled through him in equal measure. Then like lethal arrows shot into the night, they sped toward their unsuspecting target.

Alana stirred in her sleep, unaware of the danger.

Chapter 13

The small caravan snaked slowly along the California coast. The wagons were heavily burdened with every conceivable item: furniture, cookware, farm implements, bags of seed and grain. While Alana admired Trey's thoroughness, she wondered just how remote this ranch of theirs actually was. He had planned for every eventuality. And with all the other details he had to contend with, he hadn't forgotten to collect her few prized possessions from the Gilded Lily. Her antique Spanish brass beadstead and delicate Queen Anne dressing table were packed in the lead wagon.

Alana traveled in the carriage driven by Paco, one of Trey's hired hands. Trey, mounted on a magnificent bay, rode alongside with the dozen or so men he had hired. They were a taciturn, bleary-eyed group who looked as though they had spent the previous night reveling until dawn in the Stingaree. Having never learned to ride herself, Alana marveled at how they could actually doze in the saddle without falling off. Brought up in a large city, she had never found the inability to ride a hardship. Her family always kept a carriage and a driver available. When she confessed her lack of expertise, Trey had been nonplussed and assigned one of his men to drive the carriage. Maybe once they were settled, she would learn to ride. Perhaps even have a horse of her own someday.

The day was mild and sunny. For a diversion, Alana concentrated on the passing scenery. To her left were breathtaking vistas of the California coastline—rugged and unspoiled. Mighty swells crashed against gigantic boulders, then dissolved into white foam. To her right, the distant mountains formed a violet blur against an unblemished azure sky. Beyond the Rockies stretched the Mojave Desert, the wheatfields of the Midwest, and the place she used to think of as home. Resolutely, she turned her face to the road ahead and the future that beckoned.

North of La Jolla, Paco pointed to a tree silhouetted against the sky. "Look, *señora,* a Torrey pine. That tree is hundreds of years old. It was here when Cabrillo first sighted land." Having acquitted his task as tour guide, Paco lapsed back into silence.

The first night they spent at a picturesque inn along the coast. Alana assumed Trey would join her on the wide feather bed, but she fell asleep waiting for him. In the morning there was no sign that he had been there. She had slept alone. His absence hurt like a knife wound, the cut deep and painful. Although he appeared after breakfast and rode near her carriage all day, there was no opportunity to question him about it.

They arrived at the old mission at San Juan Capistrano at dusk on the second day of their journey. After sharing their simple meal in a communal dining room, the monks showed Alana to a small cell with a narrow bed. The instant she saw it, Alana knew she would be sleeping alone again. Once they reached the ranch, it would be a different story, she assured herself as she snuggled between the covers. She grew warm at the thought of falling asleep every night wrapped in Trey's arms, the taste of his kisses still on her lips.

The following morning, they left Capistrano before sunrise and angled inland away from the ocean. With bone-jarring brutality, the carriage bounced over a rutted road that was little more than a trail. Alana longed for the arduous journey to end.

Trey rode up and matched the pace of his mount to that of the carriage. "We'll reach Rancho Prado del Sol by late this afternoon." He rode off again before she could reply.

Since leaving San Diego, they had scarcely exchanged more than a dozen sentences. Alana tried to excuse this odd behavior by reminding herself how busy he was. He must have a thousand things on his mind. After all, he, too, was facing a drastic change. He was a businessman, not a rancher, no doubt with only a limited knowledge of raising cattle or whatever else people raised on a ranch. No wonder he seemed distant and preoccupied. He must be worried. It took courage to leave behind a comfortable life for the unknown.

Trey even looked different since leaving San Diego. He had abandoned his impeccably tailored coat and trousers in favor of serviceable Levi's, a white cotton shirt, and a black leather vest. A black Western-style hat, its brim pulled low, shaded his expression. She couldn't help but notice the dark curling hair that peeked from the open neck of his shirt. He looked rugged and, if possible, even more attractive.

"Prado de Sol." Alana said the name out loud, liking the way it rolled off her tongue.

"It translates Meadow of the Sun, *señora,*" Paco supplied with a wide smile.

The caravan stopped briefly near noon for a meal of cold meat and biscuits. By the time the sun had started to sink, Alana felt her patience wearing dangerously thin. After three days of bone-shaking journey, her body ached with fatigue. The traveling outfit that had seemed so chic in San Diego had a thick coating of dust she doubted she could ever remove.

"How much longer?" she asked when Trey galloped up alongside the carriage. She probably sounded like a petulant child, but at this point she didn't care. All she wanted was a hot bath and a soft bed.

"We've been on our property for the last hour."

Her eyes widened. An entire hour, and still the hacienda was nowhere in sight? "How big is Rancho Prado del Sol?"

"Thirty thousand acres. The rest of the land was sold off to pay the previous owner's debts."

"Thirty thousand acres?" Alana echoed in amazement.

"It was originally part of a grant from the Spanish crown dating back a century ago."

The road led through massive wooden gates which stood open. A rut-filled, weed-choked drive shaded by an overlapping canopy of fig trees looked as though it hadn't seen traffic in years. Trey frowned, muttering about the condition. Alana sat straighter, fatigue giving way to anticipation. A wheel of the carriage dipped into a hole that sent her nearly bouncing off the seat, and she righted herself.

"Sorry, *señora*," Paco apologized as they entered the outer courtyard.

Alana eagerly viewed the sprawling one-story adobe hacienda that was to be her new home. Beneath a red-tiled roof, the lines of the house were simple, yet pleasing to the eye. A wide veranda ran the entire length of the front. A series of small arched windows cut deep into the adobe were tightly shuttered against intruders. A recessed intricately carved oak door was secured by a stout padlock. No servants appeared to greet them. Indeed, the place looked deserted.

The horses stomped restlessly. The men glanced uneasily among themselves, then looked to Trey for direction. He swung down from the horse. "Stables are around the back. Unload the wagons and see that the horses are fed."

Alana sat unmoving, staring at the house. A curious mixture of eagerness and dread swept through her.

Trey strode over to the buggy and lifted her down. "Allow me to give you a tour of the hacienda."

Taking Alana's elbow, Trey guided her to the front door. While he searched through his pockets for a key, she traced the detailed carving of fruit, flowers, and birds on the oak panel, admiring the fine craftsmanship. Trey inserted a key in the padlock and the heavy door reluctantly opened with a creak of protest. He placed his hand at the small of her back and urged her forward. *"Mi casa es su casa."* This time the mockery in his voice was unmistakable.

Cautiously, Alana stepped inside. Deep within the murky shadows, she heard the skittering of small animals. Rodents, she realized, shuddering in distaste. She halted so abruptly that Trey slammed into her back. He was about to mutter an apology when he heard the sound, too. He cursed loudly. "Wait here. I'll find a lantern."

Alana stayed rooted to the spot, afraid to move for fear of what she might discover. A musty odor tickled her nostrils, and she sneezed. She clutched her handbag and fought back a tide of disappointment. This place was the antithesis of her dreams.

Though it seemed like an hour, Trey returned in a

matter of minutes carrying a kerosene lantern. He held it out in front of him and swung it in a slow arc. Shocked, Alana followed the path of the light with her eyes. A broken chair rung and a chunk of pottery were among the debris that littered the floor. Bulky shapes huddled beneath a filthy sheet in the center of a spacious room. Cobwebs streamed from the ceiling, covering the wrought-iron light fixture like a tattered bridal veil.

"Follow me," he ordered. He stalked off, not waiting to see if she followed. Tight-lipped, she gingerly picked up her skirt and hurried after him.

Trey stood in the middle of what she assumed to be the salon. "This fine example of Spanish architecture originally belonged to the Montoya family. However, in the aftermath of the Mexican War, the Montoyas were unable to settle the question of their ownership to the satisfaction of the land commission. As a result, the family lost a home that had been in their family for generations. The more recent owners, like many ranchers, fell on hard times after the Great Drought of '65. They held on to the place as long as they could but were finally forced to put it on the market. The house has stood vacant for years with only an old Indian couple as caretakers."

"The Indian couple—are they still here?"

He nodded. "They live in a small cabin out near the stables. I understand the man, Antonio, is quite old and infirm. His wife, Isabel, takes care of him. They have nowhere else to go."

Trey remained grimly silent as he led the way from room to room. Besides the central structure, which included the salon, dining room, library, and formal parlor, two wings extended on either side. These wings housed the kitchen quarters, various storerooms, and many bedrooms. The Montoyas, Alana mused, either had a very large family or entertained on a lavish scale. She was delighted to discover that all the rooms opened onto covered verandas that ran along the three sides of the inner courtyard and were separated by a broad patio. A majestic stone fountain graced the center of the patio like a crown jewel. She pushed open the door for a better look and sent a chicken squawking from its nesting place.

"This place is a hovel. A pigsty!" Trey exclaimed in disgust.

Alana sought to placate Trey's fury. "Once it's cleaned, it will be lovely. You'll see."

She placed her hand lightly on his arm, but he shook it off. "I arranged for a party of servants to make this place clean and ready for our arrival. When I discover why nothing has been done, there will be hell to pay."

She started again to reassure him, but instead her stomach gave an unladylike gurgle of hunger.

"I'll see what I can find in the way of food," he muttered.

Alana watched Trey cross the inner courtyard and vanish through a tall iron grillwork gate at the far end. While he went in search of a meal, Alana was drawn to the fountain. She sank down on its wide tile ledge, dipped her handkerchief into the cool water, and used it to scrub off the grime of travel. She gazed wearily in the direction Trey had disappeared. The sun was setting behind a spectacular display of brilliant pink clouds outlined in fiery red. The gurgling fountain sang in the background like an unfinished melody. A peacefulness, a sense of inevitability, stole over her, and with it came renewed determination. This was their home. A place where they would raise their children and grow old together. Always together.

While she waited for Trey, Alana's mind began to spin with plans. She'd asked him to have the men unload their bedding. Tonight they'd sleep on the wood benches that ringed the veranda. In the morning, her first task would be to thoroughly scour one of the bedrooms.

Trey returned with two plates heaped with beans and a savory meat concoction. A jug of wine was tucked under one arm. Alana cleared off a spot for him next to her, and they hungrily consumed their meal in silence.

Trey scooped up the last of his beans with a tortilla and popped it into his mouth. "Tomorrow, I'll leave at daybreak for one of the neighboring ranches. Hopefully they might have a house servant or two to spare."

"Tomorrow?" The question slipped out before Alana could stop it.

Trey continued as though he hadn't heard her. "In the meantime, Isabel, the Indian woman I mentioned earlier, will see to your needs."

"How long will you be gone?" she asked, her dismay mounting.

"No more than a day, two at the most. In less than a week, the cattle I purchased are being shipped. There's much to be done before then."

Alana nodded, then quickly outlined her plan. Trey and several of the men unloaded a pile of bedding, and Alana padded the pine benches with the thick quilts. The wine she had consumed with her dinner, combined with three grueling days of travel, made her fall asleep minutes after her head hit the pillow, lulled by the bubbling fountain and the chirping of cicadas. In the distant hills, a coyote howled. Alana snuggled deeper in the covers, knowing even in her sleep that she was safe with Trey close by.

* * *

The next morning, Alana rolled over and stretched to ease the kinks caused by a night spent on a hard narrow pallet. Sleeping in a real bed again would be a luxury. A hot bath would be paradise. She raised up on her elbow, and as she had expected, there was no sign of Trey. Rolling to her feet, she stared down at herself in disgust. Her clothes were not only soiled beyond redemption, but hopelessly rumpled as well. A sorry-looking bride she presented. It was just as well Trey wasn't there to see her.

At the metallic click of a gate opening and closing, Alana looked across the courtyard. A stooped old woman wearing a sun-bleached apron over a plain black dress was coming toward her holding a tray. Her wizened face was as brown and creased as a walnut. A thick white braid was coiled neatly around her head. When she spied Alana watching her, the old woman broke into a wide, toothless grin.

"Señora." She bobbed her head and held out a shallow wooden bowl. *"Bienvenida."*

"Gracias." Alana smiled and accepted her offering, silently bemoaning the fact that her Spanish was woefully limited to a few simple phrases. It definitely wasn't fluent enough to conduct a conversation of any merit.

The old Indian woman, whom Alana assumed was Isabel, shoved the tray at her. Alana set it beside her on the bench. Cautiously, she peeked into the bowl and sniffed. It contained a thick substance that looked like porridge and smelled like corn. There were also an orange and a mug containing delicious-smelling hot chocolate. Isabel waited expectantly while Alana sampled a spoonful of cereal.

Isabel grinned happily when Alana took a second spoonful.

"I'm Isabel. I cook for you, *señora*." She motioned with one hand toward the hacienda. "I help clean, yes?"

Alana shook her head, alarmed at the thought of the frail old woman tackling such a monumental chore. Though the woman looked game to try, Alana was firm. "Thank you, Isabel, but no. Your job is to cook. *Señor* Trey will return with help for the heavier chores."

"If you change your mind, *señora*, just call me. I will return later with your noon meal."

The old Indian woman had probably learned English at one of the mission schools, Alana reflected. Isabel definitely spoke English much better than Alana spoke Spanish. She relaxed back against adobe and peeled her orange. Isabel was a dear to offer her help. Alana had hoped her refusal hadn't offended her. Cleaning the hacienda would take days, possibly weeks, of back-breaking labor to make it habitable. As she finished her hot chocolate, she felt a surge of energy and optimism. Perhaps after she looked at her new home in broad daylight the picture might not seem as bleak.

After removing the jacket of her traveling suit, Alana rolled up the sleeves of her frilly white blouse and prepared to go to work. As she did so, she spotted her traveling case near the edge of the bench where she had spent the night. Trey must have placed it there. How thoughtful of him. The idea of a fresh set of clothes was appealing, but then she remembered the filthy state of the hacienda and wisely decided to wait until later to bathe and change into something more suitable.

Alana methodically inspected each room. Upon opening the shutters, she realized that the interior was in worse shape than she had imagined. In her wanderings, she found a straw broom, a wooden bucket, a tub of lye soap, and a scrub brush. She selected the largest of the bedrooms as a place to start and set to work. Trey would be pleasantly surprised at the change when he arrived home.

Dusk was falling once again. Alana sat back on her heels and surveyed the results of her labor. Her arms ached from the unaccustomed strain of scrubbing and sweeping, but the effort was worth it. As a final touch, she had applied a fresh coat of whitewash to the walls. The tile floor gleamed; the walls glistened. The room was fresh, clean-smelling, and inviting. She wiped a strand of hair out of her eyes with the back of her hand, adding yet another smudge of dirt to her cheek.

"A woman on her knees. What a pretty picture." Alana's head whipped toward the softly accented Spanish voice. A stranger stood in the doorway that led into the corridor. His footfalls had gone undetected beneath the swish of her scrub brush.

Her heart hammered painfully against her ribs. "Who are you? What do you want?" she asked, her mouth dry.

"Did I frighten you, *chica?*" He laughed, but there was only menace in the sound.

Alana rose stiffly to her feet, trying to disguise the fear that was running through her like wildfire. She was alone in the house, too far away for Isabel to hear her cry for help. "Kindly state your business and leave."

He clucked his tongue. "So proper for a kitchen maid."

"Get out of here!" she ordered with false bravado.

"And if I choose to stay? What will you do?"

She squinted to discern the features of the man

half-hidden in the shadows. He was still, watchful, and gave the impression of coiled strength ready to strike. He wasn't a tall man, she noted, but slender, sinewy. Beneath a broad-brimmed hat, his black hair was clipped short. His eyes were black, too, glittering ebony set in a narrow, clean-shaven face with high cheekbones and a thin mouth. Part of her brain registered these details while another part searched for a way to convince him to leave.

He advanced into the room. She retreated a step, scrub brush clutched to her breast. "I'm not a kitchen maid," she said, summoning her haughtiest tones.

He looked her up and down with insulting thoroughness. "Could've fooled me, *chica*. But then, I'm partial to kitchen maids. Like I said"—a wolfish grin split his face—"I like to see a woman on her knees."

Foreboding feathered down her spine like cold fingers, making her shiver.

"Alana, there you are. I've been looking all over for you."

Trey bounded across the veranda. Close on his heels followed a striking brunet in a low-cut peasant blouse and a full skirt of red cotton. Alana was so relieved to see her husband that she practically threw herself into his arms.

He stopped short at the sight of her. "What on earth have you been up to?" he demanded, scowling in disapproval. "You look like a chimney sweep."

Belatedly, Alana was conscious of how she must look, covered with grime and sticky sweat, her hair straggling down her back. Her cheeks stung with humiliation. Her recent fright was converted into anger. She gestured impatiently with her hand. "What does it look like I've been doing?"

Trey's gaze swept over the room. He acknowledged her efforts with a curt nod. "You're the mistress of Rancho Prado del Sol," he reminded her coldly. "In the future, I expect you to act the part. You are the lady of the manor, not the hired help."

The stranger shifted his weight from one foot to the other and addressed Trey for the first time. "I arrived at the rancho before you did. I knocked, but the *señora* musn't have heard me. I didn't mean to frighten your wife, *señor.*"

"The *señora* doesn't frighten easily." Trey tugged off his leather riding gloves. "Alana, may I present Hernando Alphonso Pablo de la Vega, or simply Vega as he prefers to be called. Vega has agreed to become my overseer."

Vega's lips curled at Alana's look of dismay.

Chapter 14

"He has mean eyes, that one." Hands on her hips, the dark-eyed woman stepped out from behind Trey and watched Vega saunter off.

Trey scowled at the woman, then made introductions. "Alana, this is Consuelo Lopez. Consuelo will act as housekeeper and help Isabel with the cooking. This will have to do until I can make other arrangements. He looked around the room that had been cleared of debris and scrubbed until it shone, then nodded grudging approval. "I'll have some of the men bring in your things and set up your bed." He turned and left the two women to get acquainted.

"The *señora* would like to soak in a nice hot bath, *si?"*

"Si," Alana echoed. Closing her eyes, she felt weariness overtake her.

"Consuelo will take good care of you."

It felt wonderfully decadent to let Consuelo pamper her. The woman's energy seemed boundless. In short order, she found a tub for bathing, had water steaming on the cookstove, and directed the men where to put Alana's bed, dressing table, and the trunks of clothing.

Night had fallen by the time Alana had stripped off her dirt-encrusted skirt and blouse and let them drop into a heap, the garments soiled beyond redemption. She sighed with pure pleasure as she stepped into a steaming tub of water scented with the soap Consuelo had found packed among her things. Resting her head against the rim of the tub, she let hot water soak away grime and soothe stiff muscles.

Consuelo chattered as she spread clean linens on the bed and plumped the pillows invitingly. "This place used to belong to the Montoyas. *Mi madre* worked for them many years ago. When Señor Trey came to the Alvarezes asking if they could spare anyone to help at Rancho Prado de Sol, I was quick to offer my services. Señora Alvarez is a *bruja*. A witch," she quickly translated, seeing Alana's confusion. "I was glad to leave. Besides"—she shrugged philosophically—"my lover Pedro was making eyes at Elena Estevez."

Alana watched Consuelo from beneath half-closed lids. Thick black hair worn long and loose fell over one generously rounded breast as she bent to tuck in the corner of the sheet. The woman was probably a year or so older than Alana, but they were total opposites in every other way. Where Consuelo was dark, she was fair. Where Consuelo was full-figured, she was slender. While Consuelo tended to be gregarious, she tended to be reserved. And no one, Alana knew with certainty, ever questioned Consuelo's need for breast enhancers.

"Did it bother you that Pedro chose Elena over you?" Curiosity prompted Alana to ask.

Consuelo's eyes shot fiery sparks. "Never! Pedro is a fool!"

Alana kept silent.

Consuelo didn't seem to notice. She smoothed the folds from a nightgown of delicate lawn and laid it across the foot of the bed. "It was me who was tiring of him. Pedro has the stamina of a stallion, but the brain of a flea. My next man will have brains and be a stallion, too."

Alana's jaw slackened at the woman's blunt speech, then she snapped it shut. Along with shock she felt a smidgen of admiration. Consuelo not only knew exactly what she wanted, but had the courage to admit it.

"Here's the last of your things." Trey entered the room and halted abruptly at the sight of Alana sitting in the tub.

Consuelo's black eyes darted from one to the other. A knowing grin spread over her face. "I will go find the cook—Isabel, is it?—and check on dinner."

Alana felt heat envelop her that had nothing to do with the temperature of the water. She welcomed Trey with a sympathetic smile. "You must be exhausted after your long ride. As soon as I finish my bath, I'll have Consuelo heat water for yours."

He lowered her bag to the floor. "Don't bother."

His curt tone wiped the smile from her face, stripped the joy from her heart. "What's wrong? Are you angry that I embarrassed you in front of the hired help?"

"I didn't bring you here to toil like the lowliest chambermaid," he snapped.

"There is much to be done before this place will be truly habitable," she countered. "Far too much for Consuelo and one old woman."

He clenched his jaw. This woman sat in a tin washtub as if it were some kind of throne, and she a smudge-faced monarch. Yet she had the audacity to defy him! He hooked his thumbs in the waistband of his pants and sauntered closer to the tub.

Alana slid lower in the water until only the tops of her shoulders were visible. But her expression was anything but subservient. "If I'm the mistress of the house as you claim, then I'll do whatever I deem necessary for its upkeep."

"You're my wife, not a charwoman."

"And it's a wife's duty to take care of her home and family."

Unable to refute her logic, Trey swore angrily under his breath. He had vowed to make this woman suffer for what she had done to his family. It should have given him great satisfaction to return and find her dirty and disheveled, working harder than a lowly field hand. But it hadn't. She wasn't a delicate hothouse bloom, but a woman unafraid to roll up her sleeves and do what needed to be done. He had been astounded by the discovery. He grudgingly admired her spunk—and found that admiration in any form was galling.

"I'm not afraid of hard work." Alana's tone became conciliatory. "I promise not to interfere with the way you choose to run the ranch. I simply ask the same consideration when it comes to managing the household."

Trey took off his hat and tossed it onto the bed. Dammit, he had been worried more than he cared to admit about leaving her alone and unprotected. That knowledge didn't set well either.

"What are our neighbors like?"

"Aristocratic Spaniards who can trace their ownership of the land back to the Spanish crown in 1788. They don't harbor any fondness for Americanos." He tunneled both hands through his hair. "They were outwardly cordial, but insisted they had no house-servants to spare. In fact, I was about to leave when Consuelo offered her services."

"What about Vega? Did he work for the Alvarezes, too?"

"No." Trey cleared his throat. It was becoming increasingly difficult to carry on a conversation when the sweet, delicate fragrance of lily of the valley teased his senses. Clusters of soapy bubbles skimmed the water's surface like fluffy clouds, parting to reveal tantalizing glimpses of her nakedness. He knew he should walk away, but couldn't. Not when wet skin gleamed pale ivory. Not when impudent pink-tipped breasts rose and fell with each breath she took. He felt the almost uncontrollable urge to lift her boldly out of the tub, carry her to bed, and bury himself in her softness. "Meeting Vega was pure coincidence."

Alana subtly shifted her position, sending water sloshing from side to side in the narrow tub. A lock of hair fell over her shoulder, the end dipping below the surface of the water to curl against one breast.

Slowly, Trey reached out and brought it to his lips. Through heavy-lidded eyes, he saw her rapid intake of breath, watched her pupils dilate. And felt the impatient stir of desire. Then, reluctantly, he remembered his vow of vengeance. He had to learn to steel himself against her allure. To be strong instead of a weakling. He dropped the golden strand as though it were a rattler and stepped back.

"Sleep well," he rasped.

"I don't understand," Alana cried, shaking her head in confusion. "Where are your things? Where will you sleep?"

He wheeled around and stalked away. At the door leading onto the patio, he turned. "It won't be with you. Tomorrow, I'll have Consuelo prepare a room for me in the opposite wing."

He stomped across the patio, his boots ringing on the worn stone. He had nearly allowed the golden-haired witch to cast her spell over him. He despised himself for the weakness that threatened to overcome him every time he was near her. His body betrayed him without fail. If it was the last thing he did, he would exorcise her power over him, and in doing so, would avenge Robert. He had witnessed just now how his cruel rejection had brought tears shimmering to her eyes. Unwittingly, she had handed him the key to the ultimate revenge. By rejecting her, he could cause her the same grief, the same anguish, she had brought down upon Robert.

But instead of feeling pleasure, he felt only emptiness.

The days that followed were lost in a flurry of activity. Alana disregarded Trey's admonition. She worked alongside Consuelo from daybreak to sunset, clearing cobwebs and sweeping out debris until she fell into bed each night exhausted. She didn't want time to think, to feel, to ache with longing.

Little by little, bit by bit, the hacienda seemed to take on a personality of its own. Wood and tile floors gleamed with a healthy patina. Under a fresh coat of whitewash, the walls looked bright and inviting. She and Consuelo gleefully discovered items the previous owners had abandoned: a huge Moorish chest, a massive carved sofa and high-backed chairs, and, shoved into a corner of a guest room, a magnificent mahogany armoire. After each new acquisition, the two women would congratulate themselves and engage in a lively debate over where to put the pirated piece. Then, at sundown, Alana would bathe and change into one of the fine new gowns she had purchased expressly for her life as Mrs. Trey Matthews.

Tonight, she decided to wear a sapphire-blue gown

of shot silk that had no girlish pretensions, her favorite among her newly acquired finery. She planned to capture Trey's attention with all the care of a general planning a strategic battle. It was an occasion that called for the heaviest artillery in her feminine arsenal. All afternoon, she had bolstered her courage. The tension between them had become almost unbearable. She needed to discover why they didn't share a bedroom. Why he avoided her bed.

Consuelo seemed to divine her thoughts as she fastened the tiny buttons down the back of the gown. "Why don't you and *Señor* Trey sleep together?"

Alana tried to keep her tone casual. "It isn't unusual for a husband and wife to sleep in separate bedrooms. That's the way it's done in many upper-class homes."

"You ask me, it don't seem natural. Men and women should share the same bed. That's the way God intended."

"As a matter of fact, my parents each had their own bedroom." But their rooms weren't in opposite wings of the house, Alana acknowledged sadly. Their bedrooms were adjoining, separated by an unlocked door.

"How long you and *Señor* Trey been married?"

"Not long."

"How long is not long?"

Alana fussed with a tendril of hair and avoided meeting Consuelo's curious eyes in the vanity mirror. "We were married New Year's Eve."

"*Dios!*" Consuelo sounded shocked. "How will you make babies if you do not sleep together?"

"Enough, Consuelo!" Alana's voice was sharp. "This does not concern you. Let it rest."

"Gringos!" Consuelo threw up her hands in disgust. Mumbling under her breath, she fastened the last of the buttons. "I will see if Isabel needs any help."

After Consuelo bustled out, Alana morosely paced the room. As much as she hated to admit it, the woman was right. It wasn't natural for a newly married husband and wife to sleep apart. Trey had wanted her once. When had it changed? And why?

By the time the dinner hour approached, her nerves were frayed. Mustering her courage, she walked down the long, lonely corridor to the dining room where Trey waited. For an instant, she thought she saw an unguarded flicker of desire burn in the emerald depths of his eyes, but then it was mercilessly doused. Nevertheless, it lent her hope.

"Care for some Madeira?" He raised a fluted wine bottle in invitation.

Alana smiled and nodded. "Is this a special occasion?"

His mouth curved upward, but the smile didn't reach his eyes. "You might call it a celebration of sorts." He handed her a stemmed glass of the amber-colored vintage. "A rancher from San Bernadino has just agreed to my purchase price for a prized bull. This should greatly improve the herd I want to build. I'm sending Vega to bring him back."

"To your success." Alana raised her glass, secretly relieved Vega would be traveling to San Bernadino and not Trey.

"Is that what you plan to do? Make Rancho Prado del Sol one of the best cattle ranches in the state of California?"

Trey shrugged. "At one time this was only one of many great California cattle ranches that lined the San Gabriel front—Rancho San Jose, Rancho Santa Anita, Rancho La Canada—to name only a few."

"What happened to them?"

"The Great Drought of the sixties ruined most of them. Water had to be hauled down from the mountains by mule team. But even that failed. The parched bones of cattle were scattered all over the plains. Many ranchers were forced to sell dirt cheap the land that had been in their families for generations. No wonder many Spaniards resent the Americanos who virtually stole their birthright."

Alana shuddered at the vivid picture he painted. But she was eager to hear more about this land that was now her home. She was equally eager to have Trey share his dreams with her. It made her feel closer to him, made him seem less remote.

"Dinner is ready, *señor, señora,*" Isabel announced from the doorway.

Alana took her seat opposite Trey at a long table that would have comfortably seated eight. Once again, more than distance kept them apart. Orange flames danced atop candles set in a wrought-iron candelabrum. Shadows hugged the far corners of the room. Instead of intimacy, she felt alienation.

Isabel lifted the lid of a covered container and spooned a spicy meat dish onto the plates. The old woman waited expectantly while Alana cautiously sampled a forkful. "It's delicious, Isabel."

The woman's lined face beamed with pleasure at the compliment. "*Gracias.*" After serving Trey, she left the room with quick shuffling steps, still smiling.

Considering conversation preferable to the uncomfortable silence that so often prevailed at meal times, Alana tried to engage Trey's interest. "Is that what you hope to do? Build up the livestock so the ranch can regain its former glory?"

"Times have changed. The new gold in California

isn't the sort miners found at Sutter's Creek back in '48. It's citrus."

"Citrus?" Alana repeated blankly.

"Oranges." Trey helped himself to a tortilla. "As far as the eye can see, there will be acres and acres of orchards. Now that railroads have arrived, citrus can be quickly transported back East. There are already groves of oranges here on the rancho. Though they've been left untended, they will soon bear fruit. Vega learned Paco is experienced in growing citrus and placed him in charge."

With Alana's subtle encouragement, Trey was still expounding on the merits of growing citrus when Isabel returned, carrying a tray with coffee and dessert. "*Señor* Vega has arrived. I told him you and the *señora* weren't finished with dinner and asked him to wait in the kitchen."

Trey pushed back his plate. "I've been expecting him. Show him in."

Alana tried to stifle her disappointment. She instinctively distrusted the man Trey had selected as his foreman and fervently hoped he wouldn't stay long.

Vega strolled into the dining room, hat in hand. Ignoring Alana, he addressed Trey. "Said you wanted to see me tonight. Sorry if I interrupted your dinner. I can come back later."

"We just finished." Trey motioned to the chair next to him. "Join us for coffee."

"*Gracias.*" He turned an ingratiating smile on Alana. "If the *señora* doesn't object to a humble peasant sitting at her fine table."

The man's obsequious manner set her teeth on edge. She forced a strained smile, not wanting Trey to think her inhospitable. "Of course not. Isabel was just about to serve dessert."

Vega slid into the vacant chair at Trey's right before she even finished speaking. His ferret-bright eyes darted about the room, taking in every little detail. "Very nice, *señora,*" he complimented. "You must be pleased. All your hard work, all that scrubbing on your hands and knees, has been worthwhile, has it not?"

There was something in his words—an undertone, an implied threat—that made her skin crawl.

"I'm glad you're here, Vega. There's something I wish to discuss with you." Trey leaned back in his chair and waited while Isabel poured coffee, then left the room.

"What's on your mind, boss?"

"I just completed an agreement with another rancher to purchase a prize bull. I want you to go to San Bernadino and transport him back here."

"Me?" Vega sat up straighter. "You want me to go?"

"That's right." Trey leveled a cold stare at his foreman. "Is there a problem?"

"Of course not." Vega belatedly realized his mistake and tried a different approach. "But, boss, are you sure that's such a good idea? There's still a lot here that needs my attention, things you have no experience with. I don't think my being away from Rancho Prado del Sol right now is a good idea. One of my men can handle the bull, *no problemo.*"

"You'll leave first thing tomorrow."

Vega's wiry body grew as taut as a finely tuned guitar string, then visibly relaxed. Smiling, he imitated a careless shrug. "Whatever you say. You're the boss."

"Good. Let's consider the matter settled."

As the Spaniard reached for his coffee mug, Alana

caught the faint gleam of smoldering resentment in his dark eyes. Uneasiness trickled along her nerve endings. This man meant trouble. She was certain of it. But could she convince Trey?

Chapter 15

Cursing herself for a spineless fool, Alana tossed and turned upon her lonely bed. Before Vega's untimely arrival, she had had every intention of asking Trey point-blank why he refused to sleep with her. Perhaps she should go to him right now and demand an explanation. Demand to know why he ignored her night after night. But pride held her tongue.

Then, as it did quite often, Colin's warning echoed in her head. *He doesn't love you. I don't know why he's marrying you, but it's not out of love.* True, Trey had never told her he loved her. But, she argued stubbornly, if he didn't care for her, why did he ask her to marry him? He was a wealthy man, and more attractive than most. He could have had his pick from any number of young women from respectable San Diego families. Yet he had chosen her. Why marry her, then ignore her? It just didn't make sense. Try as she would, she just didn't understand his actions.

An unfamiliar sound drew her attention. Her body tensed, listening, waiting. Then she heard it again. Muffled voices barely above a whisper. She strained to make out the words. She was beginning to think it was only her imagination when half-shuffling, half-running footsteps passed beneath her partly open bedroom window. Not giving herself time to reconsider, Alana threw back the covers and slid out of bed. Padding over to the window in bare feet, she peered out. The moon hung low in the night sky like the blade of a reaper's sickle. A southernly breeze sent clouds chasing one another, crowding out the meager light. But not before Alana glimpsed two hunched figures moving stealthily across the patio.

Alarm sped through her veins. None of the ranch hands had any business being within the gated courtyard of the hacienda at this hour of night. Who were these men and what did they want? She had to find Trey. He would know what to do. Her bare feet skimmed the smooth tiles as she raced toward his room in the opposite wing.

"Trey!" She burst into his bedroom, the door banging against the frame.

Startled from a sound sleep, he bolted upright and squinted in her direction. "Alana? What the devil are you doing here?"

"I heard voices," she explained breathlessly. "When I looked out, I saw two men running across the patio."

He climbed out of bed and rooted through clothes piled on a nearby chair for his pants.

Alana drew in a quick breath. Naked as the day he was born, Trey looked magnificent. Though she had seen him undressed before, the sight stole her breath away. He was the epitome of male power and grace. Well-muscled and long of limb, he could have posed for a sculpture in one of her mother's Italian art books. He was her own private version of Michelangelo's *David*, Alana thought, feeling fiercely possessive.

Trey stepped into his pants. "Two men, you say. Did you recognize either of them?"

"Who?" Distracted, she had forgotten the reason for her pell-mell flight to his room.

He sighed in exasperation. "The men you claim to have seen."

"No." She shook her head to clear the sensual fog. "It was too dark to see their faces."

"Stay here," Trey ordered. "I'll go take a look around."

"Trey . . ."

He paused, one hand on the door leading to the patio.

"Be careful."

He disappeared into the night while she was left to anxiously await his return. Her imagination conjured up all sorts of evils that might await him. She paced the length of the room then stopped short, gnawing her lower lip in indecision. Trey hadn't even taken a weapon, she realized in dismay. What if the men were part of a group of *banditos* that preyed on isolated ranchers? The waiting was wearing on her nerves. She had to find out what was happening.

She stepped over the sill and saw Trey reenter the patio through the tall iron gate at the far end. She sagged against the door frame, weak with relief that he was unharmed.

"Where do you think you're going?" Trey took her by the arm none too gently, then steered her back into his bedroom and closed the door firmly.

"Did you find them? Who were they? What did they want?" Her eager questions spilled out in a rush.

"The only person I found was Vega enjoying a late-night cigar and a swig of tequila."

"But surely Vega must have seen any strangers lurking about."

"He was there the whole time and claims he saw no one." Trey's words dropped like stones.

Alana shook her head in disbelief. "Then he's lying!"

"What possible reason would Vega have to lie?"

Alana was at a loss to explain. "I don't know," she admitted stubbornly. "But I tell you I saw two men prowling about."

"Vega suggested that perhaps you were dreaming. I'm inclined to think along those lines myself. Or . . ." He left the thought unfinished.

Trey studied her through narrowed eyes, making her acutely aware of her own state of undress. In her haste, she had neglected to don her robe. All she wore was a revealing flame-colored nightgown of silk and lace that sheathed her body like a second skin before flaring around her hips. It had been part of her trousseau.

The silence between them spun a sensual web.

A weakness stole over Alana as she watched Trey lounge indolently against a bedpost, arms folded across his chest—his broad, bare chest covered with crisp black hair. She took a step forward, then another until they stood almost toe to toe. Almost of its own volition, her hand reached out to stroke that hard-muscled wall, her fingertips raking though that tempting mat of dark curls. One touch fueled the need for another.

While Trey didn't return her caresses, neither did her pull away. Emboldened, Alana stole a glance upward. The expressionless face staring back at her could have been carved from marble. Only the eyes glittered with life. "Are you sure this isn't what you had in mind all along?" he asked, his voice hard and unyielding. "Since I didn't come to your bed, you'd come to mine?"

Alana's hands fell to her sides. She stared at him, aghast at his suggestion. But he continued in the same cruel vein.

"You're an expert in the art of seduction, aren't you?" With a fingertip he slowly traced the low-cut neckline of her flame-colored silk nightgown.

Alana felt her nipples pucker into tight buds and knew they must be visible under the filmy material. Her body automatically responded to his slightest touch.

Pity that Robert's taste in women had leaned toward sirens sheathed in scarlet silk, Trey thought. If not, he might still be alive. Thoughts of his brother helped Trey clamp down on the hot tide of desire rising within him. "You've grown accustomed to men fawning over you, haven't you? Does it hurt your feminine pride that I'm not one of them?"

"No," she replied too quickly to be convincing.

"By merely batting your eyelashes, you had all those men at the Gilded Lily clamoring for your attention. Colin O'Shea heeled like a puppy dog. Only I offered you something different, didn't I? I offered you the one thing none of the others had—marriage and respectability."

"That isn't why I married you." She shook her head in vehement protest, her hair swaying around her shoulders.

"Isn't it? Don't make the mistake of playing me for a fool, Alana."

"I married you because I love you." The admission was torn from her.

Trey straightened and stepped away. "You delude yourself, my dear, if you believe love had something to do with it when in fact you sold yourself to the highest bidder."

Alana wanted to press her hands over her ears, to

blot out the hurtful words, but she could only stare at him in disbelief. Each word was like the flick of a knife.

"I knew if I waited long enough, you'd come to me. You concocted some phony story about strange men lurking about and used that as your excuse. Imaginative, but transparent as glass. Too bad Vega couldn't give credence to your little melodrama. For a moment, I must confess, I almost believed you."

"You arrogant bastard!" she hurled, wanting to strike out, wanting to hurt him in return. "I don't know why you choose to accept the word of Vega, a virtual stranger, instead of mine, but that's your mistake. If Vega didn't see two men sulking about, he's either blind or a liar!"

"I say he's neither."

"What makes you so certain that I am? That this was all a ruse manufactured so we'd end up in bed together? Tell me." She blinked back tears. "Do you really believe my morals so lacking that I bedded every patron of the Gilded Lily who flirted with me? Do you really believe Colin and I were lovers?"

"Don't bother to deny it. O'Shea implied as much shortly before our wedding."

Doubly betrayed, doubly wounded, she realized Colin would have gone to any lengths to prevent her from marrying Trey.

Trey shrugged. "I told him it didn't matter. You're a beautiful, desirable woman. I didn't expect you to be virtuous as well."

Alana didn't stay to hear more. Feeling as if her very soul had been ripped out and trampled on, she stumbled from his room and down the corridor. She had never expected Trey to be capable of such cruelty, such callousness.

Heartsick, she threw herself into the bed and burrowed beneath the blankets. The chill she felt went bone-deep. All she had ever wanted from Trey was the chance to prove her worthiness as his wife. It had seemed so simple, so uncomplicated. She loved him and foolishly hoped he returned that love. Hurt beyond tears, she stared at the ceiling and mourned the death of a dream.

"What is it, *señora?* Are you ill?" Consuelo asked, concern in her dark eyes.

Alana didn't looked up from the laundry she was folding. "No, I feel fine."

The two women sat side by side on a bench outside the kitchen door in the late-afternoon sunshine, a wicker basket between them. "You don't look fine to me." Consuelo reached into the hamper. "Ah," she murmured knowingly. "You and *Señor* Trey must have had a lovers' quarrel."

Alana kept silent as she neatly folded one of Trey's shirts. "Did you hear or see anything unusual last night?" she asked finally.

"No, I see nothing. Why do you ask?"

Alana needed someone to confide in. She took a chance, hoping that maybe Consuelo would believe her. "Last night, I heard a noise just outside my bedroom window. When I looked out, I saw two figures running along the patio toward the back gate."

"*Dios!* Did you see who they were?"

"No. It was too dark."

"Did you tell *Señor* Trey what you saw?"

"Yes." All the misery of the previous night flooded back. "But he didn't believe me."

"But why not?"

"Because Vega claims he was outside the whole time and saw no one suspicious."

"Vega." Consuelo spat the name. *"El serpiente,* the snake."

The two women traded looks over the wicker basket. Words were unnecessary. Neither woman liked or trusted Vega.

Isabel came out of the kitchen, drying her hands on her apron. 'There is someone here to see the *señor."*

"Send him out here, Isabel. I will talk to him." Alana had no idea where Trey might be, but she could at least find out what the man's business was.

Isabel bobbed her head and left to return minutes later with a lanky cowboy in faded denims and a plaid shirt. *"Señor* Noah Stone."

"Howdy, ma'am." Noah Stone smiled, displaying a pair of deep dimples, and stuck out his hand. "Pleased to meet you."

Alana returned the handshake while studying the stranger with interest. Nearly as tall as Trey, Noah Stone had a shock of sun-bleached hair that dipped charmingly across his forehead, and the guileless blue eyes of a choirboy. His shirt was open at the throat, and he held a flat-brimmed felt hat in his hands. "Didn't mean to bust in on you like this. Awful good of you to see me."

"I'm Alana Matthews. My husband isn't here at present, Mr. Stone, but perhaps over a cold drink you'd care to tell us what brings you here."

"That's mighty good of you to ask, ma'am. Nothing I'd like better than a cold drink after a long ride. And please call me Noah."

Consuelo tossed her dark hair and gave him a coy smile. "Isabel just made some lemonade. If you like, I will fetch you some."

Noah flashed his dimples. *"Gracias, señorita."*

An answering smile curved Consuelo's red lips as she left to see about refreshments.

Alana motioned Noah to have a seat. "What is it you wish to see my husband about, Noah?"

"Frankly, ma'am, I'm here lookin' for work."

"What kind of work are you interested in?"

"Folks said your husband is building up a herd. I'm good with livestock. Never met a horse or cow I couldn't get along with." He gave her a lazy grin. "Animals are a hell of a lot—excuse the expression, ma'am—easier to get along with than some two-legged critters."

"Nice cold lemonade and a plate of Isabel's sugar cookies." Consuelo reappeared with a swish of her colorful skirt. As she bent to offer Noah a cookie, she afforded him a tantalizing view of her deep cleavage.

"I've been working on a ranch down in Texas, but got a hankerin' to see what California was like. I think I'll like it here real fine."

"Tell us about Texas, *señor,*" Consuelo coaxed. "I have heard many stories. Is it true . . ."

The next hour flew by. Noah Stone regaled the women with stories of life on the Texas frontier. His outrageous flattery aside, Alana felt herself responding to his charm. In some ways he reminded her of Colin. Animation made Consuelo's dark eyes sparkle and her laughter was blatantly flirtatious. Even Isabel was not immune to Noah's charm. The old woman giggled like a schoolgirl when he lavishly complimented her on the fragrant smells emanating form her kitchen.

"My husband should be home soon," Alana said. "We'd be pleased to have you join us for dinner. Afterward, you can discuss your business with him."

"I'd be honored, ma'am, if you're sure your husband won't mind sharin' his fine table with a simple cowhand."

"I'm sure my husband will be more than happy to talk with someone who shares his enthusiasm for livestock." After their bitter exchange the night before, Alana welcomed Noah to act as buffer between her and Trey. All day, she had been dreading their next encounter.

"As soon as I finish my chores, I'll be happy to show *Señor* Stone the rancho and a place where he can wash up before dinner." Consuelo generously volunteered.

"I'll put the laundry away, Consuelo. Go ahead and entertain, Mr. Stone."

Over Consuelo's token protests, Alana picked up the armful of neatly folded laundry and went inside. As she shoved open the door of Trey's bedroom she assured herself there was no reason to feel like an interloper. Yet she felt uncomfortable. A wife should not feel guilty for entering her husband's bedroom. If Trey should come upon her, she would simply explain she was helping Consuelo with her chores. In a hacienda this size, everyone was needed to pull a share of the workload. She would quickly put away his clean laundry and leave.

She stepped across the threshold and looked around. Last night's hurtful scene had been played out against a backdrop of darkness. Now, she looked about the room in the waning daylight, really seeing it for the first time. The furnishings were spartan, mere props to fill an empty stage. To her left stood a massive oak bedstead, its four posts soaring nearly to the ceiling. A chair with a woven seat sat next to the bed. A plain oak bureau occupied the opposite wall. It was a place to sleep, nothing more.

Crossing the room, Alana opened bureau drawers, replacing socks, undergarments, and shirts. Searching for the place he kept his handkerchiefs, she pulled out the uppermost drawer. A silver-framed photograph lay facedown among the folded squares of linen. Curiosity prompted her to pick it up and carry it to the window for a closer look. Two young men and a handsome older woman stared back at her. She recognized Trey instantly. Even so, there were subtle differences in the young man he was then and the man he had become. In the photograph, his expression was more open, less stern. The beautiful mouth that rarely smiled was pleasantly curved as though he was enjoying a private joke. The woman, probably his mother, had strong features that showed pride and strength of character rather than beauty. The type of women, Alana surmised, who grew more attractive with age. The third person in the photograph was a youth of about fifteen, with fair hair, light-colored eyes, and an open smile.

"Who gave you permission to snoop through my things?"

The photograph slipped from Alana's fingers and crashed to the floor.

Muttering a soft curse, Trey crossed the room in long strides. He picked up the picture and examined it almost reverently.

Alana breathed a sigh of relief to see that although one corner of the frame had been slightly bent, the memento had sustained no serious damage. Her gaze shifted from the damaged frame to her irate husband. An apology clogged in her throat. Clothed in black, his expression fierce, Trey resembled a fallen archangel in the encroaching twilight, sword in hand ready to collect reparation. "I-I wasn't snooping," she stammered.

"Then why were you going through my belongings?"

She lifted her chin proudly, refusing to be cowed by his anger. "I wasn't aware that a wife needed to ask her husband's consent before putting his clean clothes in a drawer." When he made no retort, she ventured a question. "Is that your mother and brother with you in the photograph?"

"Yes."

Alana watched him replace the picture. She noted that once again he laid it face down, as though he couldn't bear the sight of his loved ones and the memory of his subsequent loss. Sympathy welled inside her. He had cared for his family deeply, of that she was certain. She wanted to reach out to him, ease his pain. "You never mention your family," she said softly.

He slammed the drawer shut so violently that Alana jumped. "I no longer have a family. They're dead."

Alana was frightened by the green fire blazing in his eyes. She sensed the fury that climbed close to the surface, ready to spew forth. Suddenly, she felt frightened. It was as though he held her personally responsible for their demise. Intent on escape, she edged toward the door.

"Alana!" His voice cracked like a whip, stopping her in her tracks. "In the future, stay out of my room."

She fled his bedroom for the second time in less than a day, not caring whether he thought her a coward or not.

Dinner was a strained affair. Alana could not help but be aware of the fact that Noah Stone's questioning glance bounced between her and Trey. To his credit, Noah tried to keep the conversation going, but in the end he, too, fell victim to the malignant silence. Alana toyed with the food on her plate. A nearly forgotten memory clamored to be recognized. She sensed it had to do with the photograph on Trey's bureau. In spite of Trey's warning to stay out of his room, she had to get another look at that picture. She would have no peace of mind until she did.

The seemingly interminable meal finally came to a close. Trey finished the last of his wine and shoved himself away from the table. "Well, I'm satisfied, Stone. You seem to know a good deal about ranching. You can move your things into the bunkhouse."

"You've got yourself one grateful cowpoke." Noah stuck out his hand, and the two men shook hands.

"You'll take orders from my foreman, Vega, but I'll let him know you're to work with the horses."

Noah turned to Alana. "You were awfully quiet tonight, ma'am. Sure hope it wasn't the company." His bright blue eyes bored into hers, and for a fleeting moment, she imagined she read concern in them.

She summoned a smile. "No, of course not."

"Good." He picked up his hat. "Then I'll be seein' you around. Thanks for the invite to dinner."

Alana watched him leave, his movements surprisingly graceful and fluid. Noah's sunny smile was a heartstopper, and he had enough charm for six men. Simple, uncomplicated, happy-go-lucky. Too bad Trey couldn't be more that way, she thought wistfully.

"I suspect our new ranch hand meets with your approval."

Though Trey's tone was casual, the gleam in his eyes was intense. Alana chose her words with care. "Noah Stone seems like a nice man. I'm sure you wouldn't have hired him if you didn't think he was capable."

"I have work to do in my study," he said in dismissal. He strode down the corridor, leaving her alone in the deserted dining room.

Alana stood in indecision, her mind busily plotting. Trey would be occupied for hours going over ledgers or reading journals. This would be a perfect time to get a better look at the puzzling photograph. Before her resolve—and her courage—failed her.

Chapter 16

A compulsion too strong to deny propelled Alana past the closed door of Trey's study and down the long hallway. The lamp she carried sketched grotesque shadows on the adobe walls. With each step, tension mounted inside her. Mounted until her nerves stretched taut. She hesitated in the darkened hall just outside his bedroom, then, drawing a steadying breath, slipped inside and quietly closed the door behind her. She set the lamp she carried on top of the bureau. Slowly, she pulled open the drawer, and with an odd reluctance, withdrew the photograph.

She stared first at the woman, taking in her silver-streaked hair, strong jaw, and no-nonsense gaze. The somewhat formidable countenance could have belonged to any of countless society matrons from Baltimore to San Diego. Her gaze slid to Trey's younger brother. An insidious familiarity nudged at the edges of her memory. Frowning slightly in concentration, she examined the image closer. The youth and Trey bore no physical resemblance. Indeed, the pair were as different as night and day. Yet there was something about him. Something about his smile . . .

Alana tapped her fingernail impatiently against the frame. Her frown deepened. Someone she had known a lifetime ago in Baltimore. A person with a similar smile. Then a name materialized to go with the photograph—Robert Prescott. Robert had had the same endearing smile with one front tooth slightly overlapping the other. Whatever had happened to Robert Prescott?

Could Robert Prescott and Trey's younger brother be one and the same?

Impossible.

Not only did they bear no physical resemblance, but also their surnames were different.

Dear, sweet Robert. He had been so earnest, so sincere, and so in love with her. But from the moment he had introduced his friend Phillip Fairchild to her, Robert had lost his place in her affections. He had been crushed, heartbroken. While she, on the other hand, had been so infatuated that Phillip had filled her entire world. Nothing else had mattered, not family, not friends, and certainly not Robert's broken heart—only Phillip. What a strange quirk of fate, she mused, if she were to discover herself married to Robert's brother. Trey had said his family was dead. How tragic that both Trey's brother and Phillip should die at such a young age.

She was too engrossed in reminiscing to hear the door quietly open and close.

"So you came back. I wondered if you would."

Eyes wide with surprise, Alana spun to face her husband. Like a child caught with her hand in the cookie jar, she knew guilt was written across her features in bold letters. She fought the temptation to hide the photograph behind her back. "I know you told me to stay out of your room, but the likeness in the photograph bothered me all evening. I had to look at it one more time."

He rested his back against the door.

Alana found his silence more unnerving than any

recriminations might have been. She replaced the photograph, taking care to lay it facedown, conscious that Trey studied her every move. "I'm sorry. It was wrong of me to enter your room when you expressly forbade me to." She slid the drawer shut.

Trey made no move to step aside so she could leave. Neither did he speak. A frisson of unease swept over her as lightly as a feather, making goose bumps rise on her flesh. She ran her tongue over lips that were suddenly dry. "Your brother bears an uncanny resemblance to someone I once knew."

"Really?"

"It's the smile. The crooked front tooth."

"Rather unusual, don't you think?"

Alana nodded warily. "What was your brother's name?"

"Robert."

"Robert," she echoed faintly. "How strange. That was also my friend's name."

"What a coincidence."

Alana's look sharpened. Had she detected bitter sarcasm in his tone? "Other than telling me you were raised in the East, I don't think you ever mentioned what city your family is from."

"No. I was saving that bit of information for just the right moment." His lips curved in a sinister imitation of a smile. "I'm from Baltimore."

"Baltimore?" she gasped. Her mind scrambled to assimilate this startling new fact, along with his reasons for keeping it a secret. "Then Robert Prescott *was* your brother?" she blurted.

"Congratulations, wife. I wasn't sure how to tell you. Your curiosity solved the problem for me."

"But how can that be? You both have different surnames. You're totally different in personality and appearance." There were so many questions clamoring for answers, and paramount among them was his reason for secrecy.

"Robert was my half-brother." Trey doled out the information in a miserly fashion. "Did you know him well?"

She lifted one shoulder in a small shrug. "He was one of my suitors."

"One of your suitors," he mused thoughtfully. "I'd wager the last of my railroad shares that Robert was only one of *many* ardent admirers." When Alana remained silent, he continued. "And how did you feel about him?"

"I was fond of Robert."

"Fond?" Frowning, Trey drew out the word as though puzzled by its meaning. "*Fond* is such a bland term when it comes to describing affection, don't you think? One is fond of an aunt who brings you presents, of a certain food, or a favorite pet. Was Robert *fond* of you, too? Or did his feelings run deeper?"

Alana eyed Trey warily. He showed no indication of leaving his post by the door, his large body easily barring the exit. She was reminded of a sleek black housecat patiently baiting a field mouse.

"Could it be you had so many suitors you can't even remember how my brother felt about you?"

She restrained the urge to squirm under his cross-examination. "Why are you badgering me? All this took place more than a year ago. It no longer matters."

"Oh, but I disagree, my dear wife. It matters a great deal."

"I don't wish to discuss this any longer. If you'll kindly let me pass, I would like to retire to my room."

He didn't budge an inch. "Was Robert in love with you?" he asked in a silken voice laced with steel.

Raising her chin a fraction, she met his gaze with a bravado she didn't feel. "He professed to be."

"And what was your reaction?"

"I told him that while I was flattered by his attention, I didn't return his feelings. I told him there was someone else." A defensiveness had crept into her tone.

Trey was persistent. "Just who was this someone else?"

"Phillip Fairchild," she snapped. "The man I married."

He pushed away from the door and advanced toward her. In a heartbeat, Trey ceased being a harmless housecat and became a stalking panther, relentlessly moving in for the kill. The urgency to flee drummed through her veins. Fighting the desire to run, she took an involuntary step backward and connected solidly with the oak bureau.

He towered above her, his features cast in harsh planes. Only his eyes were alive with a bright feral gleam that made her cringe. "A woman like you was born to flirt and tease. One man isn't enough to satisfy your love of the sport. Then, when you tire of the game, you carelessly toss one lover aside in favor of another."

His vicious accusations slashed her soul. "What is it you want from me?" she asked in a tortured whisper. "An apology for rejecting your brother's proposal?"

"An apology would be much too simple—and far too quick. I want you to experience the same pain—the same hurt—that Robert did."

"Why?" she cried in confusion. "I don't understand . . ."

"Why don't you ask me how Robert died?" His voice was low, raspy. "Or don't you care?"

The ominous softness of his tone was as chilling as the bay breeze in the hours before dawn. "No," she cried, casting a longing glance toward the door. "I don't want to know."

"Damn you! Ask me how Robert died!" His hands roughly circled her upper arms. "Ask me!"

Alana's mouth opened, but no words came out.

His grip tightened painfully. "*You* killed him, Alana."

Alana grew very still. It seemed that her heart ceased to beat. Her brain wasn't functioning properly. Trey's accusation didn't make any sense.

"What!" he jeered. "Don't you want to hear the gruesome details?"

She shook her head from side to side. If this were some horrible nightmare, she prayed she'd wake up.

"When you so callously broke his heart, Robert couldn't bear the pain. He put a gun to his head and blew his brains out."

"No . . ."

"Oh, but it's true, every word. I can describe the scene for you in gory detail. Just ask me. I'm the one who found him slumped over his desk, the gun cold in his hand. Blood—Robert's blood—was splattered everywhere. It was the same color as the rose I brought you the night I asked you to marry me. Fitting symbolism, I thought."

"No . . ." All vestiges of color drained from her face. Trey's features blurred and the room began to revolve slowly. Only the pain from Trey's fierce hold on her was real. Alana forced herself to focus on it to keep from fainting.

"But that isn't all the damage you did," Trey continued. "You also destroyed my mother."

Alana pressed her hands against her ears. "D-don't," she pleaded brokenly. "I can't bear to hear any more."

"Ah, but you will." Mercilessly, he manacled her wrists and dragged them downward, forcing her to listen. "The night of the funeral, Mother collapsed from a stroke after cursing the name Alana Van Dorne. It would have been a blessing had she died then. But she didn't. She lingered for nearly a year, her right side paralyzed. She was a helpless invalid, unable to utter a word. Only her eyes mirrored the woman she once was. They burned with the same light as they had when she denounced your name."

Aghast, Alana could only stare at him, tears brimming in her eyes. What could she say in her own defense? Words couldn't restore his family, couldn't restore what her actions had unknowingly destroyed. She hung her head and asked the only question left that still mattered. "If you hate me so much, why did you marry me?"

"Because you killed my entire family. I want to see you suffer, to make you pay. I want you to hurt, to feel sick with remorse, and to know that nothing you can ever do will bring back two lives." His eyes blazed with a fervency as hot and unforgiving as the Santa Anas.

"You never loved me at all, did you?" The words were wrenched from her.

"Love?" he snarled. "I despise you. You can't seriously think I cared about you even for a minute. I used you like a man uses a whore."

A sob escaped her bloodless lips. Alana's entire world shattered around her.

Trey smiled coldly. "Rumor had it that you and your lover had run off to Europe. I had detectives scouring all of London and half the English countryside looking for you. I had almost abandoned hope of ever finding you. Then, as luck would have it, I discovered you singing in a San Diego saloon, of all places." He let go of her suddenly, as though he could no longer stand to touch her.

Alana stared up at him through a haze of tears. She had never meant to harm anyone, yet she had killed Robert and was responsible for turning his mother into a bedridden invalid. So much destruction, so much pain. Suddenly, it was too much to comprehend. A paralyzing numbness bordering on shock crept over her.

Trey watched desolation deepen the hue of her eyes and wondered grimly why he didn't feel elation. This was what he wanted, wasn't it? To bring this woman to her knees. It should be the ultimate victory. But instead of gloating, he felt only a vast void. "Go," he ordered, his voice flat. "Get out of my sight."

Tears streaming down her cheeks, Alana stumbled from the room.

A profound weariness settled over Trey as he watched Alana, blinded by tears, grope her way down the darkened corridor and disappear from view. He crossed the room with heavy steps and sank down in the chair. Resting his head against the backrest, he closed his eyes. But all he could see behind his closed lids was Alana's stricken face. He had wanted to hurt her—and he had succeeded beyond his wildest dreams. Why, then, did he feel . . . lost?

Eyes gritty and burning, Alana lay on her back and stared up at the ceiling. It had been two days since her fateful confrontation with Trey. Two days racked by guilt, remorse, and despair. Days spent pacing;

nights haunted by dreams. Robert's guileless smile taunted her every moment.

With an effort, she had recalled Robert's proposal. After they had attended one of her mother's musicales, Robert had persuaded her to accompany him on a stroll through the garden. While he prattled on, she had mentally reviewed her plans to elope with Phillip later that very evening. All that remained to do was pen a farewell note to her parents. As soon as the house quieted, she would steal down the stairs to meet Phillip. By the time her mother and father discovered she was missing, she would already be a married woman on a train bound for California. Suddenly, Robert had grasped her hand and stammered a proposal. "You'll find someone more suited," she had told him, dismissing his ardor with a sisterlike pat on the cheek. Then she had left him standing amid the roses while she merrily went off to elope with her dashing young Englishman. How heartless her actions now seemed.

Tears she had thought were spent trickled down her temples. Robert had placed a gun to his head and ended his life. She had killed him as surely as if she had pulled the trigger. And the tragedy hadn't ended there. Distraught with grief, his mother had been condemned to a living death, robbed of her ability to speak, confined to a body that no longer responded to her commands. Alana's tears rolled faster. No wonder Trey hated her. No wonder he sought revenge.

I used you like a man uses a whore. Trey's cruel words had cut like a sword. Just as she had broken Robert's heart, Trey had broken hers. Would time mend a broken heart? she wondered bleakly. Somehow, she didn't think hers could ever be made whole.

"*Señora!*" Consuelo's voice carried from beyond the closed door. "It is nearly dinnertime."

"I'm not hungry."

"*Señora*, it's been two days. You've barely touched your food."

Alana wiped her tears. "I'll have Isabel fix me a tray later."

"To lock yourself away like this is not good." Consuelo walked off, clicking her tongue in disapproval.

Alana rolled onto her side, her arms hugging her waist. She knew she was being a coward, but she didn't care. She dreaded her next meeting with Trey. She would have to face him eventually, but hoped to delay it until she regained control over her emotions.

"*Señora*." Consuelo was back. "The *señor* insists that you join him for dinner. If you are not in the dining room in one hour, he said he will come for you himself."

Alana shuddered, remembering the fierce determination burning in Trey's emerald gaze. She knew with certainty that his wasn't an idle threat. He was determined to show her who was the master. If necessary, he would break down the door and drag her out, screaming and fighting every step of the way.

"I have water heating for your bath." Consuelo called, then her footsteps retreated down the hall.

Feeling old beyond her years, Alana dragged herself from the bed, shuffled to the dressing table, and peered into the mirror to assess the damage. She almost didn't recognize the woman staring back at her with the puffy eyes and tear-ravaged face. With a trembling hand, she shoved the tangled mane of hair behind her ears. Feminine pride asserted itself. She didn't want Trey to see her this way—didn't want him to witness her abject defeat.

"Dios!" Consuelo exclaimed when Alana opened the door to admit her ten minutes later. "You look terrible! Get in the bath. I will find something to help your eyes."

Alana stripped off the dressing robe and stepped into the steaming water. She laid her head against the rim of the tub. Consuelo left, then returned with cold compresses with a faint herbal scent. "Close your eyes," she ordered, placing the moist cloths over Alana's closed lids.

The combination of hot water and cold compresses had a wonderfully soothing effect. When the bathwater grew tepid, Consuelo held out a towel. As Alana rose from the tub, Consuelo's dark eyes fastened on the purple bruises that banded Alana's upper arms. Alana tensed, embarrassment and humiliation warring for dominance. She was immensely grateful when Consuelo didn't comment. She selected a demure gown of lavender striped silk, its square-cut neckline trimmed with blond lace. Consuelo fastened her hair in a sleek chignon low on her neck. Alana applied a judicious touch of rouge to each cheekbone to disguise her pallor. At last she was ready.

Her heart in her throat, she slowly approached the dining room, where she knew Trey waited. She found him seated at the head of the table, absently tracing patterns on the damask tablecloth. He looked up at her approach. Eyes narrowed, he scrutinized her as though searching for some hidden flaw. Alana stiffened and suffered his inspection in silence.

Slowly, he rose to his feet. "You're late. I was about to go and get you."

"I saved you the trouble."

Alana took her place at the foot of the table. Isabel appeared carrying a pottery baking dish. She beamed a broad smile at Alana as she heaped her plate with chicken and spicy rice. To please the old woman, Alana took a bite. *"Bueno, señora."*

After serving Trey and refilling the wineglasses, Isabel left them alone. The only sound in the room was the faint clink of cutlery against china. Alana tried another small bite of chicken, but the food, delicious though it probably was, tasted like glue. Reaching for her glass, she took several swallows of wine to wash it down. Glancing at Trey from under her lashes, Alana noted he was having no such problem with his dinner. Alana pushed the food about her plate. At length, she put down her fork and abandoned all pretense of eating. The situation between her and Trey was untenable. It couldn't continue.

A calm settled over her as she reached a decision.

Chapter 17

"I intend to leave here as soon as I can make the arrangements."

Trey calmly helped himself to another portion of rice. "Perhaps you didn't hear me," she said. "I'm leaving you."

He tore off a piece of tortilla. "Oh, I hear you, all right."

She tilted her head to one side and studied him. His complete lack of emotion baffled her. "I didn't expect you to be so agreeable," she said at last. "I was prepared for an argument."

He shrugged. "There's no reason to argue because, quite simply, you aren't going anywhere."

His continued indifference made her nervous and confused. "You're mistaken. I plan to return to San Diego as soon as possible."

"How?"

The single word dropped like a stone into a still pond.

How? Alana repeated silently. She frowned. Why did she feel this was a trick question? She stared at Trey, who leaned back in his chair and unblinkingly returned her regard. Apprehension crawled along her skin. "Why," she answered slowly, "I'll ask one of the men to take me."

"And why do you think they'd do as you ask? Aren't you forgetting one vital fact?"

Her mouth suddenly dry, she reached for her wineglass and took a swallow. "And what fact is that?"

His smile, like the sun on a cold winter's day, lacked warmth. "The men take their orders from me."

"And you've ordered them not to take me anywhere?"

He nodded. "Precisely."

"You have no right to hold me here against my will," she cried, lashing out in frustration.

"As your husband, I have every right in the world to detain you. I even have a license."

Anger raced through her, purging fear, temporarily obliterating guilt and depression. She shoved back her chair, jumped to her feet, and advanced on him. "I'm *not* going to stay here. I'll find someone who is willing to take me."

He arched a brow. "And what will you use to pay him with?"

She halted abruptly. A sudden chill doused her anger. She hadn't a dollar to her name. She had withdrawn every penny she had managed to save while working at the Gilded Lily and spent the entire sum on a wardrobe befitting the wife of an influential man like Trey Matthews. What was left over had gone for household items to bring to her new home. She had assumed her husband would provide for her.

"I see you finally understand the predicament you're in." Trey smiled with satisfaction. "I have you in my power, Alana, totally dependent on my benevolence for every stitch of clothing, every morsel of food."

"You're mad!" she gasped. "Your mind is so twisted with hatred you can't see beyond your need for revenge. None of this will bring Robert back."

Tossing down his napkin, he leaped to his feet. He grabbed her arm before she could flee and spun her around. "You're right," he said through clenched teeth. "None of this will bring my brother back to life, but I'll have the satisfaction of reminding you every single day of the suffering you caused."

"You're obsessed. Hasn't it brought you enough pleasure to know that by making me fall in love with you, you hurt me every bit as much as I hurt Robert?" Her voice shook with suppressed rage and bitterness.

"Love!" He laughed. "Is that what women like you call spreading your legs?"

She slapped him, the palm of her hand loud against his cheek. Both appalled and surprised by her reaction, she stared at him. The violent urge to retaliate had raced out of nowhere, consuming her, too powerful to control. Tight-lipped, Trey caught her wrist before she could strike him again.

They glared at each other. The imprint of her hand on his tanned cheek turned from white to red.

"Women like me?" she asked, her voice strained. "You don't know me at all."

"Don't I? I watched you all those nights in the Gilded Lily. You smiled, and men swarmed around you like bees to honey. Nothing you can say will convince me I was the only one you bedded."

"Let go of me!" She struggled to break free, wanting to draw blood, to wound him as his words wounded her pride.

Though his grip on her wrist wasn't painful, she was unable to extricate herself from his hold. He brought his face down closer to hers. "You're deceiving yourself if you think you're any different from Candy or the others who ply their trade in the Stingaree District. You came with a price tag. Only yours wasn't money, it was marriage."

"That isn't fair," she choked, her face as white as paper.

He released her. Tension thick in the air, they confronted each other as adversaries. Alana shrank from the contempt carved in every grim line of Trey's features. Her anger dissipated as quickly as it had appeared, leaving her desolate. Trey's harsh words stripped away all her defenses. True, escape from the Stingaree was an added benefit, but love had been the driving force behind her decision to wed. But even if she could convince Trey of that, he would never forgive her for Robert's death.

Their wordless duel was broken by Isabel's agitated chatter. "No, no, *señor* . . ."

"Get out of my way, old woman," a man snarled. "I need to see Matthews—now." Vega roughly pushed past the Indian woman, who tried to bar his entrance.

"It's all right, Isabel." Trey scowled at his foreman. "What is it, Vega?"

Vega directed his remarks to Trey, as though Alana weren't present. "You told me I'd do all the hiring. Yet the first thing I hear when I get back from San Bernadino is that you signed on a drifter."

Alana absently rubbed her aching wrist and, morbidly fascinated, watched the scene between the two men.

"I assume you're talking about Noah Stone," Trey said evenly.

"Damn right that's who I'm talking about." Vega's manner was belligerent. "How do you expect me to run this place if I don't have any say in the men who are hired?"

Trey eyed him coldly. "Just because I've given you free rein until now doesn't give you license to barge into my dining room uninvited."

Vega hitched his thumbs in his belt and shifted his weight from one foot to the other. He visibly banked his fiery temper, as if beginning to realize he might have committed a tactical blunder. "No offense, boss, but you're a railroad man, not a rancher. A greenhorn." He gave a feeble chuckle.

There was no answering glint of humor in Trey's expression. "Railroad man or rancher, I've hired a good number of employees in my day. Don't make me regret that I hired you."

Vega swallowed, his Adam's apple bobbing.

"If you're not happy here, Vega, you're free to leave."

"No, no, *señor,* I like it here. I did not mean to anger you." He made a conciliatory gesture with his hands. "You said you wanted to make this ranch something to be proud of. I try to pick the best men for the job. I hire only the ones with the right experience. There's something about Noah Stone I don't trust."

"He stays."

"Whatever you say, *señor.* I want only what's best for the *rancho.*"

His ingratiating tone set Alana's teeth on edge. Slowly, she let out the breath she wasn't aware she'd been holding. Trey had called Vega's bluff as coolly as he had Colin's that long-ago night at the poker table at the Gilded Lady.

"Vega!" Trey stopped the foreman as he turned to leave. "In the future, don't make the mistake of forgetting that *I'm* the owner of Rancho Prado del Sol."

"No, *señor.*" As Vega started out of the room, his attention fell on Alana for the first time. He gaze swept over her, insulting in its thoroughness, then lingered on the way she cradled her wrist. His reptilian black eyes shifted to the telltale marks on Trey's cheek. Careful to keep his expression impassive, he bobbed his head. *"Buenos noches."*

Alana watched Trey sink down in his chair and drag a hand through his hair. For an unguarded moment, he looked weary, vulnerable. He had set himself the difficult task of converting a neglected piece of land into a showplace. *Enough,* an inner voice warned. *Don't start feeling sorry for him.* Hardening herself against a rush of sympathy, she straightened her shoulders. Her concern was laughable. She, better than anyone, knew that Trey could be utterly ruthless when the situation demanded it. Should Vega challenge him, Trey would crush his resistance as effortlessly as he had crushed hers.

But her resistance was still intact, she realized in amazement. She refused to live with a man who was driven by hatred. Her determination to escape stronger than ever, she stiffened her spine. She left Trey to his solitary brooding, her head unbowed.

She would find a way to get away. If not today, then tomorrow, or the next day, but she would find a way. Alana dug the trowel deeper into the rich soil. Consuelo hadn't been much help. Under Alana's careful questioning, she had only confirmed what Alana already feared. Few of the ranch hands spoke English. And if the language barrier wasn't enough to discourage her, what could she offer in exchange for their help? Surely they would lose their jobs once Trey discovered that they had helped her flee. As she pulled weeds and replanted flower beds that had been long-neglected, she mentally inventoried her assets. They were appallingly few. Only her jewelry was of any value: a single strand of pearls her parents had given her on her sixteenth birthday, a small sapphire brooch that Colin had won in a poker game, and the diamond ring Trey had given her when he proposed on Christmas Eve.

Setting aside the trowel, Alana sat back on her heels and stared at her left hand. The diamond winked up at her. The facets captured sunlight in a shimmering rainbow of colors. In her mind, rainbows stood for hope and happiness. This beautiful ring and its spectrum of dancing color represented just the opposite. It was a travesty, a mockery. A vehicle for Trey's vengeance. A half-sob ripped through her as she jerked the ring from her finger.

She sniffed back tears and studied the small circle of gold in the palm of her hand. She could use the ring as a bribe, her practical nature asserted. Surely, no one would refuse such a valuable bauble. Then sentimentality rose to the surface. The thought of parting with her engagement ring made her fingers curl around it possessively. A realization—unwelcome and unexpected—crystallized. While the ring meant nothing to Trey, she treasured it. It was her own personal rainbow of hope for the future. She'd never give it up. Her eyes blinded by tears, she jammed the ring back on her finger and picked up the tool. She resumed her gardening as though her very existence depended upon it. How ironic, she thought. She wouldn't be here long enough to see the flowers she planted grow into full bloom. The trowel glanced off a rock, scraping her knuckles and eliciting her cry of pain.

"Drat!" she swore in agitation as she inspected the

damage. One fingernail was broken to the quick. The skin on two knuckles was abraded.

"Now there, ma'am, fingernails have a way of growin' back."

Her head snapped up and she met Noah Stone's laughing blue eyes. She managed a wan smile in return. "That will teach me. Next time, I'll wear gloves."

"There ya go. Then all you'll need is a raggedy straw hat like my Aunt Liddy used to wear in her garden." His dimples winked in and out. "Blackbirds used to take 'er for a scarecrow."

The notion of herself in an outrageous gardening costume drew a genuine smile from Alana. Setting down her trowel, she got to her feet. In the process, the neckline of the white peasant-style blouse Consuelo had loaned her dipped low on one shoulder. Automatically, she reached to pull it up, but Noah shoved her hand out of the way.

His sandy brows puckered in a frown. His usual amiable expression vanished in the blink of an eye. He looked different somehow. Older, experienced, like someone used to giving orders rather than taking them. Amazed at the transformation, she watched him for a long moment before her eyes slid to the object of his scrutiny. His gaze was fixed on the purple bruises banding her upper arms, livid souvenirs of the night Trey had told her of Robert's suicide.

"What happened?"

"N-nothing." Alana was reluctant to tell the truth, although it was plain to see. "I tripped. If Trey hadn't caught me in time, I could have injured myself." She hitched her blouse back in place.

Noah caught her wrist and held it up for his inspection. More bruises formed sooty bracelets around her slender wrist. "How do you explain these?"

Alana snatched her arm back, but refused to meet his eyes. "It was an accident. I was unpacking a trunk and the lid dropped on it. It's nothing."

Noah captured her chin and forced her to meet his steady gaze. "I don't take kindly to men who beat their women."

"It's not what you think. Trey wouldn't—" She stopped in midsentence, astonished at how instinctively she came to Trey's defense. Startled, she realized she spoke the truth. Trey had no need to resort to physical abuse when he had much more subtle methods of inflicting pain. "Trey wouldn't beat me."

Noah released her chin. "Sure glad to hear that, darlin'. Your husband didn't strike me as a low-bellied snake, but you never know what goes on behind closed doors. Just remember, if you ever need me, you know where to find me."

Alana's mind raced. Here was the answer to her prayer. The solution to her problem stood in front of her wearing scuffed cowboy boots and speaking with a Texas twang. She spoke quickly before she could lose her courage. "Noah, I do need your help. I need to get away from here . . . to go back to San Diego. I don't have any money, but I can give you jewelry."

"Whoa, slow down." He stepped back, hooked his thumbs in the waistband of his pants, and cocked his head to one side. "Why are you in such an all-fired hurry to leave here? Didn't you just tell me your husband didn't mistreat you?"

Belatedly, Alana realized her error. "I don't like it here. It's too remote. I miss my old life, my friends, the shops. I was raised in a city, not some godforsaken wilderness."

Though battered, her pride was still intact. Better

to let Noah think her a petulant wife than bare her soul with the truth and confess she was fleeing Trey's hatred before it could destroy her.

Noah tipped back his hat and flashed a boyish grin. "Honey, all you need to do is to give this place a little time. Once you get used to it, you'll love it as much as that husband of yours does."

Pride be damned. "Please, Noah, I beg of you. I just have to get away from here."

"Sorry, honey, but your husband would skin me alive if he even got wind we were talkin' like this. He'd send me packin' before nightfall. Can't afford to lose a good payin' job like this one. I got responsibilities that need tendin'."

Alana was instantly contrite. She hadn't stopped to consider the ramifications Noah would have to face if he agreed to her request. Nevertheless, she was disappointed, and it showed.

"It pains me to see a pretty woman like you so down in the mouth." Then he snapped his fingers. "Know what always cheers me up when I'm feelin' low?"

Alana shook her head.

"Saddlin' up my horse and takin' a nice long ride. With the wind at your back and the sun in your face, pretty quick you don't have a care in the world."

"It sounds wonderful, but I don't know how to ride a horse."

He displayed the smile Consuelo found so fascinating. "Well, I can remedy that. Come down to the corral tomorrow afternoon, and I'll give you your first lesson."

She stooped down, picked up her trowel, and resumed planting geraniums. "Thank you, Noah. I just may take you up on your offer."

If I'm not on my way to San Diego!

* * *

According to Consuelo, Paco had an unquenchable fondness for tequila. The unwitting remark had been all that was needed to set Alana's plan in motion. When she had shown the pretty sapphire brooch to Paco, his eyes had gleamed like polished agates. Undoubtedly, he'd been thinking of the countless bottles of liquor it would buy. He had insisted on payment in advance, and against her better judgment, she had complied. Once again, the pretty bit of jewelry was lost in a gamble, but as far as she was concerned, the rewards outweighed any risk. In a few minutes, she would be leaving Rancho Prado del Sol—forever.

Alana fastened the top button of her dark woolen wrap, then draped a black rebozo over her head. She cast a lingering glance around her bedroom. Regret slammed into her, its blow so strong and unexpected she had no time to shield herself against its stunning force. She didn't want to leave the ranch. Didn't want to leave Trey. In a short time, she had grown to love the age-mellowed adobe house with its sprawling vistas and sense of timelessness. She had arrived on its threshold bursting with optimism for a bright future. Somehow, Trey's dreams of citrus and cattle had become her dream. He would be all alone now—alone with his hatred.

Her heart leaden, she picked up the bag holding her belongings, then quietly slipped out the door. Keeping to the shadows, she soundlessly crossed the patio, unlatched the back gate, and hurried toward the stables where she had agreed to meet Paco. He had promised to have a wagon waiting, had bragged he knew the route like the back of his hand. The air was cool and crisp, making her grateful for the warmth of her woolen wrap. Ahead of her the stable appeared dark and deserted. Alana tried to allay her apprehension.

Cautiously, she stepped into the stable and tried to peer through the blackness that enveloped her. The place smelled of hay, saddle soap, and horseflesh. In the belly of the stable, horses stirred restively in their stalls.

"Paco!" she called tentatively. When there was no answer, she called again.

Still no answer.

A figure emerged from the shadows. "Paco sends his regrets."

"Trey!" Her suitcase thudded to the floor.

"You sound disappointed." He advanced toward her. With studied casualness, he flipped an object in the air, then caught it. "You've grown careless with your jewelry. I think I'll have to lock this away for safekeeping."

Bereft of words, Alana gazed at her brooch cupped in the palm of Trey's hand. She felt trapped. A crushing sense of betrayal weighed heavily on her shoulders. Not only had she lost her brooch, but with it her last chance of ever securing transportation back to San Diego. Her plans had borne bitter fruit. There was no hope of escaping Trey's web of vengeance. Not now, maybe never.

"Nothing to say in your defense? You didn't believe me when I said I wasn't going to allow you to leave. Perhaps now you will."

"How did you know?" she asked in a subdued voice.

"I appealed to the men's greed. Should you try to bribe them, I promised to double your offer."

"How long do you plan to hold me against my will? Forever?"

"Forever isn't long enough."

His voice was cold and frigid, his expression bleak. She wrapped her arms around herself to ward off the chill. "You thought of everything, didn't you?"

He shrugged. "For the past year, I've had nothing better to do than imagine ways to make you pay for what you did to my family."

"Can't you see that hatred is eating away at you like a cancer? I'll always regret the role I played in Robert's death. It'll be a blight on my conscience until the day I die. I've thought of little else since you told me he committed suicide. But the truth is, I didn't kill him. Robert—and only Robert—pulled the trigger." She swept past him and out of the stables.

A muscle worked in Trey's jaw. He scooped up her suitcase and quickly caught up with her, matching his stride to hers. Neither spoke. Outside the door to her room, she snatched her suitcase from his grip. Girding herself against his wrath, she dared to look at him. Moonlight etched his cleanly chiseled features in tones of silver and pewter. She was prepared for anger, even contempt, but not this stark resignation.

"I pity you, Trey Matthews," she whispered. "In your self-righteous quest for vengeance, you've destroyed two more lives—yours and mine. I wish things could have been different between us." Tears magnifying her eyes, she stepped into her bedroom and closed the door behind her.

Trey turned and walked slowly across the veranda to his own quarters. His hands balled into fists. It had taken every ounce of willpower he possessed not to reach out and wipe away the single tear that had trickled down her cheek. Even with her hair severely pulled back and hidden beneath a shawl, her face held the haunting purity of a Madonna. Would her beauty never cease to taunt him? Though a personal vendetta made him spurn her, he ached to possess her—both body and spirit.

It was more than physical beauty alone that attracted him. With each passing day, with each added tribulation, he was continually discovering new dimensions of her character that he admired in spite of his resolve not to.

He knew he couldn't hold her hostage forever. But for reasons he didn't care to examine too closely, he didn't want to let her go.

"You may find this hard to believe, vixen," he muttered softly to himself, "but I, too, wish things were different. I wish I was the one you met in Baltimore—not Robert."

Chapter 18

Alana watched surreptitiously as Trey sliced off a piece of meat, then left it untouched while he traced wet rings made by his water glass. Something was dreadfully wrong. She could sense it.

Finally, when she could stand his brooding silence no longer, she cleared her throat to draw his attention. "If you don't finish your dinner, you're going to have to listen to one of Isabel's lectures instead of me."

Trey glanced down the table. A fleeting smile softened his mouth, momentarily erasing the lines of tension.

His infrequent smile did queer things to her insides. It made her feel warm, wanted. Alana fervently wished he would look at her like that more often. "Something's troubling you. Care to talk about it?"

Conflicting expressions flitted across his features—doubt, denial, indecision, resentment, and finally resignation. He slouched back in his chair, the meal forgotten. "Guess I'll have to take my chances with Isabel."

"I've never noticed you suffer from a lack of appetite before. The problem must be serious."

"It is." He dragged a hand through his hair.

Alana waited patiently for him to continue. Just

when she was certain he had changed his mind about confiding in her, the words reluctantly spilled forth from him.

"Ever since we arrived at the ranch, there have been a steady stream of incidents. A more sensible, or less determined, man would almost think someone was trying to drive him off."

A frisson of apprehension drifted across Alana, chilling her. "What type of incidents?" she asked, frowning slightly.

Trey leveled a look at her. "The hacienda remained a pigsty even though the real estate agent hired a crew to clean it thoroughly prior to our arrival. The staff of houseservants I arranged for never appeared. Ranch hands I personally hire disappear during the night without any explanation. And now . . ." His voice trailed away.

Her mouth suddenly dry, Alana leaned toward him. "And now . . ." she prodded.

"My fences are being cut. Cattle vanish faster than I can replace them."

"Rustlers?"

"That was my first thought," Trey confessed, then shrugged. "Funny thing is, none of the other ranchers are plagued by the thieves. So far Rancho Prado del Sol is their sole target."

Alana sipped her wine, needing time to think. "Surely there must be something we can do. What about the law?"

"I filled out a report, but the local marshal claims he doesn't have the manpower to oversee such a vast area. Vega has assigned men to night patrol. Our only hope is to catch the culprits before it's too late." On that discouraging note, he pushed away from the table and excused himself.

For a long time after Trey left, Alana sat at the dining room table deep in thought. Two incidents might be considered a coincidence, but not this rash of problems. She tried to convince herself that she didn't care, shouldn't care. After what Trey had done to her, she didn't owe him any loyalty. She tried to persuade herself that only idle curiosity spurred her interest. But in the end, she had to admit it wasn't curiosity, and she did care. Whether it pleased her or not, what concerned Trey concerned her as well.

She rose from the table when Isabel arrived to clear it. Restlessly, she prowled the sprawling hacienda, searching for a distraction. Finding none, she returned to her bedroom and tried to read. The book she had found so engrossing earlier no longer held her interest. Snapping it shut, she left her room and headed for the kitchen, hoping to find Consuelo or Isabel for companionship.

To her disappointment, she found neither. Usually the hub of activity, the kitchen was deserted. She stood undecided in the center of the empty room. Her gaze drifted while she pondered how to spend the long hours until bedtime. Copper kettles, scrubbed and gleaming, hung from rafters. Strings of red peppers trailed from hooks, their spicy scent filling the air. A wooden bowl heaped with fruit occupied the center of the scarred trestle table.

Alana reached into the bowl and broke off a bunch of grapes just as Trey charged through the door. One look at his expression told her something serious had happened. "What is it? What's the matter?"

"Everything," he muttered, breezing past her.

Alana dropped the grapes back into the bowl and followed him, almost running to keep up with his long strides. "Is there anything I can do to help?"

"It would take the Almighty Himself to get us out

of this mess." He strode down the hall toward his room with Alana at his heels.

"What happened?" She felt caught up in the sense of urgency that was driving him. "What are you going to do?"

He threw her an exasperated look over his shoulder. "Try to save the citrus crop—if I can."

"I thought Vega put Paco in charge of the orange groves."

"He did. Therein lies the problem." Inside his bedroom, he tore a thick woolen jacket from a peg behind the door and jammed his arms through the sleeves. "I found Paco dead drunk with an empty tequila bottle in one hand. Earlier, he assured me he had taken the necessary precautions against a deep frost tonight. Now I find out nothing's been done—absolutely nothing."

"What about Vega? Can't he help?"

Trey yanked open a drawer of his bureau and rummaged through its contents. "Vega and a handful of men left to take delivery of a shipment of cattle at the railroad depot, a full day's ride north of here. There's only a skeleton crew left to tend to business. Most of them speak little or no English. And since I speak only rudimentary Spanish, I can't make them understand what needs to be done."

"Noah could."

Trey stopped searching for a pair of gloves and whirled to face her. "What could Noah do?"

"Noah speaks fluent Spanish." Hope as brief as summer lightning flashed in his eyes. Encouraged, Alana elaborated. "I heard him talking to Consuelo. Noah's words were flying as fast as hers." She didn't add that she strongly suspected they were saying things not meant for her ears.

In his excitement, Trey grabbed her shoulders and

gave them a squeeze. He cursed softly when she flinched from his touch. "Thank you."

Stuffing his gloves in a pocket, he dashed off.

Alana ran after him as far as the back gate. There she saw Trey and Noah engaged in earnest conversation. Then Noah issued a volley of Spanish and a half-dozen men came running from different directions. Consuelo, hugging a shawl around her shoulders, came out to stand next to Alana.

"What are the men going to do?" she asked. Each word formed a puff of white vapor in the chill night air.

"They are going to build small fires in the orange groves, *señora,* to keep the oranges from freezing."

"Surely that will be dangerous." Fear crept into her tone as she remembered the devastating fires that swept down the mountains fanned by the Santa Ana winds. "What if they set the entire ranch on fire?"

"They will be careful," Consuelo replied. "The men will use whatever they can to contain the fires, and they will guard them all night."

As the women watched, men darted about, rounding up every available pot and pail along with an assortment of tools and tossing them in a wagon where they landed with a clang of metal striking metal.

"Wait!" Consuelo called out suddenly and waved wildly when Noah glanced her way.

"Come." She turned with a swish of skirts and hurried off, not waiting to see if he followed.

Noah's long strides ate up the ground as he drew near. A worried frown had replaced his usual affable expression. "Where is that woman off to? I don't have time to waste on foolishness."

Alana motioned him toward the kitchen. When Noah didn't slacken his stride, she picked up her skirts with both hands and tried to keep pace. The stays of her corset dug into her ribs as she half-ran to keep up with him. "Whatever she's doing," she said, gasping for breath, "I'm sure it's important."

At the kitchen doorway, they heard Consuelo's voice coming from an adjoining pantry. "Here—you can have these."

Alana peeked over Noah's shoulder and saw Consuelo proudly point at six large iron kettles. "Years ago when this was one of the great cattle ranches, these were used for rendering fat," Consuelo explained. "Isabel claims they were bartered from a whaling ship."

"They're perfect—and so are you." While Alana looked on in amusement, Noah caught Consuelo up in a bear hug and gave her a sound smack on the lips. After setting her back on her feet, he picked up a kettle in each hand, the heavy weight bunching the muscles in his arms. "Manuel! Juan!" he called from the doorway. When the men came on the run, he directed the pair in rapid-fire Spanish to collect the remaining kettles and add them to the precious cache of containers.

By the time Alana and Consuelo returned to the courtyard, all the ranch hands were piling into the wagon. Trey had already mounted his bay. The horse snorted and pawed the ground impatiently. Noah vaulted gracefully into his own saddle. Then, with a jingle of harnesses and a crunch of wagon wheels on hard-packed dirt, the small caravan rolled off.

Trey's gaze swept over Alana as he rode past her. The brim of his hat was pulled low, making it impossible to decipher his expression. She wanted to call out after him, to wish him well, to let him know she cared. But the words locked in her throat. Instead, she watched him go in silence. With her arms wrapped around her waist to ward off the chill, she stood shivering outside the courtyard gate until his figure was swallowed by darkness.

"Will the fires work?" Alana hadn't realized she had voiced her concern out loud.

Consuelo shrugged. "The men won't know till morning. They will try. That is all they can do. The rest is in the hands of God."

Alana bit her lip to stop the shivering. It was more than the cool night air that chilled her. All that stood between Trey's dream and utter destruction were a few meager bonfires. The knowledge brought a coldness that sank bone-deep. "I feel so helpless. I wish there was something I could do."

"We can pray, *señora.*"

Consuelo returned to the hacienda, and Alana followed. In minutes, Consuelo had a small fire blazing cheerily in the kitchen hearth. While Alana prowled the room, Consuelo took a bowl from the cupboard and began shelling beans. The rhythmic sound of dried beans dropping into a wooden bowl marked the passage of time as effectively as a second hand on a clock. An hour crawled by, then another commenced. The bowl filled. A second was started.

Alana sighed. "I pity the men. It's going to be a long night. They're going to be cold . . . hungry. Consuelo?"

"Señora?" Consuelo replied, not looking up from her task.

"Do you know how to harness a horse to a buggy?"

"Si," she replied absently.

"Do you know the way to the orange grove?"

"Si."

"Do you know how to cook?"

"Si!" Consuelo's head came up with a snap.

"Since neither of us is going to get much rest tonight, why not make ourselves useful?" Before Alana could finish speaking, Consuelo set the beans on the table with a satisfying *thud*. Of one accord, the women got busy. Imitating what she had seen Isabel do, Alana made her very first pot of coffee. While waiting for it to come to a boil, she gathered cups and packed them into a basket. Consuelo, meanwhile, sliced leftover beef into a cast-iron frying pan, then added refried beans, tomatoes, chiles, and seasonings. When these were simmering, she found a stack of tortillas in the pantry and added them to the basket.

When everything was ready, the women loaded the food into the back of a wagon and set out for the citrus grove. The night was cold and clear. Millions of stars spangled the night sky like diamond dust on black velvet. A orange glow hovered above the citrus grove, guiding their way. Consuelo clucked to the horse, which responded by quickening its pace down the rutted trail. Alana clung to the seat as the wagon swayed from side to side, thankful they had packed the food securely to keep it from spilling.

Upon reaching the outer fringe of the grove, Consuelo drew back on the reins. "Ay," she muttered under her breath.

Alana sat motionless and gazed at the dreamlike scene before her. Smoke trailed like heavy fog through the trees. The air was redolent with woodsmoke along with the pungent, more offensive odor of kerosene. Misty figures of men with *sombreros* pulled low and bandanas tied over their faces moved in and out of the precisely planted rows. Evenly spaced along the ground, bright red blossoms of fire bloomed in pots and tubs and circles surrounded by stone. The rasp of a saw and *thunk* of an ax formed a discordant tattoo of sound.

A single man separated himself from the tableau. Alana felt her stomach muscles tighten as her husband materialized. Even with the lowered brim of his Stetson and a handkerchief covering the lower half of his face, he was easily recognizable from his size alone. Even his gait was distinctive, full of the masculine grace and self-assurance that never failed to have an odd effect on her heartbeat.

Trey raised a gloved hand and jerked the bandana down. "What are you women doing here? This is no time for a social call."

Alana fought back an angry retort, along with a quick stab of hurt. "We brought you coffee and something to eat."

"Mighty good of you, ma'am." Noah came up behind Trey, his grin a slash of white in his dirt-streaked face.

Alana shot him a grateful smile before starting to swing down from the buggy. Noah took a half-step forward to assist her, but Trey nudged him aside and, putting his hands on her waist, lowered her to the ground. For the first time since their wedding night, there was no animosity in his touch. Alana felt the sensual pull, a silken cord of desire, being spun between them as intricately as a spider's web. Her breathing became shallow, her pulse quickened—and the fingers at her waist tightened their grip.

"The men must eat quickly, or the food will grow cold." Consuelo clamored down and went to the back of the buggy, where she began unpacking the basket.

Trey let go of Alana's waist and dropped his hands to his sides. With a shout, Noah summoned the men from the fires they tended. The sound of ax and saw ceased while singly and in pairs the men gathered around the buggy.

Alana cleared her throat, feeling self-conscious and

awkward. Stepping around Trey, she went to help Consuelo. While she poured coffee, Consuelo scooped the beef concoction on top of tortillas. The men murmured their thanks, then congregated a short distance away, where they ate and talked among themselves.

Alana poured coffee for Noah, then realized Trey was no longer part of the group. She finally spotted him feeding a chunk of wood into one of the small fires near the end of a row of trees.

"Your man has not eaten yet. Here, take this to him." Consuelo thrust a tortilla into Alana's hand.

Noah leaned against the buggy wheel. "Maybe he's not hungry."

"Of course he is," Consuelo contradicted cheerfully. "What man who works so hard wouldn't be?" She pressed a steaming mug of coffee into Alana's free hand.

Alana felt Noah's eyes probing hers. From the grim set of his mouth and the frosty glint in his eyes, she knew he remembered the bruises on her arms. Knew that he suspected Trey of abusing her. *I'm here if you need me. Just holler.* He was sending her the message as clear as any telegram.

"Go!" Consuelo gave her a little shove. "Your man's waiting."

Determined to show Noah that he was wrong about Trey, Alana drew a steadying breath and walked toward her husband. Trey looked up at her approach. As each step closed the gap between them, Alana felt buffeted by a strange blend of reluctance and eagerness.

"I brought you something to eat. You'll need it to keep up your strength before this night's over."

He pulled down the bandana, whipped off his gloves, and stuffed them in a back pocket. "Thanks," he muttered, accepting the tortilla bulging with meat and beans.

She watched him wolf down the food while her mind cast about for something to say. All the while, she sensed Noah behind them watching the exchange with uncanny shrewdness. "Do you think you'll be able to save the oranges?"

He frowned before swallowing. "There's a fighting chance, but we won't know for sure until morning."

"I see," she murmured, and handed him the coffee.

He nodded his gratitude, then took a big gulp and sighed. "Remind me, will you, to give Consuelo a bonus. The pots she unearthed were a godsend."

Envy ripped through her. Alana wished with all her heart that she, not Consuelo, had been the one to offer the iron kettles.

"I only hope we have enough fuel to keep the fires burning until dawn. We're burning every bit of brush, every stick of firewood we can find. Not to mention a month's supply of kerosene. I don't know what we'll do if it doesn't last through the night."

"If anyone can beat the odds, you can. After all"—she offered a tentative smile of encouragement—"I've watched you play poker."

"There's a lot more at stake here than money."

"I know." At the simple acknowledgment, their differences were temporarily set aside. In the ensuing silence, they were bound together by a mutual concern. "If anyone can succeed, you can. You're not a man to give up and admit defeat."

He quirked a dark brow. "What? A compliment? After all that's passed between us, I hardly expected flattery."

"Not flattery," she corrected with a shake of her head. "Merely an observation." As she reached out to take the empty mug from his hand, her fingers brushed his. A pleasant tingle raced along her nerve pathways clear up to her shoulder.

"Alana . . ."

Trey's voice was husky, and she wondered if he, too, had felt the electricity that arced between them.

He shifted slightly to block her retreat. "It was good of you to do this. I know the men appreciated it. Hell . . ." He dropped his eyes and kicked a clod of dirt with the toe of his boot. "*I* appreciated it."

This was a new side of Trey Matthews, stripped of his customary arrogance and self-assurance. No longer impeccably groomed, he stood before her with his face streaked with soot and his clothes reeking of woodsmoke. Yet never had he seemed more attractive or appealing to her. "I wanted to help," she answered simply, and tried to convince herself the choking sensation in her throat was caused by the smoke from the smoldering fires.

"Thank you."

As she walked away cradling the empty coffee mug against her midriff, she accepted the fact that the warmth surging through her had been generated by his wry smile rather than the heat of a dozen bonfires.

The sun inched toward the horizon. Tones of magenta and vermilion stained the sky, the colors as garish as a whore's party dress. But in Trey's mind the colors were beautiful, for they heralded daylight and sunshine—warmth that would dissolve the night's chill. He had narrowly cheated the elements.

His bootsteps rang hollowly against the tiled courtyard. Fatigue dogged his heels. He was dirty, cold, and bone-weary, but he had done it. They had done it. The orange crop was safe.

And Alana had helped.

Trey smiled in spite of his fatigue. She had appeared like some midnight angel out of the heart of the night with food and coffee to sustain the men through their long, cold vigil. His smile slowly faded. Instead of gloating over his misfortune, she had rallied to his side. Her generosity had been as unexpected as it was undeserved in light of his treatment of her. The thought shamed him.

But your treatment of her is justified. Think of Robert, think of your mother, before you grow soft.

His expression hardened with resolve.

At the fountain in the center of the courtyard, he stripped off his jacket, dipped his cupped hands into the icy water, and sluiced it over his face, scrubbing away the grime. Shivering, he shook himself. Droplets of water flew in all directions. The shock of the cold water drove some of the cobwebs from his mind. Refreshed, he turned toward the hacienda. In the kitchen, he shrugged out of his shirt to rid himself of the disagreeable odor of woodsmoke that clung to the fibers and carelessly slung it over his shoulder. Later, when he was rested, he would soak in a tub of hot water. Right now, all he wanted was to kick off his boots, stretch out on a bed, and get some sleep.

He started down the hallway toward his bedroom, but got no further than the study when he paused. The door stood ajar. Peeking inside, he saw Alana curled in a chair, a woolen shawl draped over her lap, a book lying on the floor with the pages splayed open. Careful not to awaken her, he entered the room.

He stood for a while, staring down at her. A honey-gold tendril of hair had escaped the once tidy coil at the base of her neck to curl softly against her cheek. Trey intended only to smooth it back, but instead ran it through his fingers, savoring its silky texture. In repose her face held a childlike innocence and purity. Regret surged through him, as swift and sharp as a scalpel. If fate had been kinder, she was the sort he would have chosen to love. A woman of beauty and spirit and passion. A partner through life.

Around and around his finger, he wound the silky strand. In spite of his resolve, he was touched by her concern. She had kept vigil here just as he had done in the orange grove. Then he cursed under his breath. Damn! He was doing it again—going soft. It must be from lack of sleep. There could be no other possible explanation.

He released the lock of hair. It lightly brushed her cheek, and she batted it away. As he watched, her eyelids fluttered open and she blinked up at him.

"Trey!" She pushed herself upright, shoving the wayward curl behind her ear. "The orange grove. Will it be all right?"

"Yes. No thanks to Paco."

"I'm so relieved." She yawned broadly, her eyelids drooping, and snuggled deeper into the chair.

Trey sighed in resignation, then picked her up. Her eyes wide in surprise, she let out a startled gasp. Without another word, he carried her out of the study and turned in the direction of her room. One of her arms stole around his neck. The palm of her right hand rested lightly against his bare chest. Her head nestled in the crook of his shoulder as though it were a pillow created expressly for her use. He felt her relax against him, all warm woman and soft, feminine curves. And though he was loath to admit it, he liked the feel of her in his arms. Liked it too much.

He shouldered open the door to her bedroom, and placed her none too gently on the bed. Instead of letting go of him as he expected her to do, she reached up and experimentally traced the lines that bracketed his mouth.

"You know, you look quite fearsome at times. Rather like a pirate, or perhaps a mercenary—a very tired one."

He caught her fingers as they skimmed his stubbled jaw. "Any pirate or mercenary with an ounce of common sense should be forewarned not to tangle with you. You can be one dangerous lady in more ways than one."

She smiled drowsily, and he experienced a powerful urge to lie beside her, to take her in his arms, to hold her, to sleep in her sweet embrace.

He hadn't planned to kiss her, but the kiss seemed as inevitable as the next beat of his heart. One moment he was staring down into her slumberous blue eyes, the next he was sampling a mouth as lush as ripe strawberries. His lips played over hers, lightly tasting, savoring. She made a sound deep in her throat, like the contented purr of a kitten. He took the kiss deeper. His tongue traced the seam of her lips, and when they parted in eager anticipation, his tongue deftly slid inside to duel with hers in ancient loveplay. At last, he reluctantly drew back and straightened.

"Buenos noches," he whispered.

He carried the thought of her with him as he left. What had come over him just now? Where was his willpower? His self-control? Chalk it up to exhaustion, he told himself. Or perhaps he was lonely. Loneliness, so he had heard, could do strange things to a man.

Memories drifted through his mind like tumbleweeds across a windswept plain. Memories of Robert. Skipping school in the spring to attend baseball games. Sailing in Newport every summer. Robert's weekend visits to Cambridge, where Trey was attending college. Ski trips to the Adirondacks. It didn't matter that they were only half-brothers; it mattered that they were friends. The two of them shared the rarest bond of all—uncomplicated, unconditional friendship. Trey had intended to set in motion their plans for a ranch as soon as he returned from Spain. They had been so close to realizing their dream.

"If only you had returned from Europe sooner," his mother had upbraided him the evening of Robert's funeral. "You could have talked sense into Robert. Your brother idolized you. You should have been here." His mother's recriminations had echoed his own. *And it was true. He should have been there.*

If only he had completed his business sooner . . .

If only he hadn't lingered in Barcelona . . .

If . . .

Chapter 19

The ranch was unusually quiet the following afternoon. Everyone still seemed to be recovering from the long, sleepless night. Everyone except Alana, who had slept most of the morning and was now wide-awake. She wandered aimlessly with no particular destination in mind. She had sent a yawning Consuelo off for a siesta immediately after the midday meal. Trey was nowhere about, she discovered with a pang of disappointment. She had resisted the urge to sneak into his bedroom to see if he, too, was sound asleep. How wonderful it would be to curl up next to him on the wide feather mattress. She sighed. Wonderful, but impossible.

Milder temperatures had returned. The day was sunny and warm, the sky a cloudless blue. Much too nice to sleep away. Bored, Alana slipped out the back gate and strolled along a walkway that was shaded with a grapevine-covered trellis and led to the stable and outbuildings. When she emerged, she was struck by the deserted appearance of the outer courtyard. Most of the ranch hands were probably enjoying a well-deserved siesta, she decided with a wry smile. Upon entering the stable, she was surprised to find Noah crouched in a stall grooming one of the horses.

Looking up, he flashed his engaging grin. Twin dimples winked appealingly in his cheeks. Alana leaned across the half-wall separating the stalls and smiled back. "You were up all night. How come you're not taking a siesta like everyone else?"

Noah shrugged and resumed his task. "Never could sleep much after sunup. Ma used to threaten to skin us kids alive if she found us sacked out when there were chores to be done. There'll be enough time for sleepin' after you're dead, she used to tell us."

"Did you come from a large family?"

"There were six of us. Four girls and two boys."

"Ah." She smiled in satisfaction. "That explains it."

Noah slanted her a bemused look. "I lost you somewhere. What does it explain?"

"With four sisters, no wonder you're such a ladies' man."

"Shucks, ma'am, not me." His innocent expression could have put a choirboy to shame.

She laughed. Unlike Trey, Noah was easy to be around. He was the sort she would have chosen for a big brother. Someone who was fun to be with, an overgrown tease, but with a strong protective streak. "Being surrounded by sisters, you and your brother must have been very close."

He drew the brush down the mare's flank. "Closer'n most, I reckon."

"Is he back in Texas?"

"Yes, ma'am."

"Do you hear from him often?"

Noah concentrated on currying the horse with unhurried, circular strokes. He was silent for so long that Alana thought he wasn't going to answer her question. "No," he finally replied, his voice low. "My brother got caught up in a gunfight. He's buried back in a Texas churchyard."

Alana mentally fumbled through a collection of standard cliches, all the while berating herself for her insensitivity. When would she ever learn to curb her impetuous tongue? She struggled to find an appropriate response, simple and sincere. "I understand exactly how you must feel."

Noah hurled the brush into a corner of the stall. "How could you possibly know what it's like to lose a brother in a senseless gunfight?"

Every word was stitched in pain and laced with hurt. A lump rose in her throat. She wanted to go to him, put her arms around him, comfort him. "I've never lost a brother, but I did lose a husband."

His head whipped around. He stared at her, his eyes a pale, piercing blue. Bitterness drained from his face, replaced by remorse. "I'm sorry. Here I am wallowin' in self-pity and lashin' out at you. I ought to be horsewhipped for speakin' out like that."

"Don't apologize. You couldn't have guessed."

He stepped out from around the mare. "You're so young and all, I just figured you hadn't been married before."

"I fancied myself madly in love at the time. Phillip and I eloped and caught a train headed West, all in the same night. We got as far as Dodge City." Memories caused her voice to snag and grow husky. "He died there in my arms a week after we were wed."

Now it was Noah's turn to search for words of consolation. Silence lengthened as ghosts whispered in the cobwebby recesses of the stable. Time was measured by the swish of the horse's tail against the stall's rough planks.

Finally, Alana roused herself with a shake of her head. "Would it help you to talk about your brother?"

His Adam's apple bobbed once, twice. He cleared his throat. "Someday maybe, but not now. It's still an open sore."

Alana could accept that for the time being. She remembered the months following Phillip's death when she broke down and wept at the slightest provocation. Yes, she agreed silently, open sores needed time to heal. In time, she prayed, Trey's wounds would heal, too, but she feared their scars would run deep. "When you're ready to talk, Noah, I'm ready to listen."

"Thanks." He dusted his hands along the sides of his Levi's and reached for his hat. "How about that riding lesson I promised you?"

"I don't know if that's such a good idea."

"How come?" He tilted the brim of his Stetson over one eye.

"I've never been around horses very much. Actually," she said with a deprecatory laugh, "I've never been around them at all."

He cocked his head to one side. "You scared of 'em?"

"Yes—er—no. Maybe . . ."

"Darlin', you gotta talk straighter than that to this dumb cowpoke. Which is it gonna be—yes, no, or maybe?"

"My mother was kicked by a horse when she was just a girl. She never let my sister or me go near them for fear it might happen to us."

"I see." He nodded as though this explained her uncertainty. "You just never got a chance to make up your own mind how you felt about horseflesh. Seein' how you live on a ranch, don't you think it's high time you did?"

She studied him for a moment in indecision. Her mother's fear had been communicated to her daughters at an early age. Yet there was something innately appealing about the freedom the ability to ride a horse offered. She glanced doubtfully at her sprigged muslin dress. "I'm not dressed properly, and I don't own a riding habit."

Noah rubbed his jaw thoughtfully, then snapped his fingers. "Consuelo and I went ridin' just the other night. She was wearin' an old pair of Levi's she claimed once belonged to her brother. She's a bit broader in the hips than you are, but I think they might fit if you cinch 'em at the waist." He disappeared into the tack room and came out seconds later holding a pair of blue denims. "Here ya go!" he said, tossing them in her direction.

Alana caught them with one hand. "All right. You've got yourself a pupil." All of a sudden, the idea was too tempting to resist. Learning to ride could prove just the distraction she longed for as well as an outlet for her energy.

"Good," Noah grinned. "You can change in the tack room while I saddle a horse."

Alana hurried before she could change her mind. The door to the tack room groaned open on rusty hinges. Horse paraphernalia, all of which was unfamiliar to Alana, hung from hooks randomly nailed to beams. Sunlight streamed through a window set high in the far wall and illuminated a low wooden bench beneath it. Along with Consuelo's denim pants, Alana found a loose peasant-style blouse. Stripping off her dress, she stepped into the Levis' and pulled on the blouse. Just as Noah had speculated, the pants were a little large, but a long strip of leather used as a belt solved the problem.

Feeling a little shy but at the same time reveling in the newfound freedom, Alana went to join Noah.

He looked her critically up and down, then gave her a slow grin of approval. "Never could figure why womenfolk hide themselves under miles of petticoats. Those darn fool bustles make 'em look wider across the beam than a whalin' ship."

"What do we do first?" She glanced about, both nervous and eager for her lesson to begin.

"You watch while I saddle. Next time, I'll see how much you remember." He led a placid-looking mare from a stall. "This here is Sarafina. She's a calm, surefooted critter. A good one to learn on. Later, after you're more experienced, your husband might want to find you a more spirited mount."

Alana bit back a denial. If Trey even suspected that she was learning to ride, he'd more than likely forbid it, viewing it as a possible means to escape his domination. Better her lessons were kept secret.

She observed with interest as Noah forced a bit in the mare's mouth and fastened the bridle. He threw on a saddle blanket and saddle, then tightened the cinch and adjusted the stirrups. She followed him as he led Sarafina out into the corral. His own horse was already there, saddled and waiting patiently.

"For today, I'm going to teach you how to mount. If that goes well, I'll let you ride her around the corral at a slow walk."

"And that's all?" She had envisioned herself riding off into the hills.

"Honey, you gotta be patient. You need to learn to walk before you can gallop."

Chastened, she nodded.

Easygoing Noah turned out to be a strict taskmaster. "When you mount a horse, always stand by its left shoulder, facing its rear. Grasp the reins like so in your left hand along with a lock of mane," he said, demonstrating. "Put your left foot in the stirrup. Grab this thing here, the cantle, with your right hand, spring up on the ball of your right foot, balance a second, then swing your right leg over and place it in the other stirrup. Reverse the procedure to dismount. Let me show you." He proceeded to mount and dismount several times. "Want to give it a try?"

"Ready." She wiped her sweaty palms on her Levi's, then took a deep breath. Mimicking Noah's actions, she swung up into a saddle for the first time. When viewed from the back of a horse, the world took on a whole new perspective. She felt inordinately pleased with her accomplishment.

For the next hour, Noah instructed her on the rudiments of how to a make horse respond to simple commands.

"I think that's enough for one day," he finally announced, wheeling his horse toward the stable.

Alana opened her mouth to protest, but he cut her off. "Darlin', if you don't stop now, you'll regret it later. Trust me. In another day or two, I'll give you another lesson.

"What about tomorrow?"

Grinning, he swung down. "Tomorrow, you may decide you never want to look at a horse again."

"Why do you say that?"

"You'll see." He held the mare's reins while she dismounted. "Go ahead and change. I don't think your husband would be too happy findin' his pretty little bride wearin' a pair of man's pants."

Alana didn't care to dwell on Trey's reaction. Leaving Noah to tend the horses, she disappeared into the tack room and quickly changed back into her petticoats and sprigged muslin.

Cheeks flushed from exercise, she emerged with her head bent as she tried to subdue her windblown hair into some semblance of neatness. "Thank you for the lesson, Noah."

"Whatever the lesson, *señora,* I could give better."

Alana's head came up with a snap. Her hair ribbon slipped to the floor. She stumbled to a halt as she found Vega, not Noah, waiting for her. "Noah was giving me a riding lesson." She didn't know why she felt compelled to explain.

"A riding lesson, eh?" He strolled closer, leering. "If you want to ride a stallion, *chica,* you have only to ask. I will be happy to accommodate you."

Alana gasped at the man's audacity. Before she could react, Noah returned.

"I found this stone jammed—"

Vega hooked his thumbs in his pants, his black eyes shifting between Alana and Noah. His narrow mouth curled in a knowing smirk.

"Look here, Vega, I know what you're thinkin', but you're dead wrong." Noah's hands clenched and unclenched at his sides. He looked angry enough to tear the smaller man apart.

Vega's smile grew wider, nastier. "I'm not *loco.* I know what happens between a man and a beautiful woman. But don't worry, *señora.*" Vega dropped his voice to a conspiratorial whisper. "This will be our little secret. I won't say anything to *Señor* Matthews—at least for now." He winked and sauntered out.

"That slimy bastard!" Noah pitched the pebble he had pried from the hoof of Vega's horse clear across the stable, where it ricocheted off a post and landed in the hay. "I'll set him straight."

Noah started after Vega, but Alana caught his arm. "Don't! That will only make matters worse."

"It would sure make me feel a sight better to plow my fist into that bastard's face."

Alana watched anger cross his features like a passing storm, making her realize that in spite of his breezy charm, this man was still a stranger in many ways.

Noah drew in a great lungful of air, then blew it out. "Sorry, ma'am," he apologized. "Ma would wash my mouth out with soap if she ever caught me speakin' like that in front of a lady."

A lady? The novelty of the word struck Alana. It had been a long time since anyone had referred to her that way. Would Noah Stone still consider her a lady once he found out she was a former saloon singer? she wondered. She suddenly needed to know. "I've heard much worse language when I worked at the Gilded Lily."

Noah pushed back his hat, perplexed, and scratched his forehead. "Gilded Lily, huh? Sounds like the name of a saloon back in El Paso."

"San Diego," Alana corrected as Noah's sandy brow quirked in surprise. "Before I met Trey, I earned my living singing in a saloon."

"Were you any good?"

"Yes, as a matter of fact, I was," she answered, surprised at her response. "It's no mean feat to quiet a bunch of rowdy men long enough for them to hear the lyrics of a song." She felt a certain satisfaction in knowing that night after night, she had won their attention.

"Good for you. Wish I'd been there to hear you."

Alana tried to smile but couldn't. Her thoughts were still on Vega. "Consuelo calls Vega *el serpiente*, the snake."

Noah chuckled. "That woman sure has a way with words."

Alana turned and started walking away. "We haven't done anything to feel guilty about. If Vega should say anything to Trey, I'll just explain that you were giving me a riding lesson."

"What if he chooses not to believe you?"

She paused at the door and smiled grimly. "Then I suppose I'll have to give him a demonstration of my riding skill."

She finished reading *The Adventures of Huckleberry Finn*, drank a glass of warm milk, and brushed her hair a hundred strokes. Nothing worked. It was nearly midnight, and she was still wide-awake. The brush crackled as she drew it through her loose curls. Her hair formed a golden halo around her face, then tumbled around her shoulders and down her back. With a sigh, she flung the hairbrush onto the bed.

As she paced the length of her bedroom, her white cambric nightgown swirled around her ankles. Absently, she toyed with the narrow baby-blue ribbons that trimmed the rosepoint lace yoke. Her mouth curved in a wry smile. Trey couldn't possibly accuse her of trying to seduce him if he could see her wearing this. High-necked and buttoned nearly to her chin, the gown was as modest as a nun's. But Trey couldn't see her. Didn't want to see her.

A heaviness settled in her chest, making the air thicker, harder to breathe. The walls seemed to shrink around her, hemming her in.

Impulsively, she snatched up a woolen shawl and headed out the door. Once outside, she leaned against the rough adobe wall and sucked in a deep draft of cool night air. The night was hushed, peaceful. Starless, moonless, the sky soared above her like the vaulted ceiling of a Renaissance cathedral. Slowly, her tension ebbed.

Soundlessly, she strolled the perimeter of the inner courtyard. She envied men who could gain physical release from manual labor. Now that the hacienda was in order, there was little for her to do. Consuelo lectured and scolded whenever she caught her doing what she considered to be her chores. How could she make the woman understand that she desperately needed to be busy? That she needed less time to think. Less time to hurt.

Drawn by the musical tinkle of the fountain, she crossed the patio and perched on its wide tile ledge. Water flowed like quicksilver from the upper basin to a larger one below. She dipped her hand into the water, then, tipping her palm, watched the drops roll off and drip into the fountain. The water droplets reminded her of tears. Tears reminded her of Trey. Her eyes filled, and she blinked back moisture. She had tried to flee from him, but what was the use? She would be leaving her heart behind. Could a body survive without a heart? Hers couldn't. Pride dictated that she leave. That she prove Trey couldn't hold her hostage. But the truth was, she didn't want to leave. She wanted to stay.

A second truth rocked her; whether they were together or apart, she loved him.

Loved him with quiet desperation. . . and always would.

If only he would forgive her role in Robert's death . . . But the prospect seemed hopeless. She was destined to love a man who hated her.

Melancholia seeped through her. Her shoulders sagged beneath its oppressive weight. Alana's thoughts drifted to what might have been, to what could never be. Alone in the darkness, she mourned the loss.

Her tears fell like midnight rain.

"Please don't cry."

Startled, she looked up. Trey's figure, clad in a silk dressing robe, wavered behind a watery curtain of tears. Distraught at his seeing her that way, she choked back a sob.

"Don't . . ."

To her astonishment, Trey bent down and tenderly wiped the moisture from her cheeks. The action, totally unexpected, totally uncharacteristic, unraveled her. A freshet of tears slipped from beneath her lids.

Trey knelt in front of her on one knee. Burrowing his fingers in her thick curls, he cradled the base of her skull in his hands, and using his thumbs, tilted her face to his.

She closed her eyes in defeat. She didn't want his pity, couldn't bear having him see her anguish.

"I thought I'd rejoice in your suffering, but I don't," he admitted, his voice low, gruff. Leaning forward, he gently kissed away the tears that squeezed from beneath her fragile eyelids.

Starved for the solace he offered, Alana twined her arms loosely around his neck. A small sound that was half-sob, half-sigh escaped to meld with the liquid notes from the fountain.

Trey dusted petal-light kisses over her closed lids, across her delicately sculpted cheekbones, along her jaw, and down the ivory column of her throat.

Alana's entire being quivered like a harpstring. With her eyes still shut, her other senses became heightened. His warm breath was like a balmy breeze on skin that suddenly felt flushed and feverish. The slight rasp of bearded stubble against her skin whispered of erotic longings. The faint scent of sandalwood wafted to her nostrils, as heady as French perfume. The falling water sounded like a melody played by a symphony.

"If this is a dream, don't wake me," she murmured, as reality shifted, then dimmed, leaving only the two of them and the night's dark promise.

"Ah, vixen." He nuzzled the sensitive spot behind her ear, drawing a shudder from her.

"Trey . . ." she breathed, his name a sigh, an invocation.

"This is far better than any dream I've ever had." His fingers nimbly unfastened the row of tiny pearl buttons and slid the filmy nightgown down her shoulders.

Cool air christened her overheated flesh. Alana's breathing quickened.

With kisses as light as a butterfly, as evanescent as morning dew, he sketched the delicate line of her collarbone. When the kisses ceased, he dipped the tip of his tongue into the delicate hollow at the base of her throat to flick lightly the pulse that fluttered there.

Her world reeling, Alana gripped Trey's shoulders to steady herself. Her nails bit through the silk of his dressing gown and dug into his flesh. The warmth of his body radiated through the thin fabric. Just as she suspected, he wore nothing underneath.

His mouth settled over hers, the touch light. Cajoling, teasing, savoring. Then, when Trey felt her lips part, he deliberately deepened the kiss.

Mindless pleasure surged through her as their tongues tangled in a timeless duel of passion. When he cupped her breast, she thought she would die of pleasure. Deep in her throat, she made a sound much like the purr of a contented feline.

Trey massaged her nipple with his thumb and forefinger and was rewarded instantly when it puckered into a tightly furled bud. He marveled at how quickly her body responded to his slightest provocation. Sparks flew whenever they touched.

His hand slid up her thigh and hugged the rounded curve of her hip. "Mm," he murmured, nuzzling the soft fullness of her breast, "your skin feels like warm satin." She smelled like a garden. And tasted like sin. He wanted to make her forget all the other men she had ever known—Phillip, Colin, and faceless others. He wanted to be the one—the only one—to make her blaze with passion.

He pivoted her so that her legs straddled his hips. With unnerving slowness, he trailed wet kisses down her neck, then lower still. His tongue circled the rosy aureole of her nipple. Then he gently took the tender bud between his teeth, drawing it into his mouth with a strong sucking motion.

"Trey . . ." She gasped as searing heat shot through her. His name was like a drumbeat pounding through her veins. It became a chant echoing off every cell in her body. Loud. Insistent. Drugging. She flung her head back in mute surrender. Her hair, a shimmering torrent of gold, pooled on the fountain's broad ledge. Her slender neck arched, exposed and vulnerable.

He dipped his head and traced moist, lazy circles across her abdomen.

"Love me . . ." Her plea, barely audible, was carried away on a light zephyr.

Governed by the overpowering need to possess her, he rose to his feet, bringing her with him. He intended to carry her into the house, to make love to her until they were both sated and senseless, but her legs locked around his waist, holding him fast. Her mouth fastened greedily on his. They got only as far as the doorway to her room before he stopped and leaned against the door sill. Desire raged through him, scalding, pulsating, alternately making him as weak as a kitten and as strong as Sampson. "God, I want you," he groaned against her mouth.

"Then take me," she whispered, her voice a sultry caress. Sensuously, she slid one bare leg down his thigh. She curled her hand around his manhood. His shaft felt as strong as finely tempered steel, yet sheathed in costly silk. She guided the blunt tip unerringly to the portal of her femininity.

His breathing became ragged. A sheen of perspiration gilded his body. She was hot, sleek, ready.

Alana knotted her fingers in his hair as he entered her and held tight.

Love me, love me, she begged silently until there were no words at all, only sensations, swirling and sucking her into a tempestuous vortex.

Cleaving to each other, they rode out the storm of their passion.

Chapter 20

Alana stopped pacing the veranda long enough to pluck a dead leaf from a geranium in one of the clay pots that lined the walls. She examined it absently before she let it drift to the tiles. It was withered and dead. Just like her dreams.

A week had crawled by, then two. Fourteen long days. Fourteen even longer nights. All during that time, she had hoped—no, prayed—that things would be different between her and Trey. She desperately wanted to believe that the night they had made love by the fountain would begin a time of healing. It had seemed much more than a lustful joining of two bodies; it had seemed more like the spiritual communion of two souls. Their lovemaking that midnight hour had seemed special, so very special, a crystalline moment of unsurpassed beauty. It had been for her; she thought it had been for Trey. Obviously, she had been mistaken.

Sighing, she resumed her walk. Trey, though no longer abrasive or abusive, maintained a polite distance. Every night, she fell asleep listening for his footfalls in the hall. Twice, she had sat by the fountain in the wee hours of the night, alone and dry-eyed.

As she passed the kitchen, she could hear Isabel humming to herself while she prepared dinner.

Consuelo was busy elsewhere pressing clothes. She had made it abundantly clear she didn't need Alana's help. Alana kicked a pebble out of her way with the toe of her shoe. If she didn't find something to do, she'd lose her mind from sheer boredom. She had read until her eyes burned and the print blurred. Needlework was out of the question. She had found it tedious as a girl and equally tedious as an adult. The only thing that had kept her sane were the riding lessons with Noah. She eagerly awaited them. Following their last lesson, they had taken a short ride into the hills.

Suddenly, the idea of a ride, however brief, perked her interest. Perhaps Noah had some free time. As she hurried across the courtyard, she glanced at the sky. The afternoon was cool, the clouds gray and sullen. Later, the heavens would probably open and release a torrent of rain just as they had for the past week. The rains in southern California weren't the gentle, steady, saturating type she associated with Baltimore. Here they were often dramatic and passionate, brutal in their assault on a sun-parched land. She quickened her step. If she was lucky, the rains would hold off until after her ride.

Emerging from the trellised walkway, she found Paco waiting in a buckboard, the reins slack in his hands. Eyes shut, body slouched, he was obviously sound asleep. After the incident with the citrus grove, she had been surprised that Trey hadn't dismissed the man. When she had questioned Trey, he had explained that Paco sent all of his money to a wife and family back in Mexico who were dependent on him. In view of this, Trey had decided to give the man a second chance.

Before Alana could decide whether to proceed or to retreat, Vega strode out of the stables. Instinctively, she took a step backward into the arbor, hoping to meld into the shadows unnoticed. But like the snake Consuelo compared him with, Vega's black eyes missed nothing.

"Buenas tardes, señora."

"Good afternoon, Vega."

Instead of climbing into the buckboard, he approached her slowly, a mirthless grin curling his mouth. She felt as if she was being stalked, but resolutely held her ground.

"Looking for someone, *señora?"*

Noah had echoed her own thinking when he'd warned her against mentioning her riding lessons. *Your husband might not approve,* he had cautioned. He had explained that while he didn't normally condone wives keeping secrets from their husbands, under the circumstances, silence might be the most prudent course. "I thought I might find my husband," she lied.

"Ah," Vega said, "the beautiful *señora* is lonely for her husband. How touching."

She gritted her teeth against a strong desire to slap the smirk off his swarthy face, and remained silent.

"If you are lonely, *señora*"—he dropped his voice—"I will be happy to keep you company. I know all the ways to pleasure the beautiful *señoritas."*

Vega made her skin crawl. Alana was grateful that Paco, even though asleep, was within calling distance. "Save your talent for the *señoritas,"* she snapped. "I'm not interested."

He sidled closer, his black eyes gleaming, his manner bold. "Talk has it you and the *señor* do not sleep together. That you have separate bedrooms—in separate wings of the house. How convenient should you take a lover."

"Enough!" Raising her chin haughtily, she glared

at him. "If you ever dare speak to me again in this manner . . ."

"You will what?" He appeared amused rather than intimidated by her threat.

"I'll tell my husband exactly what you just said. Your bags will be packed and you'll be out of here by sundown." She was so furious her voice shook.

"Oh, *señora*, you scare me. I am shaking." His grin of supreme confidence mocked his words.

El serpiente. Cunning, dangerous, deadly. But snakes often warned their victims before attacking. Would this man be so honorable? Alana doubted it. She regarded him warily and tried to ignore the tight coil of dread in the pit of her stomach.

Vega seemed to relish her fear. "If you should be so foolish as to tell *Señor* Matthews about our little conversation, I'll deny it. Who will your *esposo* believe? You or me?"

"Why shouldn't he believe me?"

"I'll tell him that you're lying to protect yourself. That you're afraid I'll tell him about your affair with the Texas cowboy. He already suspects as much. While he may not want you himself, he doesn't want another to have you."

"You vile, loathsome man!" The warmth drained from her limbs. "How dare you threaten me?"

"Such fire beneath all that ice." He chuckled. "Has anyone ever told you that you're beautiful when you're angry? If your husband is not man enough to melt such ice, I am."

He stepped closer. Alana itched with the desire to back away, but a stronger instinct prompted her not to give any ground. This man would use any sign of weakness to his advantage. "Paco's waiting," she said coldly. "No doubt my husband will be wondering what is keeping you."

Vega smiled. "I don't think so, *señora*. Your *esposo* has much more important things to occupy him."

"What do you mean?"

His dark eyes glistened malevolently. "His prize bull, *señora,* has met with an unfortunate accident. The bull was found dead this morning, its throat slit. Such a shame." He clucked his tongue. "The *señor* had such high hopes."

Another mysterious incident? Uneasiness coiled in the pit of her stomach as Vega sauntered off.

"By the way, *señora,*" he said over his shoulder, "if you are looking for Noah Stone, you won't find him."

All sorts of dire possibilities sprang to her mind. "Why not?"

Vega paused alongside the buckboard. "Your husband has decided *Señor* Stone does not have enough work to keep him busy. He asked me to assign him other duties. In the future, every minute must be accounted for. There will be no time left for entertaining the boss's beautiful but neglected *esposa.*"

Heartsick, Alana watched Vega climb into the wagon and, flicking the reins, bring it into lumbering motion. While she didn't trust Vega for a minute, she knew intuitively that he was telling the truth when he said Trey suspected that she and Noah were lovers. It didn't surprise her. On numerous occasions, Trey had rendered his opinion regarding her supposed lack of morals. He was convinced she had slept with more men that she could count. Spending the night in Trey's hotel room that long ago evening after *The Mikado* had been a grievous mistake—one she had paid for dearly. She had proven to be easy prey, just as Trey had suspected all along. From the first look, the first kiss, the first touch . . .

She walked slowly toward the stables. A sadness

welled inside her that went beyond tears. Mistakes, so many mistakes. She had certainly made more than her share. But the most serious of all had been her callous insensitivity that had broken a young man's heart and resulted in his suicide. An entire family had been destroyed. Both Robert and his mother were dead, and Trey was emotionally scarred. She, too, was a victim of her youthful carelessness. Every fiber of her being ached to change what could never be changed.

The futility of it all weighed heavily on her spirit.

Wandering into the stable, she found it deserted. Suddenly, she longed to get away from the ranch, even for a little while, to put distance between herself and the problems it represented. The notion was too appealing to resist. Imitating Noah's careful directions, she quickly saddled Sarafina, the gentle little mare, and, before anyone could stop her, mounted and headed for the hills behind the ranch.

She proceeded cautiously at first, keeping the house in sight, but her care faded as a newfound sense of freedom settled over her. She crested a hill and urged the mare on. This was farther than she had explored with Noah, but she was reluctant to return to the ranch just yet. The countryside grew more rugged. Thunder rumbled ominously in the distance. Sarafina pranced nervously, tossing her mane.

"Whoa, girl," Alana soothed. She sawed on the reins and fought to control the skittish animal.

When the horse calmed, Alana glanced worriedly at a sky the color of tarnished silver. Plump drops of rain spattered her upturned face. Dismayed, she realized her folly. She had strayed too far from the hacienda.

Thunder rumbled again, louder this time. Rain

pelted from the heavens, saturating a landscape that was already saturated. A brilliant flash of lightning zigzagged across the murky sky. Frightened, the mare bolted and set off in a wild gallop.

Alana ducked in time to avoid the low-hanging branch of a poplar. Scrub pine and chaparral tore at her skirt; wind whipped the pins from her hair. The little horse veered left and charged down a rocky slope. Alana forgot all of Noah's instructions and held fast. Above the fury of the storm, she heard an ominous sucking noise. She gasped in horror as the earth shifted. The ground beneath was her no longer solid but a quagmire. Soil, as slick and black as lava, started its stealthy slide, uprooting everything in its path.

Sarafina struggled valiantly to maintain her footing, but her hind legs skidded in the slimy ooze, and she canted sideways. Alana, terrified she would be crushed, shifted her weight. The saddle slipped.

Strangely detached, Alana watched the earth come up to greet her. Sarafina's shrill whinny rent the air. Then, mercifully, there was silence.

Consuelo waylaid Trey the moment he entered the hacienda. "The *señora,*" she blurted. "I cannot find her."

"What do you mean you can't find her?"

She flung up her hands. "I have looked. She is not here."

Before she could finish speaking, Trey brushed past her and stormed down the hallway toward Alana's bedroom. He sent the door to her room banging against the wall. He stalked across the room and rifled through the drawers of her chest and looked in the armoire. Her belongings appeared intact. A surge of unbridled relief swept through him. He thought he had lost her. Surely if her clothes were here, she couldn't have gone far.

"I am worried, *señor.*" Consuelo stood in the doorway, wringing her hands. "A storm is brewing, and it will soon be dark."

Trey's fleeting sense of relief vanished. "I'll find her."

He left the house, Consuelo close on his heels. After questioning a stablehand, he discovered that one of the horses was missing. Moments later, the buckboard rolled in with Paco and Vega aboard. Noah rode alongside them.

"My wife is nowhere to be found," Trey stated without preamble. "Do any of you know where she is?"

"Last time I saw her, she was hanging around the stable." Vega cast a sly look at Noah. "She said she was waiting for someone. She would not say who, *señor.*"

"One of the horses is missing. Could any of you enlighten me as to what that might have to do with my wife's disappearance?" He speared each man a look, the same look that on more than one occasion had made his business associates squirm.

A guilty expression crossed Noah's face. He cleared his throat, then dismounted and approached Trey. "Mrs. Matthews might have taken a notion to go for a ride."

"How could she? She doesn't even like horses." Trey's voice was silky smooth.

"I've been teachin' her. She's a right quick learner."

"Who gave you permission to do any such thing?"

Not the least bit cowed, Noah met Trey's gaze. "I didn't know I needed any permission. And while we're askin' questions, what would make the lady take off without tellin' a soul? Did you tie into her again and get her all upset?"

"Why you—"

"Gentlemen, please." Consuelo placed herself between the two angry men. "You can settle your differences another time. We must first find the *señora*."

A muscle ticked spasmodically in Trey's jaw. "Consuelo's right. We're wasting time." He issued a rapid succession of orders, and the men scattered to obey.

All the available ranch hands were divided into three groups. Vega and Noah were each delegated the task of leading a search party, while Trey led the third. The first group to find her would fire a single shot, wait five seconds, then fire again.

The light was fading fast under dun-colored clouds as Trey urged his horse along the crest of a ravine. Once the ranch was out of sight, he ordered the men to fan out, knowing they could cover more territory singly than as a group. He tugged the brim of his hat low against the fresh onslaught of rain and pulled the collar of his jacket around his ears. What if they didn't find her? He pushed the thought aside.

His eyes sharp, his mind alert, he scanned the rugged terrain for any sign of his wife. She was lost somewhere, probably cold, wet, and scared out of her wits. She could be hurt . . . or worse. The pit of his stomach burned like a smoldering coal.

Just when he was beginning to think the situation was hopeless, he heard the strident cry of an animal in distress. The high-pitched screech rose above the howling wind and driving rain, permeating the semi-darkness with its despair. Trey felt his hackles rise and his heart bound.

"Alana!" he shouted, then strained to hear a response. There was no reply. He quieted his restive bay and shouted again. Still no sound. He swore in frustration. He had to find her—he just had to. He'd canvass every square inch of land until he did.

He cupped his hands around his mouth. "Alana!" From a narrow ravine clogged with debris came the distressed whicker of a horse. In the dim light, he discerned a slight movement. Dismounting, he scrambled down the steep incline as quickly as the brambles and mud allowed.

There at the bottom was the mare he had planned to breed that spring. The little horse feebly attempted to rise only to crumple back to the ground. Agony was evident in the whites of her eyes. Trey decided he'd deal with the horse later. Fear for Alana's safety superseded all else in his mind. Like a man possessed, he tore at the brush, calling her name, terrified of what he might find. His heart pounded fiercely against his ribs. He pulled at the branches of an uprooted sapling and found her almost hidden beneath a pile of brush.

He knelt in the mud and smoothed the wet tangle of hair from her ghostly pale face. "Alana," he pleaded, a husky catch in his voice. "Please be all right." His fingers came away red and sticky.

Her eyelids fluttered, then opened. Her eyes glazed and unfocused, she stared up at him.

Gratefulness engulfed him, leaving him weak and shaken. She was alive. Safe. Gathering her close to his heart, he scolded, "What were you thinking of? Don't you know it isn't safe to ride off without telling anyone? Crazy little fool, you could've been killed."

"My head hurts," she muttered. Raising a hand, she pressed it to her temple, then stared uncomprehendingly at the bright smear of blood on her fingers. "I'm bleeding."

"You took a nasty spill." he explained. "Hold still. I need to see how badly you're hurt." He deftly examined her arms and legs for broken bones, then explored her rib cage with a tender, probing touch. Other than the gash at her temple and a lump the size of a goose egg on the back of her head, he found no further injuries.

"What happened?"

Trey gently wiped the rain from her face. "You took the mare Sarafina for a ride. You were either thrown or fell."

"Sarafina? Is she all r-r-right?" she managed through chattering teeth.

Trey shrugged out of his jacket and draped it over her. She was chilled to the bone. He had to find shelter and find it quickly. After lying out here in the cold rain, she might easily develop pneumonia. He couldn't bear the thought of losing her after he'd just found her. "As soon as I take care of the horse, I'll get you somewhere warm and dry."

Trey stood and reached for the pistol strapped to his hip. "Don't watch!"

Alana dragged herself to her feet and took an unsteady step forward. She halted at the sight of the mare lying on is back in the mud. A shiny white bone protruded from one of her forelegs. Bile rose in her throat, and she swallowed it back.

"Turn your head and cover your ears," Trey told her.

Eyes wise with the sudden realization, Alana stubbornly shook her head and bit her lip to keep it from trembling. Tears streamed unchecked down her pale cheeks.

Trey had wanted to spare her this, but it couldn't be helped. Turning his back on her, he leveled the gun barrel, aimed, and fired. The mare's body jerked convulsively, then lay unmoving. Trey waited a full five seconds, then fired again, the prearranged signal that his wife had been found. He slid the gun back into its holster and turned toward Alana.

She was doubled over, arms wrapped around her waist, heaving up the contents of her stomach. She vomited until only dry heaves racked her.

Trey swiftly crossed to her and dabbed her face with his handkerchief. When the spasms subsided, he placed one arm firmly around her shoulders. Weakly, she leaned against him.

"It's my fault," she murmured in a small, bewildered voice. "Robert . . . Sarafina . . . It's all my fault."

Her eyes were inky dark and enormous, but it was their vacant look that most frightened him. She teetered on the verge of collapse. Enough time had been wasted. Sweeping her into his arms, he turned and trudged up the ravine. The rain fell more heavily now. A northernly wind plastered their wet clothing to their skin. Even in the near darkness, Trey noted the bluish tinge of her lips. Near the top of the ravine, he spied a shallow cave carved from beneath an overhang that afforded protection against the wind and rain. At that given moment, a suite in the finest hotel wouldn't have looked more welcoming.

Inside the cave, he gently set Alana on her feet. He hated to leave her even for the few minutes it would take to get his horse and the supplies in his saddlebags. "Don't worry, vixen. I'll be right back," he whispered. If she heard, she gave no indication. Eyes shut, she sat down and curled into a tight ball on the hard stone floor.

Trey returned as quickly as he could, leading the bay. The cave opening was wide enough to accommodate the horse. Trey loosened the cinch and unpacked the few supplies Consuelo had insisted the searchers bring with them. Along with a blanket, canteen, and matches was a small package of the ubiquitous tortillas. He confiscated a pile of sticks and dry brush that some animal had stockpiled for a lair from the back of the cave. He was thankful the animal was nowhere in sight.

Once he had a small fire blazing, he returned to Alana. He took one of her hands and chafed it. It felt small, limp, and icy-cold in his larger one. "I have to get you out of these wet clothes, vixen." He kept up a soothing monologue while he stripped off her wet clothing. She made no effort to resist, her body as limp as a rag doll. He wrapped her snugly in the blanket, then spread her skirt, shirtwaist, and underthings to dry in front of the fire. He quickly did the same with his own clothing before he lay down beside her. Taking her in his arms, he pressed the length of his body to hers, sharing his body's heat.

Alana released a shuddering sigh and snuggled closer.

Trey bit back a groan. The feel of her naked flesh pressed to his was almost more than he could stand. He was aware of her every subtle curve, every hollow. She molded to him like a glove. It was sheer torture holding her that way, feeling her voluptuous breasts crushed against his chest, the cradle of her pelvis wedged against his manhood. Blood rushed to his groin, and he felt himself harden. He gritted his teeth. He wanted her. God, how he wanted her. He had wanted her from the first time he had laid eyes on her in that damn saloon. If he made love to her every morning, noon, and night of his natural life, he didn't think he could slake his thirst. She had become his addiction.

"Some men have whiskey, some opium, but I have you," he murmured against her tangled hair.

His hands splayed against the small of her back, his thumb absently tracing the knobby protrusions of her spine. She felt slender and delicate. Fragile. But she wasn't fragile at all, he mused. She was as strong and resilient as tempered steel. He had tricked and deceived her, then betrayed her love with cruel rejection. She had suffered his abuse, and though bowed, she hadn't broken beneath its weight.

He brushed a kiss across her temple. Tenderness sprang up from a secret well deep inside him. Alana had countered his cruelty with unquestioning loyalty. If anything happened to her, the blame would be his. Vengeance was a vile and vicious emotion, not at all satisfying as he had once thought it would be.

God, what had he done to her? What had he done to them?

Glancing down, he was surprised to find her watching him, her eyes lucid.

"How do you feel?" he asked softly.

"I have an abominable headache." She managed a wry smile. "Other than that I feel wonderful."

"You took a nasty spill. Do you remember what happened?"

She swallowed hard, then nodded. "I remember. Where are we?"

"In a cave I happened to find." He smoothed back her hair and pressed his lips to her temple. "Hush now, try to sleep. We'll go back to the ranch in the morning."

"Trey . . ."

He shifted slightly and tucked her head under his chin. "Hmm . . ."

"Sarafina . . ." The words were muffled against his chest. "Did you have to . . .?"

"She broke her leg. I had no choice."

"I'm sorry." Her voice caught.

"It was an accident," he soothed. He planted a kiss on the top of her head. "The mare lost her footing. With all the rain we've had, the ground slid out from under her. There was nothing you could have done."

"I shouldn't have gone riding. If I hadn't, this wouldn't have happened."

And if I hadn't lingered in Barcelona, Robert wouldn't have taken his own life. "Unfortunate things happen."

He thought she had gone to sleep when she spoke again. "Like with Robert?"

Pensively, he stared into the flickering flames. "Yes," he answered after a lengthy pause. "Like what happened to Robert."

Alana sighed. "I had no idea Robert would react so violently when I refused his proposal. I didn't mean to be unkind. I received at least a half-dozen proposals. All of my suitors professed to be heartbroken, then all soon found another girl to court. I never dreamed Robert would be any different. He was a nice boy. I liked him. But I loved Phillip."

Outside the cave, the rain continued to fall steadily. Inside, firelight danced along craggy walls; flames crackled hungrily around bits of dry wood. "What about afterward?" Trey's voice was low, intense. "Have you loved a lot of men since Phillip?"

She curled closer, instinctively seeking his warmth. "No." She sighed, her breath a soft caress across his skin. "Just you."

He remained awake long after she drifted back to sleep. Was she telling the truth?

The possibility pleased him in a way he couldn't voice.

Chapter 21

Alana stirred in her sleep and reached for Trey. Her hand encountered hard, rocky earth instead. Feeling a sudden rush of panic, she opened her eyes and looked around. She spotted him fully dressed, standing with his back to her, one arm braced against the opening of the cave. She raised herself on one elbow, every muscle in her body protesting a night spent on the cold stone floor. Beyond the cave's entrance, she could see that the rain had ceased and a new day was dawning.

Dragging the rough woolen blanket around her bare shoulders, she hauled herself to her feet and walked across the cave to stand beside Trey. The sight that greeted her literally stole her breath away. The sky was awash with a magnificent palette of vivid hues. Magenta, gilt, and fiery pinks smeared the eastern horizon in a spectacle so stunning that no artist—no mere mortal—could capture it on canvas. She stood next to Trey and together they silently paid homage to the lavish display of nature. Unthinkingly, she placed her hand on Trey's arm. Words were unnecessary.

Trey turned with a smile, his eyes glinting with an affection he rarely displayed. Alana started to return the smile, but sneezed instead. A loud, unladylike sneeze.

A frown of concern quickly replaced his smile. "I'd better get you back to the ranch before you take sick. Your clothes are dry. I'll saddle the horse while you get dressed."

Sniffing, Alana nodded, then hurriedly pulled on her clothes.

Trey led his bay from the cave, swung up into saddle, and extended his hand. After a second's hesitation, Alana accepted his outstretched palm, placed her foot in the stirrup, and swung up behind him. As they rode off, she kept her face carefully averted from the ravine. "What about Sarafina?"

"I'll have a couple of the men come up and bury her." He didn't want the little mare torn apart by the wild animals that roamed the hillside, but he kept this thought to himself.

Alana hugged his waist and tried to keep her mind blank. Her head still ached. She didn't want to think about the gentle little mare at the base of the ravine. Not now, not yet, maybe never.

The mild, sunny weather she associated with southern California had returned. Early-morning mist clung to the hills and distant mountains, turning them into blue-green smudges on the horizon. Water from the recent rains rushed through the arroyos. The air had a crisp, freshly laundered scent. A new day. A new beginning. The thought brought a lump to her throat.

She wished that she and Trey could have a new beginning. He had been unexpectedly kind and gentle with her during the night. This was a side of his personality she had rarely been privileged to see, an untapped font of tenderness and caring. All this time, though, she had sensed it was there. His ability to love was evident in his devotion to his family. He was a man capable of deep, undying commitment. A man worth waiting for. She would rather sleep on a hard stone floor with his arms securely around her than alone between silk sheets on a downy mattress.

After a while, a lassitude crept over her. Resting her head against Trey's back, she closed her eyes.

When they arrived at the hacienda, Consuelo and Isabel rushed into the courtyard to greet them. Consuelo fired off a round of questions, in a mixture of Spanish and English. Noah hurried out of the stable, his expression both anxious and relieved.

Vega followed, looking bored. Ignoring Alana as he usually did, he addressed Trey. "So you found her, *señor.* Did she say why she ran off?"

Noah didn't wait for Trey's answer. A frown creased his brow as he tipped back his hat and stared up at Alana. "You all right, ma'am?"

Trey answered for her. "She's fine."

"I'm fine, really." Alana gave Noah a wan smile before catching Trey's hand and swinging to the ground.

Noah stepped around Vega and, ignoring Trey's dark scowl, placed his hands on Alana's waist to steady her.

"Fine?" Consuelo clucked her tongue. "She don't look fine to me."

Alana sneezed. "I just caught a little cold. It's nothing to worry about."

Their conversation was cut short when Paco galloped up on his piebald horse and reined to a stop. Anything that stirred Paco from his usual slow pace must be serious indeed. Alana glanced quickly at Trey to see if he shared her alarm. Judging from his expression, she could tell that he did.

"What's wrong?" Trey barked.

"The cattle are dying, *señor.*" Paco clamored down

from his mount. "We found two dead cows this morning."

"Where?"

"In the north pasture," Paco said, pointing in that direction.

"Were there any signs on the carcasses of what might have happened?"

"Some blood, *señor*, from the mouth, and"—he looked at the ladies, a red flush staining his olive skin—"and other places."

"Sounds like anthrax," Vega proclaimed importantly. "I'd better go take a look for myself."

"Anthrax?" Trey repeated, stunned by the blow. "That could wipe out the whole herd."

"I'll go with you, Vega," Noah volunteered.

"No," Vega snapped. "Stay here and tend the horses."

Noah appealed directly to Trey. "I witnessed an anthrax outbreak back in Texas, Mr. Matthews. I might be of some use."

Trey nodded. "Saddle up and meet us."

Vega shot Noah a fulminating stare as he strode off, muttering under his breath.

Trey turned to Consuelo. "See that my wife gets a hot bath, then spends the day in bed."

Alana was touched by Trey's concern, especially when this new crisis must weigh heavily on his mind. "Trey . . ." she said, stepping forward.

He paused, his hand on the pommel, ready to swing into the saddle.

Now that she had his undivided attention, she couldn't find the appropriate words. She wanted to tell him that everything would be all right. That she, too, cared deeply about the ranch. That she would be there when he needed her. That she loved him. Instead, she simply said, "Good luck."

His eyes met hers, searching, probing. Then, his mouth set in a grim line, he nodded and mounted his bay.

Moments later, the men rode off. The three women watched as they disappeared over a rise. They waited until the pounding hoofbeats faded into silence. The feeling of impending disaster hung in the air like ozone after a storm.

Finally, Consuelo put her arms around Alana's shoulders and steered her toward the house. "Isabel, put water on to boil. What the *señora* needs is a hot bath and cup of tea with lots of honey and a bit of whiskey. *Pronto, pronto.*"

"Si." Isabel bobbed her head in rapid agreement and scurried off.

At Consuelo's insistence, Alana spent the next few days in bed, allowing herself to be fussed over and coddled. Her throat was scratchy, her voice husky, her nose red, and her eyes watery. An energy-draining fatigue sapped her strength, leaving her perfectly content to spend most of the day napping.

On the evening of the second day, she sat propped up on pillows, a book open in her lap. Her attention strayed from the printed page. She had seen Trey only briefly the night before when he came to inquire how she was feeling. Though he hadn't said much, he had seemed distracted and withdrawn. She knew even without asking that the situation with the cattle was serious.

A slight sound drew her attention. Trey stood in the doorway, hands jammed in his pockets, feet slightly braced. He stood partially concealed in shadow, making it impossible for her to read his expression. Instead of his usually proud carriage, his broad shoulders slumped in dejection. Her heart squeezed painfully at the sight.

She smiled and held out her hand in welcome. Trey advanced into the room. Alana was appalled by the change in him. His face was drawn and haggard. Though his cheeks appeared freshly shaven, the hollows were pronounced, the planes sharp. Anxiety etched deep brackets around his mouth. His usually brilliant green eyes had lost their luster.

"Consuelo said you were feeling much better. I'm relieved. I was worried about you."

"Yes, I'm much better, thank you."

It was the stilted conversation of strangers. She loathed the awkwardness that so often sprang between them. Was that all fate decreed they be—intimate strangers? Was intimacy too much to achieve except in the throes of passion? "The cattle . . ." she began hesitantly, searching for common ground.

"We found two more dead cows this afternoon."

"Do you still think it's anthrax?"

"I don't know what else to think," he said with a weary sigh. "Vega insists it is. Even Noah admits the disease can follow this course. He said that sometimes there are no symptoms. Cattle simply die."

"I'm sorry . . ."

He looked at her with an odd expression for a long time. Yes, he believed she was sincere. In spite of the worst he could do to her, she wanted him to succeed. Did she speak the truth when she said she cared? The possibility added to his already deep guilt. She looked positively angelic in her high-necked nightdress with her soft blond curls cascading around her shoulders, but no angel had ever had a mouth like that—full, luscious, and as tempting as the devil himself. Lamplight limned her exquisite features with a gold patina. And her eyes, those incredibly blue eyes . . . The clear, unclouded blue of a summer sky.

"Tell me more about it. Talk to me, Trey." She patted the empty space beside her on the bed.

He sank down on the edge of the mattress near the foot of the bed. If he sat any closer, he might succumb to the urge to take her in his arms. He wanted to hold her, nothing more. Just hold her and unburden the doubts and uncertainties that plagued him. "Whatever name you give this sickness, it could decimate the entire herd—along with everything I've worked for, planned for."

"If we have to, we can start over. Build up a new herd, plant more citrus trees, do whatever it takes to save the ranch. The truly important things in life are worth fighting for."

He pulled his fingers through his hair and sighed. "This ranch has been a dream of mine since boyhood."

Alana kept quiet, afraid to say anything that might staunch the flow of his words. She had long suspected how much the land meant to him, but she wanted to hear it from his own lips. She wanted him to confide in her. To trust her.

"Robert and I dreamed of having one of the best ranches in the West—not necessarily the biggest, but the best. A place that we could mold with skill and vision. A place to make our own mark. We both wanted wide open spaces and fresh air, not dark-paneled boardrooms thick with cigar smoke.

"I read everything I could get my hands on about livestock and crops. I delayed doing anything about it for years. After I graduated from college, I took over the family business. It was originally a shipping firm, but we began to get more involved in railroads, especially transcontinental lines. It was my duty to keep things going until Robert came of age and mother was financially secure. Then . . ." His voice trailed off.

He didn't have to explain; Alana already knew the rest. Fast on the heels of Robert's suicide came his mother's stroke. Trey wouldn't abandon his mother when she desperately needed him.

"When I learned that many of the large Spanish land grants were being divided and sold, I knew this was the opportunity I'd been looking for. I jumped at the chance to come out to California and investigate this golden opportunity for myself."

"And you found me."

"Yes." He gave a humorless laugh. "I couldn't believe my good fortune. The property of my dreams, and the woman who haunted them. All tied up in one neat package. It seemed perfect. If I could persuade you to marry me, I'd sequester you in this remote place, miles removed from stage footlights and your crowd of admirers. I was certain you'd hate this place."

"But you were wrong. I love it nearly as much as you do."

"Yes, I was wrong again." He massaged the back of his neck to relieve some of the tension. "Where you're involved, I have a talent for sorely underestimating you. And now it seems I'm in danger of losing everything. Most of my assets are tied up in the ranch. I narrowly escaped losing the citrus crop. Now the entire cattle herd is threatened. If I were superstitious, I'd take this as an omen. Maybe I should pack up and return to the boardrooms."

"No!" Her response was swift and emphatic. "Surely there must be something we can do."

Trey's shoulders rose and fell in a weary shrug. "We've separated the healthy cattle from the sick ones in the north pasture. We've taken every precaution in the disposal of the dead carcasses. I don't know what else to do, unless . . ."

"Unless what?"

He hesitated, plucking absently at the coverlet. "Noah came up with an idea, but I'm not sure it's sound."

"What is it?" She leaned forward in her eagerness. For the first time since Trey had entered the bedroom, a note of hope had crept into his tone.

"Noah claims he read about a vaccine that was developed by the French scientist, Louis Pasteur, that's reputed to be effective against anthrax. I gave him permission to ride all the way to Los Angeles if that's what it takes to find this miracle cure."

Reaching out, she covered his hand with hers and squeezed. "Then let's pray Noah will be successful."

"You really do care, don't you?"

"Yes, very much."

The low, smoky pitch of her voice never failed to stir his senses. It tempted him with a promise of sultry heat and silken limbs. He stood to leave while he could still summon the willpower.

Her eyes filled with regret. "Stay." She tried to catch his hand, but he stepped beyond her reach.

"I can't."

"Why?" Her voice broke.

She thought he wasn't going to answer, but he paused in the doorway and looked back. Without benefit of lamplight, his expression was once again masked by shadows, but when he spoke, the pain in his voice was unmistakable.

"Because I betray my brother's memory every time I hold you in my arms. I can't bear the guilt."

His admission scored her soul, immobilized her

with anguish. Blinded by sorrow, she stared sightlessly at him.

Then, recovering, she flung aside the bedclothes and raced after him, intercepting him midway down the darkened hallway. She caught his arm and forced him to face her. "Can't you accept that I didn't kill Robert, and neither did you?" Each word throbbed with conviction. "Robert killed himself."

"I shouldn't have stayed on in Barcelona." His face contorted in agony, Trey shook off her touch. "I could have stopped him. *I should have been there.*" His breathing was ragged, the confession torn from him at great personal cost.

Again, Alana tried to make him understand. There might never be another chance. "You can't continue to blame yourself any more than you can continue to blame me. You have to forgive yourself. There was no way you could possibly have guessed Robert would take his own life. Just as I couldn't have . . ." She wanted to shake him, to make him accept the logic of what she said.

Their gazes fused, challenged, warred, refused to retreat, refused to surrender. Time hung suspended by a delicate thread. Finally, Trey shook his head, as though to negate her words. "I should have been there," he repeated, his voice flat. He turned and left her standing in the dark, staring after him in despair.

Alana sat on a worn wooden bench on the sun-dappled veranda, a basket of mending at her side. Though still suffering from a lingering fatigue that caused her to sleep later each morning, nap every afternoon, and retire early at night, she felt much better. The number of dead cattle now totaled twelve. Trey was at his wits' end—and she felt powerless to help him. She aimed for the hole in the button and speared her finger instead. Sucking her injured flesh, she allowed herself to be diverted by a goldfinch perched among the vines that climbed the pillars of the veranda. Head cocked to one side, she listened to the small bird's melodious warbling.

"Señora!" Consuelo burst from the house like a whirlwind, startling the finch, which flew away with frantic flapping of wings. "Noah has returned with the medicine. *Señor* Trey has given the men orders to corral all the cattle. They are going to start shooting medicine into the cows."

The shirt Alana was mending dropped from her lap as she jumped to her feet. The veranda spun like a carousel for a moment before it stilled. She shook her head to clear the last vestiges of dizziness. "What marvelous news! Let's go and watch."

"Are you *loco?"* Consuelo clucked her tongue. "You are still not well."

"I'm going—with or without you."

"Loco," Consuelo declared, wagging her head in exasperation. "I will get the buckboard. You find a hat to wear. The sun is strong today."

During the short ride to the corral, Alana was forced to endure Consuelo's incessant praise of Noah Stone. "He is *macho,"* Consuelo said, making a sweeping gesture.

"Macho? What is *macho?"* Alana asked, amused by her friend's exuberance.

Consuelo skillfully steered the buckboard around a rut in the trail. "He is a real man, not a strutting bantam rooster or low-bellied slithering snake." She didn't have to mention Vega by name; Alana knew whom she referred to.

Macho. Hmm, Alana mused. It was a term she'd

have to remember. Noah Stone wasn't the only man the word applied to, she thought as she instantly picked out her husband mounted on his dependable bay, overseeing the operation.

Dust kicked up by hundreds of hooves formed a brown haze over the corral. From a distance, the scene resembled a sepia photograph. As they drew nearer, however, Alana realized the initial impression was deceptive. The sight greeting them was one of controlled chaos. Cattle lowed their agitation at being herded into pens. Men shouted at each other to be heard above the livestock. Some ranch hands worked the pens; others on horseback kept the cattle from straying. Lariats hummed through the air with grace and precision before settling around the necks of unsuspecting animals. As Alana and Consuelo looked on, cows were led toward a narrow enclosure where Vega and Noah injected the rump of each animal.

Consuelo reined the buckboard to a halt within earshot of the pair.

"This is a foolish waste of time and money," Vega grumbled, his face set in sullen lines. "There's no guarantee this'll work."

"It'll work," Noah replied cheerily. "You've got my guarantee. This Frenchman Pasteur first tried it out on sheep and later cattle. The results were impressive."

"Yeah, we'll see." Vega viciously jabbed a needle into a cow's hide.

Trey rode over to the enclosure and addressed Vega. "This can't be all the cattle. What about those from the north pasture? They make up at least half the herd. I gave orders the men were to include them in the inoculations."

"I told them not to bother." Vega stopped and

wiped the sweat from his brow with a dirty bandana. "They're already contaminated with the disease. No sense in taking a chance they might infect the rest of the herd."

The muscle in Trey's jaw bunched angrily. "Dammit, Vega! How dare you countermand my orders? I specifically stated all the cattle."

"I was only trying to protect the healthy ones." Vega glared at Trey defiantly.

"Reports state that even affected animals in the early stages of the disease benefit from the vaccine," Noah said without looking up from his task.

"Tell the men to bring them in. Pronto," Trey ordered. His bay danced restlessly, as though sensing its rider's anger.

Vega lowered his heavy lids to conceal the furious glitter in his black eyes. He turned on his heel and stalked off.

Trey wheeled his horse around and approached the buckboard. He greeted Consuelo, then turned the full force of his stare on Alana. She tilted her head and returned the look, prepared should he challenge her right to be there.

"You still look a little pale. Shouldn't you be resting instead of being out here in the hot sun?"

Ready for criticism, she was taken aback by his solicitude. "I had to see for myself how the inoculations were progressing. Do you really think they'll work?"

"I don't know," he answered honestly. "I wish I had Stone's confidence. I heard of Pasteur's work when I was in Europe. He's a brilliant scientist. Let's hope his vaccine solves our problem. Now I want you to let Consuelo take you back to the hacienda so you can get some rest."

Consuelo nodded her agreement. *"Si, Señor* Trey,

that is what I try to tell her, but the *señora* insist on coming."

Trey managed a dry chuckle. "My wife has never learned to sit on the sidelines if she can be in the thick of things."

Alana gaped at Trey in disbelief. He'd only chuckled, not laughed outright, but she was reminded of her long-ago desire to make him laugh.

Consuelo grinned mischievously, her dark eyes dancing. "*Señora* Matthews needs a houseful of little ones to keep her busy." She flicked the reins, and the wagon rolled off.

By the time they returned to the ranch, it was late afternoon. Alana could barely keep her eyes open. "There's nothing more we can do, *señora*. Go rest," Consuelo advised, giving Alana a gentle nudge toward her bedroom.

Consuelo and Trey meant well, Alana knew, but she resisted the idea of taking a nap. She seemed to be spending entirely too much time sleeping these days. Alternately tired and restless, she roamed the empty rooms before finally settling in the cozy book-lined study. She could understand why Trey favored this room with its shelves of leather-bound volumes and big comfortable chairs. His massive oak desk stood in front of the window, its surface covered with neat stacks of papers and journals. Pens and inkwells were meticulously aligned along the upper edge. Everything was neat, orderly, and in control—just like the man.

Idly, she trailed a fingertip over the spines of the books. History, philosophy, horticulture, and botany were well-represented. Much to her delight, she had long ago discovered that Trey shared her fondness for fiction. The works of Charles Dickens, Nathaniel Hawthorne, George Eliot, and Mark Twain all shared shelf space. To her surprise, she now found a copy of *Ramona*, a novel by Helen Hunt Jackson that was currently enjoying immense popularity.

After a brief debate, she selected *The Bostonians* by Henry James, then, tucking a woven blanket around her, curled up in one of the big chairs. Minutes later, she was asleep. The book slid from her lap unnoticed.

Nightmares invaded her sleep. Faces, at first vague, then with disturbing clarity, paraded through her dreams. She was walking down a long narrow corridor with many doors, then the corridor twisted and changed into an alley. Her footsteps echoed hollowly against the hard-packed dirt. Sensing she was being followed, she increased her pace, but her feet felt as if they were encased in lead boots. Her heart thumped with fear as she almost stumbled over a body. A Chinese man lay in a crumpled heap at her feet, his throat slit ear to ear in a macabre grin. His long braided queue lay coiled like a serpent in a pool of blood.

A man wearing a derby set at a rakish angle stepped from behind one of the closed doors. "Nowhere to run, my pretty." He tossed back his head and let loose a chilling peal of laughter. "Time to pay the piper."

She turned and raced mindlessly toward a light at the end of the alley. She was almost to safety when a second figure blocked her exit. Her chest heaving with fear, she stared into Vega's sly, smiling face. "Nowhere to run, *chica?*"

She bolted upright. Disoriented, she looked around. A man's figure appeared in the doorway. She pressed her hand over her mouth to stifle a scream.

"Alana, what's the matter? Are you all right?" Trey asked from across the room.

She gave a small gasp and fell against the cushion. "I must have fallen asleep and had a nightmare. My father always accused me of having an overactive imagination."

Trey came into the room and lit a lamp on the desk. "You must have been exhausted to have slept all this time. You missed dinner. I'll have Isabel fix you a tray."

"I'm not hungry."

"Nonsense, you need to eat something. You've lost weight since coming here." He perched on the edge of the desk and regarded her thoughtfully.

He made her conscious of her rumpled state. While he, on the other hand, looked extremely attractive in a crisp white shirt open at the throat and black pants tailored to fit his lithe form. Lines of tension had been erased from his face. He looked more at ease than he had in weeks—and very appealing. Alana got to her feet, her legs rubbery, and smoothed her wrinkled skirt. "Did all the cattle get vaccinated?"

He nodded. "Only thing to do now is wait, but somehow I feel more optimistic."

"I'm glad." There didn't seem to be anything left to say, so she turned to leave, but stopped midway to the door. "Did Vega's attitude this afternoon strike you as a bit odd?"

"In what way?"

She gnawed her lower lip, trying to choose the right words. "It was almost as though he didn't want the vaccine to work. That he wanted the experiment to fail."

Trey dismissed her concern with a shrug. "He was

probably jealous that Noah came up with the idea, and he didn't."

"I suppose," she replied doubtfully.

But deep inside she wasn't so easily convinced.

Chapter 22

Alana punched her pillow. She had no idea of the hour, only that it was sometime after midnight and before dawn. With a sigh, she flopped onto her back and stared up at the ceiling. Tossing restlessly was just punishment, she thought, for napping away the afternoon. But a small, insidious voice insisted otherwise. Her afternoon nap, the annoying voice stressed, wasn't to blame for her sleeplessness.

For weeks, she had waited for her monthly flow. While sometimes it was a little irregular, it was never this late. Scalding tears trickled down her temples to dampen the pillow. What was it about the still of the night that made one admit truths that could be denied in the course of the day? Sniffing, she hugged the bedclothes to her chest.

She was pregnant—and she wasn't happy about it.

Before the Santa Anas swept through the canyons next fall, she would bear Trey's child. As much as she wanted children and a family, the circumstances were wrong. It was too soon. She needed more time to convince Trey that neither of them was responsible for Robert's suicide. She needed time to convince Trey that Robert—and Robert alone—was ultimately responsible for his act.

She wiped her tears away with trembling fingers. She had to be strong, not weak. She had to plan for the future, not wallow in self-pity. Knowing how Trey hated her for what she had done to his family, she couldn't remain there. And he wouldn't let her leave. The situation was hopeless.

Tears threatened again. How could she bring a child into this world, then stand by helplessly as Trey poisoned the child's mind against her? Something inside her would surely die if that happened. How unfair to ask a child to pass judgment on a mother's deeds. How unfair to make it choose sides. How could any child thrive and grow in such an atmosphere? Doubts and fears hardened her resolve. She wouldn't allow that to happen. The child must be protected regardless of personal cost. She refused to subject a child to such an evil, unhealthy environment.

A faint cry broke into her tearful brooding. It sounded like the squall of an infant. Alana strained to hear it again, but there was only silence. She sniffed back tears, feeling foolish. Already she was hearing babies cry when it was more likely the meowing of Isabel's cat. Her stomach gave an unladylike rumble. Like her moods of late, her appetite was unpredictable, shifting from total disinterest in food to odd cravings. Tonight was no exception. A light snack would be a welcome distraction. Swinging her legs out of bed, she reached for her wrapper. Just as she did so, she heard the soft patter of footsteps outside her window—and froze.

She caught her lower lip between her teeth. What should she do? Stay here and pretend she heard nothing? Or investigate? She was certain of one thing. She couldn't—wouldn't—run naively to Trey as she had done last time she had heard strange noises late at night. That had been sheer folly. She could still recall the vile scene in which he had hurled unfounded accusations at her. His vitriolic attack had left her shaken and confused. If she went to him again, he'd only accuse her of fabricating stories to gain his attention. Swallowing hard, she reached a decision. She'd check out the situation first. If she discovered anything, then and only then would she go to Trey with her findings.

Quickly, before she had a chance to change her mind, she crossed the room, opened the armoire, and took her trusty little derringer from its hiding place. The hard cold metal filled the palm of her hand. It was the same gun she had carried to protect herself against Ling Ho's killer. It had reassured her then; it reassured her now. Gun in hand, she quietly opened the door to the patio and slipped outside. Cautiously, she looked around but could detect no movement in the thin light from the quarter moon. Scarcely daring to breathe, she crept along the veranda.

She was about to pass the kitchen when she noticed that the door was partially open. She gingerly pushed the worn wood and the door swung wide. The butt of the gun felt slick in her sweaty palm. Drawing in a steadying breath, she stepped back inside the house once more. Nervously, she scanned the room. Everything seemed neat and orderly, just as Isabel left it each night. Her breathing was returning to normal when she heard a muffled cry from the pantry.

Her index finger hugged the trigger. "Come out or I'll shoot," she ordered, hoping her voice didn't quaver.

Nothing happened.

"I'm counting to three. One . . . two . . . three . . ."

Her ultimatum went unheeded.

She took a step forward, her knees wobbling precariously. "One more chance. Come out or I'll shoot.

Uno . . . dos . . . tres . . ." she repeated in her limited Spanish.

A figure emerged hesitantly from the pantry.

Alana's heart skidded to a stop. God help her, she didn't want to have to fire her gun.

"Por favor, señora . . ."

Alana couldn't follow the rapid Spanish that followed, but two facts registered immediately in her mind: the intruder was a woman and more frightened than she. Immense relief surged through her. She relaxed her grip on the derringer. "Do not be afraid. I will not hurt you. *Por favor, señora . . ."*

The figure moved slowly forward. Even in the dim light, Alana could see that the woman was young, hardly more than a girl, pretty, with long black hair, and obviously beside herself with fright. She clutched a bundle firmly to her chest. Alana gasped in astonishment as the bundle squirmed and let out a mewling cry. It wasn't stolen goods at all, she realized, but a baby!

Alana tried to allay the girl's fear. She gestured toward the infant and smiled. *"Nena?"* she asked, borrowing a word she had heard Consuelo use.

"Nene," the girl corrected with an emphatic shake of her head.

Alana impulsively laid her hand over her own stomach. *"Nene."*

A tentative smile broke over the girl's face. Alana approached her cautiously. When she was close enough, she peeled back a corner of the blanket. As she watched, the infant jammed his tiny fist into his mouth and sucked noisily. Seeing the fretful baby with his mop of dark hair made her want to smile and cry at the same time. The moment was bittersweet, one she would always remember. For the very first time, she thought of what it would be like to hold her own baby. For the first time, she welcomed the thought of Trey's child—even if it meant leaving him.

Afraid that at any second the baby would tire of gnawing his fist and demand something more substantial, Alana hurriedly left the house, beckoning the girl to follow her. She eased open the back gate and instinctively headed for the stable and the privacy it afforded.

The stable smelled of straw and horses. One of the animals stirred restlessly in its stall. Lifting a lantern from a peg on the wall, Alana lit it, trimmed the wick low, then moved toward a stall at the far end. The woman trailed close behind her and sank gratefully onto the pile of straw. Unselfconsciously, she began to nurse the hungry infant.

Alana watched, fascinated. Once she conquered her initial embarrassment, she felt privileged to watch the intimate ritual as old as time itself. The baby suckled greedily, one little fist kneading his mother's breast. A look of contentment so pure that it stole her breath away passed over the infant's face. Alana suddenly longed to see that same expression on the face of her own child.

When the baby finished nursing, the woman reached in her bundle and brought out a stack of tortillas wrapped in a checkered cloth. Alana recognized the cloth as one of Isabel's. The woman flashed her a guilty look, then stuffed a tortilla into her mouth, hunger far outweighing any pangs of conscience. Motioning the woman to stay where she was, Alana got up and left the stable. She returned minutes later with a jug of cold milk, which she offered to the woman.

"Gracias." The woman accepted the milk readily and took a long swig.

Alana made a rocking motion with her arms. The woman smiled shyly and relinquished the baby to Alana's care. While the woman ate, Alana cuddled the infant. She began to hum, softly at first, and then with growing confidence. The lilting tune of a lullaby drifted through her mind, and the words formed on her lips. Her voice clear and sweet, she sang as she would do someday for her own child.

When she finished the tune, the baby was sound asleep.

"That was right pleasin' to the ear. By the looks of 'im, the little fella enjoyed it, too." Noah Stone stepped into the small circle of light.

Alana let out a startled gasp. The woman scooted back and might have bolted, had it not been for the fact that Alana held her child.

"No need to get spooked on my account." Noah grinned disarmingly. He hunkered down next to Alana and gently touched the baby's hand. Instantly, the tiny fingers curled around his large one and hung on tight. "Did your friend say what she was doin' here in the middle of the night?"

Alana shook her head. "No, she doesn't speak English. I don't even know her name."

Noah favored the woman with another smile, but she continued to regard him warily. Quietly, he began to question her. The woman spoke rapidly, her hands flying, animation in her voice. When the exchange was finished, Noah turned to Alana.

"Well . . . what did she say?" Alana asked, impatient for an explanation.

"Her name is Maria." He shifted his weight. "She's following her husband, Miguel. She claims an *amigo*, a friend, told her he might pass through Rancho Prado del Sol."

"I don't know of any ranch hand by the name of Miguel. What will she do if he isn't here?"

He shrugged. "She will look elsewhere. She's very determined to join him."

"But she can't just wander the countryside hoping to find him. Especially not with a baby."

"I offered to do what I could to help."

"Perhaps Trey—"

"No," he said sharply, cutting her off. "No one else must know that she's been here. She made me promise and insisted you promise, too."

Alana glanced at Maria.

"*Por favor, señora . . .*" The rest was lost in a passionate outburst that Alana was unable to follow. But the pleading in Maria's large, dark eyes spoke eloquently.

Reluctantly, and against her better judgment, Alana agreed to remain silent. The woman reached out and, clasping Alana's hand, brought it to her lips and kissed it. "*Gracias. Muchas gracias, señora.*"

"Ouch!" Noah exclaimed, pulling his finger from the baby's mouth. "This little tike's teething. My sister's kid did the same thing when he was about this size. No wonder he's fussin'."

Noah turned again to the child's mother, but Maria was already curled on her side fast asleep. Alana rose and carefully laid the baby next to her. Noah found a horse blanket and spread it over the two of them.

"*Mañana,*" he whispered to Alana. "Tomorrow will be time enough to sort things out."

Alana extinguished the lantern, and together they tiptoed from the stable. Once they were outside, she turned to Noah with a list of questions.

"What made Miguel leave a wife and baby? Why would someone say he came here? She's all alone.

She has no money, no friends, and can't even speak the language. How will she survive?"

Noah shoveled both hands through his sun-bleached locks. "I suspect that she entered the country illegally, as did her husband. That's why she insisted we tell no one. She's afraid that if the authorities find out, they will send her back."

Alana shook her head. "I don't understand. What would make a man abandon his wife and family?"

"Her husband is trying to find a better life for them. Maria said Miguel was promised a lot of money to leave his home and head north."

Alana thought back to the first time she had heard footsteps late at night. She had also heard voices. Spanish-speaking voices? She frowned, trying to remember. It was entirely possible. Were those also voices of men who had been promised a great deal of money to leave their families? Had they been illegal immigrants? If so, was their passing through Rancho Prado del Sol a coincidence? Or was it part of a plan? The thought was disturbing.

Her mouth dry, she moistened her lips with the tip of her tongue. "Who would pay these people to leave their homes?"

"People are always on the lookout for cheap labor. Everyone from ranchers in the West to the cotton growers in the South. Even the New Mexican coal mines aren't exempt from the practice. Now that East and West are connected by rail, crops picked in California will be brought to New York. Migrants desperate for money will be grateful for the work. Since Congress passed the Chinese Exclusion Act, no more Chinese are allowed to enter the country. It's only natural that businesses will look to Mexico to fill the void."

All at once Alana realized that Noah's lazy Texas

drawl had disappeared, replaced by urgency and eloquence. She studied him. It was almost as though the amiable drifter had vanished, replaced by a fierce crusader. "How do you know all this?"

"Sorry, didn't mean to get up on no soapbox." Noah took her elbow. "It's late. Let me escort you safely back to the house."

"That isn't necessary. I can see myself back."

"A body never can tell what kind of varmints are prowlin' around at night."

Was he referring to Vega? she wondered with a shiver. Did he distrust the man as much as she and Consuelo did?

"You sure do have a right pretty voice, ma'am. I could sit and listen to you sing all night. Back in the days when you were singin' at that saloon, I bet the place was packed every evening." Noah gently steered her toward the hacienda, matching his pace to hers.

Afraid he might leap to the same conclusion that Trey had, she attempted to set him straight. "If the place was packed, it was only because they enjoyed hearing me sing . . . and no other reason."

"I never suspected for a minute that there was another reason, ma'am."

At Noah's injured tone, Alana was instantly contrite. "I don't know what came over me. I had no call to lash out at you. And please stop calling me ma'am. My name is Alana, as you well know."

"Pretty name, Alana. Suits you. Sounds like a right proper name for a lady like yourself."

"A lady?" Alana's mouth firmed into a bitter line. "I wish my husband thought of me in those terms."

"Some men are just more hardheaded than others." He unlatched the back gate and stood aside for her to enter. "Give him time, he'll come around."

They paused near the fountain. She rested a hand on his arm and looked up at him beseechingly. "Do you really think so, Noah?" A wistful quality crept into her voice.

"A man would have to be a fool not to see the treasure right under his very nose. I don't take Trey Matthews for a fool."

"So there you are!" Trey thundered as he burst from the hacienda. Even in the limited moonlight, his expression was as dark as that of some ancient war god.

"Trey!" Nearly speechless with surprise, Alana let her hand fall from Noah's sleeve.

Trey caught Noah's shoulder and spun him about. Before Noah had a chance to defend himself, Trey slammed a fist into his jaw, sending him sprawling. "I should have known better than to trust you, Stone. Vega warned me about you, but I wouldn't listen. I didn't think you were the kind to cheat with another man's wife."

Noah wiped the blood from his mouth with the back of his hand. "Give me a chance to explain, Matthews. It's not the way it looks."

Hands balled into fists, breathing heavily, Trey towered over Noah, who made no attempt to stand. "Let me be the judge of that."

"Trey! What's gotten into you?" Alana asked, horrified by the sudden violence. She reached for his arm. His bunched muscles felt like steel beneath her fingers.

"Shut up, you faithless bitch!" He shook off her touch so forcibly that she stumbled backward, nearly falling.

Noah leaped to his feet in a flash. He landed a vicious punch to Trey's midsection that knocked the breath from his body and made him double over in pain. Another blow sent Trey reeling backward. Trey's knees connected with the bench that circled the fountain, and he toppled into the water. Spray cascaded in all directions, liberally drenching all of them.

Awakened by the brawl, Consuelo came running. She took in the situation at a glance. "What is going on? Are you men *loco?*"

"Stay out of this, Consuelo," Noah ordered, his voice low, taut. He reached into the fountain and jerked Trey upright. "That's no way to talk to your wife, Matthews. Time someone taught you a lesson."

"You sonofabitch!" Still not ready to admit defeat, Trey hauled back his arm, but he was no match for Noah's reflexes.

Anticipating his opponent's move, Noah whipped Trey around and twisted his arm behind his back. Using his other arm as leverage, he applied pressure against Trey's windpipe. "Some men don't have the sense God gave a mule," Noah drawled, not even winded.

"Get your hands off of me, Stone."

"Maybe you're not nearly as smart as I gave you credit for, Matthews. If I ever hear of you mistreating your wife again, so help me God, I'll find you and break your arm."

"Stop it!" Alana cried. "Both of you. Let go of him, Noah, before someone gets hurt."

"I'll release you all right, Matthews, but only because your lady asked me to. I hope you understand her loyalty. I sure as hell don't." He let go of Trey's arm and stepped back.

Alana stood rooted to the spot and eyed the two men warily. Trey's eyes glowed like green coals. He looked as though he'd like to tear Noah limb from limb. Noah, on the other hand, appeared unruffled.

But she knew that under that placid exterior was a man who was not to be trifled with, which made him all the more dangerous.

"Pack your things, Stone. I want you out of here by daybreak."

"Trey, you're being hasty," Alana warned.

"It's something I should've done the first time Vega came to me with his suspicions."

"One last word of advice, Matthews," Noah said as he turned to go. "Be careful who you put your trust in."

Consuelo exchanged an unhappy look with Alana, then, looping her arm around Noah's waist, walked off with him. Alana knew Consuelo would miss Noah. For some time, she had suspected the pair were lovers. She turned to see Trey's reaction, but he was already stalking toward the house.

Alana ran after him. She couldn't leave the situation as it was without trying to explain. "Trey, it's not the way you think."

"Tell, me, wife," he said, striding into his bedroom. "What do I think?"

"Noah and I are friends. *Only* friends."

"Two friends innocently strolling in the moonlight while everyone else is sound asleep? How stupid do you think I am?" He stripped off his wet shirt and hurled it into a corner. "How do you explain the fact that you're wearing a nightgown?"

"I couldn't sleep."

"I saw the way you two were looking at each other. Sleep was the last thing on your minds."

They stood almost toe to toe. He glared down at her, accusing, condemning. Alana was tempted to confess about Maria, but she remembered her pledge. There was no telling what Trey might do in his present state of mind. What if he reported Maria to the authorities? She might never be reunited with her Miguel.

Finally, Alana's own temper kindled and burst into anger. Why should she always have to defend herself? Why did Trey always choose to believe the worst? Well, if he wasn't willing to listen, she wasn't ready to talk. She flung her hair over her shoulder. "Think what you will." She marched past him, head high.

Her haughty manner infuriated him. If she was guiltless, shouldn't she be pleading with him to believe her? Instead *she* acted like the one who'd been wronged. He reached out and caught her arm. "Wait just a minute. Where do you think you're going?"

"To bed. Arguing with you is a waste of time and energy. Once you get an idea in your head, you never let go—no matter how wrong you are."

"Is that so?" He stared down at her, green eyes gleaming. A muscle ticked in his jaw. "Maybe you're right," he said, his voice deep, raspy. "I've had an idea all evening that won't let me rest." Grabbing a handful of her hair, he held her head still while he pressed his lips against hers.

The tight wet pants he was still wearing molded him like kid leather. She could feel the steel shaft of his manhood hard against the softness of her stomach. She struggled against his hold, but it was inexorable. A strangled sob tore from her throat. She wouldn't give into the heat surging through her. She wouldn't give him the satisfaction—even if it meant denying her own.

At last he released her. She stared up at him, her eyes brimming with hurt and confusion, her mouth red and swollen from his kisses. "Why tonight, Trey? How did you know I wasn't in my room?"

"I came to you for the most fundamental reason a

husband seeks out his wife." He gave a harsh laugh. "The joke's on me. You got tired of waiting and took yourself a lover."

She rubbed her mouth as though to expunge his kiss. "It wasn't me you wanted. Any woman would have served the purpose."

This time he didn't try to stop her as she swept out of the room. Oh, but she was wrong, dead wrong. No other woman he'd ever met could compare with her. Damn! He slammed his fist against the wall. He had sought her out in the tentative hope that they could begin to breach the chasm he had willfully gouged between them—only to wrest her from Noah Stone's arms. His mouth twisted at the bitter irony.

Chapter 23

Trey scowled at his face in the mirror above the washbasin. His reflection scowled back. He hadn't slept a wink—and it showed. His face was pale beneath the tan, with dark circles under his eyes. He applied the razor to the bearded stubble covering his cheeks and scraped a path from ear to jaw. Damn! He grimaced. His body hurt like the devil. Even the limited movement required to shave reminded him of Noah's blows the night before. Stone had been ferocious in his defense of Alana. The man landed a punch as soundly as John L. Sullivan. Hell, it even hurt to breathe.

Doubts assailed Trey. Was he guilty of maligning his own wife? Had Stone been justified in defending Alana's honor? What if she had been telling the truth? What if she and Noah were only friends? "Sure," he grunted. "When cows fly."

You're so besotted with your own wife you'd swallow any cock-and-bull story she dished out. What possible reason would she have to be strolling on the veranda dressed in her nightclothes with a man at one o'clock in the morning? He nicked himself with the razor and cursed softly. Whether he wanted to believe her or not, the answer was painfully obvious.

It galled him to admit that he wanted to believe that she and Stone were not lovers. Wanted to believe it so badly that the ache superseded any physical discomfort from last night's thrashing. But the evidence against her was staggering. With her hair loose and flowing, she had worn that tousled, just-made-love-to look that he knew all too well. She looked so damn desirable, he couldn't blame Stone for taking what was offered—almost.

And he couldn't blame her for turning to another man—almost. He sure as hell hadn't been much of a husband. First tricking her into marriage, then either treating her shabbily or ignoring her altogether. What could be more natural than for a woman to turn to someone who was more sympathetic, more compassionate, more attentive? He had gone to her room to—

Trey's hand froze in midmotion in the act of shaving. To do what? Talk? He had gone to her room because he was tired of sleeping alone. Because he wanted to make love to her, hold her, fall asleep with her in his arms. Instead he had found her missing. His anger flared anew.

He finished shaving, grabbed his shirt from a peg on the wall, and strode from the house, stuffing his shirttails into his pants as he headed for the stables. He needed to inform Vega that Stone was no longer welcome at Rancho Prado del Sol. As he was about to enter the stable, he nearly collided with Alana coming out. Automatically, he reached out to steady her.

For a long moment, they stared at each other.

Alana berated herself for not paying more attention to where she was walking. Intent on studying the object in the palm of her hand, she hadn't seen him approach until too late.

Trey recovered from his surprise first and dropped his hands to his side. A malignant sense of betrayal grew inside him and refused to be ignored. "What are you doing out here? Looking for you lover?"

"I refuse to dignify your insulting questions with a response," she replied haughtily.

His eyes blazed green fire; his countenance looked daunting. "If Stone knows what's good for him, he'll never show his face within fifty miles of here."

"That's bold talk after the way he bested you last night." Alana knew she was playing with fire, but she felt reckless. How could he hurt her any more than he had already?

"He won't do it a second time. I never repeat my mistakes."

Trey didn't speak boastfully, but with a chilling conviction. Alana decided it would be wise not to provoke him further. She took a half-step backward.

"What are you holding in your hand?" he demanded.

Her fingers curled more tightly around the precious object. "It's none of your business."

"I'm making it my business." He caught her wrist and exerted gentle but concentrated pressure on the delicate bones until her fingers reluctantly opened.

A string of pretty silver beads lay nestled in her palm. He raised a skeptical brow. "How touching," he ground out. "Stone left you a necklace to remember him by."

"Wrong," she contradicted, her voice tight. "You're not very observant."

Picking up the beads between his thumb and forefinger, he held them up for a closer inspection. "Prayer beads!" he said in disbelief.

"A rosary." In one smooth movement, she jerked her wrist free and snatched the rosary back. She turned toward the hacienda. "Sorry to disappoint you," she called over her shoulder. "It's a gift, but not from Noah."

Trey didn't deserve an explanation, she thought. Besides, she had given Maria her word not to tell anyone that she and the baby had been there. When she had gone to check on them just now, she had discovered that they had vanished as mysteriously as they had appeared. Instead, she had discovered the rosary carefully placed in the bed of straw where she was sure to see it—Maria's way of showing her gratitude. Alana slipped the beads into her pocket and offered up a prayer for their safety.

"What the hell . . ." Trey stood in the center of the bunkhouse and looked around him in amazement. Sunlight filtered through the dusty panes and formed pale golden rectangles on the worn pine floor. Mattresses had been stripped to bare ticking. An empty whiskey bottle lay on its side in one corner. Flies feasted on a half-eaten plate of beans. He rubbed the back of his neck as though to erase the growing unease. Something was wrong. Radically wrong.

Yesterday, he had observed fewer and fewer men working about the ranch. Vega had shrugged off his concern, saying he had given the men chores elsewhere. But today, the ranch was virtually abandoned. There was no sign of the ranch hands, no sign of Vega.

"Psst, *señor,*" a voice called softly.

Trey whirled around as Paco slipped furtively inside. "Paco! Where's Vega? Where's the rest of the men?"

Paco glanced around nervously. Sweat beaded his upper lip. "They are gone, *señor*. Vega told them they must leave, or they would be dead men."

"What are you talking about? What's going on?"

"Vega is one mean *hombre, señor*. I think he plans to harm you and the *señora*. That is why I stay to warn you."

"Tell me what you know."

Paco spread his hands. "I know little. Only that Vega does not want you here. He tried to make you leave, but you do not go."

Trey resisted the urge to shake the information out of the man. "How did he try to make us leave?"

"By causing *problemos, señor*." Shamefaced, Paco scuffed at the floor with the toe of his boot. "That night in the orchard, Vega gave me the tequila, knowing I will drink until it's gone and not take care of your oranges. And that is not all."

"Go on," Trey encouraged.

"He cut the fences and ordered Juan to slit the throat of your bull." Paco glanced anxiously at the door as though half-expecting Vega to burst through, then spoke in a low voice, his words tumbling over one another. "It was not the disease that killed your cattle, *señor*. It was Vega. I saw him give your cows something to make them sick. He did not want you to come here. I overheard him brag that he scared off the servants sent to clean the hacienda for your *esposa*."

Trey raked a hand through his hair. "Why would Vega go to so much trouble to drive us away?"

Paco shrugged his shoulders. "I do not know, *señor*. I only know he wishes you harm."

"Why do you tell me these things?"

"You and the *señora* have been kind to me. I do not want your deaths on my conscience."

Deaths? Foreboding descended upon Trey like a dark shade as the full import of Paco's words sank home. Rancho Prado del Sol was isolated and remote, the nearest help miles away. There were only two women, an elderly couple, and he. How could they hope to stave off enemies, should Vega attack? "Will you stay, Paco, and help us?"

He backed toward the door. *"Lo siento mucho.* I have an *esposa* and *muchachos* in Mexico who need me."

Reaching into his pocket, Trey pulled out a handful of bills and thrust them at Paco. "I owe you a debt I can never repay, Paco. *Vaya con Dios."*

"Gracias, senor. Muchas gracias."

Trey ran to the hacienda. Isabel's mouth opened in surprise as he burst through the kitchen door. He clasped her shoulders and spoke distinctly to eliminate any chance that she might misunderstand him. "Go to your husband. Stay there. Barricade your doors and windows, and don't come out if you hear gunfire."

The elderly cook's eyes rounded in terror. *"Banditos, señor?"*

"Yes, Isabel, *banditos."*

He rushed down the hallway, nearly stumbling over Consuelo, who was on her hands and knees scrubbing the floor. He hesitated, debating briefly what to tell the woman without causing her to panic.

Consuelo sat back on her heels, wiped a strand of hair out of her eyes with her forearm, and solemnly returned his regard. "Well, *señor,"* she said at last, "are you going to tell me what is wrong?"

Trey impatiently drummed his fingers against his thigh. There was no easy way to tell her, so he plunged ahead. "The men have all gone. Vega, too. Whatever his reasons, I think he's planning to attack us."

"El serpiente." She spat the epithet, then rose to her feet. "What do you want me to do?"

"Take care of my wife. See that she doesn't get hurt. Lock yourselves in the bedroom, then move the heavy pieces of furniture in front of the doors. Bolt the windows. And whatever you do, don't unlock the door unless you're sure it's safe. Here," he said, pulling out a revolver. "Use this if you have to. You do know how to use a gun, don't you?" he asked.

"*Si.*" Consuelo tucked the gun into the waistband of her skirt and ran off in search of Alana.

Trey raced to the locked cupboard in the library where he kept the rest of his guns. He pulled out his Winchester and a box of shells, then strapped on a holster with twin Smith and Wessons. At one time, he had entertained the notion of collecting firearms, never dreaming that someday they might save his life.

With methodical thoroughness, he went through the house securing the shutters. He shoved the bar in place across the heavy oak door to the outer courtyard. It was stout enough to withstand a battering ram, he noted with satisfaction. Even the small recessed windows with their iron grillwork and shutters were an asset against invasion. When the attack came, and Trey felt it would come soon, in all likelihood it would be through the gate guarding the inner courtyard. He was determined to make it as difficult as possible for Vega and his cutthroat band.

After rummaging through a storeroom off the kitchen, he located a sturdy length of chain and a padlock that looked like a relic from the Inquisition. All that remained to do was lock the courtyard gate.

Alana was waiting for him in the kitchen when he came out of the storeroom. "Consuelo told me everything. Do you think we can keep them out with that?" she asked, gesturing to the lock and chain.

"It's a start. Go back to your room where it's safe."

But even as he issued the order, Trey knew it was useless. He had seen that glint of steely determination in her blue eyes far too many times to mistake it. Even if he had had a shred of doubt, the small derringer in her right hand would have dispelled it.

"If you expect me to cower in my room, then think again. Wherever you are, I'll be right beside you."

"Alana . . ."

She cut him off. "Three people have a better chance of holding off attackers than one."

With a sigh of resignation, he pulled a Smith and Wesson from his holster and handed it to her. "If you're going to guard my back, you'll need more than that little peashooter you're holding." He quickly left the house.

Gripping the revolver in both hands, she watched as he darted the length of the veranda. He hugged the wall, stopping periodically to scan the rooftops before hurrying toward the back gate. She released a pent-up breath as he doubled the chain around the tall wrought-iron gate and snapped the huge padlock shut, then sprinted back toward safety.

They shared the vigil from the dining room at the far end of the house. A shutter was cracked wide enough to accommodate the barrel of a gun. Consuelo kept watch in the north wing.

"Keep a lookout while I load the guns," Trey ordered. Alana knelt beside him on the floor and did as he asked, her eyes roaming anxiously from the back gate to the rooftops for any sign of Vega or his men.

"I don't suppose that if I asked one more time, you'd reconsider and barricade yourself in the bedroom with Consuelo."

"Not a chance."

"Didn't think so."

Alana's head whipped around at the unexpected humor in Trey's voice. He shot her a grin, which she returned automatically.

"At times you can be as obstinate as a mule." He finished loading the rifle and picked up a pistol. Maybe *courageous* would be a better term, he mused, shoving bullets into the empty chamber. Instead of hiding where it was safe, she demanded to be in the thick of things, there at his side, ready to protect and defend him with her life if need be. Since the beginning she had surprised him at every turn. He had fully expected to despise the woman he blamed for Robert's suicide. He had done his damnedest to hate her. Yet . . . Resolutely, he lined up the guns on the floor within easy reach. This wasn't the time to examine how he felt. Later, maybe, when this latest crisis was behind them.

If they survived.

Alana gnawed her lower lip and peered through the crack in the shutter. "Perhaps we should've tried to make a run for it."

"And risk an ambush? That would only make Vega's task easier."

"What if we could make it to our nearest neighbors?" she asked hopefully. "Surely they wouldn't refuse to help us."

"We'd never make it there alive." The calm certainty in his voice made her shiver. Trey saw her reaction and felt a sharp pang of regret. It was his fault that she was in danger. He never should have brought her here. He had been too intent on revenge—and lust—to think straight. "Don't worry. We'll get out of this all right. The hacienda is well fortified. We have food, water, and a good supply of ammunition. By the way," he added, his dark brow raised questioningly, "have you ever fired a gun before?"

"Of course," she returned.

"I should've known," he muttered in resignation. "Let me ask another silly question. Did you actually hit your target?"

"Sometimes," she admitted tartly, then grew serious. "After I witnessed the murder in the alley, Colin took me out into the hills, and we practiced shooting at tin cans."

"If it comes down to a situation where it's you or them, just remember to stay calm, point the pistol, and gently squeeze the trigger. The most important thing is not to panic."

Alana nodded, hoping she wouldn't need to recall that piece of advice, but knowing she probably would.

Waiting commenced in earnest. The world beyond the closed shutters and thick adobe walls teemed with its usual vitality. Birds flitted in and out of the vines. The fountain in the courtyard tinkled merrily. Buttery yellow sunlight bathed the veranda in a mellow glow.

In stark contrast, the hacienda was dim and cool, its mood brooding, pensive. Every sound, no matter how slight, seemed magnified. Alana's nerves felt stretched as taut as piano wire. But perhaps that's what Vega intended all along, she thought grimly. He wanted to make them sweat, to make them squirm, to make them taste fear.

She stole a sidelong glance at Trey. Fierce determination had hardened the line of his jaw. A lock of hair fell across his broad forehead. She wanted to reach up and brush it back. A lump wedged in her throat. In spite of all that had passed between them—the harsh words, the bitter accusations, the anger and the tears—she loved him. Hating him would have been less painful. But it would be easier to reverse the tides than to change the way she felt.

"Trey . . ."

He kept his gaze riveted on the gate and beyond.

She dredged the depths of her courage to ask a question that had plagued her since the night she had discovered Robert and Trey were brothers. She knew she was risking Trey's wrath, but her need to know was great. She had to ask. There might never be another opportunity. "Robert . . ." she began hesitantly. "You knew him much differently than I did. What was he really like?"

He slanted her a look, carefully weighing her request. "Why do you want to know?"

"I've had a lot of time to think, and I realize how little I knew him."

"Did you have so many suitors that he was just one of a crowd?"

She flinched inwardly, but ignored the barb and forged ahead. "Robert must have been very special for you to have loved him so much."

Trey swallowed hard and looked away. "He was."

The simple, unadorned statement told her more than a treatise. The depth of his feeling was betrayed by the sudden huskiness of his voice, by the rigid line of his jaw as he struggled to control his emotion. "Talk to me, Trey," she coaxed softly. "Tell me what made you care so much."

He stared out toward the gate, his eyes narrowed, haunted. He was quiet for so long that Alana didn't think he was going to answer her question. Finally, he sighed and began to speak. "Robert was good . . . kind . . . sensitive. Perhaps too sensitive. He had the gentle soul of a poet."

Trey's words sharpened her hazy memory of the

earnest young man. Guileless blue eyes. A shy smile. An eagerness to please. Alana felt the prick of tears behind her eyelids as she listened to the unfulfilled hopes for a future that had never materialized. "I remember he once gave me a book of poems by Elizabeth Barrett Browning. I still have it."

"He always loved poetry," Trey said quietly. "When we were kids, Robert used to follow me around. At first, I got mad at him. Called him a pest, told him to get lost. But he'd look so hurt, so sad . . ." Trey's voice choked. "After a while, I just let him tag along. As we grew older, we became friends, then best friends. Actually, owning a ranch was originally his idea. Whenever life became . . . difficult . . . for him, he'd talk about running off, heading West.

"His dream was to find a place with a bluff that afforded a view of the distant mountain ranges. He believed the most beautiful sight in the world would be the sunrise from that bluff. He talked of spending afternoons in the shade of a tree reading poetry.

"Robert was constantly urging me to wind up business matters and head out to California, but I was always too busy. I kept putting him off. I told him that maybe when I returned from Europe." Trey's voice roughened, caught. "Then, instead of coming home as I planned, I decided to spend the summer in Barcelona. If I hadn't, I would have been there when he needed me. He would still be alive."

The anguish in his voice tore at Alana's heart. At last she understood the truly special devotion that had existed between the two brothers, and why Trey had directed all of his fury over his brother's suicide at her. In his heart, he blamed himself. *He* felt responsible. How horrible it must have been to find Robert's body. She couldn't imagine the pain.

She placed her hand on his arm. "Please, Trey.

Don't torture yourself this way. If you must blame someone, blame me."

Trey turned his head. There was no antipathy in his gaze . . . only sadness.

She ventured a timid smile. "Does the ranch have a view like the one Robert once dreamed of?"

Trey nodded. "I would have bought Rancho Prado del Sol for that reason alone."

"Where is it?"

"There's a bluff not far from the cave where we spent the night of your accident. It even has a shade tree. Robert would have loved it . . ." Trey's voice trailed off and he looked away.

An hour crawled by. Minutes filled with memories. Seconds filled with regret. Alana debated whether to tell Trey about the child she was carrying. The words formed on her tongue, but she swallowed them back. Trey didn't need to carry a heavier burden. If they survived this crisis, there would be plenty of time for revelations. If not . . . She resolutely banished the unpleasant thought.

But as the angry scene they had played out on the veranda the night before sifted through her thoughts, she realized she sorely needed to set one matter right before it was too late. "Should anything happen . . ." Her voice faltered. Clearing her throat, she tried again. "If anything should happen to either of us, I just want you to know that I love you—and I always will."

He started to speak, but she silenced him by placing her fingers lightly on his mouth. "Please hear me out. Nothing happened between Noah and me. He's a friend, nothing more. I swear to you there's been no other man in my life except Phillip, and—God forgive me—I never loved Phillip half as much as I love you."

Trey's eyes seemed to plumb the depths of her soul. Then his gaze wandered over her face, as though fixing it in his memory. A second stretched into an eternity as she willed him to accept the truth. Tension turned into electricity of a different sort until the air crackled with awareness. Slowly, he reached out. His hand curved around the nape of her neck, then exerted tender force to bring her close.

Alana's heart hammered like a caged bird's as Trey dipped his head and slanted his mouth over hers. Her lips parted with a sigh, a sound that was part pleasure, part anticipation, part homecoming. Her eyes closed. She leaned into the kiss—and was lost, caught in a maelstrom of sensation too powerful to resist: the texture of his lips, the taste of his mouth, the beating of two hearts.

Suddenly, repeated blasts of gunfire shattered the stillness.

The sound of galloping hooves and war whoops filled the air. Alana and Trey jerked apart. Alana picked up the revolver, then, crouching low, moved to her post at a window. Next to her, she heard Trey flip down the lever of the Winchester and click it back into place.

"Alana . . ."

Her eyes luminous with fear and hope, she turned toward him.

Trey kept his gaze fixed on the view of the gate, his expression one of fierce concentration. "Be careful," he warned gruffly.

"You, too," she replied softly, heartened that in spite of their desperate situation, a reluctant show of concern had been forced out of him.

Recalling Trey's advice, Alana drew in a calming breath as panic threatened to unravel her. She needed to stay collected, to keep her wits sharp. She wondered if Consuelo in the opposite wing of the house was experiencing the same fear. She hoped her friend was safe behind a barricaded door with a stockpile of ammunition for protection. Cautiously, she edged open the shutter and peered out. She shuddered at the sight that greeted her.

A groups of gunmen, or *banditos*—perhaps six or eight, she couldn't be sure of the exact number—were gathered behind the locked gate. Heavily armed and brandishing pistols, the bandits wore sombreros pulled down over their foreheads and bandanas tied over the lower halves of their faces. Bandoliers studded with ammunition crisscrossed their chests. The leader, whom she recognized as Vega, gestured angrily at the locked gate. As she watched, he aimed his gun at the heavy lock. Before he could fire, a blast from Trey's rifle knocked one of Vega's men out of the saddle. The group scattered amid a flurry of Spanish oaths.

To Alana, the waiting that followed was even more grueling than the time that had preceded it. She could see nothing out of the ordinary, yet knew the bandits were regrouping just beyond the gate. Finally, she heard the sound she dreaded most. A *thud* overhead was followed by scrabbling noises on the roof as heavy footsteps tromped across the tiles. "Dear God," she gasped, fear spurting through her, "they're on the roof." Her heart beat in triple time. A shot rang out from the opposite wing—and the noise stopped. Consuelo, Alana realized, as she expelled a sigh of relief. Later, if they all survived, she'd be sure to commend her friend on her excellent marksmanship.

More time passed, each minute eons slow. Still nothing happened. She cautiously eased her cramped muscles. "Do you think Vega is abandoning his plan?" she whispered hopefully. "Maybe he's decided to retreat."

Trey gave her a pitying glance. "Don't worry, vixen. As long I'm alive, I won't let anything happen to you."

Suddenly, Vega's face illuminated Alana's memory like a bolt of lightning. His cruel mouth flashed an evil, mocking smile. His eyes glowed dully—flat, obsidian, snakelike. *El serpiente*. He'd never give up, she acknowledged desolately.

Daylight was waning. Shadows elongated, their hue deepening from lavender to mauve to purple. Compared with a day fraught with tension, night would be intolerable.

Glancing up, Alana spotted a man crest the peak of the roof opposite her. Both she and Trey fired, but the intruder flattened himself against the tiles and dodged the bullets. In a blur of movement, riders repeatedly charged the gate, then quickly retreated. Vega's band seemed to be coming at them from all directions. Eyes darting from gate to rooftop, Alana fired repeatedly. Judging by the number of gunshots she heard, she knew Consuelo was doing likewise. From the hallway outside the bedroom, she detected running footsteps. Before she could make sense of them, she heard a heavy scraping sound. Dazedly, she recognized the noise as the oak beam that barred the main entrance being shoved aside. A scream clawed its way up her throat; sheer willpower held it at back.

"Hurry! Hurry!" Vega hollered as he rallied is men to the front.

Alana was drenched in a cold sweat. The enemy had gained entry.

Chapter 24

"Halt, Vega, or I'll shoot."

Alana picked up her skirts and sprinted after Trey. She rounded the corner of the south wing and stopped as she saw Trey with his pistol drawn. Vega was standing, arms raised, gun in his right hand, with his back toward Trey.

"All right, Vega. Turn around slowly and drop the gun."

Alana marveled at Trey's composure. He sounded as unruffled as he had when bluffing Colin across a poker table.

"Ah, *señor,* what do you plan to do now? Shoot a man in the back?"

Alana caught her lower lip between her teeth. If Vega was scared, he didn't show it. In fact, if anything, he sounded belligerent.

"Turn around! Now!"

Vega turned, though none too quickly. "You cannot win this game. My men have you outnumbered. You should have left the rancho while you had the chance."

Trey pulled back the hammer on his pistol, the metallic *click* ominous in the gathering shadows. "Skip the advice, Vega. Just toss the gun down."

"Whatever you say, *señor,* you are the boss." With studied deliberation, he lowered his right arm and casually tossed the gun to the floor. A sudden flick of his wrist brought a thin knife to his hand. A split second later, the sliver of steel sang through the air with deadly precision.

Trey moved to one side, but too late.

Alana's eyes widened in horror as the blade embedded itself to the hilt in Trey's shoulder. The impact drove him to his knees. His revolver clattered noisily to the floor.

Vega kicked the gun out of reach, then shoved aside the bar and flung the door open, allowing his henchmen to pour through. One of the bandits, seeing Trey on his knees, the knife protruding from his shoulder, raised his rifle butt and brought it crashing down against Trey's head.

"Stop!" Alana cried. "Get away from him." Using both hands to hold the pistol steady, she pointed it at the man nearest Trey.

The men froze, noticing her for the first time at the end of the hall.

"Ah, *chica,*" Vega cajoled. "Put that thing down before you get hurt." He took a step toward her.

Though her instincts cried retreat, she held her ground. "Take one step closer, and I'll shoot. I swear I will."

"You are very brave, *señora,* but also very foolish. You cannot shoot all of us. We are too many." Arrogantly ignoring her warning, Vega started toward her.

Alana sucked in her breath, pulled back the hammer, and squeezed the trigger. A hollow *click* signaled an empty chamber. The men howled with laughter at her look of dismay. Trey struggled to rise, but before he could get to his feet, the bandit struck him a vicious blow across the temple. He crumpled in a heap.

Another of Vega's band leveled his gun at Trey's inert form. "No, please," Alana cried.

Grinning, Vega pushed his cohort's arm aside. "No need to waste a good bullet, *amigo*. He'll wake up with the angels."

Alana shook her head, silently refuting Vega's words. Vega smiled cunningly. "Ah, *señora*, finally our day has come. Vega will show you how a real man makes love to a woman."

She took a step backward, then another, and another. Vega's grin broadened. Turning, she fled with Vega in close pursuit. His men scattered in the opposite direction, eager to loot and plunder. Vega reached out to catch her skirt but missed by a hair's breadth. Panting, heart racing, Alana ducked back into the dining room. Knowing Vega was right behind her, she slammed the door closed, then, summoning strength she didn't know she possessed, shoved a small chest in front of it. It wouldn't keep him out for long, but it would buy her precious time. Her eyes darted around the room, searching for a means to defend herself.

All the bullets Trey had given her were piled on a small braided rug beneath the window where she had kept guard. She ran over to them and, scooping them up, tried to jam them into the cylinder. Her hands trembled so that two of the bullets dropped to the floor and rolled across the room. She nearly sobbed in frustration.

Vega kicked at the door. The small chest proved a flimsy barrier against his determined onslaught. The door crashed open and Vega charged through. Alana pointed the gun and fired. But her aim was wide and the bullet lodged harmlessly in the wall. Vega rushed at her. He backhanded her across the face. Her head snapped to one side. The force of the blow sent her crashing against the wall, then sliding down, to land half-sprawled, half-sitting at his feet, the Smith and Wesson still clutched in her outstretched hand.

Vega planted his booted foot on her wrist. "Let go of the gun, *chica*, or I'll crush your hand."

She stared up at him, not understanding. It was hard to think. One side of her face felt as if it were on fire.

He increased the pressure.

Agonizing pain shot outward from her wrist into her palm and fingers until she grew faint and nauseated.

"Let go, *chica*."

Slowly, reluctantly, she loosened her grip.

Vega bent down and jerked the gun from her slack fingers. He grabbed a fistful of hair and yanked her head back, so hard that it felt as though her hair would be ripped out by the roots. Her eyes smarted with tears, and she furiously blinked back the moisture. Vega lowered her face to hers until he was so close she could count his oily pores. His fetid breath almost made her retch.

"It's just you and me, *chica*. When I'm finished with you, maybe I'll let each of my men have a turn. After they're done, you'll be food for the buzzards."

From a distance, she heard a door being smashed and Consuelo's scream. New terror assaulted Alana. "If it's money you want . . ."

"You're hardly in a position to bargain. There's nothing you can give me that I can't take for myself." Still gripping her hair, he stepped between her legs and fumbled with the buttons on his fly.

Alana scooted away until her back was flush with the wall. Fear tasted as real as the coppery blood from her cut lip. She kicked out at him, but he slapped her again until her ears rang, and she subsided with a whimper.

"Puta!" he spat. His hold on her hair tightened, cruelly forcing her head up and back. With a malevolent smile on his lips, he hooked his fingers into the neckline of her bodice and ripped downward. The fabric split from neck to waist, buttons flying in all directions. Her chemise suffered the same ill treatment, and her breasts were bared to his greedy gaze. He covered one breast with a callused hand and squeezed roughly.

She gazed at Vega in raw terror. Lust chiseled his features into a wolfish mask. He meant to rape her, then kill her—just as he had killed Trey. And she felt completely, utterly helpless to stop him. He pushed her down and forced her legs wider. She felt a hard object nuzzle the small of her back.

The derringer. Somehow, it must have slid between the braided rug and the floor.

Hope rekindled, she bucked, trying to dislodge Vega while her hand groped for the small gun. "Get off me, you filthy swine." Mindless of his reaction, she clawed his face with her nails.

He yelped in pain as her fingernails plowed deep furrows in his pockmarked cheek. He shifted his weight to escape her attack. The slight movement allowed her to roll and twist beneath him, spilling him onto his side. She scrambled to her feet, the derringer firmly in hand. "Don't move," she panted, her chest heaving. "At this range, there's no way I'd miss a target your size."

His black eyes glittered with amusement. "Would a fine lady like you shoot an unarmed man in cold blood?" he taunted.

"She might not, *señor*, but I would."

Alana gasped in disbelief. She turned slowly toward the sound of Trey's voice, scarcely daring to believe that her husband was still alive. What if this was just a dream. A cruel hoax perpetrated by sheer desperation? The tears shimmering in her eyes blurred the beloved figure filling the doorway. "Trey . . ."

"My men and I will take charge from here on in, sir."

Trey stepped aside and allowed Noah Stone entry. Alana's jaw dropped in surprise as Noah strode across the room, jerked Vega to his feet, and handcuffed him. His face was familiar, but gone were the distinctive Texas drawl and the easy manner. A silver badge glimmered on his chest. "This culprit will be out of commission for a long time. His partner in San Diego has already been arrested."

Clutching the frayed edges of her garments together, Alana moved toward Trey like a sleepwalker. As she drew closer, relief gave way to alarm. Even in the dusk-filled room, she could see the effort that standing was costing him. His skin was chalky. The white ring around his mouth testified to his iron control against the pain that racked him. Blood dripped down the fingers of his left hand and puddled on the floor. One side of his light blue chambray shirt was stained dark crimson and plastered to his chest. Blood matted his hair where the bandit had struck him.

She slid her arm around his waist, lending her support; he leaned against her, accepting her help. Their eyes met for a brief moment. They had survived—not unscathed, not without cost, but they had survived. Then they looked away. Their last exchange aside, the yawning chasm formed by a single deed was not easily breached.

And in the end, as it had in the beginning, it all came back to Robert.

They had reached an impasse. An unbearable longing ripped through Alana as she thought of what could never be. She thought of the dreams, the hopes, the happiness that had died unborn.

"I'll get this snake out of your sight, then be back to take your statements." Noah hustled his prisoner out of the room. Vega, his face sullen, passed them a final time with a look so evil that Alana cringed. From the voices elsewhere in the house, she determined that Noah's men were corralling the rest of his band.

"Your wounds need tending." Alana tamped down emotions that threatened to rise up and overwhelm her. Purposely, she kept her tone businesslike. "I need to get you to bed."

A small smile tugged at the corners of Trey's mouth as he allowed her to lead him toward the bedroom. "That was my thought, vixen, the very first time I saw you."

Consuelo, looking a little bruised, a little tattered, but nonetheless intact, charged into the room with a lamp. "*Dios!* What a day this has been."

Still deathly pale from his ordeal, his chest swathed in bandages and another bound around his head, Trey sat propped up by pillows. Alana, Noah, and Consuelo had gathered at his beside, eager to review the day's events.

Alana was the first to speak. Turning to Noah, she asked the two questions that were uppermost in all their minds. "Who are you?" she demanded. "And how did you know what Vega was planning?"

"Noah Stone, ma'am." He affected his Texas drawl and flashed his dimples. Then his smile faded, and he dropped all pretense. "I'm Noah Stone, Mrs. Matthews, federal agent appointed by a special governmental committee to investigate illegal immigration."

"Illegal immigration?" She shook her head in confusion. "What does that have to do with why Vega tried to kill us?"

"Hernando Alphonso Pablo de la Vega, or Vega as he calls himself, is a labor contractor who works with several partners to recruit cheap Mexican labor to work in the mines and fields here in the United States. A congressional act passed last year outlaws labor agreements with foreign immigrants prior to their arrival here in the United States. This makes what Vega and his friends were doing illegal. One of the senators got wind that this scheme was going on and organized a group to quietly investigate. Officials have suspected Vega for a long time, but we needed more evidence. It was my job to collect the proof."

"I never realized a few Mexicans in search of work and better wages would be of such interest to the government," Trey observed thoughtfully.

"This activity, while limited at present, is rapidly gaining momentum. Ever since the 1880 Chinese Exclusion Act barred the entry of Chinese laborers, there has been an ever growing demand for more workers. Americans have always depended on a constantly replenished supply of cheap labor to perform unskilled and unattractive tasks. The railroads, the mines, and now agriculture are desperate for manpower. They're willing to ignore federal laws if it means more money in their pockets. Vega was hauling in a tidy profit for his trouble."

"But why did he try to murder us?"

"Your ranch is a perfect spot for his activities. He tried to drive you out, and when that failed, he resorted to more drastic means to remove you."

"Then Paco was right." Trey shifted, trying to find a more comfortable position. "Vega poisoned the cattle, then claimed it was anthrax."

Noah chuckled. "There really is an anthrax vaccine, but there was no way I could get hold of it in time to save your livestock. What we really gave your cows was plain old water. I suspected what Vega was doing and hoped to call his bluff. Luckily we did, although I'm afraid you'll lose more of your cattle. Vega has admitted he poisoned twenty-five head. We won't be able to save them."

Trey grimaced. The effort caused a fresh paroxysm of pain to explode in his head. His shoulder throbbed unmercifully.

Attuned to his discomfort, Alana placed her hand over his on top of the counterpane and squeezed sympathetically. The laudanum she had given him earlier should soon take effect.

Consuelo patted Noah on the back and beamed her approval. "I always said you were one smart *hombre.*"

"Shucks, ma'am," he drawled. "All those pretty words are gonna make me blush."

Alana leaned forward, serious despite Noah's attempt at levity. "Maria and her baby. Are they all right?"

"They were fine yesterday when I left them with the padres at the mission. The little fella even sported a brand-new tooth. Maria was able to supply the rest of the information I needed to form a case against Vega. In exchange, she and her husband will be allowed to remain in the United States."

"Who's Maria?" Trey asked.

"Just a wife trying to be reunited with her husband regardless of cost." Alana smiled at Trey, remembering the young woman's bravery and determination.

"I found her stealing tortillas the other night. I hid her in the stable, but Noah discovered us. She disappeared by the next morning when I went to check on her. She left the rosary as her way of saying thank you."

Trey closed his eyes briefly and nodded. What a jealous fool he had been to accuse Alana of having an assignation with Noah. No wonder she had been so furious—and so hurt. Could she ever forgive his stupidity? Where she was concerned it was only one in a chain of stupid acts that he had committed.

"What happens now?" Consuelo asked, her dark eyes dancing with glee. "You put Vega in the jail and throw away the key?"

"Bloodthirsty piece of baggage, aren't you?" Noah grinned at her affectionately. "Vega is under armed guard. In the morning, my men and I will escort him back to San Diego, where he'll be charged. He committed a federal offense, with additional charges tacked on for attempted murder. I suspect he'll be spending a long time in a federal penitentiary."

Alana breathed a sigh of relief. The man was vicious, a menace to society. It was good to know he would no longer prey on the innocent and vulnerable. "You mentioned he had a partner in San Diego. What part did he play in all this?"

Noah leaned back, stretched his long legs, and crossed one ankle over the other.

"Vega's friend worked in a position where he often overheard businessmen complain about how much trouble they were having finding cheap labor. Afterward, he'd approach them and offer to supply as many bodies as needed to fill those jobs—for a hefty fee, of course. A third man worked the cities of the Mexican interior, recruiting impoverished young men who wanted a better life."

"So your work is all finished?" Consuelo asked, unable to conceal her disappointment at the prospect of Noah's departure.

"Not really." He slumped further down in his seat. "Not unless the Diaz regime in Mexico improves life for the poor in rural areas. Until then, Mexicans will continue to cross the border to eke out a subsistence. But by clapping these culprits in jail, we will send a message to the others that the government is serious about prosecuting offenders."

The day's events had exacted a heavy toll on the room's occupants. Consuelo yawned. Noah fell silent. Alana felt as though her limbs were weighted with lead. She glanced at Trey and discovered he had fallen asleep. The medication had finally taken effect.

Of one accord, the three looked from one to the other, then rose and left the room.

Once in the hallway, Noah draped his arm over Consuelo's shoulder. Dropping his voice, he addressed Alana, "Are you going to be all right?"

She nodded, not trusting herself to speak. Sensing they wished to spend a final night together, she bid them goodbye and returned to her room.

Though her body was exhausted, her mind refused to rest. She sat alone in the dark with her thoughts. It was time to leave. Now, while Trey was too weak to prevent her. Now, while her resolution was still strong. She didn't want to go, but knew she must. If she waited, there might not be another chance.

She wrapped her arms around her waist and rocked back and forth. *Dear God, why did loving have to hurt so much?* But her eyes remained dry. Her grief went beyond tears.

Long before dawn stained the sky with a riot of brilliant color, Alana's bags were packed. She sat at her dressing table, pen poised in hand, and pondered what to write. At last, the words flowed freely.

We both know I'm not what you need. I'm only a reminder of the pain and suffering I brought you and your family. It's time we stop allowing past mistakes to rule the present and get on with our lives. I hope the ranch brings you all you ever dreamed of.

I will always love you,
Alana

She folded the note, placed it in an envelope, and sealed it shut. She thought about leaving it in her room for Consuelo to deliver, but the opportunity to see Trey one last time was too great to resist. Her footsteps were like muffled echoes against the tiles as she made her way through the darkened house that she had come to regard as home. Cautiously, she turned the door handle to Trey's bedroom and peered inside. Although the room was steeped in darkness, she could make out Trey's still form on the bed. Careful not to awaken him, she tiptoed closer.

Even in sleep, his eyes appeared sunken and ringed with dark circles, attesting to the amount of blood he had lost the day before. One eye was swollen shut. Blood stained the dressings at his shoulder and around his head, but she was enormously relieved that the stains weren't fresh. He looked defenseless, and infinitely dear. A vast wealth of tenderness surged through her, nearly undermining her resolve to leave.

But she shoved the treacherous feelings aside. She placed the envelope on the small chest between the water pitcher and basin where he was sure to see it later. Unable to stop herself, she laid her hand lightly on his whiskered cheek and brushed her lips across his.

"Goodbye, my love," she whispered, then left before she could change her mind.

She returned to her room and lay down on the bed, hoping to get a few hours of sleep before it was time to leave. At first light, Noah would discover her waiting for him just outside the rear gate. If he didn't agree to take her with him, she'd follow him. Either way, she was leaving Rancho Prado del Sol. Leaving Trey. He had nothing to give a child but hate and anger. She couldn't bear the thought of her child becoming an instrument of his malignant vengeance.

Chapter 25

Trey drifted in and out of sleep, feeling as weak as a newborn kitten. The dull ache in his head throbbed in counterpoint to the sharp stabbing in his shoulder. When he did pry his good eye open, the other seemed glued shut, and the room always looked dim with either closed shutters or a low-burning lamp. He imagined Alana there nursing him, coaxing small sips of cold water past his parched lips, spooning a vile-tasting medicine down his throat when the pain become unbearable.

Faces from the past flitted through his dreams. Robert—easily hurt and overly sensitive. His mother—critical and accusing. He muttered incoherently and called out to them, but both turned away. Neither seemed to hear.

Trey awakened at midnight, his body drenched in sweat. Disoriented, he looked about the bedroom. The house was quiet, the wick from the lamp trimmed low. Rain pattered softly on the tiled roof, its gentle cadence soothing, lulling, peaceful. He slumped back against the pillows, his mind still fuzzy, but clearer than it had been since the attack.

The dream had exhumed old memories. Estelle Matthews Prescott had been a formidable, domineering woman with rarely a kind word for either of her sons. Her constant barrage of criticism had always been prefaced by the phrase, "I'm only telling you this for your own good . . ."

While his mother's admonitions had strengthened his character, making him determined to prove her wrong, her approach had had the opposite effect on Robert. It had undermined his confidence, filling him with doubt and feelings of rejection. He had wanted so badly to be accepted, to be loved, first as a boy and later as a young man. No wonder he had fallen apart when the girl he loved turned down his ardent proposal. If it hadn't been Alana, it could as easily have been someone else.

Alana . . .

Ever since Robert's suicide, Trey had made her the scapegoat. *If it wasn't for her, Robert would still be alive.* He had repeated his mother's litany so often, it had become his own. For a long time, Trey stared sightlessly at the ceiling. The fogginess slowly left his brain, revealing a clarity to his thinking that hadn't been present since the day he had found Robert's body. Truth dawned unclouded by emotion.

Finally, after all this time, he could accept the fact that Robert, and Robert alone, must take responsibility for his actions. While Alana's rejection of his marriage proposal had surely been painful, most young men would not have reacted by ending their own lives. Robert's suicide wasn't Alana's fault. And neither was it his. A single tear trickled down his cheek. Then, before he could gain control, the dam burst. Hoarse, raspy, gut-wrenching sobs broke the stillness.

Alone in the dead of night, weak and hurting, Trey finally released the healing tears that until now he had denied himself.

Physically and emotionally spent in the aftermath of the storm, Trey dried his face. Peacefulness enfolded him, surpassing anything he had ever experienced. In that microcosm of time, he forgave Alana for any role she might have unwittingly played in Robert's death—and in so doing, forgave himself.

Alana . . .

His beautiful, beguiling, bewitching wife. He wanted to go to her and beg her forgiveness. If the hour wasn't so late . . . If every ounce of his energy hadn't been sapped . . . In the morning, after he had rested, he'd go to her, implore her understanding.

Admit that he loved her.

A smile stole across his face. He had loved her for so long, he didn't remember when hatred had withered and love had begun to bloom. He fell into a dreamless sleep, the smile still on his lips.

Trey woke before daybreak, aching in every bone and muscle of his body. The sound of birds chirping outside the bedroom window made him wince with pain. Paramount in his mind was the need to find Alana. There were so many things he had to tell her. He'd apologize for the abominable way he had treated her, get down on his knees if he had to.

He swung his feet to the floor. The banging in his head increased. His left arm felt heavy, useless, and hurt like the devil. Calling on his reserves of strength, he stood up. The room spun like a top. He staggered and grabbed the chest alongside the bed for support. The pitcher and washbasin crashed to the floor. A white envelope slipped unnoticed behind the chest. He managed to take a half-dozen steps across the room before his legs buckled, sending him sprawling.

Consuelo rushed in, dark hair flying in wild disarray, and knelt beside him. "*Señor*." she scolded. "Let me help you back to bed."

Trey's head felt stuffed with cotton, making it difficult to think. His mouth felt as dry as the Mojave. "Where's Alana?" he demanded, his voice a croak. He wrapped his hand around Consuelo's wrist, his grip surprisingly strong for his weakened condition. "Where's my wife?"

"I'm here," Alana herself answered. He looked across the room and saw her standing in the doorway. Even in his delirium, he could see that her face was filled with anguish.

"I dreamed you left me," Trey gasped, trying to push himself into a sitting position.

Alana unfastened the bonnet of her traveling outfit and went to him. "No, I haven't left you. I'll be here for as long as you need me. As long as you want me to stay."

"You must get back into bed, *señor.*" Consuelo took one of his arms, Alana the other. Together, the two women half-carried, half-dragged Trey back to bed. Consuelo pushed him down on the edge of the mattress. "*Dios!*" she exclaimed. "Your skin feels like it's on fire."

"Your shoulder," Alana murmured. "It's bleeding again."

Consuelo grabbed both of Trey's ankles, lifting and pivoting him as she did so, while Alana gently but firmly pushed until once again he was flat on his back.

"I have to get up. See to the cattle, repair the fences," Trey mumbled.

Consuelo wagged a finger beneath his nose. "You will be going nowhere for the time being, *señor*. Unless you remain in bed, the *señora* will be two times a widow."

Trey was in no condition to argue. Willingly, he submitted to their ministrations.

Alana tore strips of cloth to press against the widening stain on his shoulder. He had lost a great deal of blood. Fear raced through her. She couldn't bear the thought of losing Trey; he meant the world to her. How could she ever have imagined living apart from him?

She had come so close to leaving him. She'd been stepping cautiously down the corridor, suitcase in hand, when she'd heard him fall and had come to see what had happened. From the moment she had seen him lying there hurt and helpless, his body racked with fever, she had known she couldn't leave. Along with the knowledge had come an overwhelming sense of relief. Deep in her heart, she had never really wanted to say goodbye. She shivered, thinking how dangerously close she had come to abandoning hope of a future with him.

Consuelo bustled out but soon returned with a basin of water and a cloth. She began to wipe Trey's face. "We have to get his fever down."

Within minutes, Alana was satisfied the bleeding was under control, and she took over for Consuelo, tenderly bathing his body with the tepid water. Consuelo picked up the broken glass on the floor, then left after promising to find Isabel, who was a skilled healer. Alana continued to sponge Trey. A single phrase kept playing through her mind like the fragment of a song.

He needed her.

Thinking Trey was asleep, she turned away from the bed to open a shutter, but he caught her skirt in his fist and held tight. "Don't go," he rasped.

Leaning over him, she brushed a kiss across his brow. "Never, my love."

With a ragged sigh, he succumbed once again to sleep, her skirt still clenched in his hand.

* * *

The next week passed in a blur.

Twice a day, the old Indian woman applied her evil-smelling poultices to the angry red wound on Trey's shoulder, then redressed the site with clean strips of cloth. When the fever was upon him, he restlessly thrashed from side to side. His mind played strange tricks on him. At times, he was still fighting off Vega and his cutthroat band. Other times, he called out Alana's name—or Robert's. To quiet him, Alana spoke in the low, soothing tones one would use to settle a fretful child. When all else failed, she sang to him: lullabies and ballads, songs from battlefields, theaters, and churches, anything and everything she could remember to allay her ever-present fear that in his agitation he'd break open the knife wound and start bleeding again.

When the fever loosened its hold, she changed the sheets and fluffed his pillows. Then she spooned liquid between his parched lips and coaxed him to swallow. She refused to leave his bedside except to bathe and change her clothes.

"You will make yourself sick, *señora,*" Consuelo scolded after finding her slumped in a chair. "If you will not think of yourself, you must think of the *bebé.*"

Alana's weary eyes widened in surprise. "How did you know I was pregnant?"

"A woman isn't as easily fooled as a man." Consuelo shrugged philosophically, then offered a smile.

Alana smiled for the first time in days, happy to be able to share her news, but her smile faded quickly as she realized she wouldn't be able to keep her condition a secret much longer. She had began to suffer occasional bouts of nausea. The sickness hit suddenly at unexpected times of the day or night, causing her to make a headlong rush for the chamber pot. During those episodes, she was grateful that Trey was too sick to notice. Her gaze slid to his still figure on the bed. How would he react when she told him about the child? Assuming he survived. The fear slithered across her mind, making her recoil in terror.

The slight motion didn't escape Consuelo's shrewd eyes. She squeezed Alana's hand reassuringly. "Do not worry, the *señor* is strong. You will have many *muchachos*."

At Consuelo's suggestion, a cot was set up so that Alana could be available when Trey needed her and could rest while he slept.

Alana was beginning to despair of Trey ever getting well. She lost all track of time. Day flowed into night and night into day in a never ending cycle. She couldn't see the slightest improvement in his condition. Each day, his face grew more gaunt, his eyes more sunken. She smoothed a damp lock of hair from his brow and bit her lip to keep from crying.

"Please get well, my love," she whispered. "Give me a chance to prove I'm worthy of your love."

Fever became a faceless enemy, stealing Trey's strength, robbing her of hope. As she sat next to his bedside late one night, she fought the urge to put her head in her hands and weep. She was so tired, so very tired. Resting her head against the back of the chair, she fell into a fitful sleep. At the sound of Trey's restless tossing about, she sat bolt-upright.

Knowing the actions by rote, she wearily dragged herself to her feet and began to sponge his body with cool water. His skin fairly sizzled beneath the cloth. It had never felt so hot.

"I've got to go . . ." He kicked off the covers, leaving his body naked across the wrinkled bedding.

"Shh, my love," she soothed. "I'm right here."

"Need to find . . ."

He twisted and turned, his actions growing more agitated in spite of her efforts to calm him. His green eyes were glazed, uncomprehending. One look into them told her that none of her words were penetrating the feverish haze clouding his mind. Alana dodged just in time to avoid being struck by the arm he flung suddenly outward as he struggled to push himself into a sitting position.

"Trey, don't," Alana pleaded. "You'll hurt yourself." She placed her hands on his shoulders and tried to force them to the mattress. Regardless of his weakened condition, he was amazingly strong. She wished Consuelo were there to help, but she didn't dare leave Trey alone even for the few minutes it would take to fetch her.

Not knowing what else to do, she climbed onto the bed and used her own body to physically restrain him. He tried weakly to dislodge her weight, but she held tightly to the wrist of his uninjured arm with both hands. Using her legs, she anchored Trey's securely beneath hers.

All the while, she kept up a monologue. Deliberately keeping her voice low and even, she let her words flow smoothly, assuming a rhythm that was almost musical. While he hovered in delirium, she told him truths she had never dared tell him when he was conscious. She talked of Phillip . . . and Robert. Of meeting Colin O'Shea and how frightened she had been at being alone and penniless. Of how hurt she had been by her father's denial of her. She told him about the baby—his baby, their baby. And when all other subjects were exhausted, she began to recite poetry.

" 'How do I love thee? Let me count the ways . . .' "

She smoothed her hand tenderly over his cheek. Beneath the bearded stubble, his skin felt hot, but no longer searing. She breathed a sigh of relief and offered up a silent prayer of thanks.

The demon fever left Trey's body by slow degrees, and she felt him relax beneath her weight. Grateful and exhausted, she told herself that in just a minute she would return to her cot, but her supple length instinctively molded against his.

She awoke with the vague unease that she was being watched. Her eyes flew open to find sunlight streaming into the room through the partially opened shutter. She stirred and found herself pressed the length of a hard male body, one arm resting against a broad chest covered with a thick mat of dark curls and her leg flexed familiarly across a heavily muscled thigh. Leisurely, her eyes measured the breadth of the torso that was swathed in white linen, then wandered up the strong column of his throat to trace the stubborn angle of his jaw. Her gaze rested on the tempting cleft of his chin. Before she could stop herself, her fingers lightly touched the slight indentation that intrigued her so.

A lean hand caught her wrist. Startled, her gaze flew upward to find Trey watching her, his eyes clear and lucid, his mouth curved into a faint smile.

"Trey?"

His smile broadened. "Were you expecting someone else, or will I do?"

She blinked back sudden tears. So great was her relief that she wanted to laugh and cry at the same time. "N-no," she stammered. "I mean yes. You'll do perfectly."

"Glad to hear that, vixen." He chuckled. "For a

while there, I was afraid Noah Stone was going to ride off with your affections."

Alana brushed her knuckles across his stubbled jaw. "No chance of that happening—ever."

He hugged her closer, then grimaced from the effort it had cost. "Speaking of Noah, we ought to get up. I want to thank him before he leaves."

Alana's hand stilled. Concern colored her eyes a deeper shade as she looked up at him. "It's too late for that, Trey. Noah left with his prisoners a week ago."

"A week?"

"You've been very ill," she hastened to explain. "You lost a lot of blood from the wound in your shoulder, then infection set it. You haven't been yourself since the night of Vega's attack."

Trey started to rise, only to fall weakly back against the pillows. Stunned, he tried to assimilate the information. He had no clear recollection of anything that had happened since that night, only snatches of memory, like fragments of broken glass. But through it all, he knew Alana had always been there, talking to him, singing, touching, cajoling.

The door burst open, and Consuelo breezed in. Upon seeing the two of them in bed together, she stopped in her tracks. Trey automatically drew the rumpled sheet over both of them. Consuelo placed her hands on her hips, a wide grin spreading across her face. "*Santa Maria!*" she exclaimed in satisfaction. "Finally, you two in one bed."

Convalescence was a slow, tedious process. Trey chafed at his inability to perform his usual activities. Thankfully, Paco, along with several ranch hands, had straggled back. They could at least keep the place running while he recuperated. This period, however, provided ample time for him to reflect on past mistakes. He had been a bastard. Driven by thoughts of revenge and goaded by physical desire, he had treated Alana abominably. Yet through it all, she had remained steadfast and loyal. As soon as he regained his strength, he would try to make things right between them. Every day, he forced himself to sit up when he wanted to rest, made himself eat though he had little appetite. And every day, his strength returned.

"Ah, *señor,* the wound no longer festers." Isabel's seamed face broke into a pleased grin. "A few more days, and you will feel like yourself again."

"If I spend one more day cooped up in this room, my brain will fester and I'll go mad."

Alana and Consuelo exchanged glances, then nodded as one.

"But only as far as the veranda," Consuelo cautioned.

"And only if I go with you," Alana added.

Isabel held out a thick sweater. "Wear this, *señor.* There is a chill in the air."

Trey acquiesced, knowing it was senseless to argue. With Alana's arm around his waist, he leaned lightly on her, enjoying the feel of her, inhaling the delicate flowery scent that she made uniquely her own. After seeing him comfortably situated in a large chair in a sunny corner of the patio, Consuelo and Isabel left them alone. Alana settled on a bench next to him.

Sunlight leaked through the vines to form a spidery mosaic on the worn tiles. Birds twittered noisily as they hopped among the branches. Alana placed her hand on her abdomen and smiled dreamily, thinking of her unborn child. Optimism and contentment enveloped her. Then her contentment vanished.

If only she could reconcile her role in Robert's death, her happiness would be complete. He had offered his heart, wanted her to share his life, yet she had callously, insensitively turned him away. If she could turn back time, she would be kinder, gentler, more caring. She sighed, wishing she had known him better. Robert must have been a fine young man for Trey to care so much, to mourn so long. She wished she could beg Robert's forgiveness, tell him she was sorry.

"Such a gloomy expression will drive the sun away," Trey teased.

With a shake of her head, Alana pushed past mistakes into a far corner of her mind, where she could examine them later in privacy. She smiled at Trey, marveling at the changes in him since the siege on the ranch. He, at least, seemed to have put his ghosts to rest. No longer angry, hostile, or resentful, he seemed at ease with himself—and with her. She could also put aside ghosts from the past. She need no longer fear that English might reappear in her life. Colin's letter had arrived yesterday afternoon stating that a man matching English's description had been found in the alley behind the saloon with his throat slit.

She felt something soft brush against her legs. Glancing down, she found a furry gray kitten rubbing against her skirt. She scooped it up and set it on her lap. "Isabel's cat just had a litter of kittens. This little fellow is going to be a mouser when he grows up."

Trey watched her slender hands slide from the kitten's head down its back with languid ease—and envied the kitten. He felt his body tighten at the thought of being stroked in such a fashion from head to heels. She'd made him purr just as she did the kitten. As much as he enjoyed being near her, watching her, it wasn't enough. He wanted her back in his life. Back in his bed. But he was a patient man.

He'd wait until he was fully recovered, until he felt like a man again, not some cosseted, gruel-fed invalid. It wouldn't be much longer. He felt stronger every passing day. In the meantime, he would bide his time.

Reaching over, he scratched between the kitten's ears. "We still have unfinished business between us, vixen, but it can wait."

Alana's head came up. All sorts of questions paraded through her mind. Was he still bent on revenge? What if he had tired of her? Or had he guessed her secret? Did he know she was pregnant? "What do you mean?" she asked, fear and emotion making her voice husky.

He merely smiled and refused to elaborate.

As had become her habit since Trey's recent brush with death, Alana found she couldn't fall asleep without checking on him at least once or twice. She slipped into her robe and crossed the veranda to his room. He was curled on his side, sleeping peacefully. She touched his forehead, but could detect no trace of fever. As she tenderly brushed a lock of dark hair from his brow, she wondered which of them their child would favor. Would the baby be dark or fair? Have blue eyes or green?

The slight reminder of her condition was enough to unsettle her stomach. Her hand flew to her mouth in distress. She feared she'd never make it to her room in time. Whirling, she fled. She was halfway across the veranda when she lost her dinner in an empty clay plot. When the spasms subsided, she walked unsteadily to the fountain and sank down on the ledge. Cupping her hands, she rinsed her mouth, then took a long drink of the clear, sweet water.

She started in surprise when she felt a strong, protective arm around her shoulders. "There, there, vixen," Trey murmured into her hair. "Let me take care of you this once."

Over her token protests, he drew her to her feet and guided her toward the house and into his bedroom. "Just until you feel stronger."

Alana lay down on the bed and closed her eyes. Trey wiped her brow with a cloth that felt wonderfully cool. She felt the mattress sag as his weight joined hers. Being careful not to jostle her, he gathered her in his arms. "I just want to hold you, vixen. It's been much too long."

She cuddled closer, seeking his warmth, his closeness. "Much too long," she agreed, her voice muffled against his chest.

"This is the way it should be." His lips brushed her temple. "A man ought to take care of his wife, not the other way around."

"No, you're wrong." She shook her head in protest. "People, especially man and wife, should take care of each other. A team is stronger than any single member."

Trey was silent for some time before he spoke. "Men may be the stronger sex," he mused with bitter irony, "but I think women are the wiser."

Alana drifted to sleep with her head on his shoulder. For a long time, Trey was content to cradle her gently against him. It seemed right somehow. As though the two of them had been destined for each other since the beginning of time. First, though, their union had had to be tried and tested. But it had withstood the challenge. Trey pulled her closer as he experienced a sense of completeness so profound that it left him shaken.

He recalled what she had said about their being a team. Soon there would be an addition to their team. She was carrying their child. Tonight's bout of illness had confirmed his suspicions. Though she was still as slender as a ballerina, her breasts were fuller, and her skin glowed like a ripe peach. Impossible though it seemed, she was more beautiful than ever.

The notion of a son or daughter pleased him immensely, he discovered. But why hadn't she told him about the pregnancy? Surely, she didn't think she could keep the news from him indefinitely. Maybe, as he had, she, too, awaited the right opportunity. Even though he hadn't put his thoughts into words, she must sense how his feelings for her had changed. They had grown so close recently, sharing smiles and laughter, exchanging possessive touches and lingering glances. He didn't think he needed to take out an ad in the *San Diego Union* to broadcast how he felt about her.

Minutes ticked by. Alana stirred. Trey pressed a kiss to the top of her head. "Feeling better?" he asked.

"Much." She sighed. Her fingers raked through the thick mat of black curls that covered his chest.

Trey stiffened and bit back a groan. "Ah, vixen, you're playing with fire."

"Then make me burn," she whispered achingly.

Trey needed no further encouragement. Shifting onto his side, he captured her face between his hands and raptly studied her exquisite features, as though they were a priceless work of art. Ever so slowly, ever so tenderly, he lowered his head. Kisses as whisper-light as gossamer drifted across her temple, along the pure line of her jaw, to the shell of her ear.

Delicious quivering sensations rippled through her. Alana turned her head, seeking his mouth with hers. Still he teased and withheld what she sought. The maddening flurry of kisses continued. Her breath caught when the tip of his tongue delicately outlined her lips. Then instead of the kiss she craved, he drew her full lower lip between his teeth and bit gently.

She plunged both hands into his hair and brought his wandering mouth to hers, opening greedily, hungrily for his possession. She was breathless when he dragged his lips from hers. "Trey . . ." she moaned. It was half-sigh, half-plea.

He loomed above her like a dark archangel. Alternately controlled, then impatient, he kissed and caressed every inch of her body, adoringly, lovingly, all the while whispering words of endearment. His breath was a balmy, erotic zephyr against her overheated, sensitive skin.

Pleasure built within Alana until it became so intense she clutched the bedding to keep from crying out. Her body arched spasmodically against his, and she felt the swollen shaft of his manhood, mute testimony of his arousal.

Wearing a smile that was both tender and predatory, he grasped her writhing hips and entered her in one powerful movement. A low keening sound escaped her slightly parted lips.

He stilled. "Did I hurt you, vixen?" he asked, instantly concerned.

She shook her head. "No, don't stop," she gasped.

Her nails lightly scored his back; her pelvis tightened spasmodically, urging him on. A shudder ripped through him, and he plunged farther into her velvety vault. Deeper and deeper. Again and again.

Alana felt herself explode in a shower of fiery sparks.

Trey burned, too, incinerated by a passion made even greater by the love he felt for the beautiful woman in his arms.

Later, as the fire of their passion cooled to glowing embers, he curved his body protectively around hers. "Call me a fool for being so slow to realize it, but I love you, Alana Matthews," he whispered. "I love you beyond reason—beyond life itself."

Disappointed when there was no response to his declaration of love, Trey realized it had gone unheard. Alana was fast asleep.

Chapter 26

Trey reached out in his sleep to pull Alana closer, only to discover she was no longer beside him. He sat up, thinking perhaps she had been ill again and, afraid of disturbing him, had returned to her own room. Tossing aside the covers, he swung his legs to the floor. He found matches and lit the lamp on the chest at his bedside. His hand accidentally knocked over a water glass, which he deftly caught inches from the floor. As he began to straighten, he noticed a white square of paper wedged between the chest and wall, and reached out to retrieve it.

Frowning, he stared at the envelope bearing his name. For some unknown reason, he felt loath to open it. Then, slowly, he slid his fingers beneath the flap and extracted the single sheet of paper. Alana's handwriting filled the page with graceful strokes, free of frilly curlicues or other affectations some women were so fond of.

Numb with disbelief, he read and reread the note until he had memorized it.

Alana had left him.

Fast on the heels of shock came pain. Piercing. Absolute. Eviscerating. It rendered him helpless. He slumped on the bed, staring blindly at the crumpled letter in his hand. How could she claim she wasn't what he needed when she was so perfect for him?

She complemented him in every way a woman could complement a man. She possessed a courage and spirit that surpassed her matchless beauty. And physically, their bodies were in perfect harmony. Certainly last night had proven just how attuned they were to each other's needs.

But he didn't deserve her. He had treated her shamefully. She had suffered his abuse with dignity, standing by his side, rifle in hand, during Vega's attack, then nursing him back to health when he had fallen.

He scrubbed a hand over his unshaven jaw. Perhaps, he reflected dazedly, Alana was wise when she said that it was time she get on with her life. If he wasn't such a selfish bastard, he would step aside and release her with his blessing.

"Damn!" He stood suddenly and beat his fist against the wall. He couldn't—wouldn't—give her up without a fight. He wasn't a saint; he was a sinner. And a selfish one to boot. He had to find her.

He hurriedly pulled on his clothes, stuffed the note in his shirt pocket, and raced across the veranda to her bedroom. He found the bed linen mussed, but her belongings appeared to be undisturbed. His knees felt weak with relief. If she was traveling, she was traveling light. Outside, the sky was beginning to lighten. She couldn't have gone far, he reasoned, feeling a glimmer of hope for the first time since he had found her note. He'd find her, bring her back. He'd beg, plead, promise her anything if only he could convince her to stay.

In his preoccupation, he failed to notice Isabel as he charged through the back gate. The two collided, sending the oranges that had been heaped in Isabel's basket spilling in every direction. Cursing the delay, he bent to help her pick them up.

Their eyes met as they refilled the basket. "Isabel, the *señora* is missing. Have you seen her? Do you know where she is?" His questions tumbled out with growing urgency.

With infuriating calm, the Indian woman reached for an orange that had rolled under a bush. "She is not missing, *señor.*"

"Then you've seen her? She's safe?" He had to restrain himself from shaking the information from her.

"Si, señor." Isabel stood, her movements slow and stiff, and looked at him as though he had taken leave of his senses. "I just saw the *señora* ride off."

Trey's fragile hope plummeted. At this very moment, Alana was intent on putting miles between them. "Did she ride off in the direction of the mission?" he asked dully.

Isabel wagged her head. *"El bien no es conocido hasta que es perdido."*

"Speak English, Isabel," he ordered impatiently, then was instantly contrite at his sharp tone. He felt ashamed of himself for taking out his frustration on a helpless old woman.

"It means, *señor,* good things are not appreciated until they are lost."

Trey groaned aloud and dragged his hand through his hair. Even Isabel, a simple serving woman, had more sense than he. How could he have been so careless as not to recognize Alana's true value until it was too late?

"The *señora* was heading toward the hills, *señor,* not the mission."

"The hills?" Trey repeated, scarcely able to believe what he had heard.

Isabel broke into a wrinkled grin. "If you ride quickly, *señor,* you can catch up with her."

Trey swept the woman up in a bear hug that almost sent the oranges spilling for a second time. Laughing, he released her and raced toward the stables.

Alana stood on the bluff just as the first rays of dawn tinted the horizon. She clutched a small oilskin package to her breast and gazed eastward, toward the distant mountains and the great plains beyond.

"I'm so sorry, Robert," she whispered brokenly. "I never meant to cause you such pain. I can't give you back your life, but I can give you sunrise and poetry."

She smoothed her hand over the slim volume of sonnets that Robert had once given her. While the sunrise was in its full glory, she planned to bury the book of poems in the shade of a tree. It would be a small memorial, but somehow fitting. Though Robert wasn't there to partake of the moment, his dream would finally become a reality.

Alana waited. A star winked from the heavens in solitary splendor. The sky faded from black to dusky blue. Then, distant mountain peaks magically materialized, bathed in shades of peach and pearly pink. The breeze played with her unbound hair.

"Alana!"

She spun around at the sound of Trey's voice. She had been so lost in reverie that she hadn't heard his approaching footsteps, which were muffled by the damp earth.

"What are you doing here, alone and in the dark?" he demanded. His fear has been transformed into unreasoning anger. "Do you have any notion of the scare you gave me?"

"There was something I had to do," she replied quietly.

"So urgent it couldn't wait for daylight?"

"I came here to make peace with Robert."

Her words stopped him. He paused near the summit to gaze at her. Like some ancient goddess, she stood proudly silhouetted against the magnificent backdrop of mountains and sky as the first rays of sun limned her hair until it shone like spun gold. Never had she seemed so desirable, so beautiful. So precious.

"I brought the book of sonnets he once gave me." She showed Trey the small oilskin package she held. "I thought I'd bury this under the tree in his memory," she explained, her voice breaking. "This way part of him will always be here—just as he wished."

Trey nodded, touched by her thoughtfulness. "I think Robert would have approved." He forced the words past the lump in his throat. It was time, he realized, time to put the past behind them and look to the future, just as her note suggested. Slowly, he walked the rest of the way up the bluff to join her. "We'll do it together."

He closed the gap that separated them, and took her in his arms. "I was afraid you had left me," he confessed, his voice raw with emotion.

"Left you? Whatever for?"

"Because I've been a bastard. And a stupid one at that." He held her tighter. "I couldn't bear the thought of losing you. When I found your note, I was afraid it might be too late."

"What note?"

Trey pulled the crumpled sheet of paper from his pocket. "I found this behind the chest in my bedroom where it must have fallen."

Her breath escaped in a rush as she recognized the farewell note. "I forgot all about it."

"Then you did intend to leave me?" Fresh pain washed over him.

"Yes." She pulled back slightly and angled her head so she could see him better. It distressed her to see the bleak expression etched upon his beloved features. "I planned to leave after Vega's attack, while I still had the courage. It was the hardest decision I've ever made in my life."

"Why, Alana? Why were you going to leave me?" He cupped her face between his hands. His eyes bored into hers, plumbing the depths of her soul.

"Because I'm going to have a baby." She bit her lip to keep it from quivering. "Knowing how much you resented me, I didn't think it would be fair to bring a child into a home where there was hate instead of love."

Trey closed his eyes briefly. No, it wouldn't be fair to inflict that on a child. A child needed to feel secure and loved. He had seen firsthand the disastrous results when those needs weren't met. He caressed her delicate cheekbones with the pads of his thumbs, as though to reassure himself she was real. "What made you change your mind?"

"I was about to leave when I heard you fall. You were so ill, and . . ." Her love shone in her eyes, their brilliance rivaling the rising sun. "You needed me."

"I'll always need you, vixen." He raised her hand and, turning the palm upward, pressed a kiss into its center. "As long as I draw breath, I'll always need you. You're a part of me, as necessary as food and water, light and air. I love you, Alana, now and forever."

Joy streamed through Alana like liquid sunshine. She flung her arms around his neck, wanting to laugh and cry at the same time. "I was afraid I'd never hear you say those words."

"I plan to spend the rest of my life showing you just how much you mean to me. Starting now." Trey lowered his mouth to hers, his kiss tender, loving, possessive. A covenant sealed.

The sun stole higher above the mountains. Dawn heralded a new day.

A bright beginning.